A
KISS
OF
FLAME

BOOKS BY JESSICA THORNE

A
KISS
OF
FLAME

JESSICA THORNE

SECOND SKY

Published by Second Sky in 2024

An imprint of Storyfire Ltd.
Carmelite House
50 Victoria Embankment
London EC4Y 0DZ

www.secondskybooks.com

ISBN: 978-1-83790-927-8
eBook ISBN: 978-1-83790-926-1

For Pat, still my hero, always my hero.

GLOSSARY

Asteroth (country) [Ass-te-ROTH], Asterothian (adjective), capital Pelias – currently ruled by a regents' council in the absence of Aeryn, Queen of Asteroth, Chosen of the Aurum, 'The Lost Queen'

Aurum, the [OR-um] – one of two powers formed from old magic in the cataclysm, the Aurum represents light. It sits in opposition to the Nox and takes the form of flames. The centre of its power is held in the Sacrum in Pelias. In each generation it selects a woman from the royal family of Asteroth as its Chosen and she becomes the queen

Aurum-forged steel – metal forged with the power of the Aurum, the opposite of shadow-wrought but the same thing

Castel Sassone – fortress within the walls of the lower city of Pelias, held by the Earl of Sassone and the Tarryn family

Cellandre – forest in the northwest of Asteroth/southeast of Ilanthus

College of Winter, the – independent college for the study of all magic, located to the north, beyond the borders of Asteroth and Ilanthus

Darkwoods – parts of wild forest infected with traces of the Nox where bargains can be struck and shadow kin roam

Hedge witch – a witch living in a rural setting, administering to the needs of a village or small local community, generally unaligned, regarded as lesser by the College of Winter, the maidens and the sisterhood

Ilanthus [Ill-AN-thus] (country), Ilanthian (adjective and inhabitant), capital Sidonia – currently ruled by Alessander of the line of Sidon, King of Ilanthus

Knightsford – fortified town on the edge of Cellandre with a garrison of knights

Knights of the Aurum – sworn warriors in the service of the Aurum. Once the power (or light) of the Aurum runs through them they become Paladins

Line of Sidon [Sid-ON] – bloodline of the royal family of Ilanthus. Spilling the blood of Sidon in a place of old magic is said to summon the Nox

Maidens of the Aurum – society of witches dedicated to serving the Aurum – currently led by Sister Maryn. By law in Asteroth all women with magic must submit to the Maidens of the Aurum and serve through them while all men must return their magic to the Aurum

Nightbreaker – Aurum-forged sword of the Grandmaster of the Knights of the Aurum

Nox, the [Noks] – one of two powers formed from old magic in the cataclysm, the Nox represents darkness. It sits in opposition to the Aurum and is said to take many forms, but it is worshipped as a goddess by the people of Ilanthus

Old magic – primal magic torn into two opposing forces by a magical cataclysm long ago, now passed into legend

Othertongue – secret language of magic known primarily to witchkind

Pact, the – peace agreement between Asteroth and Ilanthus which ended the last war

Paladins – senior Knights of the Aurum, touched by its light and blessed, filled by the light when its power is invoked which makes them stronger, faster and lethal. Servants of the Aurum, and the queen of Asteroth, her protectors

Pelias [Pel-EE-ass] (city) – capital of Asteroth

Rebel witchkind of Garios – witches who have refused to serve either the Aurum or the Nox but seek independence, freedom and rights of their own

Sacrum, the [Sak-RUM] – a stone circle now enclosed by the temple in the palace at Pelias which houses the flames of the Aurum, the most holy site of the Aurum

Sanctum, the [Sank-TUM] – secure compound in the royal palace in Pelias housing the Maidens of the Aurum

Seven Sisters, the – a stone circle near Knightsford

Shadow kin – creatures formed from shadows which can beguile, infect and overpower humans, turning them into monsters serving the Nox. They use music, illusion and brute force to hunt and trap their prey. When a bargain is made, shadow kin often claim the price

Shadow-wrought steel – metal forged with the power of the Nox with the intention of containing or harnessing magic. The sisterhood are skilled in this art, forging the weapons to fight and capture others

Sidonia [Sid-ON-ee-ah] (city) – capital of Ilanthus

Sisterhood of the Nox – society of Ilanthian witches dedicated to serving the Nox

Thirbridge [THUR-bridge] – village in the forest of Cellandre near the border with Ilanthus

Witchfire – a magical spell which conjures flames, used primarily as a weapon as very difficult to control

Witchkind – people able to wield magic, able to command or cajole the powers of light and dark, or attuned to old magic in some way

PROPHECY OF AELYN THE FIRST

When the Nox is scattered across the land,
Sidon's walls come down.
When the Aurum sleeps in silent flames,
Pelias gives up its crown.
When shadows take the Aurum,
the Nox will take the throne.
When the Nox is crowned in the Sacrum,
the lost queen stands alone.

PROLOGUE

ROLAND

The hostile glares of the rest of the regents' council greeted Roland as he entered.

They were all here waiting for him then. Of course they were.

Three senior regents and three minor – that was how it worked. Three to govern in the queen's absence and three to advise. In theory anyway.

Two of the minor members were constantly changing depending on the whims of the other regents – Ylena, and Sassone. Urdel had been Ylena's favourite for some time now, while Leyborne was a newcomer, the earl's man to the core.

Regent was a role Roland had never asked for. Rather it had been thrust on him as Grandmaster in the chaos following the war. He didn't believe in using a role on the council as a reward. His representative here, Yvain of Goalais, sat still and silent, as watchful as Roland himself, his right-hand and trusted compatriot ever since Dain had died in battle.

Lady Ylena's expression was unreadable. She'd seemed so relieved to see Elodie return to Pelias that Roland felt sure it was real. People had been cheering in the streets, laughing and crying. They had been throwing flowers, for the love of the light. Ylena herself had embraced Elodie like a long-lost child.

The coldness in her now was something else, something that belied the performance she'd put on in the courtyard that day. Her white hair was elaborately dressed and she wore a chain of office from the royal treasury. Sister to the former queen, aunt to the current one, her life had been a study of power, living one step away from the throne, until Elodie had vanished.

Roland wondered if she intended to take that step back now. It didn't look like it.

And as for the Earl of Sassone...

Foremost noble of the kingdom, and descended of men who would have been kings in their own right had the Aurum not chosen Elodie's family instead. The line of Tarryn threaded itself around the royal family like a vine, always there, defending the city in the same way the Knights of the Aurum defended the crown and the kingdom. If the crown held the kingdom of Asteroth then the earls of Sassone held Pelias. Some said it was balance, some said a threat.

The current earl was Anselm's father but that mattered little. Roland had been more of a father to the young knight over the years. Thickset and heavy, with shoulders of corded muscle, and a bald head, Sassone resented everything about Roland. That much had been clear for many years now.

'Your report, Grandmaster,' Ylena said.

He pushed aside his thoughts. 'The girl, Wren, was discovered by Finnian Ward and rescued from an Ilanthian incursion force.' A force led by the crown prince Leander, who had been intent on killing his half-brother. A detail he didn't bother going into for now. They had been turned back, Leander fleeing with his tail between his legs.

'The queen had been in hiding with Wren in Cellandre, a remote area seldom visited.' No need to say how she had been earning her living. The outrage that would cause wasn't worth it. A lowly hedge witch, indeed. 'Queen Aeryn deigned to return with us.'

'*Deigned*,' Sassone interrupted, his tone scathing.

He had a point. Elodie hadn't spoken to Roland since they'd left Knightsford. She probably never would again. They had once loved each other far more than was wise. But she had fled the city when she defeated the Nox, leaving them all to war and destruction, and unbeknownst to him taking with her their child.

Wren was a miracle, one he had never thought to experience. He really did not know what to do about her.

He pushed on, not wanting to mention his daughter again right now.

'The queen is with the Maidens of the Aurum, under their care until such time as we decide—'

'Until her trial and conviction,' Sassone cut in again. 'Let's not beat about the bush. She deserted us in our time of need, flung her people to the Ilanthian wolves and forsook her vows before the Aurum. The flames are too good for her.'

A brittle silence met this outburst.

Roland glared at him, but what could he say in response? Sassone wasn't exactly wrong. The charges would have to be answered. Lesser transgressions had seen monarchs judged guilty by the Aurum and given to the fire.

The thought of it though, of Elodie, his Elodie, burning...

He forced himself to uncurl his clenched fists. She wasn't his Elodie anymore, hadn't been for years. But she was his queen.

'Perhaps she had good reason,' said Ylena softly. 'It will be decided. There will be a trial. A *fair* trial.' She turned her icy gaze from Sassone back to Roland until both of them subsided.

'And she brings with us her heir. That is something to be celebrated. I hear the girl raised a beacon and touched the Aurum. She is powerful. Perhaps even more powerful than Aeryn.'

The girl. It made her sound like an infant, not a grown woman in her own right. And yet Roland couldn't help thinking of Wren as a girl himself, which wasn't fair. She had summoned the light of Aurum into the knights, giving them strength and speed unmatched in years. She had channelled the Aurum and saved Finn's life with its power. There was more than that though, something which had bound the two of them together, a love so powerful that it couldn't be natural. Roland had raised Finn as his own son. He couldn't bear the thought of the same kind of enchantment that had claimed Roland, ensnaring his ward too.

He had saved Finn from the dark fate the Ilanthians had for him. He wasn't going to just hand him over to another form of magic.

'Indeed, Princess Wren is a talented witch in her own right,' he found himself saying, in tones far calmer than he'd expected. Someone whispered something. Someone else laughed under their breath, hurriedly silencing themselves.

Oh, let them gossip. They knew nothing. Better they talked about him as a gullible fool than Wren as a... a what? A byblow? His child born out of wedlock to another man's wife? The witch-queen's bastard?

Yvain cleared his throat. 'I have no doubt many of us there in Knightsford owe her our lives. Certainly our victory.'

Yvain had been the commander of the Knightsford garrison when the shadow kin had attacked. He had fought at Roland's side, his brother-in-arms, and every inch the Paladin Roland was. He knew better than most how many lives had been saved that day due to Wren's raising of the Aurum's light in their blood.

Not least Finn's life. And as a prince of Ilanthus, even one held hostage and raised in Asteroth, Finn's death would have caused a war. Did no one else see that?

Ylena smiled. 'Then there is hope no matter what. The trial date will be set and all traditions followed.'

Lord Leyborne cleared his throat nervously. He was Sassone's man to the core. '*All* of them, my lady regent?'

Ylena didn't flinch. 'Of course,' she snapped. 'We are not so far fallen that we will not follow our most sacred traditions. Delegations will be invited, our neighbours will see that our law applies fairly to all—'

'You're going to invite the Ilanthians?' Roland asked, unable to stop himself blurting it out in his surprise.

Ylena's face didn't change but her eyes hardened. 'That is what is expected and that is what we will do. No exceptions. Not even for Queen Aeryn.'

'How can we—' Sassone thundered and for once Roland agreed with him.

'Enough!' Ylena slammed her hand down on the table. 'This is how it is done, my lords, and this is what we will do. It is written. If you will try a queen and a Chosen of the Aurum, it must be seen to be fair. There are steps that must be taken and witnesses who must be here. None of them will come anyway. Why would they? Except perhaps to gloat. It doesn't matter. What we are talking about is the gravest of situations and I will have this done correctly. Now, are there any more complaints?'

No one said a word. No one wanted to cross her. The anger in her voice was unprecedented. The bravest among them held their tongues.

Elodie had betrayed her too, Roland thought. She had loved the queen as her own daughter, perhaps even more than her own daughter, truth be told. She had helped negotiate Elodie's marriage to Evander which had ended in such disaster.

How was Elodie even to hope to have a fair trial here in Pelias? How was Wren to hope to have any kind of life?

Elodie had begged him to let them go back to the forest, her and Wren, to forget he had ever found them. He should have listened.

CHAPTER 1

WREN

Wren hated Pelias.

She had never thought she could hate anywhere quite so much.

Oh, Pelias was beautiful and refined, and her every need was catered for. She lived in a palace of white marble, perched above the perfect city, overlooking the sea. It had blue tiled roofs and golden domes. The sun always shone on fair Pelias.

But it was also shallow and petty and cruel in so casual a way. And she was trapped here.

She caught sight of Finn at the far end of the banqueting chamber and something in her chest stuttered as she tried not to call out to him or make her way directly to him. Too many people were watching. His stormy-blue gaze snagged on hers and he shook his head, barely perceptibly, before turning away.

And something in Wren died a little bit more.

She wished a thousand times every day that she was back in the forest of Cellandre, living half wild and half witch, with only Elodie as a companion.

Or Finn.

When she had been discovered and brought back here, she

had thought that maybe she would be fine. She had Finn and he would never leave her. And Elodie would be here as well. And maybe, just maybe, she could get to know the man behind the austere and formidable front her father presented to the world.

But the austerity seemed to be no front. It went all the way through the Grandmaster of the Knights of the Aurum, Roland de Silvius, right to his stony core. And Elodie wasn't with her. She was locked up in the Sanctum of the Maidens of the Aurum, awaiting a trial which was seen as a foregone conclusion. No one was allowed to visit her.

And now Finn was like a ghost on the edges of her life. He had to be, he said. It was for the best. But it didn't feel that way.

She let him go on ahead before pushing her way towards the doors to the gardens, heedless of those petitioning her, or trying to ingratiate themselves with her. Or even just trying to get into a perfect position to stare. Wren knew the rumours were flying about her. And about Finn as well.

But most of all about Elodie.

The royal palace of Pelias perched high above the harbour city, built into the mountain. It was a rabbit warren of a place, full of corridors and galleries, chambers hewn from living rock and balconies hanging out over the ocean. The sound of seabirds and breaking waves was its song and the wind carried the scent of the sea. Wren couldn't have found it more alien if she had been dropped into another country altogether.

That was without the court and its mysterious rhythms and rules. Everywhere she went she found people following her, people who became silent and awkward when she tried to talk to them, or got a gleam in their eyes like she could give them something.

Wren was a disaster. She was always wrong, always. In the wrong place, wearing the wrong thing, saying the wrong words. It was exhausting. She missed the forest so much it hurt, the deep green-gold light, the sway of the canopy overhead, the birdsong so much sweeter than the wailing of the gulls.

The palace itself was divided in two, one side housing what remained of the royal court and now the regents' council, and on the other the Maidens of the Aurum in their Sanctum. The Aurum's chamber, buried in the rock face, was the bridge between them, accessible from both sides, but she hadn't dared set foot in there since that terrible night.

'We have to be careful,' Finn told her solemnly that night. 'If it ever happens again...'

So now he was avoiding her. Avoiding being seen with her.

She knew he still loved her. And what she felt for him was brighter than any magical fire. They only had stolen moments and those were already getting few and far between.

Great terraced gardens filled with flowers and trees over-looked the city, climbing the mountainside in tiers. From here Wren could see all the way down to the city walls on one side and the harbour on the other, and far, far beyond, across the plain and towards the hills, almost as far as the great forests, but not quite. And here she could be alone. Or as alone as she ever could be with attendants and servants and all those people who wanted something from her.

At least the air here was fresh, unlike the hot and stuffy halls, and the audience chambers they would lock her away in for hours on end, the air ripe with perfume and sweat. Here, leaves rustled, and cut the sunlight with green, and if she closed her eyes she could almost imagine she was back in the forest with Finn. Safe with him. Curled up together under Cellandre's canopy.

Where no one could touch them. Watch them. Judge them.

She thought he would be here to meet her, but there was no sign of him. Had she got it wrong? Had he meant they should meet somewhere else?

Three women sat at the far end of this particular garden,

shaded by an array of parasols in red and gold, and attended by a host of silent servants who never made eye contact. Wren didn't know the woman clothed in the robes of the Maidens of the Aurum, but Lynette of Goalais sat beside her. And the other was Lady Ylena, Wren's great-aunt.

Wren froze as the old woman locked eyes with her and beckoned her forward. Behind her one of the attending servants murmured something between a prayer and a blessing and Wren had to fight not to turn tail and run.

But of course, she couldn't. Running was against the rules. There was no escaping this.

Finn must have seen them and beat a hasty retreat. Or else they had sent him away. Probably with no more than a glare.

Wren cursed softly.

One of the dour-faced attendants pulled out a chair for Wren, opposite the regent. Beside her, the Maiden of the Aurum sat demurely, hooded and gazing at her hands. A smile flickered over Lynette's lips, encouragement and comfort, or an attempt to convey both.

Don't cause trouble, Wren, she seemed to say with her gaze. *This is important.*

It was always important.

'Wren, what a delightful coincidence,' said Ylena. She didn't sound like she was in any way delighted. And Wren didn't imagine for a moment that this was a coincidence. The woman had a plan for everything. She had been waiting for her. The old woman carried herself like an empress. Or a bird of prey. Wren couldn't quite decide which was worse.

'The gardens here are beautiful,' Wren replied, noncommittally. 'I was taking the air.'

'You are used to fresh air and freedom,' said the maiden. Her voice was almost familiar, soft and lyrical with the accent of Pelias. For a moment Wren's heart gave a different kind of jerk. It wasn't Elodie, though they sounded similar. The woman looked up, her gaze searching, but she said nothing more. It felt like being studied by some kind of professor. 'And select companionship.'

She saw far too much with her pale blue eyes and sculpted features. She was perhaps forty, and the resemblance between her and Elodie could not be denied. Perhaps it was the bearing. Perhaps it was what Pelias did, creating women like statues with hearts made of stone.

The regent, Ylena, was no better, just older and harder. 'A princess has no need of such things, neither solitude nor select company. There is a whole court here and you need to become its beating heart, young lady. You have many duties here, Wren, and I have selected Lynette to help you, guide you.'

Lynette bowed her head graciously, accepting the role before Wren had a chance to interject. Not that it was exactly a surprise. Lynette had been angling for this since Knightsford and she was an expert in the political games of court.

'Your life has changed irrevocably,' Ylena continued, 'and Queen Aeryn clearly did nothing to prepare you for it.'

'This was not meant to be my life,' Wren said and Ylena stiffened.

The maiden in her white robes made a noise that might have been a stifled laugh and might have been a cough. Wren stared at her, but she didn't look up again. Ylena glowered at Wren, unmoved.

'On the contrary,' Ylena told her. 'It always was and now it is. Accept that and we can move on. You have ancient magic in your veins, in your soul, the very light of the Aurum. You channelled it and it accepted you. Or so I am told. I have yet to see any evidence myself... But the queen says you are her daughter.'

'Then why can't I see her?' No one answered. 'I need to talk to her.'

'She has other... duties to prepare for. You are needed here.

I will teach you how to navigate the court. Given time you will learn how to rule.' Ylena was unbending as iron.

'Elodie is the queen,' Wren argued again, undaunted.

'And she decided to abandon her kingdom, and must answer to that choice. You are her heir.' Ylena leaned forward, skewering Wren with her glare. 'This is not a discussion, child. The facts of the matter are as they are. She claimed you, publicly, and you channelled the Aurum. You woke it from slumber, if only for a moment. One day you will rule this kingdom. No one is going to risk losing another queen, so you will have to quell the headstrong ways she has taught you. You will do as Lynette, your new chief lady-in-waiting, says in all things. You will dress as she tells you to dress, learn our court and make alliances among the younger courtiers. You have the chance to rebuild what your mother squandered. You can start by taking some care of your appearance.'

That was a low blow.

'My appearance?' Wren asked, not even bothering to disguise her shock.

As if sensing the hurt, Ylena seemed to relent a little. 'You could start with your hair, child. You are no longer a wild thing. Appearances matter here.'

Wren flinched and before she could stop herself she brought a hand up to her hair. Its dark length was loose, soft and ragged as shadows, and moved in the breeze. Or at least she hoped there was a breeze. Because her hair had a tendency to move with her magic, and with her anger. When it got too long, things quickly got out of control. And she was already angry.

But that was not the danger here. She had betrayed her insecurity and now Ylena had a knowing smile on her face. It had been some sort of test. And Wren had failed.

Ylena couldn't know her secret but she was clearly an expert at finding a weak point and exploiting it. She wouldn't be the political powerhouse she was in this city if that wasn't the case. Wren tried to imagine what Elodie would say right now and failed.

'Appearances,' she murmured angrily and let her hands fall to her lap. Everything here, it seemed, was about appearances. All around her the air stirred fitfully, shadows lengthening. Wren stiffened as she felt the magic rising from the ground beneath them, unfurling in the darker corners of the garden. The air around them turned suddenly cold as if something had blotted out the sun or the wind had changed to the north. Even Ylena noticed that.

'Maryn?'

Shadows subsided as quickly as they had stirred. Not shadow kin, nothing so terrible as that. But Wren knew that the darker shades of magic followed her. They had done all her life. And that was how it always started.

Sister Maryn slowly released a breath. 'Shadows are moving,' she murmured, and this time her eyes were distant, fixed on the far side of the garden. 'But the wards hold firm. There is no need to fear.' When Wren frowned in confusion, the maiden smiled so briefly, a movement at the edge of her lips. 'The whole city has wards sunken into the fabric of the stones with which it was built. Ancient protections. The maidens restore them annually with the blessings of the Aurum. Shadow kin cannot form here, although they still try. They never learn. There is nothing to fear.'

Ylena gave a dismissive snort that was decidedly unprincesslike and glanced at Lynette. 'Back to the matter in hand then. Lady Lynette?'

Lynette's golden hair was perfect, of course. Pearls threaded through it, along with little silken flowers that matched her gown exactly. 'Of course, Lady Ylena. I have a number of plans. The princess is a beautiful young woman. There are any number of dressmakers and—'

She didn't get any further. Ylena cut her off.

'Do your best, Lynette. The families of the council are meeting this afternoon. See that she is presentable. They have children your age, Wren. Make some friends. Lynette will tell you who is worth knowing.'

Children indeed. Wren was a woman, not a child. And she didn't need friends. She had Finn and that was enough for her. But clearly Ylena was not given to actually listening to anyone but herself. Too many years doing whatever she wanted. Wren was a potential new weapon in her arsenal.

Ylena rose to her feet and the others followed suit. Wren did not. She knew that was a snub and she frankly did not care. As they were so fond of pointing out, she was a princess now. Princesses could be rude. Clearly.

Wren had learned from Elodie. And perhaps she knew now where Elodie had learned herself. She wished Elodie would talk to her, help her stand up to this woman.

Or Finn. But right now she didn't dare go looking for him. She could feel too many eyes on her.

She needed something, a choice that was hers alone...

CHAPTER 2

WREN

'Princess!' the maid gasped out loud, far louder than she was supposed to speak and in an appalled tone of voice that would probably get her beaten if anyone else heard.

They didn't like loud or opinionated servants in Pelias. Or princesses, Wren thought ruefully.

There were a lot of things they didn't like, as Wren was discovering.

'What have you done to your hair?'

Wren looked up from her work, as the little silver knife she had lifted from the dining room sawed through the last thick black strands. The poor woman's mouth sagged open as the hair turned to smoke and drifted away. Wren allowed herself to breathe a sigh of relief and put the blade down at last. Her head felt blissfully light and the sense of freedom almost made her dizzy for a moment.

'Did you need something?' she asked in as calm a voice as she could muster. She didn't even bother to suppress the smile. There was no point. She couldn't hide her pleasure.

Defiance felt extraordinarily good.

But the maid had already turned around and run from the room, shouting in horror for the ladies-in-waiting.

Because of course this had to be reported as quickly as possible.

The chaos that filled Wren's chamber moments later was only to be expected. The other maids thronged in the doorway, and the ladies in waiting all had to offer their scandalised opinion. Lynette was inevitably summoned.

For a society that was so obsessed with appearances, the idea that their newly discovered princess should mutilate her finest feature on a regular basis was horrific to them. They had actually used those very words. Mutilation. Oh, and the idea that her hair was the only thing beautiful about her was thoroughly insulting.

There was a dark magic threaded throughout Wren's existence, manifest in her abilities, and in her hair. Cutting it off was the only way she knew to keep it in check. Elodie knew that too, of course. She had been the one to set the rules about Wren's hair, about always cutting it and never letting it get too long or out of control. Along with the rules about using magic, to only reach for the light and never the darkness, to never allow the spirit of the Nox to rise again and to always try to live in the light of the Aurum. To never call on shadow kin or listen to their lies. To ignore the siren song that came in the night, enticing her to be what it would make of her. So many rules that Wren had thought it was silly, once upon a time.

It didn't seem so silly now.

But those rules took absolute precedence over anything the court could inflict on her.

She had almost lost herself. If she had gone any further into that darkness, she could have ended up enslaved to an Ilanthian prince, or a mere vessel for the power of a dark goddess.

And as it was, Elodie had been arrested and imprisoned. The same thing could well be said of Wren, for all the freedom she was allowed. Roland de Silvius and Lady Ylena were determined to put her on the throne, it seemed, and if that happened...

The prophecy about the Aurum had never seemed real until she stood in front of it, wearing a coronet someone had thought looked pretty against her black hair, and the flames transformed to shadows of themselves. Finn's face, the horror in his expression...

She'd never get that image out of her mind.

When shadows take the Aurum, the Nox will take the throne.

Oh the prophecy suddenly seemed very real indeed. And that terrified her.

'Princess, what do you think you're doing?' asked Lady Lynette, pursing her perfect lips together as she surveyed the damage. She had sent the others away, as she entered.

'I'm not a princess,' Wren replied, ignoring the obvious evidence all around her. 'Have you had any word about when I can visit Elodie?'

Maybe a change of subject would do the trick. She could only hope.

Lynette looked around the floor as if she might find the hair and stick it back on Wren's head. Wren would put nothing past the gracious, elegant and very beautiful Lynette.

On the whole, she didn't mind. Lynette meant well, and no one understood the court like she did. She was kind and had a gentleness underlying her stern demeanour. If only she didn't seem quite so disappointed all the time. Ylena expected much of her. And at least Lynette was kind.

'No, my dear. I will check again, but the maidens have decreed that no one will see her. You know that. The decree extends right up to the Grandmaster himself. Your father has been waiting at the door to their Sanctum every day so far and, every day, they send him away. He even tried to interrupt them in the Sacrum, when they were tending the Aurum in hopes of seeing her. But her majesty was not there and the maidens are not best pleased with him now.'

That sparked Wren's interest. Roland was trying to see Elodie too and failing. It wasn't just her. He was even breaking rules to do so. And still it didn't work. A small if slightly vindictive part of her brain was glad. He'd brought them here, insisted they return to the royal city. He could have let them go, let them vanish back into the forest once more, but he didn't.

'And Finn?' Wren asked and knew from the tightening of Lynette's jaw that this subject was forbidden as well. 'I mean... is he... I was hoping to see him later on, if his duties will allow it.'

'That rather depends on him,' Lynette sighed and turned away without answering any further. Subject closed.

A different maid appeared with her gown – Carlotta who, at least, was happy to talk to Wren like a human being, who sometimes laughed at her jokes and told her gossip about the others, both the nobility and the servants. She had lush chestnut hair and golden brown eyes, a sprinkling of freckles over her face, and was probably the only thing approaching a friend Wren had made here despite all Ylena's suggestions about various courtiers, nobility and their offspring.

At least Carlotta never seemed as personally affronted by Wren's behaviour as the others. Had she drawn the short straw or volunteered? Wren wondered. Carlotta hadn't been born in Pelias and often found its customs strange, she had confided to Wren once, and that had forged some kind of tentative connection between them.

That was against the rules as well. Carlotta was a servant, Lynette had explained patiently. Wren ignored her on that front out of principle. Carlotta was torn but in her eyes Wren outranked the rest of them, so that was that.

It wasn't really a good basis for a friendship but it was all Wren had to hang onto.

The gown they had picked for her today was a dark blue, shot with silver threads and embroidered with a delicate pattern like frost. It was beautiful, she knew that. She couldn't fail to admire the work which had gone into its creation but she longed for something simpler.

A good pair of breeches and a tunic, for example, some stout boots. Maybe she could find Finn and run away.

The thought of Finn made her keenly aware of his absence again. He had passed her at the banquet last night, and his hand had brushed against hers, his skin warm and soft, almost a caress. Just for a moment. It had felt like magic jolted through her entire body. And then he was gone. She hadn't seen him since.

'What tortures do you have for me today?' she asked Lynette, trying to push that sensation from her mind. It lingered in the background tormenting her, like the memories of their last kisses or making love in Knightsford.

Lynette sighed, defeated. 'Well first we'll have to do something about your hair. Some flowers perhaps? Something to disguise...'

She waved her fingers towards Wren's head indicating everything. Wren ran her fingers through it so the short style spiked up at odd angles. Wickedness made her do it.

'I prefer it like this, don't you?'

Carlotta hid her grin and turned away quickly.

Yes, Wren knew she was being impossible. But it was the one rebellion she still had.

Lynette didn't so much as smile. 'You're meeting the regents' council and their families for a reception.'

'And do any of them style hair for a living?'

'Wren!' The admonishment was hardly a surprise. But at least she wasn't using a title now. There was almost a smile on her lips. You'd have to look really hard to see it but Wren was sure it was there. 'What will they think?'

'That I'm a wild girl from the forest. They might even let me go back home, if I'm lucky.'

Except there was no home to go back to. The tower had burned to a shell. And without Elodie there, it wouldn't be home anyway.

Lynette sighed again, softer this time, with understanding, and pulled Wren in for an unexpected hug. It shouldn't have been so welcome. Wren had decided to fight the court every step of the way if she could. But Lynette was kind, and gentle, and there was nothing Wren could do against that. With Ylena's appointment of her as lady-in-waiting, she had taken it upon herself to be Wren's champion and her friend, her shield against the rest of them. Protecting her the same way the knights did.

'I'm afraid this is home now, my dear. Now please, if you must cut it all off, at least let me do something with it afterwards. They expect a princess and they can make life so difficult for you if they don't get what they want.'

They. Ylena, she meant. Wren was sure of that. And Roland, of course. And that pompous earl. The rest of the court followed the regents' leads.

Make life difficult for her. How much more difficult could they make it? She shuddered to think.

Honestly, what good was it being a princess if everyone else still got to make the rules about her life?

Lynette was right. The regents' council held power in the royal city, and until there was a queen back on the throne their word was the law. The problem with finding a queen was that meant either Wren, or Elodie, wearing the crown. Neither of whom wanted it. No one seemed to be willing to accept that.

'Fine. Flowers, just a few.'

'Or a diadem. A small one. There's a perfect one in the treasury which belonged to your great-great-great grandmother, I believe. It would be very fetching against—'

Wren shuddered. A diadem, she had discovered, was like a crown, or a coronet, or a tiara... and they all signified the same thing.

'No. Just flowers. Or a ribbon if you have to.'

And because Lynette knew if she insisted, Wren would lose whatever was put on her head at the first available opportunity, out of a window if necessary, she settled on a silk ribbon the same colour as the dress. In the mirror she didn't look like herself anymore. Another young woman was staring back at her, one who didn't climb trees, gather herbs, or race deer through the forest. One who hadn't grown up with the old magic singing to her from the trees, or the Nox from the shadows. One who would never have faced down shadow kin and commanded them, who couldn't bend the powers of light and dark to her will, to take a life or save it. How did she even begin to explain that, or what she had seen and heard in the stone circle known as the Seven Sisters?

She had a dark fate, and Leander of Ilanthus was determined to be part of it. He may have fled home with his tail between his legs, defeated by Elodie, but Wren was certain his plans were far from finished. He hated Finn and wanted him dead. And Wren represented everything that he considered to be his by right.

'You can't keep this up forever, Wren,' the lady-in-waiting told her solemnly, as she led her from the chamber. 'No one is going to put up with this rebellion for long.'

'They can try to stop me,' Wren muttered, setting her mouth in a hard line. 'Or they can let me see Finn and Elodie. I don't ask for much.'

Lynette shook her head. 'I don't think you know what you're asking at all.'

HISTORY OF THE WARS BETWEEN ASTEROTH AND ILANTHUS

VOLUME 24, CHAPTER 8

When Asterothian forces broke through Sidon's walls, and de Silvius rode into the stronghold, Hestia, Lady Rayden, was waiting for him. She begged his aid, threw herself on his mercy, and it was she who laid the groundwork for the Pact. Some say she saved thousands of lives that day, while little more than a girl herself. But she was shrewd and astute enough to understand what would happen if the Ilanthians continued fighting, the death and destruction that would follow.

Some say she had the Sight and a vision had shown her all.

Whatever she said to the champion of the lost queen, de Silvius listened. She had but one request for herself and that was that he take as hostage the youngest son of King Alessander.

De Silvius asked where the boy was to be found, for she stood there alone.

Lady Rayden led the knights to the chamber of sacrifice where de Silvius found the king standing over his young son, knife in hand, ready to spill the child's blood to call forth the Nox, though this was a futile effort and the dark goddess was no more.

He took the boy as a royal hostage and made him his ward.

CHAPTER 3

FINN

'He was with her, you know. When the Ilanthians almost took her. Maybe he led her there in the first place. They can't be trusted. None of them.'

The hushed voice wasn't as subtle as its owner thought. It carried on the breeze across the courtyard to the place where Finn was cleaning his sword. He tried not to flinch, keeping to the steady rhythm as he sharpened the blade.

It was something Roland had taught him long ago, to always take care of a weapon no matter how humble. A sword could mean your life. Even a sword as great as Roland's Nightbreaker was just a weapon and needed to be treated with care.

So Finn focused on his task and not the loose tongues around him.

Let them talk, he thought. Let them gossip. He knew the truth of what had happened in the stone circle at Knightsford. Or some of it anyway. Enough. He knew enough.

He had to find a way to make sense of it all.

And as for the moment he and Wren had stood in front of the black flames...

He pushed that firmly from his mind.

A nightmare. Or at least he wished it had been a nightmare.

Every moment since had been stolen, every glimpse of her left him hungry and hollow. Wren haunted him, and made him a shell of himself. He couldn't bear to be around the various gatherings in the palace, knowing she was so close and that to reach out to her would invite disaster.

So he withdrew. From her, from everyone. And he let the gossip grow unchecked. He tried not to care and failed at that, too.

The flames had turned black. Not for long, not forever. But he knew what he had seen. The woman who commanded shadow kin, who drew the night around her like a cloak and had filled him with such blinding light... the woman he loved...

She had done that.

And yet still he ached for her.

He couldn't help himself. And that was part of the problem, wasn't it? Because he was a son of the line of Sidon. He had been marked for the Nox from his birth. All she needed to do was embrace her power and command him and he would have no choice to obey.

How did he even know if what he felt was real?

But how could it not be?

'Are you planning on wearing that sword down to a tooth-pick?' Anselm asked with a laugh.

Finn looked up, distracted to see his friend approaching across the courtyard. When Finn had been a boy and Roland had first brought him to Pelias, he'd been terrified but defiant, a wild little thing, or so Roland had called him. An unholy terror according to everyone else. The fights had been inevitable and the scowls he cast at everyone must have made him impossible to warm to.

He recalled distinctly sitting not far from here, huddled in shadows where he felt safest, nursing bruises and grazed knuckles. And Anselm coming to find him. All golden curls and aristocratic bearing.

He'd held out his hand. 'Tarquin is an arse,' he said. He was of course correct.

Finn hadn't known what to make of that. 'I think I broke his nose.'

'He deserved it. Come on, we should get to training.'

'You... you want me to go with you?' Finn had asked. No one wanted to be around him and that suited him. He was Ilanthian and they were Asterothian. They were enemies to the core. He was a hostage here.

Anselm shrugged. 'You know how to fight. It seems a shame to waste that. The Grandmaster said you were to train with us. So I came to find you. Coming?'

They'd been more or less inseparable ever since. Training to be a Knight of the Aurum was no joke and they had needed each other countless times. It was hard not to smile back at his friend. Anselm could make anyone feel better in a moment. They had been knighted together, and side by side every step of the way. Finn didn't have many people he relied on and trusted the way he trusted Anselm. But he didn't have to let Anselm know that. He'd be insufferable.

Finn didn't so much as grin. 'Did you need something?'

'The Grandmaster wants to see us. He's in a foul mood though.'

Finn sighed, sheathing his sword and packing away his equipment. 'When isn't he these days?'

Anselm pulled that face, the expression which said he agreed but didn't want to. As one of Roland's most reliable aides he probably took the brunt of whatever was going on with Finn's guardian, whatever issue he was dealing with.

The same problem Finn had. Wren and Elodie.

Olivier was already waiting outside the chamber, tall and dark, with his perpetual scowl. He had always been there as well, as long as Finn had been in Pelias. Another knight and potential Paladin, who had squired alongside him and Anselm, his father was the wealthy Count Arrenden, and the whole family were devout followers of the Aurum. Solemn and dour, Olivier prayed daily, even now that the Aurum didn't respond, and lived an austere life. Anselm would tease him mercilessly but Olivier ignored him.

Anselm Tarryn was from similarly noble stock, his parents being among the foremost nobles in the kingdom. His father, the Earl of Sassone, was one of the three regents, and Anselm himself carried the title of Lord Tarryn though he never used it in his life as a knight. Finn forgot that sometimes, that Anselm was almost as high-born as he was. He didn't have that air about him. No more than Finn did.

'What do you think he wants?' Olivier asked Anselm. Not Finn. He rarely interacted with Finn if he could avoid it. Being Ilanthian in this court came with many prejudices. Finn liked to think that the many slights, from exclusion, to offhand comments, to outright slurs he experienced every day, flowed off him like water after so long, but they didn't. Not really. He had just got better at hiding it over the years.

'I'm sure the Grandmaster will inform us of his intentions when he's ready,' said Anselm. 'Best not to speculate or indulge in idle gossip.'

Silence fell over the group, Finn trying to focus on anything but the way Olivier kept casting sidelong glances at him. Eventually, though, the inevitable question came.

'You were at Knightsford, at the stone circle...' Olivier began, but stopped when Anselm glared at him. 'You must have heard the rumours too?'

Anselm snorted, clearly disgusted that his warning about idle gossip was being ignored. 'There have been a lot of rumours,' he said, his voice unusually cold. It wasn't like him. Finn glanced his way, surprised. The glare he was giving

Olivier made his face look different, more like his father's, a comparison Anselm would not have welcomed. The two of them had that in common. 'She saved Finn's life. She saved us all and drew down the power of the Aurum.'

'I thought the queen did that.'

Olivier hadn't been there. He had been stationed here in Pelias, guarding the Aurum. He hadn't seen or indeed felt the vast power that had filled the stone circle at Knightsford. Finn already knew that some of the knights were bitter about that, like they had missed something important. All they knew was what they had been told.

Which was probably just as well.

'She is very beautiful,' Olivier said, casting another sidelong glance at Finn. 'You must be close, the two of you. Alone, all that time in the forest.'

In constant danger. Lost. Hunted.

But the passion Wren had ignited in him still simmered away in his depths. He couldn't deny it to himself, even if he was determined to hide it from everyone else. Anselm knew, but then Anselm was no fool. He saw far more than most. Luckily he was good with secrets and understood discretion.

'She's Roland's daughter,' Olivier went on. 'I wouldn't pursue her. Not if you want to keep on his good side. Not with your reputation.'

For a moment Finn hoped Olivier was joking, which would be so far out of character they would have to check if he had been infected by shadow kin or something. But no such luck. Olivier was deeply in earnest. Finn glared at the floor as if he could make it burst into flames and curled his hands into fists at his sides.

His reputation. His background, he meant. A child of Ilanthus, the exiled son of Alessander, the hostage prince. All of Pelias knew who he was and most of them blamed him for things that had happened when he was only a child.

The problem was, they were right. He had no business being near Wren. It was dangerous for both of them. Dangerous for the whole kingdom.

He couldn't help himself. He wanted her. Needed her. She was everything to him.

He was about to tell Olivier where to go, when the door opened.

'Inside,' Roland barked, and from the look on his face, this was not good news.

CHAPTER 4

FINN

The Grandmaster wasn't alone in his study. By the window, Lady Ylena sat watching them file in, her elderly eyes still sharp and keen. She was Elodie's aunt, second in line to the throne to her mother, and had been at the side of that same throne for the last forty years – guardian and guide, counsellor, and now one of the regents. Roland didn't take a seat behind his desk as they lined up. Instead, he paced back and forth in front of them.

'These are the ones?' Ylena asked, as if she had been presented with a collection of alley cats.

'Yes,' Roland said, the answer as firm and confident as possible.

Ylena rose, moving like the royal princess she was. She inspected each of them, pausing in front of Finn for an unnecessarily long time.

'If you say so,' she said at last. 'I don't see it myself.'

'They are the best here.'

'Even the Ilanthian? Isn't that a risk?'

Finn was used to this. He had heard worse every day all his life. Even when he was a child back in Ilanthus. He knew better than to react.

Roland didn't rise to the bait. 'I have trusted Finnian Ward with my life on more than one occasion. I raised him. He was the one who rescued your niece and great-niece from those who would have taken them back to Sidonia.'

Roland was careful about not identifying who 'those' were. Finn's brother, in other words. Who had almost killed him. Roland didn't mention that and Finn was grateful. He kept his gaze trained on the wall, his jaw relaxed, his hands loose. He had to. Showing any sort of reaction at times like this just made it worse.

'And the ill-judged affection between the two of them?' Ylena went on. So that was what they were calling it? Wonderful. Finn felt the heat rise up his neck and fought against showing the embarrassment. Was this why he was here? To be humiliated by the lady regent?

'Finnian has a vital role to play as I am sure you are aware.'

Ylena didn't seem convinced.

'So long as he realises that it is impossible and cannot continue. She is heir to the throne, even if she won't accept that as yet. But she's a headstrong girl and that will have to change. If this is your decision, so be it. But I will be watching as well, Roland. Closely.'

Was it Finn's imagination or did Roland's knuckles turn even whiter?

'And, as I said, these are my best men. Their service has been impeccable, they come from the finest families, and they will do their duty. She will be protected in all things, as we discussed.'

The compliment from their Grandmaster should have filled them with pride. Perhaps it did, for the other two. Finn felt something like a noose tightening around him. He didn't come from the finest family. Not as far as the Asterothians were concerned. He might have a pedigree, but it wasn't one the regents' council would ever accept.

Ylena rolled her eyes and left the study, the heavy door banging closed behind her.

It was Anselm who cleared his throat. 'May I ask what this entails, Grandmaster?'

The three of them watched Roland expectantly as he cleared any lingering traces of annoyance from his face.

'You and Olivier are to be charged with the protection and defence of her royal highness, Princess Wren. She will be kept out of danger at all times. You will teach her to fight in her own defence. If so much as a hair on her head is harmed I will have your balls, understand?'

A hair on her head, Finn thought. Funny. But he didn't dare smile. And he was not included in this. He hadn't missed that.

The overwhelming silence crushed down on him. Surprisingly it was Olivier who broke it.

'Only the two of us? What about Ward? Why is he here?'

'I have a mission for Finnian specifically. You two are dismissed. Select your men, set up a roster, see to her protection. Your families regard this as a great honour, but I see it as a potential disaster. Make sure that I am wrong.'

Finn waited as they left, and wondered why he was being deliberately excluded. Ylena's reference to their relationship was indication enough of what was going on.

The door closed firmly.

'Wren isn't going to like having babysitters all the time.'

Roland gave a dismissive snort and shook his head. 'No, but the regents' council demanded it. It was all I could do to insist on having Anselm and Olivier take the lead on that.'

'I suppose their families were delighted.' The Earl of Sassone was one of the regents, after all. Having his own son in charge of her security would be something of a coup.

Roland almost smiled. Almost. 'It certainly helped. Would you have chosen anyone else?' Finn shook his head. He couldn't argue that. He would trust them with his life. And with Wren's. 'I know where their loyalties lie.'

He couldn't help himself. 'But not me.'

Roland looked up at him sharply. 'You think I doubt you?'

'What am I supposed to think?' He didn't mean to sound so petulant, but it was hard. He could feel something else brewing, like an oncoming storm. Roland was holding off telling him what that might be and Finn didn't like that.

'Keeping the two of you as far apart as possible until we can sort out whatever has happened between you and untangle whatever enchantments she wove would be better.' Finn made to protest but Roland raised his hand to silence him. '*Inadvertently* wove.'

For a moment Finn didn't know what to say.

'You're separating us? Like children?'

'Some would say you are children.' Roland sat down behind his desk now and Finn sank into the chair opposite him. This couldn't be happening.

'Because of the queen? Has she demanded this?' He knew Elodie didn't approve of his relationship with Wren. She had made that perfectly clear. The worst part was, Finn feared she might be right. And that made him feel like the worst kind of traitor.

A queen in prison, on trial for treason, shouldn't be in a position to make demands of anyone. Perhaps it was Ylena. The regent had lost more than anyone in the war against the Ilanthians so it was no wonder she distrusted him. Perhaps she was only trying to protect Wren. The Aurum knew that was all Finn himself wanted to do.

That brief thought of the Aurum, and the darkness that had flared in its depths when he had stood there before it with Wren, made the icy cold hand of reality crush his spiralling worries.

Roland and Ylena didn't know the worst of Wren's magic,

what it had done to the Aurum's flame. Finn didn't know how or why the flames had turned black for those long, terrible moments, but he knew what it could mean. The Nox had touched Wren in that stone circle. It had made itself part of them somehow. He'd felt it flow through them both. And maybe more of it remained than they realised.

It was the reason he had been keeping his distance, staying away from her, or at least trying to, even though it felt like physical pain to do so. He burned for her in a way he couldn't explain, like those holy flames, eternal and all-encompassing. It had to be an enchantment, his rational mind told him. Wren hadn't meant to do it, he was sure of that, but something had happened to bind him to her. He could claim it was when she saved his life with her magic in the stone circle, but he knew it had happened long before that. He'd been bitten by shadow kin. That ought to have been the end of him and if anyone found out even that much, he'd be locked up, examined and tested to madness. But Wren had cured him, riddled him with divine light and made him... made him into something else. Her creature. When she was threatened, he lost his mind with the raging need to protect her.

Perhaps it had happened even before that. In the forest of Cellandre, where he first met her. When he had lost all sense of who and what he was and she had saved him. He had kissed her. Her lips on his, her body in his arms... even that first kiss still haunted him.

Roland spoke again, more softly but still firm, the voice of command.

'I have another mission in mind for you. One for which you are uniquely suited.'

That did not sound good at all. And clearly it was something designed to keep him as far away from Wren as possible. Which... yes, he knew it had to be this way. Inevitable.

'Which is?'

'The king of Ilanthus, your father, has petitioned us to reopen the embassy as a gesture of goodwill and an overture of peace talks.'

For a moment Finn thought he might be hearing things. 'Peace talks.' The two words came out flat with disbelief. His father didn't want peace. None of his family did.

'He is sending a special emissary here and they have asked specifically for you to act as a liaison. He sent a letter.'

'What letter?'

Roland produced it, unrolled it and let Finn read. It really didn't help. Not at all.

'You can't believe any of this?'

Roland shrugged. Whether they believed it was clearly beside the point. Finn was a prince of Sidon, Ilanthian royalty, whether he liked it or not. He might have started off as a hostage here but the connections he could forge between the two courts were, as the letter pointed out, unique. It would serve them both.

His father's signature adorned the bottom of the page, a beautiful and elaborate scrawl. There was an official seal. This was not a lie.

But it could be a trap.

Finn sighed to himself.

Of course it would be a trap. For him. Or for Roland. For someone.

And it would surely mean he would be kept as far away from Wren as possible. Because an Ilanthian could never be trusted. But of course, he knew that better than anyone.

CHAPTER 5

WREN

Everything Wren had learned about magic came from Elodie, knowledge which in turn came from Asteroth and the Maidens of the Aurum. Oh, she was aware of the Sisterhood of the Nox in Ilanthus, witches bound and subjugated to the service of the dark goddess Elodie had defeated and scattered, precipitating the war. There were other witches too of course. Hedge witches, for one, those usually of little power who lived in the most remote areas, alone and prey to Ilanthian witch-hunters or whoever else felt the urge to persecute them. Usually they had a kind of symbiotic relationship with a local community and sought their protection in return for healing and herbs. Some of them could still touch the ragged remains of old magic and work charms. She and Elodie had lived as such on the outskirts of Thirbridge for all of Wren's life up to the point when she had met Finn and everything had fallen apart.

There were also the rebel witchkind of Garios, those who lived by the rallying cry: 'We are witchkind. We will live free or we die.' Wren knew less of them as they resisted any kind of allegiance but their own. They were wild and untameable, legendary, the stuff of tall tales and campfire stories.

To fall afoul of them was to suffer untold horrors. Everyone said so. They were never specific about what that entailed and Wren had always wondered. She'd never got an answer.

The College of Winter, on the other hand, seemed little more than a staid place of learning, occupying a common ground between the light and the dark. It welcomed anyone who wished to study, men and women of any lineage, but people seldom left the same, if they left at all.

The Maidens of the Aurum had taught Elodie everything she knew, had taught her forebears too. There wasn't a word of othertongue they had not trained her in, not a theory of magic or a practical charm that she had not rehearsed a thousand times. And Elodie had taught all that to Wren.

Or at least she had tried to. Wren's magic didn't work the same way. Quite the opposite in fact. Thus far, Wren had tried to keep herself as far away from the maidens as she could. She didn't know what witches of such power would be able to discern in her. Only Sister Maryn had come close to her, at that meeting in the garden. And that had been awkward enough.

But the maidens had the keeping of Elodie until the trial and if Wren wanted to see her, there was no option. She had to try.

Wren approached the maidens' doorway now, through the outer courtyard, where absolutely everyone could see her. Lords and ladies, gentlefolk and commoners, servants and stableboys, knights and squires, she didn't care. She had done it every day, and every day she had made the humiliating return journey as well.

At least she now knew she wasn't the only one. Roland was doing the same thing. Day after day.

Carlotta trailed after her, because the light forbid she should go anywhere on her own. Lynette had decreed it. Once Wren would have said that Elodie kept too firm a hand on her life. She was nothing compared to Lynette.

She couldn't doubt it was well-meant. At least there was that. But if she had to sit through one more interminable explanation of court dynamics, or dress fittings, or etiquette lessons... well, Wren couldn't be responsible for what she might do.

The gown she wore at the moment was thankfully one of the simpler ones a day-gown, Lynette had informed her in a tone that put it one step above a sack. Carlotta had been attending her this morning, thank the light, because the rest of the maids were as opinionated as their mistresses, her ladies-in-waiting. Wren couldn't stand it. She had already realised that most of them were insulted that they had not been put in charge and the in-fighting was getting out of control. In all honesty, she already feared one of them would do another an injury. At least Lynette listened to her. Sometimes.

'You might need a bodyguard,' she had told Lynette last night as they sat in the banqueting hall with the court spread out around them. Roland was somewhere else, making himself busy, she guessed. Finn was nowhere to be seen and Wren tried unsuccessfully to push him from her mind. 'Someone is going to push you down the stairs to climb the social ladder.'

Lynette had just laughed. 'They could try, my dear.'

As Wren marched across the courtyard she caught sight of a group of the younger knights filing out of the Grandmaster's hall. There was another problem she still had to deal with. Her father. His plans for her. Finn wasn't among them – she knew too well – but they all stared at her, their eyes following her like hunters.

She felt her skin flush, warming all over, and put her head down, marching onwards in as defiantly an unladylike way as she could manage.

'My lady,' Carlotta called after her, hurrying to keep up. 'Do you really want to do this again? They won't let us in. They've made that clear. And it isn't safe.'

It didn't matter. She was going to do this every single day until they let her see Elodie. Her last moment with the woman who had raised her was not going to be seeing her marched off like a prisoner. Nor was the next one going to be seeing her stand trial. It was ridiculous anyway.

But then again, a treacherous voice inside her whispered, Elodie had a lot of questions to answer. Why had she fled Pelias after the Nox was defeated? Why had she run away? And why had she not told anyone about Wren?

It was obvious that Roland was Wren's father. Neither of them would be able to stand in front of each other and deny the resemblance. But still Elodie had refused to confirm anything.

Not that it mattered. Wren was still her daughter. And therefore her heir. Paternity of the queen of Asteroth meant next to nothing. Too many Aurum-sworn knights had heard her in the stone circle claiming Wren as her own. Her daughter.

The door to the Sanctum of the Maidens of the Aurum was always closed. It was their retreat, a holy place in and of itself, where they could dedicate themselves to its service, to the practice of their magic and prayer, to devotional rituals that the world was not allowed to see. The palace took up one side of the citadel, and the Sanctum the other. In between them, the dividing line was the Aurum itself, and the Sacrum that surrounded it. Sacrum and Sanctum, people here would sometimes say, to invoke protection. No one outside the citadel could pass uninvited into either. And for the Sanctum, that included those who came from the palace.

The wards were strongest here, Wren thought, riddled throughout the palace, cunningly designed magical spells woven of light which protected the people who served and worshipped the Aurum. She could feel them in the stones beneath her feet and in the walls pressing close. If she closed her eyes she could feel them aglow with otherlight. And even now, years after the defeat of the Nox, the wards were still kept strong and whole.

The Sanctum was a place of refuge, of meditation and study. It was a place of women. And magic.

The door was heavy oak, studded with iron, with a grille that could be pulled back to see outside if needed. As she approached, the shadows around her stirred, the sense of threat rising. There was magic woven through the fabric of the door too, and the walls on either side and her own magic responded to it. More wards. Shadow kin couldn't pass through them. And the shadows that clung to Wren were weaker for it, no threat. Not here. She tried to breathe easy. It ought to be a good thing.

Wren pushed the dark magic which nested inside her down with a ruthlessness she would never have believed she possessed only a short few weeks ago. And it obeyed. Another surprise that no longer surprised her.

She was getting stronger, or the dark magic was becoming more compliant to her wishes, more malleable. That was not the comfort she would have hoped for.

Part of her, a part that still believed she belonged some-where else far away, running wild in the forest of Cellandre, wanted to hammer her fist on the door until she got someone's attention but there was a rather delicate bell hanging beside it and so, deciding to play along this time, she rang it and waited.

'*You catch more flies with honey than vinegar,*' Elodie would always say.

'*Why do you want to catch flies?*' Wren had replied and Elodie had laughed.

Great light, she missed that sound. It hadn't been that common an occurrence. But it had been sweet.

The grille in the door slid back and a sour-faced woman peered out at her.

Speaking of vinegar, Wren thought, and kept that thought very carefully unsaid.

'No,' said the maiden and slammed the grille shut again. The same way she had every other day Wren had tried this, leaving her to turn around and traipse back to the palace, in full view of everyone.

But not today. She was not putting up with this any longer. She rang the bell again, more insistently this time.

For a moment she wondered if they would ignore her entirely, but the grille opened again.

'Were you always this obstinate?' the maiden asked.

Wren tilted her head to one side and smiled as sweetly as she could muster. 'Maybe you should ask Elodie.'

The maiden snorted out a huff of air. 'No one by that name in here to ask.'

And she slammed the grille closed again.

'Maybe we should go back,' said Carlotta softly, already trying to cajole her and persuade her.

Wren's temper got the better of her. She couldn't help it. She had been trying to be nice about it, and all she wanted to do was talk to Elodie. Even for a few minutes. She had begged, wept, asked politely, everything. The woman was impossible. Before she knew what she was doing, she lashed out, not with her body but with her mind. Shadows recoiled from the bell and light burst from it. Behind her Carlotta gave a shriek of alarm.

The bell didn't so much ring as explode, leaving a pool of molten metal on the dusty ground underneath it.

CHAPTER 6

WREN

Wren stared at the puddle of molten metal, hiding the rising horror inside her, and then dragged her gaze up to the grille which was now open again.

'Well,' said the maiden. It wasn't the same woman this time. Wren recognised the familiar blue eyes of Sister Maryn, the maiden from the garden. 'I suppose Elodie might have some questions to answer after all. I've been wondering how long it would take.'

The grille closed again and Wren stood there, feeling utterly wretched and defeated.

But this time the door opened and two maidens in white stood behind it.

'Inside, both of you,' the gatekeeper snapped. 'You'll be paying for that bell, your highness.'

Wren was so relieved, she didn't even argue about the title. Or the sarcastic way it was delivered.

'With what?' she asked and the maiden gave a snort of laughter as she closed the door behind them. Carlotta stared, wide-eyed, and knotted her hands together in front of her neat apron. She was Wren's own age, perhaps selected to give her someone to confide in.

Right now, she was clearly terrified.

Wren took her hand and squeezed gently, which almost made her jump out of her skin.

'My lady... I mean, your highness... I mean...'

'Just Wren, Carlotta, please.'

Her eyes went even wider. 'We shouldn't be in here, Wren,' she whispered, far too loudly. As the maiden secured the door and turned away, Wren saw a smile quirk her lips. Oh she was loving every minute of this.

'Well, we are. I won't tell if you don't.'

'What did you do to the bell?'

Oh. That.

'A very good question,' asked Sister Maryn. She dismissed the gatekeeper with murmured thanks and the sour woman returned to her task. 'Wren melted it, Carlotta. With magic. Magic which she shouldn't really be able to use quite like that. Especially not in Pelias. The wards alone should stop it. Your princess is something of an anomaly. Follow me please. You may address me as Sister Maryn.'

A thousand excuses ran through Wren's mind, a thousand explanations that wouldn't even begin to explain what she did. Sister Maryn was right. She had melted the bell with magic. Because it irritated her.

Well, no, the maiden keeping the door had irritated her. But she wasn't about to go around melting people. At least she had that.

'They will let us back out again, won't they, my lady?' the maid asked, more quietly this time. She didn't want to attract the attention of the maidens any more than she already had. They locked witches up here the same as they did in Ilanthus. Oh they called it service but Wren wasn't sure she saw much of a difference when it all came down to it.

That was also a very good question, Wren thought. 'I think they'll have to.'

'Or the Grandmaster will come and get us? Well, you. He'll come and get you, won't he? Don't leave me behind.'

Wren squeezed Carlotta's hand again. Would Roland come? Probably. Would the maidens let him in? No. Definitely not, if they didn't want to. One look at Maryn told her that.

Would that stop him?

Well, he wanted her on the throne. He'd made that clear. Why else had he brought her here? Why else had he agreed to make Elodie stand trial? It was ridiculous.

'I'm sure he'd try,' she said as diplomatically as she could. 'And I'm not leaving you behind. I promise. Just...' She stopped and turned to the maid. Carlotta had eyes the colour of caramel, and they gazed at Wren in desperation. Wren knew that feeling right now. 'Please, Carlotta, don't tell anyone what happened to the bell? They won't understand. I can trust you, can't I?'

She hoped. There was every chance Carlotta would be straight back to Lynette to report everything the moment they left this place. Or someone else. Ylena perhaps. Sister Maryn appeared to be Ylena's creature already. Wren had no illusions that her every move was not being watched. But she had to try.

Carlotta frowned suddenly and then seemed to come to a decision. She nodded firmly. 'You have my word. They wouldn't listen to me anyway, Wren.'

Wren shook her head. Oh someone would listen if Carlotta chose to speak. She didn't doubt that.

Sister Maryn had stopped at the gates of a small internal walled garden. She nodded her head inside. 'Go on,' she said, her voice gentler than Wren would have thought possible.

Wren peered through the opening.

Elodie was kneeling in front of a bed of herbs, her hair plaited down her back, and her hands busy at work harvesting. It was so familiar a sight that Wren's heart gave a physical lurch inside her chest. She'd seen her like this a thousand times, although it had been in the forest and not in a tiny garden like this.

'Elodie!' she cried out, unable to stop herself.

The next thing she knew she was running and then she was swept up in an embrace so strong she thought nothing could pull them apart.

Except so many things could. And would. But for now, she held on as tightly as she could.

CHAPTER 7

ELODIE

When Wren called her name, Elodie had been daydreaming, and for a moment she was back in the forest, in the garden behind their tower, blissfully happy in their solitude and at peace with the world. For a moment everything was all right again.

The maidens taught contemplation and meditation, about the need for peace and isolation in order to truly let the Aurum fill the spaces in your world. She had been unprepared for the wonder that being so far from her old life would give her. This was the only place in Pelias where she could recapture even a fraction of that.

And then Wren was in her arms, sobbing against her shoulder, and the reality of the situation washed over her like a bucket of freezing cold water.

Outside these walls, the royal court had Wren in its claws.

'What happened? Are you all right?'

'Yes. Yes, I... I thought I might not see you and I... I...'

Elodie whispered calming words, watching as the shadows coiled and writhed at the edges of the garden. Sister Maryn was watching with too keen an eye, as was the girl with her, the one with the terrified expression. She at least probably didn't realise what she was seeing. One could hope.

'It's going to be all right, my love,' she breathed. 'You're doing so well. Just breathe and let it all go. Control them before they set off all the wards and draw attention to you. Make them leave.'

'But I—'

'I know. But try, for me.'

Wren trembled against her, drew in a shuddering breath and released it slowly. And all was still again. 'It's so hard. This place... the Aurum...'

'I know. But you're being so good.' Slowly Elodie moved Wren back to arm's length and studied her. She smiled at what she saw, her brave and beautiful daughter desperately trying to hold everything together and still be herself. Someone was attempting to make a princess of her wild child. Good luck with that, whoever it was.

'They wouldn't let me in to see you before.'

Elodie smiled sadly. 'What changed their mind?'

Wren dropped her gaze to the ground, as was her habit when she had done something she shouldn't have, even if only accidentally.

'I melted the stupid bell,' Wren mumbled guiltily and that made Elodie laugh. She couldn't help it. 'I didn't mean to. It just... it just happened.'

'I'm sure it did. That would do it, I suppose.' So overt a show of power would have caught the attention of the maidens. No doubt about that. They had probably been waiting for it. Everything was a test. Maryn had asked her so many questions about Wren, all of which Elodie had refused to entertain. She trusted the maiden with her life. But with Wren's life... she trusted no one. 'Come, walk with me. We can talk in private in my cell.'

That one word brought Wren's face up, horror written on her features. 'They lock you up?'

'No, no,' and Elodie laughed again. Great light, she had thought perhaps she had lost the ability altogether but a few minutes with Wren and there it was again. That joy. The sheer delight Wren had brought into her life. 'No, I mean my room. The maidens call all their rooms cells. It's a place of retreat, not a prison.' She smoothed a hand through Wren's hair, pleased to see it short, relieved to see the girl she had raised and loved so well, and to steal a little time with her.

'It sounds like one.'

'When have you ever seen a prison?'

Light, she hoped Wren had not been shown the prison beneath the mountain, with its bleak, damp cells, devoid of light and hope.

They wandered through the little garden and back towards the long row of rooms where the maidens slept.

'This whole city is a prison.' Given that all Wren knew was Cellandre, that was almost fair. And certainly from what she had been used to, to what she had to be experiencing now, a good assessment. Elodie remembered her childhood here with a chill. Only one thing had made it bearable, her friendship with Roland and that... that was something she was deliberately not thinking about. 'What's going to happen to us?' Wren asked.

Elodie shrugged as she opened the door to her room. It was very simple, as simple as the room that she had slept in back in their tower. It was a sanctuary and, from the moment she stepped inside, she could have sworn she breathed more easily. So did Wren.

'There will be a trial before the Aurum. That's unavoidable, I'm afraid.'

'And then?'

Elodie didn't answer at once. What could she say? If the

Aurum deemed her guilty they would execute her. It was not without precedent. Her great-great-uncle Alvanor had been given to the flames because he turned away from the light. She couldn't even remember why. If they thought she had done the same thing… well, there were people who wouldn't hesitate. She had fled the kingdom when it needed her most, they would say. Worse, she had taken Wren with her and if they knew the actual reason why…

She had created a power vacuum and those who had stepped in to fill her place were unlikely to give up that power easily. It should have been a negotiation, and had it just been Roland, perhaps that would have been possible. Her aunt and the Earl of Sassone, however… they were another matter. Their enemies beyond Asteroth had taken advantage of it too, of course. Not the Ilanthians for once. They had been too busy trying to rebuild their shattered realm. But the rebel witchkind had apparently thrived and part of her heart had secretly cheered them on.

Elodie swallowed hard. Once she would have been able to talk to Roland about it. Long ago. But now… now, even though he was so close, she couldn't say a word. He would never understand. She knew that now.

But it left Wren exposed, in danger. Would he protect her?

'I don't know, little bird.' It was all she could say, this confession of her powerlessness, and Wren looked stricken.

'But they can't find you guilty.'

'It all depends on what they want. I'm not exactly first choice to return to the throne for many of them. Some have had a taste of power. Some never cared for my headstrong ways. And some—'

'Roland wants me on the throne,' Wren blurted out. 'So he can cement his own rule. He's on the regents' council and if I'm the queen… I don't know anything about ruling, or about the kingdom or… they'll put a crown on my head and the Aurum…'

The way she trailed off said it all, the dread in her voice and the realisation that she had probably said too much already.

'What happened with the Aurum?' Elodie asked in a calm and quiet voice, one wreathed in a patience she didn't feel, dreading the inevitable answer.

'I didn't mean—'

'I know that. What happened?'

Wren swallowed hard and then folded up to sit on the bed, her face hidden in her hands. 'It went black. For a while. Just when Finn and I were there.'

Aelyn's prophecy.

No, this was not happening. This couldn't be happening. Not so soon.

'Did he see?' Wren nodded and Elodie sat beside her, feeling as if everything that held her upright had been cut away in an instant. 'Did he tell anyone?'

Wren shook her head this time and Elodie wrapped her in her arms again. 'He won't. I don't think he will. But he's different with me. He's avoiding me, avoiding being seen with me. I think maybe, he's scared of me... or he hates me.'

The least of their problems, Elodie wanted to say, but it wasn't the least of it to Wren, she knew that. She remembered. It was everything.

'He doesn't hate you. He's probably equally scared as you. He's from Ilanthus, remember? Of the line of Sidon? His family tried to sacrifice him to the Nox at the end of the war, to restore it. And the blood of the line of Sidon is tied to that dark power. He's probably wondering what it means for him.'

And how to exploit it, no doubt. Elodie knew the line of Sidon too well. If Evander was still alive, he would be trying everything to get Wren into his power. Oh, he would have loved this.

Finnian Ward... that was another problem. If he was avoiding Wren for now so much the better but Elodie knew it wouldn't last. Part of her said she should have killed him in that room in Knightsford. The pragmatic, calculating part. But he was just a young man and she hadn't known how deeply entwined he and Wren were already. And as for what happened at the Seven Sisters...

Tearing them apart now would never work. Even if it was all Finnian Ward wanted in this world, he would never be able to leave Wren. Not anymore. She would draw him back. He was her creature whether he liked it or not. Wren had bound them together to save his life. Elodie hoped they saw it as love.

Even if Elodie killed him now, it probably wouldn't take hold. Not for long.

She had to think. She had to work out what to do. And most of all, she had to protect Wren. That was vital.

'Listen to me, little bird, if the time comes that anyone tries to put a crown on your head, you need to get away from this city as fast as you possibly can. Use any means necessary. I don't care if you have to summon every shadow in the place to help you. You escape, you run and you never look back. Do you understand me? You make him help you. You command him.'

There was nothing else for it. For Wren's own sake, and for the kingdom.

CHAPTER 8

ELODIE

Wren's mouth fell open and her eyes glittered like shattered glass reflecting light. 'But... but you said...'

'I know what I said. I'm saying something much more important now. Tell me you understand.'

'Any means necessary,' Wren repeated woodenly, too shocked by this change to argue.

'I wish it could be different, really I do. But... Wren, they can't make you queen.'

'Of course not. You're the queen.'

'I'm the queen,' Elodie echoed and hated every syllable. She found a handkerchief in the pocket of her simple gown, and used it to wipe Wren's face. She fussed with her hair and tidied her up and did all those motherly things Wren seemed to need at this moment. All the things they had never named as part of their relationship, but that were there between them all the same. And all the time her mind whirled through her options.

There had to be a way out of this.

And perhaps there was. But she couldn't do it alone.

Elodie closed her eyes, praying for strength, for help, for anything. But she knew what she had to do.

'Now, you need to go back to the palace. Come to see me again in a few days, if you can. They'll let you in now. They'll probably want to train you which might not be a bad idea. Sister Maryn is a shrewd teacher and she can help you, but never actually show them what the shadows will do for you. Only the light, understand?'

Wren nodded, words apparently beyond her now.

'And don't show them too much of that either. They know you're powerful. They would expect that anyway, and they've interviewed everyone who was at the Seven Sisters already. But they will want your account. Just keep it simple. The Aurum helped you but you don't know exactly what you did. And maybe... maybe they'll believe us.'

It was a vain hope. Elodie knew they didn't believe her, but what did that matter?

She kissed the top of Wren's head. 'Off you go. And find a way to talk to Finnian Ward. He doesn't hate you. Not really. He will help you. He'll have to.'

He wouldn't have a choice, not anymore, but she didn't want to tell Wren that. Not yet. She had to trust that the line of Sidon ran as true in him as she feared. She knew he was brave, she'd seen that. Roland had raised him to be a Knight of the Aurum. But all the same... blood always ran true.

She walked Wren out to the main gate, with Sister Maryn and Wren's young maid trailing behind them, hugged her close again and then let her go. It was like wrenching out a vital part of herself but she had to do it. She held herself together until the door to the Sanctum closed behind her and then found herself face to face with Maryn.

The maiden wore far too insightful an expression on her face.

'Well?' Maryn asked.

'I need to talk to him,' Elodie whispered, hardly daring to say it.

'You were the one refusing to see him, if you recall. He has waited for so many years for an explanation. But why now?'

'He needs to help her.'

Maryn gave her another shrewd look.

'She's his daughter. Of course he'll help her. In all ways. Surely you don't doubt that. You know Roland de Silvius better than anyone else.'

Elodie sighed. She *had* known him. The man he was now? Not so much. He was angry, she knew that, and dour. And broken inside. And it was all her fault. But she had not had any choice in the matter and it hurt more than anything to realise that she was the one who had broken him.

'None of you understand,' she murmured and turned away. 'I'm not even sure I understand myself. But Maryn... I need to speak to him.'

'I'll arrange it. He has come here every day asking for you and I've sent him back as you requested. I could set a time piece by him at this stage. He'll be here before sunset and you know that as well. Don't pretend you haven't noticed. I've seen you watching, and I know you too well.' Her old friend smiled with a forced sweetness as Elodie frowned at her. 'Or I can go and summon him now, if that's what you want?'

Summon Roland. How many times had she dreamed of doing that?

Elodie nodded and lowered her gaze so Maryn wouldn't see what was in her eyes.

'More important than whatever her father wants or does not want,' Maryn said, eager to change the subject to one more pertinent to her interests, 'Wren's power needs to be trained, to be honed. Her abilities are already so strong and her instincts—'

Elodie nodded again because there was nothing else she could do. If she wanted their cooperation, she would have to play along. Maryn meant well, she knew that. But she would never understand what Elodie had done. None of them would.

Or why. And no one could afford it if the maidens found out the truth about Wren.

'She will agree to training. We spoke of it. But do not push her too hard, please, I beg you. She's young and she's been sheltered and—'

And that was Elodie's fault as well.

'I understand,' said Maryn gently. 'But her carefree days are over. You know that, don't you? She's your heir. In so many ways.'

Elodie couldn't deny that either. She thought back to the maelstrom of powers which had encircled Wren in the Seven Sisters stone circle. Carefree was not a word that could be applied to either of them anymore, if it ever had a place. The darkwood had always been there, right on the edge of their lives. Waiting. The shadow kin were hungry and the Nox...

The Nox lurked on the other side. Its fragments gathered around Wren, from the first time she had walked out into the storm that night they arrived in Cellandre, so many years ago. They had almost taken her right there and then and Elodie had made her choice to save her, to keep saving her, in order to save everyone. That was what she told herself. No matter what anyone thought, the Nox was far from gone. The dark goddess of the Ilanthians, the antithesis of the Aurum, was always waiting.

It wanted Wren. How could it not? And when it called to her, something inside the girl responded eagerly, something Wren couldn't control.

She would have to learn to control it, however, and the maidens were the only people Elodie could think of to teach her. The only ones she trusted.

Everyone else would try to use her for their own ends. The College of Winter would want to study her. But the maidens...

No, the maidens would want to use her too. Of course they would. They all would.

Sometimes Elodie thought she should have gone to the rebel witchkind long ago, but that would have opened another world of trouble. And what would they have done with Wren? They were busy fighting their own war. They would have seen the young girl with such power only as a weapon dropped into their hand. Elodie couldn't have that either.

Witchkind lived free or they died. Elodie had adopted their mantra herself for a while. Part a disguise, part a vain hope. Hedge witches, rebel witches, and even the College of Winter, they were all the same, standing between light and dark, just trying to survive. And using whatever came their way to do so. If they ever took the fight into the open, so many people would die.

Wren would be a spark in a room full of dry kindling.

It wasn't only the Sanctum and the Sacrum at risk now. It was more than the city. It was more than even Asteroth. It was their whole world.

Elodie needed to see Roland. She needed to make him understand. And to do that... she would have to tell him the truth.

Or a certain amount of it anyway. She wasn't sure she could bring herself to tell him everything. It would mean admitting far too much, so many things she didn't want to say, things she really did not want him to know.

But what choice did she have left?

She was about to face trial. She needed a champion. But Wren needed him more.

He would understand, wouldn't he? He had to. She closed her hand around the locket she wore and held it tight.

'Tell him I'll see him. Tell him... tell him I want to talk.'

CHAPTER 9

WREN

Wren had not expected the summons to Roland's office which was waiting for her when she got back to her chambers. Not today. There had been a number of them since they arrived in Pelias. They had all been quite cold and formal, impersonal, polite messages from a stranger. Easy to dismiss.

This time he had sent Finn and she couldn't ignore that. From his grim expression she realised that this was less invitation and more command. Making Finn deliver it was just the line to underscore that. A very different kind of message. Finn was his man, through and through, no matter what Wren thought or hoped. And clearly Roland knew Wren would not ignore him.

Carlotta took one look and stepped back out of the room, closing the door discreetly behind her.

Well, at least there was that. Wren didn't want witnesses to this. She was alone with Finn in the plush palace suite assigned to her and she didn't know what to do. Finn had been leaning against a tall-backed chair, but straightened when she entered, coming to attention like the soldier he was. He moved with that familiar lithe stealth, all fluid lines and steely muscles. He took her breath away, just by being there.

'What do you want?' she asked, the words out of her mouth before she could think of anything clever to say. So that would have to be her greeting. If the words stung him, he didn't show it. Well, he had been avoiding her. He kept his face perfectly placid and handed her the note.

She knew what it was the second she saw it. She had scrunched up and thrown enough of them away by now.

Why on earth did Roland have to send a note when he could come to ask her himself, or even send armed guards to bring her to him? There was a formality to it, an iciness, that didn't sit well with her. He was meant to be her father.

He was also the last person she wanted to know anything about her. Especially now. It was too dangerous, no matter what Elodie thought.

And Elodie, in spite of her own belief in herself, did not know everything.

'Why does he want to see me?' Wren asked.

Finn closed his eyes, clearly hearing her tone and not relishing the fight to come. Because there was going to be a fight, wasn't there? She could feel it fizzing in the air between them.

'He's your father. He's worried about you. He wants to explain why—'

Wren didn't let him finish. There was no point.

'I don't need him. I've never needed a father.'

'Only because of Elodie. Please, Wren, listen to him.'

'Why? Because you ask me? He didn't come here himself. He sent you. I don't know why. You've been avoiding me ever since...'

She couldn't say it. Even now. Turning away, she threw the letter aside, heading for the second room which was where her bed was. A mistake, she realised in an instant, but Finn was right there with her, every step matched. Of course he was. Finn had never backed down from a fight. Not even with her.

'I've been trying to work out what to do. And what happened.' He sounded as lost as she felt. It stopped her in her tracks.

'What happened when?'

Finn gave a brief laugh, little more than a huff of breath. There was no humour in it, not really. Just bitterness and despair. 'Where to begin? In the darkwood, at the stones, in the Sacrum, any time I'm with you...'

'With me?'

His hand closed on her shoulder, so warm, so strong and yet so gentle. She turned into his touch, unable to help herself. Finn was here, he was real and finally he was talking to her again. But now he didn't reply. He had no answer either.

'I wish I knew too,' she admitted, ashamed of the way her voice shook, and of the way she wanted to bury herself in his arms. 'It's terrifying. I keep thinking that any second someone will find out and then... I'll be in so much trouble, Finn.'

'They won't find out.' His voice rumbled against her and he pulled her into his embrace. She pressed her face into his chest and was swept away in the scent and the warmth of him.

Her Finn. He was hers, through and through, and she was his. She had known it from the first kiss deep in the darkwood, though she would never have admitted it then. From the moment, delirious with magic, he had pressed his lips to hers and filled her with such pleasure and desire, she had known they belonged to each other.

But he didn't deny what they both knew to be true. He didn't try to tell her that everything would be all right. She lifted her face to look at him and found him standing so still, with his eyes closed, his expression fixed and strained. As if he was fighting for control of himself.

'Finn?' she whispered.

His eyes opened and they were deep and dark, endless, their blue turned to the colour of midnight.

'Wren,' he said, his voice a growl. 'Come with me. Please.'

'To see Roland?'

He blinked, and she saw the confusion flicker over his handsome features. 'No.'

His hand cupped the side of her face, the touch so tender and carefully controlled. His fingertips brushed her skin, and made a tingling shiver run through her. She lifted herself on her toes without meaning to, as if drawn to him, as if something other pulled her forward.

Finn surged towards her, swift and fluid. A warrior in motion, every muscle trained and honed. His hands tightened their grip on her, strong but still unbearably gentle. Because he was always gentle, even in the greatest passion.

He would never hurt her. She knew that with all her heart, with every fibre of her being.

But his mouth was savage, desperate, like a starving man suddenly presented with a feast. His fingers tangled in her hair, or perhaps her hair tangled around him, and she let herself melt against him.

Great light she had missed this. She had missed him, everything about him. But his passion was her undoing.

Finn lifted her from her feet, pausing only to kick the door closed behind them, and carried her towards the bed. He didn't stop kissing her for even an instant, though his mouth moved from hers, along the line of her jaw and down her neck. Teasing her, and tormenting her, his lips on her skin, his teeth grazing the surface of her flesh. Letting her head fall back, Wren closed her eyes, revelling in the sensation of his touch, his strength, his need for her.

And hers for him, because she couldn't deny it even if she had wanted to. Her body trembled and sang with desire.

The fastenings on her gown defeated him. He looked up, confused.

'How do you...?'

Wren couldn't help but laugh. 'I don't know. There's usually someone to help. If it was just me I'd probably have to cut my way out.'

A flash of something wicked and wanton entered his eyes then and a fresh shiver ran through her. He was tempted, she could see that, and he had a knife right there on his belt. Light help her, she was tempted herself.

Their gazes snagged together, understanding blossoming, and Finn laughed, such a different laugh to before. This was a low, deep chuckle that did strange things inside her, wonderful things. The sound of amusement. Of something shared. And it made her think instantly of all she adored about him. All the ways she wanted him. 'It might be a bit much to explain,' he said at last.

Disappointment quelled her, but she smiled nonetheless. She couldn't help but smile at that expression of longing and devotion. 'You're probably right.'

She moved to sit up on the edge of the bed, but before she could, he stopped her, his body blocking her.

His voice rumbled against her skin, sending shivers through her. 'I didn't say we were finished, princess. You aren't going anywhere yet.'

CHAPTER 10

WREN

Finn took her wrists, turning each over so he could plant a delicious kiss on the inside, one after the other, and then he lifted her arms over her head, one hand holding her down. Wren wriggled, more out of habit than any actual desire to escape him.

She definitely didn't want to escape him.

'Don't move,' he told her, his voice little more than a whisper, while his other hand slid between her legs, parting them, and moved up beneath her skirts.

'Oh, but I—'

He tried to look fierce, really he did. 'Do I need to stop that mouth of yours with something?'

So this was his game?

'Yes,' she gasped, as his questing fingers found her underclothes and slid beneath them as well. 'Please, Finn, yes.'

He kissed her again, silencing her as promised, stealing her breath until her head was spinning. Her body rocked against his, stretched out alongside her, all hard muscle and warmth, implacable as he pinned her down with no effort at all.

And, for the first time since she had arrived in Pelias, she knew she was safe.

She only had to say a word or give a signal and he'd stop. But Finn held her close and gave her pleasure, cherished her and desired her. He groaned softly as his fingers found her wet and waiting. He paused only for a moment, teasing her there, and then slid deep inside. The pad of his thumb found her clitoris and circled it slowly, almost lazily, until she couldn't stand it anymore.

She broke like a cresting wave, her cries swallowed up in his kiss, her body shivering against his, closing on him, needing him.

When she came back to herself he was still holding her wrists, and his forehead was pressed against hers, his eyes closed, his face a picture of torment.

'Finn?' she whispered. She tried to wriggle free but he didn't release her. His other hand, now resting on her thigh, pressed down, stopping her.

'Just give me a moment, love. Just a...'

'But what about you?'

'I'll be fine. There isn't time. But I couldn't help myself. I needed... I needed to see that. To see you, your face, that moment. Do you understand?'

She went to shake her head, but... Perhaps she did. He looked both desperate and strangely sated. As if her pleasure had given him pleasure. That she could understand.

'But I want you,' she said.

'I know. And I you. And if you command it I'll do whatever you want, though it would get us both caught and your father—'

Wren gave a groan of frustration and the spell of pleasure snapped. 'My father,' she growled.

'He won't wait much longer. He's already been waiting all morning.'

'Then why?' she asked. 'Why waste time with—'

He kissed her again, silencing her and taking his time. When he finally drew back they were both breathless again. 'Any moment with you is never wasted, Wren. I crave you like water, or air, don't you know that? It's so strong, it... it scares me.'

She wondered what it took to make him admit that. She couldn't imagine Finn being scared of anything.

'You've been avoiding me.'

He smiled, such a sad smile that her heart gave a little lurch. 'I've been trying to regain some mastery of myself. I failed, obviously. How I thought I could keep away, I will never know. You're an addiction, Wren. And anyway, you shouldn't be associating with me here. Not as anything other than your father's sworn knight.'

Now he did release her. She propped herself up on her elbows, studying him solemnly. 'And why is that, exactly?'

Finn rolled back onto the bed, staring at the ceiling overhead. 'Remember who I am? Line of Sidon, sworn enemies of Asteroth, treacherous servants of the very dark power—'

She brought her hand up to his mouth before he could say it. Finn relented beneath her touch and his lips closed on her fingers instead. He sucked her index finger gently into his warm mouth and she felt those shivers start all over again. Reluctantly she pulled back.

'You don't get out of this conversation that easily,' she warned him. 'You've been avoiding me because you're Alessander of Ilanthus's son?'

'Yes.'

'I see, for my sake or yours?'

'Both.' He gave a bitter laugh and moved to sit up but her hand on his chest stopped him. Two could play those games, she thought. She curled her feet under herself and moved to loom over him. As much as she could loom.

'Finn, answer the question.'

'Is that a command, your highness?'

'Does it have to be?'

He let out a long breath of air, and closed his eyes in defeat. 'If you did command me, you know I wouldn't have any choice, don't you? That's the real nature of our relationship. You, being who you are, with the powers you have at your beck and call...'

Wren sucked in a breath. Elodie had suggested as much. And Finn knew that it was a possibility. The thought of it though, of doing that to him... no.

'I wouldn't do that to you.'

His eyes opened again, so beautiful in this light. 'I love that you think that, Wren, but we can never be sure, can we?' He sighed and turned away. 'And here, no one will ever forget that I'm the youngest prince of Sidon. They called me Ward and still no one forgot. Even that's a reminder. I came here as a hostage, a prisoner really. I was lucky that Roland had the keeping of me. That he trusted me, and that I had seen the nature of my family first-hand and knew that, if they did ever get their hands on me, I'd be as good as dead. But the court here know who I am, and they remember what my people did to them, and they hate me for it.'

Wren shuffled back, letting him rise a little so that they sat face to face. Something had changed. Something fundamental. 'What happened?' she asked. 'What is it?'

He shrugged, but didn't pull away. He gazed into her eyes and spoke softly. 'I have to leave.'

She framed his face with her hands, running the pads of her thumbs along the high cheekbones, like blades beneath his skin. He was more beautiful than anyone had the right to be, she thought. And he was hers.

'What do you mean, leave?' He didn't mean now. This was more. Much more. And she dreaded the answer. But it didn't come. He swallowed hard, his Adam's apple moving in the column of his throat and she longed to kiss him there, and feel his shudder.

And do so much more. To make him gasp out her name. To make him wrap his body around hers.

'Just that, my love. I can't help it. Roland can explain.'

No, she wasn't having this. None of it. He wasn't going to pull away from her because of who his father was and what others expected of him.

'You're mine,' she told him. 'Didn't we already decide that?'

'When you saved my life? Does that mean you own me now?' He was trying to be harsh, trying to drive her away and horrify her. She could see that now. Oh the pain inside him was cruel and sharp, and so very bitter. It was all turned in on himself. Great light, he tortured himself all the time, didn't he?

'Long before that, Finn. You're mine and I am yours. Nothing is going to change that. I won't let it. Neither should you.'

'They'll use me against you, Wren.'

Who? She didn't dare ask. Everyone perhaps.

She pulled his mouth to hers again and kissed him, softly now, longingly, not a kiss of wild desire but one into which she poured all her love, all her fear of losing him, all her hopes and dreams.

She pulled back only far enough to speak, lips still touching, their breath intermingled. 'Let them try.'

Finn leaned his forehead against hers and closed his eyes, defeated, broken, but still hers. Forever hers.

'Your father is waiting.'

She ran her hand down his chest, under the fabric of his shirt and then lower. Finn sucked in a mouthful of air and his head fell back, eyes closing.

'Let him wait.'

CHAPTER 11

ROLAND

What on earth could be taking the girl so long?

Perhaps sending Finn had been a bad idea.

Roland had thought she wouldn't completely ignore him as she had all of the other messages he had sent. And it would give Finn time to explain what was about to happen. He owed the boy that much, surely.

He was half thinking about going to Wren's quarters himself and giving her a piece of his mind about manners when a soft knock sounded on the door.

'Enter,' he barked.

And there she was.

His daughter. The one he had never known existed. And now the heir to the throne, through no fault of her own, a role for which she was totally unprepared.

They had done their best to make her presentable, the ladies-in-waiting, but he could see clearly that she still delighted in defying them. Her hair was a case in point, ragged and cut short. She refused to wear anything on her head, beyond a ribbon.

Lynette had told him all about it. At length. With far too

many details. And Yvain had done nothing to intervene as his wife complained.

'Better you hear it than I do,' his friend said, when Roland looked to him for aid.

And though it might have all the makings of a nightmare, of a constant political headache, Roland couldn't help but feel proud of her. She was standing her ground as best she could, he supposed.

There was no sign of Finn. Maybe he was waiting outside. Roland had told him to take his summons to her, make sure she read it and to bring her back here, no matter how long it took. And it had indeed taken a very long time. He hadn't said that his ward needed to be in the room as well while Roland explained everything to her.

It was probably better this way.

She didn't look upset. She must have taken some time to compose herself when Finnian told her he had to leave the palace. Maybe that explained the time it had taken. Hopefully, no more would be said about it. If she had come in here in tears, or demanding that he change the plans, he wasn't quite sure what he would do. There was no way he could alter anything now.

'What can I do for you, Grandmaster?' Wren asked, taking the seat he offered. She had Elodie's way of making even the grandest title sound small. It used to amuse him, he recalled.

It was a lot less amusing in the mouth of his daughter.

But still, she seemed fine. Calm. That was good.

'I've reached a decision which will affect you,' he said, deciding there was no point in beating about the bush.

'Affect me how?' Wren asked, instantly suspicious. Rightly so. At least she had some instincts that might allow her to survive at this wretched court. She would need to develop a thicker skin though. And be less transparent.

'Combat training. You will begin tomorrow morning. After

breakfast, two of my finest knights will begin your instruction in weaponry.'

She was staring at him like he had suggested she learn to walk through fire. 'Weaponry? They're going to teach me how to fight?'

'Well... yes.'

To his surprise, she was on her feet in an instant, her eyes shining, with a smile like a child given gifts for her nameday. 'I won't let you down. You won't regret this.'

Roland sat back in his chair, studying her carefully. She was delighted. Not what he had expected from her at all. Young women weren't meant to wield swords. Yet Wren did not like much of what the ladies in the palace did instead. And Elodie had trained, of course, but the court was a different place these days. Ylena didn't approve, preferring more dignified lessons for her women.

Wren was an unexpected puzzle. 'You want to learn how to fight?'

She stared at him as if he had grown an extra head. 'Of course I do. I was useless in the forest. If I hadn't had some measure of magic and knowledge of it from Elodie I would have been...'

Magic. He hadn't heard her admit to its use before. Not in so many words. Well, he had known that much. She had lit the sky on fire with it, called up the light of the Aurum and sent it flowing through each of the knights. She had saved Finn. That was the way she would fight. Didn't she realise that?

But the moment she said it out loud, her face fell and she looked truly appalled that she had admitted as much to him. Slowly, she dropped back into the chair.

'I mean...' she tried to begin. Words failed her.

Roland leaned forward, still examining the minute changes in her expression, the way she betrayed herself. She was afraid of her abilities, he realised. Or rather, afraid of what she could do with them.

Understandable. And probably wise.

'You are Elodie's daughter,' he told her in that calm voice he used with new recruits, or men shaken apart by the worst excesses of war. 'Of course magic comes naturally to you. But you are also my child, so I hope the sword will as well. Magic is not the answer to everything and it can be fickle. A sword, less so.' It was the smallest kindness. Admitting their relationship was risky in public, though everyone knew it. And besides, if anything happened to her when he had the means to give her another way to defend herself, he'd never forgive himself. It was bad enough he was already sending away the one man she trusted above all others.

'I'll... I'll try my best.'

He didn't doubt that. Not for a moment. She didn't strike him as lazy or careless in anything she did. Young, yes, but not a child. Not anymore. He felt a surprising stab of pain at not having known her as a little girl. His little girl.

Now, she was a woman, in her own right. She had held off the Ilanthians, and whatever they had called down to destroy her and Elodie. She was powerful.

And she had saved Finn.

Speaking of whom...

Finn hadn't told her. Her joy and openness told Roland as much. Roland guessed that he wouldn't have been able to. Which left him with the dubious honour. Wren might be delighted now, and he wanted to savour that. She was going to hate him again in a few minutes.

'The knights who will instruct you have also been charged to form a protective guard for you. You know Anselm Tarryn already, and Olivier Arrenden is no less a knight. They have been brothers-in-arms since they first became squires. I hope that the bonds of comradeship and brotherhood will—'

'You want me to be their brother?' She smiled as she said it. It was the first time he thought he had ever seen her smile in actual amusement or make a joke. He schooled his face to stone. This was serious.

'No. I expect you to be their princess.'

She glanced over her shoulder, couldn't help herself.

So, Finn was definitely waiting outside. Roland would have had to be a blind fool to not see the affection between the two of them, more than affection in fact. He didn't need to encourage it. But at the same time, Finn would do anything to protect Wren. He would encourage the others to do the same. She would wrap them all around those little fingers of hers, exactly the way Elodie had when they were the same age.

'Anselm and Olivier will be in command of this new unit. They will choose your guards, see to their rotation and... Wren, you will obey them. Their word is mine.'

Her smile twisted a little, as if she was trying to hold back a laugh. She was far too like her mother. Trouble. It shouldn't charm him the way it did.

'I see,' was all she said. That didn't sound like agreement, not really. Roland struggled not to give a growl of frustration.

'I mean it,' he told her. 'It could save your life one day. And theirs. They would die for you, each of them. Don't waste that.'

The seriousness of the statement reached her and the smile faded. 'Yes, I-I really do see.'

Her reply was solemn, and humble. That was good. That was necessary. She understood the weight of this. He couldn't put it off much longer. He needed to tell her about his plans for Finnian as well.

'I saw her today,' Wren cut in before he could say anything else. The words stole all sense from him.

'Elodie?' He blurted out her name, or rather the name he had always used for her in his heart of hearts. The name she had chosen to go by when she fled with Wren. That meant something as well, but he couldn't put a label to it. Elodie blamed him, loathed him, was rightly furious with him for bringing her back here and putting their daughter in danger. For putting his duty to the Aurum and the crown first.

'Yes. She... she's so sad, Roland.' She paused after using his name and he realised she had never used it before, not to his face anyway. It hung strangely on her tongue, like she was testing it out. When he didn't correct her, she drew in a breath, blinked and went on. 'They'll find her innocent, in this trial, won't they? They have to.'

He could lie, tell her everything would be all right, that Elodie would win through this like she had won through everything else in her life. But he wasn't so sure himself. There were people in this city who hated her.

Those who loved her too, but... she had made enemies. Too many of them.

He didn't have an answer. His usual self-assurance, all the ways he had cultivated his stony exterior, failed him.

'I... I hope so.' It sounded weak and helpless, something he had never allowed another soul to hear since she had left.

Wren stared at him in horror. 'You won't let anything happen to her, though. Will you? You can't.' He glanced away, aware of a sharp pain in his chest which should not be there. 'Roland!'

The snap of his name made him look back. Her outrage shamed him. 'I... I'll do what I can. I'll speak for her, stand for her. But I can't predict what will happen. I don't want to make false promises to you, Wren. The Aurum will judge her, and then the maidens, and finally the council will resolve her fate. I'm just one man. I have duties and responsibilities. The law must apply to all of us equally, Wren. Even Elodie.'

'You are the law here, aren't you?'

Was that what she believed?

He shook his head. 'I'm its servant. That's how it has to be.'

'I thought you loved her.'

It was no more than a whisper but it sounded so loud in his head, cutting into him like a hot blade.

He drew in a breath, fought the screaming in the back of his mind and the urge to throw her bodily from the room, and let the air out again in a long slow hiss. 'That was a lifetime ago.'

Wren had started to rise from the chair, and froze there, staring at him. No, at his hands.

They were clenched into fists on his desk, his blunt nails biting into the palms. This wouldn't do. He couldn't lose control like this. Not here, not in front of this... this girl... Carefully, he uncurled them.

He ground out more words, hardly caring what they were. He needed her to leave. Finn could break the bad news to her himself. He should have done it to begin with. This was not Roland's place. She hated him anyway. Why allow anything to make that worse? 'Now, if you are finished—'

But it was far too late. She was afraid of him. And like any creature afraid, she was testing him to see when he would turn on her. His own daughter was afraid of him.

And why not? He had shown her no gentleness. He didn't know how to. He had captured her mother and brought her to trial, back in the last place either of them wanted to be. Who knew what lies Elodie had filled her head with?

It struck him then that she wasn't just afraid. She was terrified. Of him, of this place, of what would happen to Elodie, and to herself. Of everything. Oh, she tried to hide it, behind bravado and impudence, but he'd seen that too many times. Finn had been the same when he'd first come here. And clearly, his ward could still be defiant.

Why couldn't he simply obey a direct order when it came to Wren?

'Wren—' Roland began, schooling his face to a calm he

didn't feel. Why did she have to make everything so compli-cated and his temper so unstable?

Because Elodie had taught her. That was why.

His breath turned to fog in front of his face as the air chilled all around them, the temperature plummeting in an instant. The room darkened, light draining away as shadows rose from the corners and the floor, sliding up the walls like water.

Shadow kin.

He knew them, knew their touch and their scent. He had destroyed enough of them to last a lifetime. How were they here, in his study, a place warded and guarded by the magic of the maidens, the very stones touched by the Aurum?

Roland rose, his fears and doubts forgotten. He had one role, one purpose, to protect the blood royal of Asteroth. Wren turned, facing this new threat, putting herself instantly in danger.

With a fluid motion he drew his sword, Nightbreaker. A grandiose name for what was really a simple tool like any other. But it was the sword of the Grandmaster of the Knights of the Aurum, forged long ago by the maidens in the sacred flames, and created to defend against just such darkness. It glowed now with its inner magical light in the darkening room.

'Get behind me, Wren,' he told her, his arm already reaching out to shield her. She glanced at him, her expression startled, and he moved before she could, putting himself between her and the shadow kin as best he could. He needed to raise the alarm. There were others, outside the door. Finnian for one, a knight who was more than half a Paladin if the events at Knightsford were anything to go by. He'd protect the girl. Roland knew that. Finn was already as in love with her as Roland had ever been with Elodie. 'When I move, I need you to run for the door, understand? Finn is out there. Get help. Tell me you understand.'

He needed her to say it. He couldn't risk looking at her for a nod or anything like that. To take his attention away from the shadow kin was to invite disaster. He knew that better than anyone.

'I understand,' she said, and her voice didn't shake. Her attention was entirely fixed, and focused on the threat before them. Like a warrior facing battle. 'But they shouldn't be here. They... they can't be here. Why won't they go away, Roland?'

'What do you mean?' There wasn't time for this. They were coming closer, almost as if they were toying with him. Stalking him like cats with their prey.

'I can't... I can't explain...'

Strain entered her voice, a hint of pain, and he turned, just for a moment, concern surmounting caution.

The shadows pounced.

CHAPTER 12

WREN

The shadow kin surged around Roland, and Wren screamed.

Not in fear, not this time. This was all rage. She lashed out, her mind and will as one, desperate to push them back. How dare they? How could they?

She hadn't called them and she didn't need them. She had already tried to make them leave but they refused. They were hungry, wild, dangerous. The darkness recognised her, and she felt them on the edge of her consciousness, the shadow kin singing in response to her touch. Sweet songs of seduction, thrilling through her blood, seeking out the dark heart of her. But they didn't obey her as they had before.

Leave, she told them again, more forcefully this time. *Don't touch him. Don't you dare!*

The shadows recoiled from her, and from Roland, rising over the Grandmaster in a gyre of hatred and desperation. Pleading with her. For him. To take him. Great light, they wanted him so badly. They seethed with animosity.

'No!' Wren yelled and the air shook with the sound.

The song turned to a lament. Enough, there wasn't time for

this. She shoved all the darkness around them away as hard as she could.

Light burst along the length of Roland's sword, burning brightly as he plunged it into their depths and the voices only she could hear became a shriek.

The door flew open and Finn was there as well, his face pale with anger as he ploughed into the fray.

It only took moments and all was still again but for their panting breath and the sound of footsteps hurrying towards them outside.

Finn pulled Wren into his arms and held her close. His free hand shook as he smoothed it over her hair, his sword still at the ready. That didn't waver.

'Were you hurt? Did they—?'

She shook her head rapidly and cut off the rest of his question. 'They're gone.'

'They shouldn't have been able to get in here.' Roland ran his hand along the length of his sword, the surface still shimmering with the light she had inadvertently imbued it with. By driving back the darkness she had called the light to their aid.

Everyone else would believe she summoned the light but it didn't work like that.

Wren had understood that, finally, in the stone circle. And perhaps she could use that. It was difficult though and left her drained. Roland turned his attention on them both then and she started at the grim determination in his features. 'Finn, I want one of the maidens here to check the wards. Now. See to it.'

Finn released Wren reluctantly and gave an obedient bow before he left. He didn't even say another word. She winced, wondering if he would always put duty first. But how could he do anything else? That was one of the things she loved about him.

'Wren, sit down,' said Roland. Still barking out orders, she thought. Did he ever stop? He had sheathed Nightbreaker once more. 'It takes effort, to do what you just did. You look like you're about to collapse.' He was stating the obvious and she was certain she felt even worse.

She sank back into the chair, unable to argue with him anymore. An unwelcome trembling had entered her limbs and if she didn't sit, she feared she was going to fall.

Had she called them in the first place? She had been angry with Roland. And afraid. And the next thing she knew...

No, she hadn't summoned them. Not even instinctively. She was sure of that.

'You did well,' her father said softly, his large hand cupping her shoulder as he passed. A simple gesture but it left her stunned. 'Take a moment and breathe.'

'I'm fine,' she told him, trying to hide the way her hands shook.

'Your mother used to say things like that. She was never telling the truth either.' He slumped back into his own chair as if suddenly carrying the weight of the world.

He should have been safe here, in the Grandmaster's study, protected by wards.

But wards could be circumvented.

'Did they... did they follow me in?' Wren asked, as carefully as she could.

'You?' He sounded surprised, which gave her a moment of hope. 'How could they have followed you in here?'

Because they had followed her every footstep her whole life. Because they were part of her and she was part of—

Wren shoved herself up. 'I should go.'

Noise outside interrupted anything Roland might have been about to say in reply and Finn entered again, followed by Sister Maryn.

'What happened? We felt it in the air and I came as soon as I—' She stopped as she clapped eyes on Wren.

'The wards failed,' Roland said. 'Shadow kin attacked but Wren repelled them.'

The woman's left eye twitched a little. 'Did you now?'

Oh light and shades, she knew. Somehow, she knew. Wren could see it as if it was scrawled on her face in red ink. She glanced at Finn who looked as lost as she was.

'How could they fail?' Roland continued oblivious. 'They were only renewed a month ago, Maryn.'

'Out,' said the maiden with an imperious wave of her hand. 'All of you. I need to concentrate.' Wren couldn't get out of that room quickly enough, but even then it was no escape. 'Not too far, princess,' Maryn called after her. 'We need to talk.'

Which left her trapped in the antechamber, stuck there with Finn and Roland, like she was awaiting judgement.

Roland had a number of hushed conversations with others who came and went. Finn stared at her and Wren tried to look anywhere but at the door to the Grandmaster's office.

'I didn't do anything,' she whispered and he reached out to take her hand for a moment, to gently squeeze her fingers and then retreat. At least, she thought, she had that.

A booming voice broke the silence that followed. 'Grandmaster? What's this I hear about an incursion?'

Was it her imagination or did Roland wince for a second before wiping his face clear of all expression and turning to greet the newcomer? Finn moved closer to her, a shield again, her guardian. Which meant he felt she was now in need of protection rather than simply comfort. This could not be good.

'Lord Sassone.' Roland's voice was a rumble. 'There's nothing to be concerned about. We have the matter in hand and a representative of the maidens is already—'

Lord Sassone didn't quite come up to Roland's eyeline, but he made up for that in sheer obnoxious presence. The clothes he wore were the most costly Wren had ever seen, trimmed with gold thread and embroidery. He had an entourage following him as well, armed men in uniform wearing a simpler form of the same livery, his personal guards no doubt. They filled the narrow antechamber and suddenly it seemed as if all the air had been sucked out of the place.

'Is the princess unharmed?' Sassone asked courteously.

'Of course,' Roland replied. 'She's perfectly safe. She was with me the whole time.'

Thankfully he didn't mention her magic or that she had used it to drive them off. At least Roland was discreet.

Sassone turned his piercing gaze on her. He might have been handsome in his youth, she thought absently. And he would have known it too. He reminded her of Pol, the boy from the village she had thought she was in love with. The one who had found out about her ability with magic and shunned her. Who had married someone else, and got her with child in the darkwood. Who had nearly killed her.

She didn't know if he was still alive. The village of Thirbridge had been destroyed by the Ilanthians led by Prince Leander, hunting Finn. The prince who had captured her and almost killed Finn. The man who served the Nox and would see Wren made its vessel in the world, filled with its power with no will of her own.

Sassone had the same air about him as Leander as well, she thought suddenly. That was who he truly made her think of. Finn's brother. Raised to rule and heedless of anyone else.

He skewered her with his gaze.

'Well, that's good news at least. Light forfend anything should happen to you, princess. You are precious to all of us in Pelias.' He was saying the right words, but every nerve in her body felt repulsed.

She didn't know how to reply to that. People like him tended to lock away precious things and never let them see the light of day.

'She needs a guard, Roland,' he went on, Wren dismissed as

a person capable of her own thought and speech. 'A reliable guard.'

'And she has a unit already assigned to protect her,' Roland ground out, clearly irritated. 'Your son is among them, as requested.'

'And Ward?' Sassone lifted the corner of his upper lip as if he tasted something unpleasant. He glanced at Finn, still so close to Wren that she could fold into his arms if needed. She didn't dare move.

Roland's jaw tightened. 'Ward has other responsibilities, as you know.'

'We had word from Ilanthus,' said Sassone. 'The Ilanthian ambassador will be here soon. You should probably take yourself off to the embassy to see it's all in order before they arrive, Ward.'

Roland let out another of those low growls but Sassone didn't seem fazed. He narrowed his eyes, and there was a light deep inside them that was almost gleeful. Oh, he did not like her father at all, did he? Nor Finn.

'It's an olive branch, Roland. I know you don't see them often in your line of work, but we need to grasp them when offered. The light knows, they are few and far between when it comes to the line of Sidon.'

At the sound of his family name, Wren glanced surreptitiously at Finn. His eyes were focused on the wall above Sassone's head as if he might bore a hole into the stone with his will alone but she was sure his shoulders stiffened.

An Ilanthian prince given in hostage to the victors of their great war, he must have heard this sort of thing a thousand times over. How could he just ignore it?

'I am aware,' said Roland quietly. Nothing more. The silence stretched on, awkward and strained. 'Is there anything else I can help you with, Lord Sassone?'

'No, I think not.' His pale grey eyes lingered on Wren again, weighing her somehow. She drew back and Finn stepped in front of her, arms folded over his chest. Sassone didn't seem worried about that either. 'It will be good to see some of your own, Ward,' he continued, a little louder than was necessary. 'I am told the last meeting with your brother didn't go so well.'

Wren lifted her hand to Finn's back and his muscles stiffened beneath her touch. Alarm, anger, grief... they came off him in a wave that only she could feel. If Finn managed a polite smile, it was fleeting and there was no trace of it in his voice. 'They rarely do, Lord Sassone. But then, I'm sworn to serve here now.'

'And you serve us well in all things. Including this new mission, I am sure. When do you leave for the embassy? I presume you'll quarter yourself there?'

It was Wren's turn to stiffen, to try to stop herself showing her dismay.

When Finn had said he had to leave, she hadn't given it much thought. Everything else had driven that from her mind. He was leaving the palace.

When had he planned to elaborate on that?

CHAPTER 13

WREN

If Finn noticed Wren's dismay he gave no sign. He spoke to Sassone calmly, the perfect knight. 'I will follow the instructions I am given, my lord. My loyalty is as ever to the Aurum and the crown.'

Sassone smiled broadly and Wren wished she could call up the shadows now to wipe that expression off his face. He took Finn and his loyalty for granted. And still despised him. 'Should you need it, you can get aid from my people. I still keep the fortress at the city walls in perfect order and it is little more than a stone's throw from your new home. The embassy is a fine building for an Ilanthian design. But it has been empty for too long. The new ambassador will be lucky to have your assistance.' He turned away, dismissing Finn from his attention. 'You raised him well, Grandmaster. That has to be said. The council will be meeting in an hour. You'll probably want to be there to go over security arrangements with us, Roland. Especially in light of—' He gestured vaguely towards the door to Roland's study and then left.

Wren's stomach roiled and the realisation of what had been so flippantly discussed washed back over her.

Had Finn been planning to tell her he was leaving the palace at all? Had Roland? Was she going to wake up one morning and find that he was gone? Her stomach tightened and the whisper of the darkness grew louder and louder. The shadows had not gone so far away as all that. She couldn't lose her temper now or let this strange pain overwhelm her.

But Finn was leaving her. It wasn't fair. It wasn't right.

Someone muttered a curse under their breath. Wren wasn't sure who it was. Her own heartbeat was deafening.

'Finnian,' said Roland after a few minutes more. 'Please escort the princess back to her rooms and perhaps, this time, you should explain—'

The study door opened and Sister Maryn appeared. 'Has he gone?'

'Have you been hiding back there to avoid him?' the Grandmaster asked. Maryn grinned at him.

'Of course I have. Wouldn't you? The wards were broken, Roland. Deliberately. Someone wanted your office to be a weak point. Someone must have summoned them somehow. Blood will have been spilled in the palace to bring it about, too. This is not good.'

'I suspected as much. And when Wren was there too. If things had gone differently—'

Maryn held up a hand. 'But it didn't. Wren needs training but she's strong and her instincts are good. She's already almost the match for Elodie at the same age.'

The age when Elodie had left. No one mentioned that. The age when she had faced down the Nox, broken it and fled Asteroth. The whole reason she was being put on trial.

Wren shifted uncomfortably. If they knew the truth of her, of the power inside her and the things it could do, they wouldn't even bother with a trial.

She glanced at Finn but his face gave nothing away. She had always known he could keep a secret. She'd had no idea until now how well, nor that he would keep something from her.

'We have her protection and training in hand, Maryn,' Roland went on. 'I've formed a guard for her and she will train in the sword and—'

And Finn would not be there. Now she knew why he'd been left off that list in favour of a knight she didn't even know. They were sending him away.

'The sword,' Maryn scoffed. 'We'll train her to use her magic. Hone it. Improve it. Make a queen of her.'

Oh she had had enough of this. Of any of it.

'And what if I don't want to be a queen?' Wren cut in. 'What if I'm the wrong person? What if—?'

'There's no "*what if*" to it,' Maryn replied before Roland got there first. 'You are who you are. Elodie has agreed.'

Elodie had mentioned training with the maidens, true, but not with a view to taking her crown. Wren growled with frustration.

'Elodie is a prisoner standing trial for betraying the crown,' Roland interrupted curtly before Wren said something unfortunate. He sounded as irritated as she felt. 'She doesn't get a say in this.'

'Wren is her heir. Of course she has a say. She has not been found guilty of anything, I would like to remind you. Oh, and Roland, she wants to talk to you.'

For a moment he didn't move. Perhaps he couldn't. He stared at Maryn like she'd said something impossible. And then he just left the room, moving as if only his innate sense of decorum stopped him sprinting.

Maryn chuckled to herself. 'Thought that might shut him up.'

'What are you doing?' Wren asked, incredulous.

The maiden rolled her eyes. 'Getting you ready for a throne. And hopefully saving those around you. Someone wanted him dead today. The wards were deliberately broken and the shadow kin summoned. If you had not been there, he would not have stood a chance. No, Finnian Ward,' she said before he could interrupt her. Loyal to a fault, that was Finn. Roland was his hero. He would defend his skill and valour in spite of everything, Wren knew that. 'He would not have stood a chance if he was alone, off his guard...'

'But I was there with Roland, when the shadow kin attacked,' Wren protested. 'If someone wanted him dead then why do it when I was there? Unless they wanted me dead too.'

Maryn shook her head, her headdress rippling behind her. 'No, they don't want you dead. You weren't meant to be there, I think.'

'We were late,' said Finn quietly. He sounded deflated now, defeated. And so very worried. 'We should have been here earlier and you would have left by the time... Sister Maryn is correct. Roland would have been alone, working, lost in thought probably, as he often is. He would have thought he was safe in there. Someone was trying to kill him.'

The thought of someone trying to summon up shadow kin to set on Roland in his own study, where he should have been protected, haunted Wren. They had been strong, those dark creatures, powerful and clever. Perhaps her fear or anger had drawn them out but they were waiting there until he was distracted, lost in concentration or simply tired.

Elodie was imprisoned. If she was found guilty, Wren would be forced onto the throne. And without the man who was, everyone said, her father to support her, who would step into the gap? Who would claim her next?

Finn was leaving her. Or being sent away. Or going willingly. She wasn't sure which.

'Were you going to tell me?' she had asked as soon as they were alone, in a corridor on the way back to her rooms. Finn stopped and then pulled her into his arms. Someone would see, she was sure of that. It seemed like there was always someone to see, always someone to gossip.

But Wren didn't care about palace gossip.

She was the centre of it anyway. It followed her like a pack of hounds on a hunt. At the banquets, at the balls and other gatherings, it lingered in the air. She couldn't avoid it. Sometimes when she walked into a room, everything went quiet for a moment and eyes lingered on her. Few of them felt friendly.

'I tried,' he admitted. 'I got... distracted. I'm sorry, my love. You shouldn't have found out like that.'

My love. How could he say that and then...

'But you're still going.'

'I have to. My duty is to the crown, to the knights. And if I can use my family connections to help end the conflict between Asteroth and Ilanthus...'

He trailed off, clearly thinking about the enormity of that task.

She gazed up into his eyes. He tried to smile. 'Do you think you can?'

'I have to try, don't I? For both our sakes.'

There wasn't really anything she could say to that. The last time he had encountered his people, his own brother, he had almost died. They hated him. And she wasn't sure this wasn't a trap. But what could she say? 'Stay safe. Don't forget me.'

He took her hand and pressed it against his chest. His skin was warm, and she could feel his heart thudding beneath the muscles there. 'I could sooner forget myself, Wren. You know that. And it won't be for long. I'm not far. Just down at the city walls. You can see it from here. Look.'

He led her to the window which had a view down over the city rather than out over the sea. The walls were a circle of grey stone, thick and impregnable. She could see rooftops and market squares jumbled together as they spilled down the slope of the mountain. But at the bottom, where the ground levelled off, there were larger structures. Fortifications and defences. And among them, smaller versions of the keep in which they stood.

'There,' Finn said, pointing. 'See the towers on that one, three of them, tall and thin? With the golden spires?' She picked it out, the decorative stonework beautiful even from this distance. It was different from the stark buildings around it, more like the palace on the mountaintop. 'That's where I'll be. You can watch me from here and I'll look for you.'

'I will,' she told him, and pulled him into a kiss which she prayed would sear him into her memory forever. And her in his. She couldn't bear the thought of losing him. 'Come back to me, Finn. Please.'

'Always,' he murmured, and ran his lips down the line of her neck as he gathered her to him. 'I swear that to you. Trust Anselm and Olivier and stay safe. And I will always find my way back to you, my love.'

She threaded her fingers with his, and drew him after her, back to her chambers.

THE ANNALS OF HOUSE
TARRYN AND SASSONE

The House of Tarryn and Sassone is older than Pelias. It is said that when the Aurum first came to the Sanctum, a member of that line stood between the Chosen and the flames. In the first days of Pelias, when the first stones were laid for its walls, Castel Sassone was already there. On the last day, the day of weighing up, when Pelias falls and the Aurum finally gutters and goes out, House Sassone will still stand.

CHAPTER 14

FINN

Rumours were circulating among the men by dawn. It had probably spread all through the night. One of the squires approached Finn tentatively, as he packed his remaining gear, and seemed in awe of him, shuffling his feet and unable to meet Finn's gaze.

'The Grandmaster took care of them, didn't he?'

He was a boy from one of the outer provinces. Finn glanced at his face, stalwart bravery and sheer undying belief in Roland vying with the fear of nightmares and stories. The shadow kin had been here, in the citadel, in one of the most warded parts of the palace. And if they could get in there, into Roland's own study, where else could they infiltrate? Who else would they try to kill?

Everyone was scared. This boy was actually hiding it better than most.

'The Grandmaster did,' Finn replied, trying to make his voice comforting. 'And the princess called on the light of the Aurum to aid him. We fight the Nox, remember?'

'With flame and sword.'

The boy nodded, swallowing hard and echoed the vow of

the knights that Finn had begun for him. 'Is she really the princess?'

'I believe so.' What else could he say? He knew she was. He had seen what Wren could do. The balance of light and dark was wavering inside her, the Nox and the Aurum vying for control. But all the same, she kept reaching for the light.

He prayed she always would. Because if Wren faltered and failed... if the temptation became too great for any reason... the Nox incarnate in her body, with her power, would be beyond terrible.

And he would still love her.

He would give up everything to protect her. Including the chance to be with her. He had no choice.

To his surprise Anselm met him by the main gates to the palace complex. He was dressed in plain leathers and carried his sword but no armour.

'Shouldn't you be guarding Wren?' Finn asked bluntly. It was early still. And Wren was asleep in her bed. He wasn't about to tell Anselm this, or how he knew. Anselm was probably aware of it anyway. The last thing anyone would say about Anselm Tarryn was that he didn't see everything that went on around him.

'Olivier is on it. He volunteered.'

Well, almost everything. Anselm didn't see what was in front of his own nose when it came to Olivier but that wasn't Finn's secret to tell. He'd seen the way Olivier looked at Anselm for years, the way they sought each other out, even if Anselm at least didn't appear to know why. And Olivier would never broach the subject himself. His family were strict and religious. He was sworn to the Aurum and nothing could come before that. Not even his own feelings. He always said he had given up everything to serve the Aurum.

'Anselm, you don't have to come with me.'

'Someone should. Just in case.'

'Wren will need you here.'

Anselm cast him an indulgent look. 'And I'm not planning on staying with you, Finn. But...' he shrugged. 'It seems wrong to make you slink off in the dawn like you've never been here.'

Finn shouldn't have felt quite as relieved as he did. He didn't have many friends. But Anselm was one.

The city beyond the palace gates pressed together, buildings on top of buildings, houses and towers of shared rooms, narrow streets which ran down in a steep spiral, like unspooling thread. The harbour to the east hugged the cliffs but towards the western gate, the richer inhabitants had spread out, taking up space, filling the lower city with gardens and plazas.

Castel Sassone had always been a huge, oppressive structure. The Earl of Sassone had charge of the city's watch and the gates. Though he was more usually found in the palace, the compound which loomed over Finn now was an ugly block of stone.

'Not so pretty, is it?' asked Anselm. 'Try growing up in there. He has dungeons of his own, you know. And he can call on an army to man the walls if we come under attack, to hold the city until the knights can be summoned. I've tried to warn Roland but...' He sighed. 'I guess they need him. Rich, powerful, a leader of men... My mother died just up there.' He pointed to a circular turret jutting out of the walls above them. 'Threw herself off the bartizan and died on the lower walls.'

He said it so casually that Finn wasn't quite sure he'd heard him at first.

'I didn't... I didn't know.'

'Why should you?' Anselm gave an unusually cold smile. 'No one talks about it. My father wouldn't have that. So we all packed it away and moved on. I haven't been back in years. I'd rather keep it that way. Why don't you show me your embassy instead?'

He was here for a reason then. Of course he was. Scope out

the Ilanthian embassy. Roland probably sent him. Find out who had already arrived, who was expected and what sort of welcome they gave Finn.

'You are going back, aren't you?'

His friend laughed softly. 'Of course I am. I certainly don't want to waste any more time in the vicinity of that monstrosity than I have to. I spent far too long escaping from it. I was sneaky even as a child, you know. I had to be.'

'Escaping?'

Anselm tapped his nose. 'Secret tunnels, Finn. Riddled with them. He'd have a fit if anyone ever found out though, so keep it between you and me. My father always has another way out. So did his grandfather before him. Once upon a time we were no more than robber barons, before the Aurum and the royal family. They built this city around my family home, swallowing it up. That's why Castel Sassone looks the way it does and why he keeps his own men. Can the Ilanthian embassy say the same?'

Possibly. Finn wouldn't know. He avoided the place even more studiously than Anselm avoided his family seat.

It was strange to walk up to an enemy stronghold in the city, turning their backs on a structure so fortified to find the building they sought to be delicate and beautiful. Finn hadn't thought he would ever see it as such. Sidon itself was like this, elegant and bright. It was a city of luxury and decadence and the embassy reflected that here, where it seemed wildly out of place. No wonder the people of the lower city hated it. It probably had little to do with living memory either.

The walls were made of shining stone, polished to a mirror-like sheen. It was decorated with touches of gold. Gold paint, no doubt, or the denizens of Pelias would have stripped it away in the night. But that hadn't stopped the Ilanthians putting it there in the first place. Almost as if they wanted to rub their enemies' faces in it.

The walls were faded now, run-down, but someone had already made a start on repairs. Which meant that someone must have already arrived, as Finn had been warned might be the case. The full diplomatic delegation would arrive over the next few days, he knew that. But some brave fool had to be first.

Finn hammered on the heavy oak gates, carved in the Ilanthian style with images of night flowers and birds in flight. Objectively beautiful again. Everything was beautiful in Sidonia, artful, skilfully wrought. He always forgot that. Seeing it here made it more of a shock. But the beauty of Ilanthus only skimmed the surface like shimmering oil. Danger lurked beneath it. He had to remember that.

A guard opened the gate, stared open-mouthed and almost slammed it shut again. At the last moment, he caught himself and tried to bow.

He looked about fourteen and the armour was far too big. He rattled.

'What on earth...?' Anselm murmured to himself.

'Your highness,' the boy stammered. 'We weren't expecting... that is... we thought you'd send word first and...'

Your highness... Finn was never going to get used to that.

He glanced at Anselm who betrayed nothing. His friend knew who he was of course. But Finn liked to think he was just Finn Ward and forget about the whole thing as much as he could. Anselm had always accepted that and played along. But he knew. They all knew.

Finn didn't respond and the poor boy looked lost, then terrified. He took a step back and opened the gate wider for him to enter. And well he might look terrified. If he behaved like this with Leander for example, he'd probably lose his head. And in an especially messy way.

'Please, your highness,' he said, his voice shaking. 'Come inside. I'll send for my— I mean, the ambassador and—'

The inner courtyard was deserted. There were boxes and

cases still strewn about the place. They must have only arrived last night which might explain a few things, Finn thought. He was aware that Anselm was taking all this in as well and felt a wash of... was it embarrassment? This would never happen in the palace so far above them. It would probably never happen in Castel Sassone either. And it would definitely never happen in Sidonia, where for all its decadence, protocol was everything.

What was going on?

Thank the light Roland wasn't here to see it. Finn had often felt ashamed of his birthplace, but never... never whatever this was.

A woman's voice came from somewhere inside.

'Laurence, when you've finished playing around out there, I need you and Ferdinand to take word to the encampment to tell them to hurry up. We need the rest of the servants here at once. Not to mention my staff. This is ridiculous. There are so many bills and requests and... I don't even know what this is...' She appeared in the doorway, carrying a sheaf of papers she seemed in the process of sorting through, a frown creasing her brow. She was wearing an Ilanthian gown, sleek and neat, which did little to hide her figure beneath the fall of silk. When the boy – Laurence – cleared his throat meaningfully, she looked up.

Her eyes were silver, her hair as pale as corn. She held herself like a queen and Finn could only stare.

'Hestia?' he said. 'What are you—?'

'Finnian!'

Of all the people they could have sent, of all the court of Ilanthus! His cousin swept across the courtyard and flung her arms around his neck. She only came up to his chest but that didn't stop her. She was a force of nature and always had been. The years hadn't dimmed her. How could they? Magic sparked along her veins, a higher member of the Sisterhood of the Nox, and she was the king's niece, with all the breeding and privilege that offered.

His cousin. His older cousin. The only member of his family who had ever cared what happened to him, who had hidden him from his brothers, tried to save him from his father, and had brokered the deal that had brought him here to Pelias all those years ago with Roland.

'What are you doing here?' Finn gasped.

'What I do best, my love,' she told him, stepping back and dusting herself down. She handed the papers to the boy Laurence and smiled up at Finn proudly. 'Brokering peace. And look at you. You've grown so tall. A Paladin.' She held out her hands to him and began to pull him inside after her. 'I asked for you specifically, did they tell you?'

'Your name never came up.'

'Well,' she said, a smug smile blossoming on her face. 'That was for good reason. These are delicate times and we are engaged in delicate matters. The household isn't up and running yet, but it will be soon. Once the rest of our party arrive. I only have a skeleton staff. Serves me right for riding ahead but they were taking so bloody long. Have you met Laurence? My son. This is your cousin, Prince Finnian.'

The boy bowed, a little more gracefully this time, and struggled to take off the pieces of armour. Anselm took pity on him and helped.

'Anselm, Lord Tarryn,' said Finnian by way of an introduction.

Hestia curtsied as Anselm bowed and there was the usual exchange of courtesy which seemed to stabilise the mood. But Finn wasn't fooled. The formality masked two experts sizing each other up. Finally she turned back to Finn with a smile.

'We weren't expecting you yet, Finnian. I thought they'd argue more, rather than just send you like this. After what happened when you left Sidonia last...'

After Leander had hunted him and tried to kill him on Asterothian soil. He wondered how much she knew. Clearly enough, from the dark expression that crossed her luminous eyes. Or perhaps she meant Wren and that was even more of a worry. He glanced at Anselm, who was giving nothing away.

'I should let you reconnect with your family,' his friend said. And trot back up the many hills of Pelias to report on all this, no doubt. Light knew, Finn loved Anselm like a brother – more so, though that wasn't hard – but he was under no illusions as to Anselm's devotion to Roland. 'We look forward to word from you, Prince Finnian, at the first available opportunity.'

And there it was. Prince Finnian. Not Finn, not his friend and comrade-in-arms. He was a prince of Ilanthus again, and the thought of that sent a chill through him.

'Anselm,' Finn called before he could vanish completely. He followed him to the gate and pulled him in close. 'Look after Wren for me,' he said softly, once he was sure Hestia couldn't hear. 'There's more going on here than meets the eye.'

'With Lady Hestia here?' Anselm would be a fool not to know who she was and of what she was capable. Hestia Rayden was a legend in the history of the war with Ilanthus. She had brokered the Pact. Finn had heard seasoned courtiers lower their voices in hushed tones of respect when mentioning her name in both royal courts. 'You are absolutely right. Be careful, my friend. You're walking on the edge of a blade here. You know that, don't you?'

In all things concerning his home and his family. Yes, Finn knew that.

Hestia was waiting for him, eyeing Anselm's retreat with a keen eye. 'Now we're alone, there's something I must show you.'

He didn't have any choice but to follow her. Once they had reached the small office she had claimed as her own, she took out a small wooden case, intricately carved with Ilanthian craftsmanship, and set it on the table.

'Close the door, please, Finn.'

He didn't want to, but there wasn't much else he could do.

When he turned back to face her she was holding out the case with a look of triumph and pride on her face.

'Here,' she said when he didn't come closer. 'It's a gift. From your father.' He still didn't move and Hestia sighed. 'Finn, it's a peace offering.'

'A what?'

'I mean it.'

Finn could think of nothing less likely. 'From Alessander?'

Hestia laughed. 'Of course. Who else? Look, it has the royal seal on the box and everything. The sisterhood was most insistent. There were signs and portents, Finn. Matters have changed and you're at the centre of it. So, your father sends this as a token of his love and he begs your forgiveness.'

Love? Forgiveness?

'No, absolutely not.' The words came out with a vehemence that surprised even him.

Hestia gave a growl of irritation. 'At least look at it. It's true. I promise. You have my word.'

'Or,' he countered, 'it's some kind of trap and I'll be killed. Or worse. I know my family well, Hestia.'

'So stubborn. Just like him.' She opened the box anyway and thrust it towards him. Finn couldn't help but look, which was her intention.

Nestled in the black velvet interior was a handblown glass pendant in black, shot with blue and green swirls, delicate and beautiful. Magic came off it in waves. Even he could feel that.

But it wasn't hostile or dangerous. If anything it soothed him, calmed him. It sang of home and safety, like the song he half remembered from his childhood, the one his mother used to sing to him.

Finn stared at it and before he knew what he was doing he had lifted his hand to touch it. The surface was smooth and cold.

'What... what is it?' he asked.

Hestia smiled more gently now. 'It's magic, Finn. My finest work, blessed by all the sisterhood and wreathed with protection for you alone. As I said, a peace offering. You are lost here among our enemies. They could turn on you at any moment. So, if you ever have need of it, all you have to do is break this, and it will bring you home.'

Finn snatched back his hand. 'Home?'

'Sidonia. The royal palace,' she told him. 'Where you belong, my lord prince. Where you have always belonged.'

CHAPTER 15

WREN

The next morning Finn was gone.

It shouldn't have hurt quite so much to wake up next to the space where he should have been and know that she wouldn't see him today and that she didn't know when she would see him again. Honour and duty made sure of that. They had made love, worshipped each other throughout the small hours of the night. He'd called out her name and she had whispered his. And now he was gone.

Wren dragged herself out of her bed far later than she should have, and made her way to the training yard where she was to meet her guards.

She was dressed now in a simple tunic and breeches instead of the gowns and dresses which had been forced on her since coming here. 'You look more comfortable in yourself, my lady,' Olivier Arrenden said.

It was the first time in weeks she had felt comfortable at all. And yet without Finn she felt like a hollow shell of what she had once been.

'But not like a princess,' she told him.

'Always that.' The tall, austere knight bowed gracefully. He was handsome but she wondered if he ever smiled. There was something terribly proper about him. A marked contrast to Anselm, who had that kind of open, honest face that had invited her to like him instantly from the first moment they met.

Where was Anselm? she wondered. She'd thought he would be here as well. The other guards were introduced but she barely noticed their names. Rude, she warned herself. She would have to make up for it later. Right now it didn't matter, she would only be training with Olivier for the time being.

'And within this square, you are Wren,' Olivier told her. 'Titles and honours will get in our way. We're here to train in combat, not politics, not magic. And while we won't hurt you, no one learns anything if there isn't some effort put into training. Pull no punches, give no quarter. We will train like your life depends on it. Because it does.'

It sounded so solemn, like another vow binding them together. She wasn't sure she liked Olivier Arrenden, but she respected him. He treated her like a person and called her by her name.

Without Finn, at least she had this.

And oh how she ached later on. Every muscle in her body, even ones she didn't know she had, made its displeasure known by the time they finished. Wren was exhausted and longed to sleep but that was not to be.

Every second of her day was mapped out, it seemed. And that helped in a way. She still missed Finn, but time went by quickly.

In the afternoon, she made her way to the Sanctum where Maryn met her at the gates, shutting those guards who had accompanied her outside.

'You're here to learn focus and control,' the Maiden of the

Aurum told her. 'You grab the power in the land like a greedy child. I'm going to teach you to be a surgeon. You need to control the magic in you, not allow it to control you.'

The afternoon was an interminable round after round of creating a glowing sphere, expanding it and then shrinking it down to nothing again, all the while listening to Maryn's instructions and then mentally trying to adjust them so that they would work for her, while never letting on what she was doing. By the time that was done, her mind was as wretched and exhausted as her body. And while Maryn treated her as a student rather than a friend, it was still better than being a princess.

At least she got to see Elodie, even if only briefly. They sat together in the garden, where Elodie brushed her hair, and trimmed it, and whispered about memories and dreams. When Wren asked her about seeing Roland, what they had spoken of, Elodie smiled and changed the subject.

Wren didn't mention Maryn's suspicion that someone had tried to kill him. Perhaps she had told Elodie herself, or perhaps Roland had but she doubted that.

The time she and Elodie had was precious. They spent it on themselves and no one else. And somehow, after all the training of her body and her mind, even half an hour with Elodie soothed her and healed her.

Elodie didn't mention Finn either. Perhaps she didn't know. But, no. Even now, there was little Elodie didn't know. Word came that Elodie had a visitor and Wren had to leave. She wondered if it was Roland and was surprised to find that she hoped it was. Because suddenly the thought of seeing anyone reunited with the person they loved was important.

She knew from Elodie's reaction to the news that it had to be someone she loved. Even if she would not admit it anymore.

In the evening there was yet another banquet, another court event Wren tried to circumvent and escape. As before, when she couldn't, she lingered as much in the background as she could and left at the first possible opportunity. She didn't have Finn to shield her, to escape with. She didn't have anyone.

Lynette was beside herself. 'You can't keep doing this,' she said as she found Wren back in her rooms just after dark.

'They don't even need me there,' Wren protested. 'All they do is stare anyway.'

'That's because they don't know you. Befriend some of them. It isn't hard.'

Easy for Lynette to say. Wren had never done anything like that. She'd grown up with only Elodie for company, and the children of the village had hardly been what you might call friends.

She had never felt so lost as the days slid by, each one the same.

Lynette had picked out a ballgown which was more ornate and ostentatious than anything so far. Wren stared at it in abject horror as they dragged it over her body and she stepped out from behind the screen to see herself in the large mirror which had been hauled in along with all the other paraphernalia which was part and parcel of this nightmare. The gown was scarlet trimmed with gold, layer upon layer of silk and lace which hardly seemed to cover her properly at all. It hugged her waist and slid off her shoulders, and there was far too much of it around her feet.

'I can't wear this,' she said.

'This ball will be the most formal event of the season, Wren,' Lynette told her, threading her fingers through Wren's dark hair as if she might make it longer through sheer will alone. 'Of any season. You can't turn up in something plain. Or in those breeches you love so much.'

Wren wished she could. With a sword too. That would be a look. Aware of how Lynette would react if she suggested it, Wren wisely stayed silent.

Lynette continued fussing over her hair. 'Guests are arriving in from the outer provinces already, and delegations from the neighbouring kingdoms will be at it too. You need to make a good impression. Dazzle them. You must be the princess you were born to be, everything they expect. And you will be. Look.' Lynette turned her towards the mirror. 'You're beautiful.'

'I look ridiculous,' Wren countered, scowling at her reflection. She didn't look like herself. She looked like something out of a story book or one of those interminable ballads the minstrels loved to sing.

'Saying things like that about yourself is ridiculous. But Wren, my dear, you are not. You're a princess of Asteroth. The heir to the throne. No one in their right mind is going to call you ridiculous. They'll be too busy picking their jaws up off the floor.'

'Do I have to go?'

Lynette's temper snapped. 'Please stop acting like a child. You're a grown woman. This is no laughing matter. Everything depends on how you deport yourself at this ball. Everything. Carlotta? Where is the girl? I swear, she's always off somewhere or the other.'

Wren watched her lady-in-waiting smooth the lines of her furrowed brow. Lynette didn't talk to her like that. Ever.

Carefully, Wren gentled her voice.

'Lynette, why is this ball so important? There have been other balls. What's so special about this one?'

For a moment Lynette said nothing. Perhaps she didn't intend to answer at all, but then she relented. 'The ball is to welcome those coming to witness the trial. It's traditional.'

Elodie's trial. It was happening then. Wren felt a wave of nausea wash through her and all the fight in her fled.

'We're celebrating the trial? With a *ball*?'

'Not celebrating the trial. The ball is a mark of respect for those who have travelled here. Even the Ilanthian ambassador is expected—'

'The Ilanthians are coming too?' Wren couldn't believe that. The very idea was abhorrent, but Lynette shrugged her shoulders in a brief and elegant gesture.

So that was why they were really here, Wren thought. Not to reopen the embassy, but to witness Elodie's trial. To see her suffer.

Wren clenched her fists in the fine fabric of her dress, twisting it around her fingers.

'They are our neighbours, after all. And this is an overture of peace. If there's any chance...' Lynette sighed, and tried to detach the material from her death grip before she damaged it. 'We have to try, Wren.'

Try? How was that possible?

But, if the Ilanthians were coming, did that mean Finn would be with them? She would get to see him, if only for an evening. That would be a small comfort.

Carlotta appeared moments later with a length of gold braid which Lynette proceeded to arrange in Wren's hair.

'Not a crown,' Wren said rapidly. 'Please, Lynette.' She couldn't keep the fear out of her voice. She couldn't wear a crown, or anything that looked like one, to a ball celebrating Elodie's upcoming trial. The whole concept sickened her.

Lynette paused in her labours and gazed at her steadily for a long moment, as if she could see into Wren's mind. 'It isn't a crown, my dear. I promise. Just a headdress, a frivolity to match the gown.' But all the same she withdrew it and handed it back to the maid. 'But you will have to get used to the idea eventually. One way or the other.'

'Not... not yet.'

Never. That was what she wanted to say. But she couldn't.

Lynette would start asking questions as to why she would even think such a thing...

If Wren was crowned before the Aurum the flames would turn black and she might let the Nox in to kill them all, that was what she was afraid of. Or whatever the stupid prophecy meant. Elodie would stand alone against her enemies and fall. How could she admit that to anyone? Who would believe her? At best, they would think her mad. Or foolishly superstitious. But if they did find out what she was, what she could do, the darkness lurking inside her, then Elodie wouldn't be the only one facing the flames.

And oh how the Ilanthians would love that. Their crown prince most of all. She could just picture Leander's triumphant smirk, and it sent a lance of ice down her spine.

'I can't, Lynette. I just can't.' It came out too loud, too sharp, and Wren tore herself free. A terrible silence sank around them and she was sure she heard laughter. The shadows moved and Wren closed her eyes tightly, willing them to go away as hard as she possibly could.

A soft voice broke the silence. 'Perhaps some flowers, your highness? If my lady will forgive me. Above the princess's ear? It's all the style in the lower city at the moment. Less formal and it would be much more becoming.'

They both turned to look at Carlotta who instantly bobbed a curtsy. Wren could have kissed her and when Carlotta straightened she gave Wren a shy but complicit smile.

'I suppose that would do,' Lynette said thoughtfully. 'Yes, very well. Good thinking, Carlotta. Fetch some flowers. We'll use them instead.'

Carlotta bobbed into a curtsy again and left, taking the gold thread with her.

Wren gave a long sigh of relief and Lynette took her hands, leading her over to one of the chairs in the corner. 'You're shaking like a leaf. What happened? Are you feeling quite well?

Perhaps you're doing too much, all this nonsense about swords and magic.'

She was exhausted. But none of that mattered. Not anymore. Not the stupid rules and regulations of her life, the cogs and wheels of the court of Asteroth which ground on around her... Neither did learning to fight, or use magic. It wouldn't do her any good. Nor would having Finn here. None of it mattered.

She couldn't explain it to Lynette. It was no use.

In a few days' time, Elodie's trial would begin and, one way or the other, Wren's fate would be fixed.

A knock on the door distracted them. Anselm stood outside, Olivier behind him. Both of them looked cagey and uncertain.

'What's wrong now?' Wren asked, before anyone else said anything.

'I need to talk to you,' said Anselm. 'I would have come sooner, but I had to be sure. It's about Finn.'

CHAPTER 16
WREN

'What do you mean, his cousin?' Wren asked Anselm. She couldn't believe it but Anselm wouldn't lie. He had no reason to and he looked no happier about this turn of events than she was.

'The ambassador they've sent is Lady Hestia Rayden, Finn's cousin. Her mother was sister to Alessander and her husband died several years ago.' He waved a list of names that must be those of the other attendants. 'The party arriving today is the rest of her staff. I know of most of the names. Finn can't trust a single one of them.'

Wren made a face and turned towards the window to try to breathe in the air. The room suddenly felt constricting and hot. 'Well of course he can't. No one can. They're Ilanthian.'

The words came out before she thought and she gasped when she realised what she had just said. Finn was Ilanthian too. He was a prince, whether they accepted that or not. But, from what Anselm had observed, it sounded like they did. Or at least this Lady Hestia Rayden did.

And that worried her.

'I didn't mean—'

'I know,' Anselm assured her solemnly. 'And you are absolutely right. We'll double your guard, especially for this ball. You shouldn't be too close to any of them. There will be a strict list of those who may dance with you and if you aren't sure, check with Lynette. Or Olivier and me.'

The lady-in-waiting bowed her head carefully. Wren had a feeling that the strict list would be getting shorter and shorter by the second.

'And Finn?' she asked.

He winced slightly, then shook his head. 'He'll be keeping a close eye on them as their liaison and their escort. He will have to. They won't let anyone else near them anyway. You must keep your distance, Wren.'

From Finn. He was warning her away from Finn. She couldn't quite catch her breath for a moment. She had been looking forward to seeing him again, hoping he would come back, and now it seemed that would only be from a distance, for one night, and in front of a whole ballroom full of people. The thought of that made her ache. Not to touch him, not to spend time with him. Not that she wanted to dance at this nightmare of a ball but if it was with him at least... But Finn was firmly embedded amongst the Ilanthians, and it sounded like his cousin intended to make sure he stayed there. And so did Anselm.

'Will *he* be safe?'

He was in the Ilanthian embassy after all, stuck there. She had a vision for a moment of a poison slipped into a glass, or a knife in the dark. And she wouldn't be able to help him. While he might not be far away, it might as well be the other end of the land. She couldn't go to him. That was clear. And now she wasn't to go near him when he was close by.

Anselm didn't try to palm her off with soft and conciliatory words. At least there was that. 'Finn can look after himself, I promise you.'

'But I don't understand why they're coming here,' she

protested. 'They hate us. They always have done. Leander tried to—'

'For the trial,' Lynette interrupted her, obviously deciding that rehashing old history wasn't helping anyone. Wren had never seen her so upset. Oh, she hid it well. Her perfect mask was still in place, but Wren could hear it in her voice, and in her words. 'The queen's trial. Everything else is a front. This so-called peace offer, the embassy, everything. They want to see Elodie suffer and they want to be here if she's found guilty. No doubt they'll want a front-row seat to any execution planned as well. This is madness. Why is Roland allowing it?'

Anselm shrugged.

'The council decided, not Roland. He and Yvain argued against it, my lady, but the others… It's traditional, as they're so fond of saying. They invited representatives of all the neighbouring kingdoms, even the College of Winter, although few of the others deigned to come. They presented him with it as a done deal and will not listen to his arguments. They say he's biased.'

Lynette shook her head as if at a great folly. 'Well of course he is. We all should be. Not so very long ago they tried to kill us all. They almost succeeded. What is Ylena thinking?'

Elodie had said to be patient, that it would all work out. But it didn't feel that way. And now there were Ilanthians in the city, shadow kin on the loose and everyone was at risk.

The last thing they should be doing was holding a ball.

'It's traditional,' Lynette sighed in resignation when Wren pointed that out, repeating what Anselm had said as if there was no way out of it. 'What can we do? Not holding it would be a huge loss of face. Especially now. So you, my dear girl, must shine like the sun itself, and keep just as far away from them.'

Especially with the Ilanthian nobility descending on them. Pact or not, this felt like some kind of trap and Wren couldn't work out what that might be.

'Who is Lady Rayden?' she asked.

Anselm answered. 'Besides being Finn's cousin, Hestia Rayden has been trained by the Sisterhood of the Nox since childhood. She studied more widely too, well beyond Ilanthus, one of the few women of power to do so. She treated with Roland to draw up the Pact when she was not much older than you. She's devious, cunning and one of the king's most trusted advisors. And powerful.'

'That's... not good,' Wren murmured, thinking of Elodie.

'No. Not good at all.' He glanced at the list and winced. 'And General Gaius will be accompanying her. He and Hestia will be the brains of the group. The others... perhaps Hestia brought them here to do the real work of diplomacy, trying to improve the conditions of the Pact and make overtures of peace, but with Gaius involved I doubt it. Finn trusts Hestia. He knew her when he was a child and counts her his saviour along with Roland. But... he may be mistaken in his trust. He may be in terrible danger there.'

'How many of these names do you actually know?' Lynette asked. She had picked up the letter and was reading it closely.

'All but five. They're all listed as attendants. But they could be spies, assassins... anything. They'll be especially watched.'

'And they're all staying in the Ilanthian embassy? They won't like that. It isn't that big.'

'That's too bad,' Anselm replied curtly. 'They aren't staying here.'

'And what do you need from me?' Wren asked.

'Do what we tell you, and you keep yourself safe. No sneaking off.' He fixed her with a particularly knowing glare. 'Not even to find Finn. Not even if he begs you. Don't react, even if they attempt to goad you. I presume they know of your abilities. Leander is hardly likely to have kept that a secret.'

Wren glanced at Lynette but she barely seemed to be listening now. But she had that skill, didn't she, and she missed nothing. 'My *abilities*...' she echoed, burying a warning in her tone.

'You know exactly what I mean.' Anselm knew it was not the Aurum. Finn must have told him.

'I can't... I can't always control it.'

'Then you need to work out how and very fast. Or they will exploit any weakness they find.' She'd thought Anselm gentle and kind. Now she saw an entirely different side to him.

They might expose her, that was what he meant, show all of Pelias that their new princess was more in tune with the Nox and its shadows than with the Aurum and its light.

'Failing that,' Anselm continued more like the man she knew, 'stay as far away from them as you can. Understand? Olivier and I will be there. And the rest of your guards. Just be careful, princess. Whatever happens we need to avoid a diplomatic incident. Between this ball and the trial... if anything goes wrong it could start the war all over again.'

She nodded. What else could she do? There was no getting out of this, apparently. But she wasn't alone. At least there was that.

But she had a horrible feeling that with the Ilanthians involved, avoiding a diplomatic incident was not going to be easy.

CHAPTER 17
WREN

Olivier could dance. That was a surprise.

He was precise and careful, and perfectly mannerly in how he held her, but all the same, he whirled Wren around the dance floor with an ease which made her head spin and an unexpected laugh bubble up in her throat. She almost forgot where she was.

Wren had always loved to dance, although her only partner, apart from the dreamlike spirits in the forest, had been Elodie. But all the same it was a joy, something they had shared, whirling around the upper room in their tower, especially when Wren was little. She hadn't realised Elodie was teaching her courtly dances, something which was most useful now. Perhaps Elodie hadn't realised either. Those dances were all the queen knew. Even when she was pretending not to be a queen anymore.

For a moment, in the music and the opulence of the ball-room, Olivier helped Wren feel graceful and elegant, and almost let her forget the host of eyes upon her. She had walked into the ballroom and immediately felt judged, and found wanting.

Anselm danced with her too, as did Roland, although that was a slow and sedate affair, more like a procession than a dance. A formality, as it turned out, because her father didn't return to her again.

She kept looking for Finn but there was no sign of him yet. Even if he had arrived, the instruction that she should avoid him only made her innate sense of defiance grow. She worried about him constantly. Anselm assured her that he was fine, that he was reporting in and there was nothing to concern her. That didn't help. He said it a little too earnestly for her to believe him. Anselm was a consummate politician, she knew that. He would say whatever was necessary. She wanted to see Finn and the more she thought about it the more determined she became.

Music filled the vast chamber, marrying with delighted chatter and laughter. It was almost as if this was a perfectly normal thing, to be here, to dance, to celebrate...

Celebrate Elodie's trial.

Oh nobody said it. How could they? But Wren couldn't help thinking it. And every time she did the joy seeped out of her, leaving a seething mass of dark anger.

'Princess?' Olivier murmured, concerned. 'Are you all right?'

He was kind, for all his austerity, she realised. He believed in duty and honour, but that didn't make him cruel.

'Just... just worried.'

'Have no fear,' he told her, slowing their pace. 'Come, we can take refreshments and rest a while. Anselm will keep anyone untoward away.'

He glanced for his comrade and as their eyes met, Wren saw something flicker in his expression.

'Have you known Anselm long?' she asked, as guilelessly as she could.

Olivier led her from the dance floor, towards Anselm. 'Since we were boys. We were squires together. When I first came to serve the Aurum, gave it my vows and surrendered my old life, he befriended me.'

'And Finn?'

She shouldn't keep asking people about him. She knew that. But she missed him and hearing the stories of his life here, his friendships, helped.

A smile flickered over Olivier's lips. He knew where this was going then. She was not at all cunning, she knew that, and her need to know about the man she loved undermined any pretence at being clever or sophisticated. 'Yes, Finnian as well. He is a credit to the Grandmaster. You have no idea how wild he was when he arrived here.'

Oh, she did. Not exactly perhaps, no details. But the wildness was not gone from Finn. It had been suppressed, and put to better use. She saw it every time, still buried deep in his tempestuous blue eyes. Great light, she missed him.

Anselm bowed as he approached and fetched her a glass of the sweet wine. Only accept a drink from him or Olivier, she had been told. No one else.

So many rules.

Someone cleared their throat behind her and she turned sharply to see the Earl of Sassone bearing down on her. It was far too late to run and she was standing there with his son and no excuse to be anywhere else.

'Your highness,' he beamed at her. 'You look radiant. What a joy to see you here.'

The gown was the colour of rubies, and Wren wore a choker studded with them around her neck. A small posy of rosebuds had been tucked above her left ear and, after all the poking and prodding from the various ladies-in-waiting under Lynette's supervision, she had finally been deemed presentable.

'Thank you,' she murmured and glanced at Anselm, but he stared ahead like a statue.

'Hardly any trace of the forest left to you. The royal blood of Asteroth will always out, or so they say.'

That was what she was afraid of. But all the same, she lifted her chin and gave him a defiant look.

'And have you spilled a lot of it?' she asked.

Someone choked on a laugh, Anselm she suspected, but he didn't show it when both Wren and his father glared at him.

Sassone smiled at her, a thin, hard expression she really didn't like. It was too calculating. 'You have your mother's wit,' he replied. 'Although she cannot be expected to use it much longer. I suppose you will learn to quell it more cleverly when the crown is yours.'

Wren drew in a breath and felt the shadows in the back of her mind stir with amusement. The sound of the whispers they brought with them almost drowned out the music. Othertongue lingered at the back of her throat but she swallowed it down.

'I'm not planning on wearing a crown,' she told him.

Sassone roared out a laugh, ignoring all the faces turning to look at them, and Wren felt her face flush. 'No choice in that matter, your highness. Sooner or later. Sooner, I'm sure. It'll all be decided in no time. The guilt of your mother is beyond doubt. Rest assured, it is only a matter of time until that crown sits firmly on your pretty head.'

Did he hear himself? How could he talk to her like that?

The whispers were getting louder, the shadows singing to her. How easy it would be to shut him up, and shut him up for good. No one should speak to her like that. No one.

She curled her hand into a fist at her side and felt the darkness twist closer around her fingers, like a weapon.

'Wren,' Anselm murmured. 'Are you all right?' He stood beside her, his hand on the hilt of his sword, glaring at his father. 'Do you need anything?'

She forced herself to shake her head. 'Some air, perhaps. If you would escort me.'

Anselm held out his arm for her and she forced herself to walk away. She could barely control the darkness now, but she had to. Right here in the middle of the ball, with everyone looking, she could not afford to lose control.

She was glad she didn't have to interact with so many strangers. Their stares were bad enough. They had come from everywhere, and all to see Elodie punished. To celebrate it, in the same way Sassone was already celebrating it.

The music had stopped and some sort of commotion was happening at the far end of the ballroom. She looked around for Roland, only to see him heading that way with serious intent. Lynette was hurrying back towards Wren now, trying to appear to be moving nonchalantly and without purpose. Only her haste gave her away, and the way her hands were suddenly knotted together in front of her. Her expression was fixed with concern.

What was wrong? Because something was definitely wrong.

An excited murmur rippled through the crowd.

The crowd parted to reveal a smaller group, stunningly attired for a ball, each of them beautiful and ethereal. Pale-haired and otherworldly, they moved like predators amid the people of Pelias, a royal court that Wren already thought cut-throat. The Ilanthian visitors put them to shame in a second.

Roland intercepted them, bowing with an elegance she would have thought impossible.

That was when she saw Finn, standing beside the Ilanthian woman at the forefront of the group. Her leaping heart stuck in her throat.

He wore typical Ilanthian court clothing. A black high-collared tunic hung open with sash in an iridescent blue which matched his eyes angling across his bare chest. It highlighted the pendant around his neck, one she hadn't seen before, a delicate twist of coloured glass on a thong. He looked darkly handsome beside the pale colouring of the woman, and positively decadent in those clothes.

Wren dragged her attention to the woman wearing the cream and gold sheathlike gown. His cousin, she had to be, and though clearly older than him, she wore her years lightly. Her hand rested on his arm, almost possessively, and Wren frowned. She didn't like that. Didn't like the tight expression he wore, or the way his eyes hunted her out across the crowd.

She started forward, but Anselm's hand stopped her.

'Something's wrong,' said Olivier softly. 'Very wrong. I can feel it.' He scanned the assembly looking for anything untoward, as if sensing something no one else could see.

Finn's voice rang out, strong and certain. If Wren hadn't seen that concern a moment earlier she would never have guessed it had been there now. 'Grandmaster, it is my honour to present the ambassador of the Ilanthian court of Sidonia and her officials.'

It sounded so formal. Like a rehearsed speech. Not like Finn at all. He didn't even look like himself. Not really.

'Of course,' Roland replied. 'The regents' council is most happy to welcome—' He stopped, as if his voice caught in his throat. Wren saw his shoulders tighten in a way that could only indicate he was preparing for an attack or...

Another figure stepped through the assembled Ilanthian visitors, pale and beautiful as the rest of them, but more so, outshining men and women alike. He wore clothes like Finn's, beautifully tailored, the colours picked with care and deliberation to look like exactly what he was, a prince. He didn't bow, but inclined his head curtly. Not exactly polite but far more so than Wren would have expected.

'Grandmaster de Silvius,' said Leander, the crown prince of Ilanthus. 'The pleasure is all ours.'

HERANDAL'S THE FALL OF
THE HOUSE OF SIDON

When Alessander of Ilanthus came to the throne, he was a young man, and he had left a trail of brothers dead behind him, as is the way of that kingdom. He fathered many sons, legitimate and otherwise, and he raised each to wear a crown, to wage their own particular war, to wade to the throne through the blood of the others. All but one.

And finally only two were left – Crown Prince Leander, beloved of his father, and the one known as Finnian, Ward of Asteroth, the lost prince – separate in every way, by light and dark, by distance, by disposition.

They only agreed on one thing.

And that caused disaster.

CHAPTER 18

FINN

Ilanthians delighted in chaos wherever they went. Finn knew that. He should have expected it. From the moment they came, he knew it was all going to go wrong.

Hestia particularly was known for it. It was a way for her to get what she wanted but she always knew how far to go and when to stop. She used chaos like an artist with an array of pigments and brushes at her fingertips.

Leander on the other hand... Leander never knew when to stop. He revelled in trouble, disruption and in doing whatever he could to upset whoever he felt like upsetting all for his own amusement.

Because he could. Because he enjoyed it. Because he would always get away with it.

Leander had arrived at the embassy the afternoon before the ball so Finn never got a chance to send warning.

When his half-brother appeared alongside General Gaius and the rest of Hestia's people, it was all Finn could do not to draw his sword there and then. It probably saved his life, or Leander's, not to mention the trouble it probably would have caused. He might be a prince within these walls, but he was still a Knight of the Aurum and that would matter. Even in Sidonia.

But the last time he had seen Leander, his half-brother had almost killed him, and had almost destroyed Wren with his rituals to call down the Nox.

'Don't,' Hestia said so softly it was a sigh, her hand resting on his arm. No magic, no coercion, but still, he froze at her touch. 'I need your help, Finn. In this as much as anything else.'

'This?' he hissed.

'Leander.'

They had squared off on either side of the main reception room in the Ilanthian embassy while Hestia hurriedly tried to speak words of welcome. And Finn tried not to give in to the lingering urge to attack.

Leander had smiled, lifted his hands into the air to show he was unarmed. 'I come in peace,' he said, the smug, self-satisfied expression enough to make Finn want to risk killing him anyway. Leander knew exactly what he was doing of course. 'Our father sent me. I'm sworn to be on my best behaviour and Hestia has the authority to make sure of that. Don't you, cousin?'

'More than the authority, your highness,' she warned him darkly. 'The ability as well.'

Leander tugged idly at the bracelet on his right wrist as if it irritated him, and scowled at her, his clever words silent now. Finn's eyes latched onto it at once, and he felt the horror in him twist to a new perspective.

Shadow-wrought steel. Designed to control magic and, when wielded by a skilled practitioner, used to inflict great pain.

Hestia was charming and Finn loved her, but she was a sister of the Nox and she was willing to use her magic on anyone as needed, even the crown prince, it seemed, so long as the king decreed it. Leander must have really pissed Alessander off this time.

And their father would never have punished his favourite son without good cause. Finn wondered what it was. It sounded serious.

Leander snorted dismissively. 'See? I'm on a leash.' He had the nerve to pout.

Hestia turned her back on him, sweeping back inside. 'Don't mind him, my dear. Alessander is furious with him because of his attack on you. What he did was unforgivable. If he had succeeded in killing you he would have spent the remaining years of your father's life in the chamber of regrets.' Which was just their charming way of saying tortured to near insanity. But only until his father died, Finn noted. After that... well, they all knew where the crown would land.

Why his father still cared what happened to Finn was anyone's guess. Perhaps Hestia knew, but Finn didn't dare ask. The very thought of what Alessander had planned for him, of what he still might have planned...

Hestia always took control of any situation. She was used to command, to being in charge, and to having people obey her. Finn had been too surprised and unsettled by his brother's appearance that he hadn't thought what it would mean in the larger scheme of things. Such as what Leander's presence here might mean.

Right now, in the midst of the most formal Asterothian ball, with Leander having caused yet another upheaval of seismic proportions, Hestia took control of the situation. Yet again.

Perhaps that was the plan. Throw everyone off balance and then Hestia would sail through the turmoil, charming and competent, smoothing over the rough edges with magic. Because she always used magic. Even the lingering scent of the shadows entwined around her made Finn's skin crawl.

At least she hadn't tried to turn her magic on him. He wouldn't put it past her, but it was the only thing that kept him there. He'd have to warn Roland and the others somehow, without saying it out loud. There hadn't been a chance, and Leander's appearance at the embassy was surprise enough.

Hestia's reputation preceded her even in Pelias. She was pale and gilded, like all the royal family of Sidon except him, her traditional Ilanthian gown the same colour as her golden hair, simple and sheer where her hair was elaborately styled with braids and beads, strands of gold thread woven through it. She was some twenty years older than Finn, though she did not show it, and had always, in his memory, been the only kind member of that family. She watched him as if he fascinated her for as long as he could remember.

It was not a comfortable position for anyone to find themselves in.

But she wasn't looking at him now. All her attention was on Roland de Silvius and on the need to stop Leander instantly making everything worse. She had begged Finn to help her. Not an easy task.

Roland already looked ready to start the war all over again. And Wren…

Wren stood on the far side of the dancers who had frozen to watch the scene. Her eyes, dark and endless, were fixed unerringly on Leander. They flickered to Finn only briefly and then back to the prince.

The last time she had seen him, Leander had opened the way for the Nox to consume her, to take her life and her existence and make her its vessel.

A twinge of concern bit into the back of Finn's neck as he scanned the crowd of staring eyes, trying not to think what the rumour-mongers of Pelias would make of his arrival with his half-brother and his cousin, dressed like an Ilanthian lordling, with a piece of dark magic hanging around his neck. That he had betrayed the knights, perhaps? That he had returned to Alessander's good graces and was back in the Ilanthian fold? Perhaps that he had been biding his time, waiting...

'Your highness,' Roland said, grinding out the title as he faced Leander. 'This is most unexpected.'

'His highness has something to say to our gracious hosts,' Hestia spoke before Leander could reply. 'Your highness?'

The look Leander cast at her could have curdled milk. He was not happy. Not in the least. He had not intended to do this here and now. And an angry or embittered Leander, who felt he had been slighted in any way, was dangerous.

But Leander stepped forward and bowed much more deeply to Roland than should have been imaginable. He was the crown prince of Ilanthus, heir apparent and the last of the line of Sidon aside from Finn, and to a lesser degree Laurence.

'Grandmaster de Silvius, I am here in penance for my egregious actions towards your queen, your daughter and your ward. I am here to make my humblest apologies. Your forbearance in the matter has been noted by my father and he bids me introduce my cousin to you, Lady Hestia Rayden, who will speak with his voice.'

Hestia sank into the deepest curtsy, releasing Finn and offering her hand to the Grandmaster. That was when Sassone, Ylena and other members of the court arrived on the scene. Once it was clear that no blood was about to be shed, of course. They weren't fools.

Sassone stepped by Roland and took Hestia's hand, raising her back upright.

'Lady Hestia, it is our honour to welcome you here,' he said.

She fluttered her eyelashes. It wouldn't work on Roland, of course, but she didn't know that. And it still wouldn't stop her trying. She was like that. Sassone on the other hand... The Earl of Sassone was immediately turned to clay in her clever hands.

Unwillingly, Finn glanced at Leander, who rolled his eyes. He wasn't buying this any more than Finn was, but Sassone was lapping it up. They knew her. Sassone did not.

But it meant Finn was able to slip away, at last.

As he made his way across the ballroom the music started up again, the rigid traditions and ceremonies of Asteroth rising in a vain attempt to smooth over any awkwardness.

Finn didn't care. All he could think of was Wren, standing there alone in the gown the colour of rubies, which cradled her body, which made her skin glow like moonlight. Rosebuds dotted her hair, and when she saw him making his way towards her that stonelike expression melted to a relieved smile.

She smiled at him, even now, and he felt his heart unfurling inside him, as if she reminded him who he really was.

It had only been a matter of days and it had felt like an eternity. She reached out and took his hands, her touch the only real and solid thing, all he needed.

Music swept her into his arms, and before he knew what he was doing they were dancing.

'I've missed you,' she said in a rush. 'Are you all right? They haven't hurt you or—'

'I'm fine,' Finn told her, cutting off the rush of questions. Because only Wren could look at him dressed in the finery of a foreign court, in the company of princes, and worry about him like this. 'You're beautiful, do you know that? You outshine anyone here.'

Wren blushed and smiled again, his Wren, the girl from the forest who had stolen his heart. The music sped up, bringing them whirling around the room again. Everyone was looking at them now, Finn realised. Of course they were. It was probably a scandal but they were used to that.

Everything they had done since they had arrived invited scandal.

The dance came to an end and Finn reached out to brush his hand against her face. Wren leaned into his touch.

'How sweet,' said another voice, far from welcome. 'But we have unfinished business, little bird. My turn, I think.'

Leander gave Wren a courtly bow, unmatched by anyone else there. He hadn't changed, in spite of his punishment. Perhaps he didn't really care. The more chaos he could cause, the more he would, especially here. He lived for it, delighted in it and he would never change.

And what Leander wanted more than anything else was Wren. And what Wren might one day be.

She stood there, her mouth open in shock as Leander stepped between them. There was nothing Finn could do to stop him, not without making it worse. Far worse.

Leander took Wren in his arms and the music started up again. The crown prince of Ilanthus whirled her away.

CHAPTER 19

WREN

If Wren had been worried about causing a scene dancing with Finn that was nothing next to what was happening now. Anselm would have a fit. Leander was graceful and powerful, and he knew exactly what he was doing. He moved like he was trying to seduce her and didn't care who saw it.

Whether his mission was to infuriate her, Finn or the entire court of Pelias, it was hard to say. He was succeeding at all three.

When Wren bristled, he smiled that knowing, self-assured smile and carried on regardless.

Oh yes, he knew exactly what he was doing.

As the dance began, he lifted her hand to his lips and pressed a kiss to her skin. His breath was warm, teasing, and as he looked up at her he smiled.

'It has been far too long,' he murmured. 'And we left many things unfinished.'

'You tried to kill me.'

But Leander shook his head with a soft, seductive laugh. 'Not at all. I tried to kill Finn. You, I would have made all powerful, immortal, a goddess.'

A goddess, indeed. He wanted to wipe her out of existence. 'Why are you here?'

'I'm a peace offering.' He bared all his teeth with his smile this time and she jerked back. As he was still holding her hand in his, his sleeve jerked back, exposing the length of his forearm and she saw the bracelet.

It was wreathed with dark magic, shadows coiling under his skin. Othersight showed her iridescent lines like veins of some monstrous creature beneath his pale flesh. The coldness came off it in waves, repulsing her.

'What's that?' she asked.

'My penance,' Leander told her and spun her around as if it was all part of the dance. It left her dizzy for a moment and his arms caught her again. 'No magic for me anymore. Not while I wear this. And how are you handling your leash, princess? No magic for you either, I see. This court frowns on our use of darkness, doesn't it? What would they say if they saw the wonders you can create?'

They stepped together, then apart, all part of the dance. There were so many people looking at the two of them now she couldn't stop dancing with him, or pull away.

Diplomatic incident. Those were the words Anselm had used. No matter what happened, she had to avoid a diplomatic incident. Leander was not making that easy.

The bracelet snagged her attention again, cold and merciless. She could see it leeching his magic out of him now, draining it away. It had to hurt. It had to. She remembered the shadow-wrought steel manacles he had used on Elodie back at the Seven Sisters and hesitated. Someone had a sense of poetic justice here.

But all the same... her eyes dragged back to the bracelet digging into his arm and her stomach tightened with disgust.

'Who did that to you?'

The smile grew thin again. 'My family. You haven't met the

worst of us yet. Not one of us is ever to be trusted, not even your beloved. My father commanded it and my cousin obeyed. She obeys him in all things. There she is, look.' He whirled Wren around so she could see the beautiful older blonde woman talking to Finn. But not that much older, not really. She had that ageless beauty that made it impossible to really guess her age, and the sheen of magic sparkled around her. She leaned in close, her arm entwined with Finn's, and she laughed. She said something earnestly to him, her lips almost brushing his earlobe where Wren knew he was sensitive.

But Finn didn't return the sentiment. His burning eyes were fixed on Wren, meeting her gaze, as she danced with Leander.

He looked furious. As if he blamed her. But this was not her fault. How could it be? And how did she get out of it? To tear herself free and run would cause even more outrage and probably that same diplomatic incident everyone was so worried about. She was trying to be a princess here, for Elodie's sake, for all their sakes.

And Leander seemed determined to make her ruin everything.

But Finn... Finn was staring at her like he didn't know her. And like he didn't want to know her.

'She's your cousin? And his?'

'Oh yes. She adores Finn.' He laughed then, that familiar cruel laugh. 'Hestia always gets what Hestia wants. And she's got her claws well and truly into my little brother already. Look, he's wearing her favour around his neck. She didn't waste any time giving him that. She made it herself. Isn't she talented?'

Wren didn't recognise the glass pendant. It was an Ilanthian design, aglow in the candlelight, shimmering with colours hidden in the dark glass. Beautiful but dangerous. There was magic tied to that as well, in it, around it, part of it, the othersight told her. She'd have to look more closely to work out what the spell was, but it couldn't be good.

Leander whirled her around and around, dragging her away from Finn's eyeline again and she could barely keep up.

Great light, she hated this dance. It ought to end by now. Surely. Her dance with Finn had only seemed to last moments but this nightmare went on forever.

'Marry me, Wren,' Leander murmured, his voice a rumble in his chest that ran through her blood. 'I'll take you away from here, take you to a place where you can be yourself, where everyone will appreciate you, and love you. Imagine their faces. Imagine the chaos we could cause together, you and I, little bird.'

Another twirl, and this time he pulled her in closer, his body pressed up against hers. He felt warm and welcoming and the shadows deep inside her seemed to purr with the thought of him. Of what they could do.

It was a trick, it had to be. She remembered the way her body had reacted to him in the forest, before... before he'd shown his true colours.

'No,' she said, as firmly as she could manage.

'Not sure I can hear you, my darling. Not a very adamant denial, is it?'

And then he kissed her.

It was just a brief brush of his lips to hers but it sent sparks through her body. She tore herself free the moment it happened but it was far too late.

Leander sank into the elegant bow that signalled the end of this particular dance and the music fell silent again.

Everything around her went horribly, expectantly still, like the whole court and every visitor there had been waiting for this all along.

Steel hissed against the edge of the scabbard, the unmistakable sound of a sword unsheathing, and the air in the ballroom shivered in expectation.

CHAPTER 20

FINN

Roland looked like he had been carved from stone, but the sword was halfway out of the scabbard already. He was watching Wren and Leander like a hawk. Finn knew the feeling but he himself couldn't do anything.

Not so the Grandmaster of the Knights of the Aurum. He paused for a long and painful moment before he turned to Hestia, his face unreadable.

'This is Nightbreaker, Lady Hestia,' he said calmly, offering her the blade flat across both his hands. 'Perhaps you remember it. Although you were very young then.' Hestia laid a hand on its length, her fingers only trembling very slightly.

'And the Aurum has touched it again, Lord Roland,' she said softly. 'It's stronger than ever. Thank you for showing me this. I understand more clearly now.'

And just like that a drawn sword was explained and a crisis averted. It was all Finn could do not to stare open-mouthed.

Hestia took his arm again, and this time he could feel her trembling, though whether from rage at Leander, fear, or a reaction to the magic imbuing the sword blade he didn't know. Finn locked eyes with Roland, who nodded curtly, and stepped back. No help was forthcoming there.

But at least he had stopped Leander in his tracks.

'Well,' said Lady Ylena. 'What a display. The wild revels of Sidonia have no place here, Lady Hestia.'

'Of course not,' Leander said a little too loudly as he swaggered back towards them. 'The light forbid anyone enjoy themselves, is that not so?' He ignored Ylena's glance of loathing and extended his hand to Hestia this time. 'Cousin, would you care to dance?'

Hestia sighed, but it was the easiest way for her to get him away from Ylena and the next round of trouble. She couldn't do anything to punish him here and now, oh, but she would. Finn knew that. And he didn't care.

Ylena, Sassone and their cohort watched the two of them go. General Gaius gave Finn a curt nod and made his way quietly to the drinks table, dealing with this nightmare in his own way. The rest of the Ilanthian party spread out, laughing, commenting, watching. Finn didn't want to know what they were doing or why. He knew he ought to care. Anything could happen.

'Enjoying your reunion, Ward?' asked Ylena in that icy voice of hers.

He pondered how to reply to that one. She'd enjoy most of the obvious options far too much. 'There are many other places I would rather be, my lady regent.'

'I'm sure there are.' She fanned herself dismissively. 'But your favoured companion appears to have fled once again. She does run so very quickly when given a chance.'

He scanned the crowd and saw that she was right. Wren had vanished. He wanted to say something, make an excuse for her or plead her history, but it wouldn't matter to Ylena.

Having an enemy prince treat you like that in front of the

whole court... and Ylena still wondered why Wren might run away. The woman expected far too much.

'She will have to learn that these things happen soon enough,' Wren's great-aunt continued. 'And a marriage might not be the worst thing for her.'

To Leander? Finn's attention snapped back to Ylena in horror. She couldn't mean it. She couldn't possibly think to repeat what happened to Elodie or to engineer some kind of—

She smiled her thin, cruel smile at him, seeing everything she needed to see. 'Well,' she said in softer tones. 'You'd better go and find her, hadn't you? Explain some things. And quickly, I think. So lovely to see you, Finnian, and looking every inch the Ilanthian prince once more. Right down to wearing the king's favour, I see.'

'Excuse me,' Finn murmured and stepped away from them. He wasn't needed there anymore, just a ward to some, a hostage, and too close to the Ilanthians for others. And the brunt of jokes and innuendo.

Where was she? He crossed the room, skirting along the edge of the dancers, and sidestepping anyone who tried to talk to him. He wasn't even particularly polite about it. He didn't care.

He found Anselm and Olivier standing by the double doors leading out onto a balcony, alert and on guard, which let him relax for a moment. That was good, wasn't it? It had to be good. They would keep her safe until they knew what this signified. She had to be outside, far from Leander, although someone ought to be out there with her.

Because Finn didn't like any of this. Not one bit.

Anselm nodded as he approached and stepped aside to let him through.

Wren, in that scarlet gown that made her skin glow like moonlight, was leaning on the balustrade overlooking the ocean, her arms so straight and taut it looked for a moment as if they were all that were holding her upright.

Anselm stepped outside behind Finn. 'Maybe you can make her see reason. She can't stay out here, Finn. They're going to notice. Appearances are—'

'How many times do I need to tell you I am not going back in there,' Wren snapped at him. Always the politician at heart, Anselm. Finn could guess how this conversation had gone already and nothing would appeal to Wren less than arguments about her duty and political expediency. 'Besides, Leander appears to have taken the whole diplomatic incident thing as a dare and I don't intend to play with him.'

'It's all right,' Finn told her, as gently as he could. 'No one would expect it.' He cast Anselm a meaningful glare but his friend shrugged as if to say if that was the way Finn wanted to play it, fine. But Finn wasn't playing. He gestured to the door leading back inside, where the lights glowed warm and the music was starting up again.

'I'll leave you then, your highnesses,' said Anselm. 'But please consider what I said. You are our acknowledged princess. In a very short time you might be queen. Such things become necessary.'

'Go away, Anselm,' Wren growled.

Finn knew that tone. Sure enough, in the corners of the balcony and out across the open air beyond the balcony, the shadows were moving, coiling and growing. Anselm didn't notice. He didn't know the risk.

'By your leave,' said Anselm with a bow.

Finn waited a moment or two, until he was sure they were alone, before crossing to her and running a soothing hand across the taut lines of Wren's shoulders. 'It's going to be all right,' he told her. 'Let go. You don't want to be calling up anything here and now, do you?'

She shivered beneath his touch. He felt it like vibrations up his arm. But the growing shadows unfurled into nothing again.

Wren sighed irritably. 'I've been trying so hard not to do that.'

'I know,' he told her. And he did. He could see the strain on her face, in her eyes. He wanted to hold her and tell her it would all be all right.

But no one could promise that. The silence dragged on, hollow and aching.

'Why are they here?' she asked at last. 'You know, don't you? What did they tell you?'

Finn leaned against the balcony edge beside her, staring out to sea. The waves moved far below them, crawling in from the edge of the night, to crash on the rocks below.

'That ostensibly they are here for the trial. Leander is here to apologise for what he did to us. For his incursion into the territory of Asteroth and his attempt to abduct you. And trying to kill me but that's secondary. He's been trying to do that for years and I don't think he's sorry about that in the least. Only sorry he didn't succeed. I think our father is more embarrassed than anything else and so he's reaching out to make peace with me, and with Asteroth. And Hestia, our cousin, is in charge of this mission so she'll have reasons of her own.'

'I thought witches in Ilanthus weren't allowed positions of power?' So Wren knew about Hestia. Interesting. How much had Anselm told her? And who else had her ear now?

Finn reached out and ran a fingertip down her shoulder. It was meant to be a simple gesture of reassurance and affection but the feeling of her silken skin made him draw in a breath so sharply it left him dizzy.

Focus, he told himself. He had been away from her for too long already. He wanted only to throw himself at her feet right now. Especially with her looking as she looked, with the fire of her anger raging in her eyes.

'Witchkind aren't. Hestia is... different. She's one of the sisterhood, and she's a favourite of my father's. She's powerful. And dangerous. And...'

Wren looked at him, a stare which was like being stabbed. 'I saw you with her. Following her like some kind of adoring puppy.'

He almost laughed. He wanted to. The idea of adoring Hestia...

But he did. To a certain extent, for all her faults. But he didn't believe a word she had told him, especially not about his father.

'I didn't have a choice. She was probably the only friend I ever had in that court. I owe her. Like I said, she's different.'

A small word for what she was. But Wren didn't look convinced.

She lifted her hand towards the pendant Hestia had given him as if it drew her to it. Her fingers trembled but she said nothing. Then she looked up to his face, a thousand questions in her eyes.

Finn leaned in closer, his mouth already seeking hers, his eyes closing with expectation. She drew him to her like a lodestone. Perhaps he could burn away Leander's kiss with his own. At least his would be welcome.

'Finn.' Roland's voice broke the spell and Wren jerked back from him, turning to face her father. 'You are needed inside. Our guests are asking for you. Wren...' His voice softened, gentled unexpectedly, a tone which gave Finn a rush of hope for the two of them. Roland could be kind. Few people knew that, but Finn did. 'If you wish to retire for the evening I will understand.'

He stood in the doorway, his features strained, his shoulders tight. Wren's hand closed on Finn's arm, the pendant and the abandoned kiss forgotten.

'He asked me to marry him,' she said, the tone revealing

what she thought of that prospect more eloquently than words ever could.

'Well that's not going to happen,' Roland replied before Finn could even protest. 'Not even if you begged me. It was a ruse anyway, a means to upset you. Pay him no mind. He's a whelp who has lost power and is trying to punish everyone around him in retribution. That scene was more designed to embarrass Hestia and me than anything else.'

'But he's still dangerous,' Finn warned them.

Roland nodded solemnly. 'I am aware, which is why we need you to keep close to him. Who knows what else might take his fancy to do while here.'

Finn gave a curt bow. What else could he do? The Grand-master commanded him and he was sworn to obey.

'Why does Finn have to deal with *him*?' Wren's voice sounded thin and stretched, ready to break. She was worried about him, he realised. Light bless her, she was trying to protect him. Even now.

But Finn already knew why he had to be the one. His birth, his blood. Everything. Because he might be the only one who could right now. With Alessander's favour and Hestia's enchantments, they might keep his half-brother at bay until he could be removed back to Sidonia, his apologies made.

'Prince Leander is not a threat at present. He is an honoured guest on a mission of reparation.' Finn's voice dripped with loathing he couldn't even begin to disguise. Roland almost smiled. Almost.

Wren was less impressed.

'I hope you're a better liar than that when speaking in public,' she snapped at him and then turned on her father instead. 'Have you told Elodie he's here yet? What do you think she'll do when she finds out?'

FROM THE TRIAL OF AERYN OF ASTEROTH BY DENEATHIAS

When the day of the trial arrived, they said the sun shone even brighter on fair Pelias. The slumbering Aurum made no sound and, as the people gathered, rumours began to spread. The queen had left her throne, abandoned her people in their hour of need, even as war broke out. She had hidden away from them for twenty years. Some whispered that the woman now coming to trial was not Queen Aeryn at all but an imposter. Or that she had entered into some kind of unholy alliance with the Nox to save it and had been irrevocably corrupted.

And a few, just a few, still believed in her innocence. She offered no defence.

The Aurum would judge her, they said. And if she was found guilty, she would be given to the flames.

No one expected anything else.

CHAPTER 21

WREN

Wren expected Elodie to be enraged, to vow retribution and break out of the Sanctum to track Leander down and expel him bodily from Pelias. But she didn't.

When Wren told her, she already knew all the details of what had happened, and she just bowed her head and nodded. Perhaps, with the beginning of the trial, there were other things on her mind. There was nothing she could do about it anyway. Not now. They were expected in the Sacrum any minute and it was the first chance Wren had managed to secure to talk to her since the ball. A kindness on behalf of Maryn and the maidens, she suspected.

Which was not comforting.

'To be expected, I suppose,' Elodie said at last. 'Alessander would not want to break the Pact. Not now. So he will humiliate Leander willingly. Perhaps even gleefully. He does so love to teach people a lesson.'

'Why not now?'

Elodie raised her face so that the sunlight fell on it and she smiled, so sad a smile. 'They want to see me suffer. They're here as witnesses. They want to see me condemned.'

'But you won't be. You aren't guilty.' Wren took Elodie's hands in hers, wrapping her fingers around them. 'Elodie, you can't give up.'

Birdsong was her only answer, the music of Cellandre.

'Do you remember the forest, Wren? Do you remember them singing to you like birds?' Elodie whispered. 'They sounded like that. If we could just go back there, they might still be able to help.'

What was she talking about? Elodie looked broken somehow. Afraid. Wren had never imagined she would see such a thing.

'What do you mean, Elodie? What's wrong?'

'It's up to the Aurum now. And the Aurum has been silent for too long. You may need to be prepared, Wren.' She pulled her in for a hug. 'This may not go as you wish.'

A deep booming knock sounded out, not from the direction of the gate, but further in the Sanctum, where it met the Sacrum and the home of the Aurum itself.

Elodie stood up, the long white gown the maidens had provided flowing around her. Her hair was like gold in the sunlight and she held her head high.

The only adornment she wore was the locket marked with the symbol of the Aurum, which held two miniatures, one of Roland and one of Wren.

She certainly looked like a queen. More like a queen than Wren could ever hope to be. But then, she always had, even when they had lived in the forest and gathered wild herbs to make cures, when it felt like the old magic tangled around the roots of the forest itself was protecting them.

The door between the Sanctum of the maidens and the Sacrum itself scraped open. It was huge, heavy oak banded with iron, and it moved on only the highest and holiest of days. The light around them seemed to dim as the glow of the Aurum spilled out.

'Aeryn, Queen of Asteroth,' the voice rang out. It sounded like Roland and the noise sent a jolt of alarm through Wren's body. Of course they would send Roland. He was the Grandmaster, the leader of the knights sworn to the Aurum and the kingdom, but he was also Elodie's champion and once her lover. It didn't seem fair.

Worse, it felt vindictive on some level Wren didn't understand. Like someone was delighting in the pain it would cause both of them. Ylena perhaps, or Sassone. Someone had decided he should do it. Perhaps both of them. They didn't seem to like him at all. In fact, she suspected all three of them loathed each other.

'Come forth and face the judgement of the Aurum. Your council demands it. Your people demand it.'

He stood there, silhouetted in the doorway with the glow of the Aurum behind him. It flickered off the gilded lines of his ceremonial armour and his bare sword. Wren couldn't see his face. She didn't want to. She knew she would see only pain and regret.

'It's time,' said Elodie.

'I'll come with you. I'll stand by your side.'

Elodie took her hands this time, and gently squeezed her fingers. 'Thank you, my love. But I need to know you are safe now. Stay away from Leander and the Ilanthians. And trust in the light. Don't... don't do anything.'

'But Elodie...' Wren didn't know what to say, didn't know how to voice her fears. She had such a terrible premonition, a feeling of dread and despair. She was going to lose Elodie. 'I can't let you—'

'You *won't*.' Elodie smiled down at her. 'You were always like this, my little bird. Stubborn to the core. My fault, I suppose. Come then. Stay close to the maidens and say nothing. Do nothing. Not even if it all goes wrong. And if it does... if they say you are to rule now... you know what to do.'

Find Finn. Make him help her. No matter what.

That was even worse.

Maryn appeared at the far side of the garden, grim-faced, her back towards Roland and the Sacrum. 'Are you ready?' she asked. Behind her the other maidens, dressed in white like Elodie, but veiled where she was not, gathered.

Elodie frowned. Clearly she had not been expecting them to come with her. 'What are you doing?'

'Accompanying you, of course. You are one of us, Elodie. You always have been. You, and Wren.'

'But you...' She looked bewildered. 'Maryn... sisters... you should be in there already, waiting for me. Ready for the judgement.'

Maryn smiled. 'And we are, my dear. The Aurum will decide. But our decision is already made and we are still with you. You are one of us. Now, let's show them a true queen, one filled with the light of the Aurum and destined to be forever.'

It was a procession with Elodie and Wren at the fore, the others falling in behind her led by Sister Maryn. A message sent to the city and to the council, and to the world. Fifty of them, from the eldest, only walking helped by their sisters, to the youngest, a fresh-faced acolyte of barely sixteen, trailing behind. They moved slowly, stepping into the Sacrum one after the other and light flared up all around them, from within them.

The Aurum danced brighter than before, welcoming them, illuminating the faces of the statues of the Chosen encircling them, all of Elodie's ancestors.

Wren felt it leaping up inside her, rising in a way it never had willingly before. It sang, surging with her blood, illuminating her from within in a way that had only happened when she was with Finn, when she had used it to heal him and keep him alive. This time it didn't hurt. It was pleasure and it was joy. It was everything.

Roland stood by the flames, his sword still bare, the light

reflecting off it. No, light was blazing from it. Aurum-wrought steel, alive with its glow, as the maidens were alive with it. As Elodie was. As Wren was.

And it was beautiful. Everything was beautiful.

For the first time, Wren thought it would be all right. The Aurum was already waking for Elodie. It was exonerating her even as she stepped into the Sacrum.

Wren hardly noticed the faces around them, ringing the outer stones, the white polished marble blazing as the flames turned incandescent. The whole room brightened as Elodie stepped inside.

The maidens came to a halt, Wren with them, but Elodie kept walking towards the flames.

'We bring our sister here for judgement,' Sister Maryn called out, her voice ringing off the roof overhead. 'Let there be honour in her treatment, and let the light decide her fate. We find no fault in her.'

Sassone stepped forward, a chain of office hanging around his neck. It gleamed in the luminous light. 'Know you that this place demands the truth, and only the truth. Aeryn of Asteroth, you are here to face judgement. Come forth and face the Aurum. Come forth and face us all.'

The Aurum rose higher as Elodie approached, her eyes closed against the brightness. It seemed to bend towards her, as if reaching out to her. Perhaps it was.

If Sassone noticed the flames and their increased activity, he gave no sign. He was like a cloud crossing the face of the sun, Wren thought and that chilled her. He didn't want the Aurum to judge too quickly, she realised. This was his moment and he intended to relish every second of it.

The light flared even more brightly and it was hard to see Elodie, as if it had already swallowed her up. Roland stepped to her side, hoping to help her perhaps, but she lifted up a hand, holding him back by that action alone.

He hesitated, and stepped back. But he didn't leave her.

'Read forth her crimes,' Sassone said, and it was Ylena who responded. Her voice didn't shake, didn't falter. There was music in her voice, no matter how cold.

'Queen Aeryn of Asteroth, daughter of Aelenor and Jonquil, Chosen of the Aurum, you are charged with deserting your kingdom in our time of need, of colluding with the shadows to hide from your rightful destiny, and of refusing the call of the light when it bid you serve. You forsook your crown and your calling. How do you plead?'

CHAPTER 22
WREN

No one would have known Ylena was Elodie's aunt at that moment. No one would have suspected she was any relation at all. She fulfilled a role, a sacred duty, and she did it well. Oh but she was cold and heartless with it. No emotion showed whatsoever as she listed Elodie's crimes.

'All this I did,' said Elodie, in a voice as clear as a bell. The sound of a host of people drawing in a shocked breath echoed around the chamber, followed by alarmed murmuring.

Wren flinched. She'd expected her to deny it. Something in Ylena's face tightened. Perhaps she had expected that too.

'But,' Elodie added once the murmuring died down, 'I never turned away from the light. The Aurum has always been with me and within me. All I have done, I did in its service.'

That was better, wasn't it? It had to be better. Wren tried to breathe.

'And did you know you were with child when you fled?' Sassone asked, his tone flat and uncaring. 'Did you deliberately take your heir with you as well?'

Elodie looked at him, her expression disdainful. 'I was not with child.'

Another shocked murmur ran around the chamber. How many people were in here, Wren wondered, crammed into the shadows, eagerly hanging on every word? And what were they thinking? Roland's face gave nothing away. Neither did Elodie's.

If she hadn't been with child when she left, then who was Wren's father? If it wasn't Roland, then... who?

Wren felt a host of eyes turning on her and she wanted to shrink back. Maryn lifted one hand to her back, a brief gesture of comfort. It held her still, something to cling to.

'Then who is this daughter you bring back with you?' the earl sneered, pointing at Wren, delighted to have caught Elodie out in an apparent lie.

Except she couldn't lie here in the sight of the Aurum. That was the rule, wasn't it? The light flooding through her wouldn't allow her to lie. That was what they had all said.

So how was this possible? Unless... unless everything Elodie had already said about Wren was a lie. Wren clenched her hands into fists at her sides, her fingernails digging into her palms. Her hair shifted warily against the back of her neck. Something was wrong here. Something was terribly wrong.

When Elodie didn't say anything, bowing her head slightly, Sassone pressed on.

'Do you deny her now, lady? Or did you take yet another as your lover? Look at her and tell us the truth. Who is she?'

Finn was here somewhere. He had to be. The Ilanthians were gathered at the far end, as far from the Aurum as they could stand, but still here. Wren could see them in their fine clothes so different to those of Asteroth, Leander and Hestia's pale hair bright in the shadows as the light played on it. But she couldn't see Finn. She wished she was with him, that she could reach out for him.

Everyone was looking at her now and she only wished she could hide. If she wasn't Elodie's child, who was she?

Elodie lifted her face again, looked over her shoulder at Wren, and light illuminated her. It flowed through her body, moving beneath her skin, the Aurum reaching out to her and through her, rising in her.

'She is Wren,' said Elodie in a calm, crisp voice that would not be argued with. It trembled with the truth, and behind her the flames surged higher again. 'And she is mine, and has been from the day she first drew breath.'

Elodie found her among the maidens and smiled at her, trying to reassure her even now. When Wren made to move towards her, Maryn caught her wrist in a grip like iron, holding her back. Wren was jerked to a halt and turned, confused. The maiden in her white veil had eyes like steel, reflecting that holy light.

'Not now, pet. Stay here.'

Deep in the flames something flickered, something that sapped a little of the light away. As Wren stepped back, horrified, it vanished. She glanced up at Maryn's grim face and the maiden nodded solemnly.

'Stay close,' she murmured. 'Anything could tip the balance.'

Stay back, she meant. Wren stared at the flames in horror, but there was no sign of any other shadows. Nothing at all. She let herself breathe again, just for a moment.

'Your question, Roland,' said Ylena, as if eager to hurry things along. 'Ask it.'

He stiffened, and Wren realised he was still staring at her, not at Elodie, his expression dark and unreadable. He cleared his throat, and slowly sheathed the sword once more.

'I have no questions left to ask,' he said in a low rumble of a voice. Elodie made a dismayed noise as if to interrupt him, or plead with him. 'Except to know what you intend now, my queen?'

For a moment everyone seemed bewildered. Something

hadn't gone according to plan. Roland was meant to take part in this interrogation but he wasn't playing along. Instead, Wren realised, he had asked an entirely different question, one not about the past but about the future.

Elodie drew in a shaking breath and stared at him as if he had somehow betrayed her more profoundly than anyone else.

'He was meant to ask about what happened in the forest,' Maryn whispered. 'Not this. This isn't... this isn't fair.'

Not fair? None of this was fair as far as Wren was concerned. But as she watched, Elodie folded her arms across her chest, as if hugging herself. Or perhaps to stop herself reaching out to him.

'I... I will serve the Aurum for as long as it wants me,' she whispered, and it sounded like her greatest defeat. 'And if my people will have me I will wear their crown. I will cleave to the light and be its Chosen once more. I made vows. We fight the Nox, with flame and sword.'

The Aurum burst forth, enveloping her and driving those close to her back, all but Roland who would not move. In that light Elodie blazed brightly, bent over slightly, as if she had flinched expecting pain. Slowly she straightened, and Wren knew that even in that blinding light, she was still staring at Roland.

He turned away. 'The Aurum has spoken,' he said, and his voice though low seemed to carry to every corner of the chamber, amplified by the Aurum itself. 'The queen is innocent. All hail Aeryn of Asteroth, our queen that was, and is again.'

Somewhere people started cheering, and from outside they could hear people shouting in delight as his words were relayed through the city.

The light of the Aurum sank back, leaving Elodie a frail and thin woman, standing alone, silhouetted by its glow. Her arms were still clenched tightly around her own body and her head fell back in relief or despair.

'Wait! We have a charge to lay at the feet of this traitor queen,' said Leander of Ilanthus. He strode forward quickly, pushing his way through the gathering of his own people, with Hestia glaring at him, but it was too late now. Everyone had heard him.

The chamber fell silent, watching this new act, too stunned to react.

Where was Finn? Wren wondered desperately. He was meant to be keeping his half-brother under control along with Hestia. Where were they? What was Leander planning?

'What charge is this, Crown Prince Leander?' asked Sassone in that horribly formal tone. No shock. No surprise. Had he known this was coming? He smiled and spread his arms wide. 'You are our honoured guests here. The Aurum will hear all charges and judge them fairly.'

Leander smiled. That horrible, arrogant smile. Wren knew it far too well.

'We charge her with the murder of her consort, Prince Evander of Sidon.'

Of course they did. Wren finally saw Finn start forward, still deep in the middle of the Ilanthian party and far too late now to intercept his half-brother. But before he got to the open area, Hestia herself stepped forward.

'Stand back, Prince Leander.' Her voice was all warning. 'This is not our place nor our agreement. We do not bow to the judgement of the Aurum and never will.'

Leander's voice turned savage. He sounded like an animal in pain. 'I will not be silenced. Not by you, not by anyone. She killed my uncle. We all know it. She murdered him right here in this chamber. She spilled his blood, the blood of Sidon, poured out his life and summoned the Nox here. She doesn't fight the Nox. She protects her.'

Elodie looked taken aback but Roland was already at her side. She glanced at him and said something. Wren couldn't make out what but it looked like denial. Roland nodded, still wearing that expression of granite, but at least he stood with her, ready to defend her.

The carefully choreographed ritual of judgement seemed to have slid sideways off its time-honoured tracks and no one seemed to know what to do about that. Confused looks passed between the spectators, murmurings and bewilderment.

'Let him speak,' said Ylena into the silence. Even more shocked mutterings followed this.

'Lady Ylena,' Hestia was close to begging. 'Please, there is nothing to—'

But the old woman held up her hand for silence.

'I say again, let the boy speak. Let Aeryn answer this charge. You are guests here, Lady Hestia, as you so wisely said. This is our way and in this place all charges must be answered. You may not bow to the Aurum, but we do. And even Ilanthian lies may show us the truth.'

Light and shade, Wren hated her. How could she? How could she do this to Elodie?

Hestia cast Leander a glance which promised something even worse than murder but she stepped back all the same, her hands falling to her sides. Was it Wren's imagination or did Leander almost wilt with relief as she did so?

The steely arrogance was back a moment later and she was far too familiar with that.

'What is he doing?' she whispered to Maryn.

'What he does best. Causing all the trouble he can,' Maryn replied. 'But I think he will pay for it this time. I'll enjoy that enormously. Maybe I should ask Lady Hestia for a front-row seat. Do you think a sister would grant that to a maiden?'

Leander approached Elodie cautiously and when she said and did nothing in response, a cunning smile spread over his features. 'Queen Aeryn married my uncle with the promise that he would be safe here in Pelias, that he could practise his worship as he would, and that no harm would befall him. She promised him a child, and did nothing to deliver that child.'

He almost glanced at Wren but caught himself.

Wren felt something cold and dark slither up along her spine. She stepped back, reaching beyond the light now, for the corners, for the shadows. She couldn't help herself. He was up to something. Something terrible.

Because that was what Leander did. Was he going to denounce her right here? What would that gain him?

On the far side of the chamber, she saw Finn's head come up, almost as if he sensed her distress and what it might do. He couldn't do anything to stop Leander now. But he sensed that she needed him. She knew that. Suddenly he was moving, leaving the Ilanthians and pushing his way through the crowd.

'Your uncle took his own life,' said Elodie in a voice tinged with regret. 'I had no hand in that.' The flames climbed up again, brightening with her truth.

'So you say. Who else is to know that? And why would he? Why would a prince take his own life? You killed him to summon the Nox here. Everyone knows the blood of our line calls her forth, gives her form.'

Elodie fixed him with a glare. 'A myth,' she said, but her voice shook a fraction. And she glanced, unwittingly, at Wren. 'You are distraught, Prince Leander.'

A slow smile spread over Leander's face, a look of triumph, as if he had just sprung a trap.

'I'll prove it to you. I'll prove it to you all.' His eyes gleamed in the light of the Aurum, the pale grey turning silver in its glow.

From his belt, he drew a gleaming knife which had looked ceremonial with its jewelled hilt and curved blade. It wasn't, Wren realised. It was wickedly sharp.

Leander steeled himself for a moment and then slashed through the pale skin of his unadorned wrist. 'Come, oh divine darkness and be made whole once again.'

CHAPTER 23

WREN

Bright red blood splashed on the white stones paving the floor of the chamber of the Aurum.

Someone screamed but it wasn't Wren. She couldn't move. Couldn't breathe. Couldn't do anything.

From far beyond them, something rose up behind her and within her like a tsunami. Something so powerful it would have brought her to her knees if at the same time it didn't seize her in its grip and close its jaws around her.

A dark shadow dived from the crowd and ploughed into the crown prince of Ilanthus, taking him off his feet and to the floor. For a second she thought it was shadow kin, racing through the darkness. It moved so fast and fluidly, ghosting across the white marble of the floor. The knife went flying, clattering across the floor until it came to a halt against the low wall around the flames of the Aurum. The prince and the second figure struggled on the ground.

Finn, Wren realised. It was Finn. He pinned Leander down, containing his struggles effortlessly.

The prince laughed at him and spat in his face, but Finn

didn't move. He held Leander's injured arm in a vice-like grip, staunching the blood flow. When Leander tried to pull free, Finn drew back and punched him hard in the face.

Everything erupted into chaos and disorder, people moving in every direction. Wren started forward towards the two princes of the line of Sidon, struggling on the floor, but the next thing she knew Anselm and Olivier were there, flanking her and making her move away, towards a simple and unobtrusive door in the wall. One through which she and Finn had once entered secretly. And fled through.

Her feet stumbled and turned sluggish. Something was wrong, terribly wrong. And all the while she heard it, heard the song ringing out through the chamber, echoing off the stones. The Nox, it was the Nox. It had to be. She would have known that voice anywhere, even if she couldn't make out the words. It echoed through her and her eyes burned in their sockets, her skin tightening about her bones. She started forward, drawn by the play of darkness and light in the reflected blood on the stones.

'Get her to safety,' Roland bellowed and the two knights didn't hesitate, seizing an arm each and manhandling her towards that small door.

She fought them every step of the way, and the shadows surged around her, falling from the roof and rising from the ground, twisting in the blinding light of the Aurum which had turned luminescent with rage at this intrusion.

A pillar like fire stepped forward, a figure walking across the stones towards her... No, towards the two men still fighting each other on the floor. Towards the blood.

Elodie. It was Elodie.

Whereas a few moments ago they had seen the Aurum's light pour through her, as if through stained glass, now it filled her to overflowing.

She burned from head to toe with the light of the Aurum,

blazed with it. Her hair was fire, and her eyes like stars. Her skin glowed from within.

Wren had never seen anything like it. Even her would-be saviours faltered, staring in wonder. Finn fell back from his brother, aghast, his blue eyes wide in wonder.

And Leander... Leander snarled something incomprehensible and dived for the knife again.

He never made it. Even as he made to rise, he convulsed in agony, his back arching, his mouth opening in a strangled scream. He dropped to his knees again and Hestia walked to him, othertongue dancing on her lips until he fell still.

'Forgive us his rashness, Queen Aeryn,' she said in rapid, placating tones. How she could stand there and still speak told worlds about her bravery. Or her desperation. 'The sisterhood had no part in this, nor did the king. I swear it on my life and my power. Scourge it from me with flames if I speak a lie. The crown of Ilanthus begs forgiveness for this transgression and... and...' Her voice failed her as she stared at the figure bearing down on her and caught up with what she was actually facing now. Elodie had not even paused. Hestia dropped to her knees. 'Lady, please. He's a rash boy. A fool. He always has been. Like your husband, cut from the same cloth.'

Still Elodie advanced, like an incarnation of retribution.

'*He wanted to call the Nox,*' she intoned and her voice made the rocks around them tremble. It wasn't her voice, not entirely. It sounded like many voices, harmonising down through the ages, a choir of Ilanthian royal women. '*Here. In our holiest place. In our Sacrum.*' The flames behind her surged higher and higher, licking off the ceiling of the chamber now. It hurt to look at them. And at her.

Wren felt something twist inside her, something small and scared, and so very dark. She wasn't looking at Elodie. Not anymore. Not really.

She didn't know what it was.

And at the same time she feared that she did. Even the darkness swirling up around her shrank back in recognition of the power it would have to face. For the first time, the Nox retreated. For all its rage and need for vengeance, here and now, it was afraid.

'Elodie.' The voice was firm and yet gentle. And tired. So very tired. The weight of the world lingered in that voice. 'Elodie, please. Come back.'

Roland was the one to reach her, to touch her, his hand on her shoulder. He was the only one who seemed able to look at her at such close proximity and not have the eyes burned from his head. He didn't even flinch or try to shade the view. Just looked at her in all her glory and terror, and Wren knew he still loved her. No one could doubt that.

She was, and had always been, everything to him.

'Elodie, it's done,' Roland tried again. 'He's been stopped. It'll burn through you. Let go. Please...'

'Wren? Princess, please,' Anselm said, recovering himself, though his voice still shook. 'We have to go. We have orders. You aren't safe here.'

She wasn't. Wren knew that. The shadows were still squirming for release. They wanted Leander's blood and they would take it by force if they needed to. And then the Aurum would know her, and force her to reveal herself. And Elodie... dear light, it would be Elodie's face that would look at her, Elodie's form which would bear down on her...

Wren knew Elodie would never hurt her.

The Aurum, on the other hand...

Did Roland know? He had to know. He stood in the way of something far beyond mortal powers. But he didn't move.

Tears flamed in Wren's eyes and she saw Finn struggling to rise. But he was of the blood of Sidon too, an Ilanthian, a prince. He loved her but she was a danger to him. A threat. She knew that now. She felt it deep in the core of her body. No wonder Roland had sent him away.

The Nox stirred again, rising with renewed interest as it noticed him, his concern for her, his love. It wanted him. It wanted his submission and his life, it wanted his blood and his will. It wanted all of him and it would make her take it. No. Not like that. She couldn't.

On seeing Finn, still splattered with Leander's blood, the Nox seemed to forget where it was and what was happening.

He will be ours for all time. His blood, his submission, his death will be exquisite. Make him come to us, my little vestige. Make him ours.

It battered against the feeble barricades she had placed in her mind, hungry, desperate, scenting that blood and that need. Fear of Elodie was no longer holding it back. The Nox surged up again.

Wren's mind whirled with darkness and endless night and need. So much need.

Elodie lifted her head, an unnatural movement, like a bird of prey sighting something in the distance, or a hound catching a scent of something to hunt. Her gaze snapped to Wren and she bared her teeth. The Aurum in her, filling her, burning through her...

Roland grabbed her arms and pulled her against him, holding her even though the light grew brighter and brighter, like a newborn star in the night. The chamber shook as if an earthquake struck, dust and fragments of stone falling like rain. Darkness spilled around her, and the light burned it away, hungry and enraged to be so threatened in its place of sanctuary, to have its home so violated.

Before Wren knew what was happening, Anselm and Olivier were running, carrying her along between them.

She tried to look back as they fell out of the doorway. The

light snapped out, leaving only the golden glow of the flames as they had been and the figure of Roland de Silvius, holding Elodie's limp form in his arms, as the Maidens of the Aurum gathered around them.

CHAPTER 24

WREN

Wren's head pounded with a headache that wouldn't quite break, but instead pressed insistently at the inside of her skull and left her in misery. No one would tell her what had happened.

Anselm still stood guard outside her quarters, and she had sent Olivier off in search of news of Elodie.

'What was he thinking?' she asked for the hundredth time. Lynette shook her head and turned her attention back to the piece of embroidery she was currently stabbing at in an effort to take her mind off whatever was happening outside Wren's rooms.

'I'm not sure Ilanthians think, your highness. Not the men, anyway.'

'Finn does,' she murmured. But Finn was another matter altogether. She was a danger to him, she realised that now. Perhaps she had always known. He lost himself in her, and she was far too eager to let him. If desire for the Nox would make Leander try to kill himself – *Leander* of all people – what would Finn do? Finn who actually cared about her...

She had felt it, felt the hunger and the need, felt the

complete disregard for anyone else in the darkness that had filled her. Felt Finn's need to obey her and serve. Even with his life, if she asked it.

How had she not seen it before? It wasn't love. It couldn't be. He had no choice in how he felt about her. He belonged to her and he had never even had a chance to consent to that.

She sank down on the bed, trying to still her whirling mind.

'Will you have something to drink, your highness?' Carlotta asked softly, her face all concern. 'You're so pale. I can make a tincture to help. Some chamomile and black haw, with skullcap, maybe... or ginger?' A hedge witch remedy, Wren thought absently. The type of thing she and Elodie would have made back in Cellandre, for headaches. Great light, she missed solutions as simple as that.

She took Carlotta's hand and squeezed it in gratitude but at the same time shook her head. A tincture was not going to help her now. She wasn't sure if anything would.

A knock on the door brought her to her feet as if pulled up by a wire. 'Come in,' she said loudly, before Lynette had a chance to say anything else.

Ylena entered, regal as any queen. Her attendants closed the door behind her. She fixed Wren with that keen gaze.

'How are you?'

Whatever Wren had been expecting, it wasn't this. 'Lady Ylena?' was all she managed to say, as she dropped into a clumsy curtsy. It seemed like the best course of action.

Someone moved one of the high-backed chairs and the elderly woman sank into it. And she did look old, all of a sudden. She studied Lynette and Carlotta in turn and then seemed to dismiss them from her mind.

'That was all far more dramatic than it needed to be. Honestly, Sassone was bad enough. He so wanted her to be guilty, the stupid man. He hates that he cannot control her. He never could, and nor could his father. I have handled things poorly. I apologise for that.'

Wren stared. Her legs began to shake so she sank back onto the edge of her bed. 'I don't understand,' she whispered.

'Your mother, the queen, is exonerated. That's all you need to understand. You are her daughter and therefore her heir. Your fate is put off for a time. But it is still your fate. I hope you accept that now.'

To be queen after Elodie, that was what she meant. The words were like a steel trap closing, its jaws digging into Wren's heart.

But what could Wren say? Elodie might not have called her daughter but it hardly mattered.

Wren decided to try formality. 'Lady Ylena... I would like to speak to the queen.'

'She is being cared for by the Maidens of the Aurum.' She held up her hand when Wren made to protest. 'Not as a prisoner, as a patient. The full force of the Aurum within her was too much. She is weak and needs healing. She must rest. You may never have seen such things before but I have. It killed my sister, you know.'

No one looked up or moved. Wren stared at Ylena who stared back, as if daring her to argue.

'Is she... is she in danger?'

'I think not. Not this time. The next time, who knows. It is a fickle thing, the Aurum, a consciousness in its own right, with devices and desires. But it forgets that the people who serve it, especially those who can embody it, are but mortal things.'

Wren thought of the Nox, of its casual disregard for her. Suddenly the Aurum didn't seem so very different from its dark sibling. Two sides of the same coin, two parts of the same old magic.

The way Elodie had always talked about the Aurum was as a distant and wise thing, a source of benevolence. But this felt different. The voice that had spoken from Elodie hadn't been her own. And it had sounded vengeful. That same force had turned to look at Wren when the Nox had almost slipped free and it had hated her.

Great light and shadows of old, what was she going to do?

'But she's going to be all right, isn't she?' Wren knew she sounded like a child. She didn't care. Panic flooded through her and she threw herself forward, dropping to her knees before the regent. 'Please, Ylena, she has to be all right. I'll do whatever you want. I'll be good. I promise, but I need to know—'

The old woman put out her hand and smoothed it through Wren's unruly hair, making a soothing sound. There was a brush of magic, like static electricity between them. 'There now, hush. Maryn has her and no one can heal like my Maryn. We'll start again, you and I. Is that fair? And when Elodie is ready, you shall see her. That much I can promise.'

'Thank you,' Wren whispered and tried to smile.

'We really need to do something about your hair though,' the old woman murmured absently. 'It really grows in fits and starts, doesn't it?'

Wren brought her own hand up to it and found it far longer than it should be, curling down to her shoulders already.

'It... it reacts to...'

'I noticed,' said Ylena calmly. 'Perhaps, Lynette, you would fetch me a pair of scissors?'

Lynette was only halfway across the room when there was another knock on the door.

This time it was just Roland. He looked grey and washed-out, a bit broken. He had never looked old before this moment, not to her. But now... now he looked like someone twice his age.

'Is she hurt?' Wren blurted out, coming up to her feet, Ylena forgotten.

'She's exhausted, that's all. Too much magic, too much power... the Aurum is... it's not kind to her. She won't be able to raise so much as a spark for days. The maidens are caring for her.'

'I want to see her.'

Roland glanced at Ylena, his face a mask. 'I don't think that's a good idea right now. Do you?'

Wren sucked in a breath to say something in reply but couldn't find words. Not in response to that. She stood there, staring at him, gaping like a fish on dry land.

'Roland,' said Ylena sharply. 'Be kind.'

He cast a look at her as if he had only just realised she was there. 'Lady Ylena,' he murmured but didn't say anything more than that.

At least it gave Wren some time to recover. She needed to know what was happening. 'Where's Finn? Was he hurt?'

Roland made a noise deep in his chest, a rumble of something like disappointment or disgust. 'He's gone back to the Ilanthian embassy with his brother and cousin, trying to smooth things over, I think. He's a better diplomat than he gives himself credit for. I think he will stay there for the time being, until we know what has become of his brother. And how this will all fall out.'

Also probably the best thing, Wren thought absently, and felt like the worst traitor. Finn was safer there than anywhere near her. But something inside her ached at the thought of not being near him. And she wasn't sure if it was her heart or something else, something darker she could never trust.

There had been royal Ilanthian blood spilled before the Aurum once more, and Wren had felt the Nox clawing its way through her to get out. Elodie had felt it too and the Aurum... oh light, the Aurum had gone wild. If she stepped in front of it again, what would it do? Would it recognise her?

'Elodie is safe, isn't she? She's... she's herself again?'

'Lady Regent Ylena,' Roland said after a pause, his voice all stiff formality. 'May I have a moment alone to talk to my daughter?'

Wren's great-aunt didn't move from her seat. 'I think it best if I stay, Grandmaster.'

There was a long and painful silence.

Roland's sigh was bitter with exhaustion and regret. He didn't even bother arguing with her, not anymore. He looked as if in that moment he dismissed the regent and anyone else from his mind, and turned all his attention on Wren instead.

'Were you or Elodie ever planning to tell me the truth?'

CHAPTER 25

ELODIE

Everything ached. That was the first thing she realised. Everything, everywhere, all through her body.

'Don't get up too fast,' said Maryn, her voice soft. 'You channelled more power than you have in many years. More perhaps than anyone has if I'm honest. The Aurum has never been so alive. We all felt it. All the maidens. I thought we'd lose you.'

'Did you?' Elodie's voice grated against the insides of her throat. She meant did they feel it, but did they think she'd been lost worked too. She hardly cared which answer she got. 'And the others?'

'They saw it. They saw everything.' Carefully, Maryn lifted her head and then brought a mug of water to her lips, helping her drink.

That hurt too. It burned as it went down her throat.

They were in the garden of the Sanctum, just beyond the doors of the chamber of the Aurum, safe within the retreat of the maidens. There were birds singing somewhere. Far off, Elodie could hear music. Someone was celebrating something. She hoped it was nothing to do with her. The other maidens had retreated, leaving her with Maryn, sitting at her side while she lay on one of the low divans they used for the infirm. Elodie forced herself to sit up and instantly regretted it.

'What was the Ilanthian trying to do, Elodie?' Maryn asked. 'Why would he do that to you?'

Elodie wanted to laugh, she really did. What was Leander trying to do? Perhaps he didn't really even know that. He wanted to expose Wren, and she couldn't allow that, so she had seized all the power of the Aurum to protect the girl. It had been a moment of madness. But she would do it again in an instant.

She had felt the surge of shadows around Wren as the summoning took hold. A moment later and it would have been too late. They all would have seen the truth, and they would have turned on her. They would have torn her little girl apart.

Or at least, they would have tried.

Elodie could not allow that to happen.

All she had wanted to do was stop it. Even if it meant destroying everything. She had to protect Wren. That had been the whole purpose of her life for twenty years. She'd give anything, even herself.

'I think *I* did that to me. Or the Aurum did. I'm not sure. Everything is... a bit blurred.'

An understatement. Roland had been there, she remembered that. He had called to her. He had brought her back.

His arms around her, cradling her. His eyes, so dark, reflecting the light that burned through her. Her Roland...

She couldn't think about that. Not now. She needed to focus. Oh, but her head ached, and all she wanted to do was ask if he was there, if he was all right. If she could see him, talk to him...

Explain.

How could she ever hope to explain?

'It could have burned right through you,' Maryn said, a gentle admonishment when Elodie didn't elaborate.

'If that was what had to happen, then yes, it would have.' She wasn't in the mood for an argument.

Maryn frowned. 'You always were obstinate.'

'So were you.'

'And the girl?'

'Almost as bad as me, wasn't that what you said? And she's a woman, not a girl. One who knows her own mind.' Maryn laughed then, a soft chuckle which drew a smile across Elodie's face. Relief bubbled up through her. 'She's my daughter, Maryn. In every way that matters. Do you understand?'

Maryn embraced her, held her close. 'Yes. More so than ever. Someone is trying to put her on the throne, El. Someone who doesn't care about the consequences of that. And they want you out of the way. Someone on the council.'

'Ylena?'

Maryn froze, and then pulled back to look Elodie in the face. 'I would put nothing past my mother. But I swear to you—'

Elodie lifted a hand to stop her. 'She was always the same. With my mother, and with you.'

'She has power now. Power she never had with you here. I hate to say it, but perhaps she doesn't want you back.'

Elodie laughed softly. 'I'm sure she doesn't. But what about you? You have a claim on the throne as well, don't you?'

Maryn recoiled, horrified. 'No. Not I. My service is here, among the maidens, in Sanctum and Sacrum. I serve you. You know that, don't you? Elodie, I would never—'

'I know, I know.' She shushed her cousin, a wash of fondness making her tears well up in her eyes.

But then Maryn looked up, her blue eyes very bright and glistening, the same wave of emotions flooding her. She pushed them down ruthlessly and stared in the direction of the door to the Sanctum.

'Someone's coming.' How she knew was anyone's guess. Elodie had long ago learned to trust in Maryn's instincts.

When the Aurum had called her, Elodie had thought she had lost her only friend. And then Roland had appeared, like a gift.

The banging sound echoed through the Sanctum. Someone was hammering on the door to the Sacrum.

Elodie steeled herself. They wanted her back in there already? They wanted to ask more questions, make more accusations. She would have thought that the Aurum igniting as it did would have been answer enough. Well, so be it, she thought. The sooner this was over the better. She struggled to her feet.

'What are you doing?' asked Maryn sharply. 'You're in no condition—'

'They're hardly here to discuss the weather, Maryn. They'll want answers more than ever. I have to deal with this quickly and protect Wren. Help me? Please?'

'But you've been exonerated. The Aurum proved it.'

'Judgement then. The council will want to have their say.'

She held out her hand and Maryn was beside her in an instant, supporting her as they made their way from the Sanctum to the door of the Sacrum. At least she would get to see Roland, she thought idly, and she smiled. Maybe she was still light-headed to think such thoughts.

But he had been there when she had almost lost herself to the Aurum. He had pulled her back. She'd wanted to tell him so, to tell him that he was all she needed and was all she would ever need in moments like that. But she had not had the strength to do it.

Neither physically nor emotionally. She was a coward, that was the problem. Especially when it came to him, and she had already hurt him far too much to bear.

But when the door opened, it wasn't Roland standing there.

The chamber beyond was dark, the flames of the Aurum were low now, as if it too was exhausted and sleeping as she wished she could be sleeping. Dust settled over everything in a thin, sparkling layer. There were stones and rock fall scattered around. Had she really done that? Well, not her alone. The Aurum within her. The Aurum enraged. Thanks to Leander. She wondered what had happened to him, what the other Ilanthians were doing. The priestess of the Nox who had knelt before her was furious as well as terrified. And the power in her was at least the equal to Elodie's own. Like knew like.

She felt so empty now. Wrung out. And that was a problem.

Armed guards spread out around the doorway. The instant she and Maryn opened the door into the Sacrum, they rushed forward and seized Elodie. Maryn cried out, furious at the imposition, but there was nothing she could do. She was dragged inside along with Elodie, mainly because she refused to let go.

They weren't knights. They weren't even palace guards. They wore the livery of House Tarryn.

The Earl of Sassone led them. Elodie had always thought him pompous and full of himself, but loyal to the crown. She had been sure he was loyal.

Perhaps too much so. Or perhaps not at all.

Where were the knights Roland had left manning the door? He would have done that, surely. What had they—

Three figures in ceremonial armour sprawled on the white marble of the Sacrum, blood pooling darkly below them. They were young. Far too young.

'What is the meaning of this?' Maryn shouted. Other maidens were hurrying towards the door but the soldiers slammed it shut and barred it, shutting the two of them in the Sacrum. Prisoners. 'You can't do this. You are violating a sacred space.'

But they did not care.

Before Elodie knew what was happening, manacles snapped closed around her wrists, and with them came the icy touch of shadow-wrought steel.

CHAPTER 26

ELODIE

The metal was dark and cold, so cold. It sapped the heat from Elodie's body, and deadened the last embers of the Aurum inside her. She could feel it, vaguely, like a distant, startled murmur, but she couldn't reach it, not properly, and certainly not as she had earlier.

The Aurum itself flickered low, uneasy, the light barely enough to illuminate the chamber.

She had worn shackles like these before. In the clearing of the Seven Sisters, on the edge of the standing stone circle where the old magic had converged to create a dark and terrible vortex which had almost consumed Wren, Leander of Sidon had put manacles like these on her wrists and she had been helpless until the light of dawn when Wren had helped her get free. Utterly helpless.

Just like now.

She looked up at Sassone's face, and saw that sneer, the disgust in his eyes.

She'd always known he hated her, or was at the very least jealous of her. 'What are you doing?' she asked.

'What the regents' council should have decreed,' he replied.

'You, Aeryn of Asteroth, will be stripped of your crown, and taken from this place to a place of imprisonment where you will be examined until you confess. Then you will be consigned to the flames in atonement for your many sins.'

Maryn rushed to her side, or at least started to. The guards grabbed her, holding her back. She struggled wildly, trying to draw on her magic. But the Aurum was too weak. Because Elodie had weakened it, as it had weakened her. Had they known? Had they realised that this was the moment to strike? With everyone else distracted, the Aurum drained and the maidens weakened? And Elodie herself next to useless even without the manacles?

Beyond the door, Elodie could hear the other maidens shouting, banging, trying to raise the alarm and desperately attempting to reach her. But it was no use. She knew it was no use.

She didn't know what was happening, how or why Sassone thought he could do this. She hadn't done anything wrong. The Aurum had awoken for her, proved that she was true and that she had not betrayed it. She never would. She had almost torn the Sanctum apart proving that.

'Why are you doing this?' she asked, bewildered. For the first time in her life, Elodie realised, she was lost. Completely lost. 'Where is Roland?'

He would never have agreed to this, would he? Not Roland. And if he had, then he would be here himself to see it through. None of the knights were here, she realised. Her Paladins, her sworn men, not a single one of them were here. These guards were Sassone's men to the core.

'Roland will learn of your fate soon enough. But far too late to avert it. No matter how much you call for your lover, he won't be able to help you. Bring her.'

Maryn broke free, scrambling to Elodie's side. She drew herself up to her full height and light swirled around her. The flames in the Sacrum rose, brightening. It wasn't the blinding light Elodie had summoned, but Maryn had power too. She had also been chosen and had dedicated herself to the sacred flames. They answered her now.

'In the name of the Aurum and all the light it holds—' she began, but got no further. Sassone lashed out, striking her face with his fist full force. Maryn's head snapped back and she fell soundlessly to the stone floor, blood pouring from her nose and mouth.

Elodie screamed more from outrage than fear. There was nothing she could do, nothing to stop this sacrilege, this injustice. To attack one of the maidens here of all places, to deny the judgement of the Aurum and impose his own – what was he thinking?

She opened her mouth to call on the light, to call on all the powers of the flames before her. Nothing happened. Of course nothing happened. The steel manacles saw to that.

He slapped her hard, open-handed and with force. She staggered back, stunned, and her face flamed where the impact fell.

'Someone should have dealt with you years ago,' he snarled. 'You and your wretched line. All the so-called maidens who think they have the only right to interpret the flames. Ilanthus has the right idea, controlling their witchkind with steel and sacrifice. This is a world of men, my lady.' The words dripped with sarcasm. 'A new world of the sword and the flame, and your sisters will soon learn their place in it. But not you, false queen. It will be far too late for you.'

'You can't do this,' Elodie tried to say, numb with shock.

'If you had stayed away it wouldn't have been necessary. But back you came with your brat in tow. Hopefully she'll be more biddable than you, if she knows what's good for her.'

'You can't put Wren on the throne,' she said, and fear for herself evaporated. Wren was all that mattered. Wren and the kingdom. She couldn't tell him why – no, definitely not him – but she had to warn him somehow. 'Listen to me. You can't—'

His hand closed over her mouth, huge and suffocating. His grip crushed her face. 'You don't get to tell me what I can or can't do, bitch. Gag her and bring her. We need to move.'

A cloth was shoved in her mouth, even as she tried to scream, even as she tried, uselessly, to use her power, to reach the Aurum and tear them all to shreds. Something was tied around her face a moment later, blinding her, and they dragged her bodily from the Sacrum.

ON THE LINE OF AELYN OF ASTEROTH

BY TARQIN ARRENDEN

What does the royal family of Asteroth know of treachery?

It lives not in their hearts. They serve the Aurum in all things, always reaching for the light. They strive to bring order from chaos, to drive away the darkness, to always stand firm on the illuminated way.

But there have been some who faltered. There have been some who failed.

Someone always has to fall in the end.

And in those days as simple a mistake as a poor marriage or trusting a faithless friend could bring about disaster. Or loving too well.

Or there could be no real reason at all. Just fate.

Aelyn the First spoke true: 'All who walk this path walk upon a knife's edge.'

CHAPTER 27

WREN

The truth. What was the truth? Where did she even begin?

Wren didn't know the start of it and Roland might have a better idea of it than her. Her hands shook and her hair seemed to stir of its own volition, longer than it had been, far longer than it should be. Self-consciously, she tried to smooth it down and tame it. There had been so much magic in the Sacrum, both light and dark, and Leander of Sidon had spilled his blood to summon the Nox and...

'I can't,' she whispered. 'Please. I don't know everything.'

'You know enough. Start there.'

But where? He was asking the impossible.

'I-I can't.'

'Is Elodie your mother?'

'She raised me.'

His temper finally snapped. He had been trying to keep it in check for so long, she realised, for her sake, for Elodie's, but even he couldn't manage the impossible. 'That's not the same thing!' he roared.

To Wren's surprise another pair of arms pulled her into a gentle embrace. Lynette held her close, protecting her.

'Enough,' said Ylena, in as quiet and crisp a tone as Wren had ever heard Elodie use. It was not to be argued with. Wren turned, hiding in the lady-in-waiting's arms, sobs breaking out before she could stop them. The lady regent glanced at her and then scowled at Roland de Silvius. 'You forget yourself, Grandmaster. You are overwrought, to speak to a girl like this.'

'She's no girl.'

Just three words and Wren's world began to crumble and fall apart. What was she then? What did he think she was? It was her worst fear, not to be human, not to be who she had always thought she was. But the events in the Seven Sisters had shown her part of it, a new truth, and she was terrified of it.

Ylena, however, didn't back down. She was not cowed by Roland and never would be. Her voice filled with scorn. 'Of course she is only a girl. Look at her. Whatever else she might be, she's a child.'

Roland ignored the old woman. 'Lynette, let her go.'

'No.' Lynette stroked Wren's hair, her body shaking with anger. 'How dare you do this, Roland? She has no lived experience, certainly no court experience, and yet you drag her back here and thrust her into this world and expect... what? What do you think she owes you? I would tell Yvain to thrash you to within an inch of your life if you spoke to a daughter of mine this way. Elodie would never forgive you.'

That seemed to steal the ability to speak from him. He cleared his throat and Wren dared to glance at him again. He looked like someone had punched him in the stomach.

Wren never imagined anyone would speak to Roland de Silvius that way. Perhaps not even Elodie. Lynette stood like a statue, glaring at him, completely unafraid, as if she was Wren's only anchor right now.

Carlotta was still pressed against the wall, staring at them in horror, clearly praying she could stay out of sight if she wished hard enough. Wren felt the same way, but that was not an option for her.

Ylena sank back into the chair as if it was a throne. 'Now take a moment and collect yourself, Grandmaster. Then we can talk like civilised people. Agreed?'

Roland raked his hand through his hair and tried to calm his breath. 'I need to know the truth. Are you my daughter?'

Wren wanted to shake her head. 'I don't know,' she whispered. More of a whimper if truth be told. 'She never said. Never called herself my mother, except recently, and never... never spoke of you to me. She woke up from nightmares calling for you though. That's how I knew your name. But she would never explain.'

His face froze, and then fell, horrified. 'Nightmares? I was in her nightmares?'

Was he? Maybe. But then Wren had always thought Elodie was looking for him rather than trying to escape him.

'No, I didn't mean...'

A hammering of mailed fists at the door spared her having to say anything else and cause any more pain.

Roland turned away, his voice hard with command once more. 'Come!'

Olivier opened the door, his face ashen. 'Sir, there's a... a problem.'

'What kind of problem?'

'The queen, Grandmaster. The queen is gone. She's been taken.'

At first it was chaos. Wren followed in Roland's wake and no one seemed to be willing to tell her not to, or to send her away. Right beside him seemed like the safest place to be right now and it seemed that the host of knights around them both agreed.

Elodie had been taken from the Sacrum itself. That should not have been possible. Sister Maryn had been assaulted and no one seemed to have an answer as to what was going on. The knights Roland had assigned to guard the door between the Sacrum and Sanctum had been murdered.

'Sassone and his men,' said Maryn, as she tried to wipe blood from her face. She winced whenever she touched it. Though the other maidens were trying to tend her, she waved them away impatiently. 'But what he's planning I do not know.' She glared at Roland. 'He said the regents' council had ordered it.'

'We did no such thing,' Ylena snapped. She was pacing back and forth in front of the Aurum. Wren watched her silhouetted by the low flames, afraid of drawing the attention of Elodie's formidable aunt. She need not have worried. The regent had no time for her right now. The kindness, however hard and unyielding it had been, was gone. Wren stood forgotten at the back of the crowd with Olivier. 'Get Leyden and the others. Someone will answer for this and if any of those snivelling fools had a part in this... Where has he taken her?'

'To her execution,' said Maryn. 'It sounded like he plans to torture a confession from her first. With Elodie out of the way—'

Ylena's sharp eyes fell unerringly on Wren, who shrank back again. She fought to keep calm. She was already too close to the power of the Aurum. It made her skin prickle and tug, as if torn between throwing herself at it and getting as far away as possible. Her hair tickled her upper back now, already growing far too fast in the presence of magic. She only prayed with everything else going on no one else noticed.

'We will find her,' said Roland, ignoring the implication. His tone was almost gentle, as if he sought to reassure Wren. But his gaze strayed back to the bodies of his knights, covered now with their cloaks and laid out, ready to be taken away, and something seemed to snag in his throat. He bent down and scooped up a scrap of metal from the floor. Wren recognised it at once – Elodie's locket. Roland closed his hand around it, making a fist. 'We have to. What is he thinking? And why now?' He raised his voice all of a sudden, turning sharply on those accompanying him. 'Anselm? Explain this to me. What is your father planning?'

CHAPTER 28

WREN

Wren had almost forgotten Anselm Tarryn was Sassone's son. He was her bodyguard, and her friend. He made her laugh and he had danced with her almost as well as Olivier. He looked after her, protected her and stood up for her in Finn's place. But the quick and clever man with sparkling eyes looked like someone had dealt him a blow to the head right now.

He was still armed, Wren noticed, still wearing his knightly attire, but he kept his eyes on the ground, his hands well clear of his weapons, and frankly, he looked shaken. His father had done this. If he'd had any prior knowledge of it and hadn't warned Roland, there would be hell to pay. One glance at Roland's face told everyone that.

If anything happened to Elodie, Wren thought suddenly, Roland would be the least of Anselm's problems.

And if Anselm wasn't involved, how could his father have put him in this position? He had to know where suspicion would instantly fall. Did he not care?

Anselm tried to clear his throat but his voice sounded broken. 'I truly do not know, Grandmaster. On my honour. I knew of none of this.'

Roland didn't look convinced. 'Where would he take her? What will he do?'

'I don't know.' Anselm shook his head, bewildered and concerned. 'I swear to you, Grandmaster...' Wren took a step forward to comfort him, but Olivier stepped in front of her, as if he sensed the movement before she made it. He stared down at her, strain showing in the lines around his eyes.

'You can't interfere, Wren,' he murmured.

'But we have to help him.'

'We... we can't,' Olivier said and his voice almost cracked. He looked away sharply, but didn't move from in front of her. He would play the wall and keep her there if he had to. No matter how much it hurt him to turn his back on his friend.

Because she realised, they were friends. More than friends. She could see the pain of that in the hard line of his jaw, the way his gaze kept drifting back over his shoulder to Anselm in panic and then pivoting away as fast as possible back to her. But never quite focusing on her.

'Relieve him of his arms,' Roland said coldly and Yvain of Goalais stepped forward. Anselm lifted his face, visibly shaken for a moment but then unbuckled his sword belt and handed it over. Yvain nodded solemnly, one single mark of respect perhaps. Anselm met Wren's gaze. He saw Olivier's broad back. The flash of pain in his eyes made her heart twist.

This wasn't fair. It wasn't his fault. His father was responsible for his own actions, not Anselm. But what could she say? He wasn't helping, not them or himself. His silence was complicity, that was what they thought.

'You will stand down from all your duties,' Roland went on as Yvain stepped back to join him. 'Until this is resolved you are remanded to the barracks. Unless you have anything else to add? Any information which will help us? Think *hard*, Anselm.'

'Grandmaster, if I knew what he was planning I would have spoken, on my very vow to the Aurum, I swear it.'

'Vows upon vows, boy,' the Grandmaster growled, his patience at its absolute limit now. 'You can only uphold so many vows.'

'And those I gave to you are the dearest by far to me. All I can think is that he plans to take her into the lower city, to Castel Sassone, our family seat. It's secure and defensible. Before the palace was even built, my family held it. It's the heart of the old city. His stronghold, his power base, where he has fostered support or claims it through our line. But you know it well. You must have guessed as much.'

Roland didn't give him an answer.

'Yvain,' he snapped. 'Ready the men. You, guard him. Nothing is to happen to him. If harm comes to the queen it will be another matter. Take him to the barracks and lock him up.'

He stalked outside, leaving Anselm standing there, three knights guarding him. A hostage, a prisoner.

'I'm coming with you,' Wren shouted as she hurried after Roland and his men, out of the Sacrum and into the courtyard beyond it. Everywhere was a whirl of motion, a flurry of activity.

'Absolutely not,' Roland snapped. 'You will stay here under guard. Olivier—' His face seemed to freeze. Had he been about to call Anselm as well? The young knight had been his protégé as much as Finn. He'd trusted him. And now...

They didn't know what they would face down there, what Sassone might have planned. But Wren didn't care. She looked into the stony face of the Grandmaster and her mind whirled with frustration. He wasn't going to agree to bring her, she knew that. She almost understood why.

But if she argued now he was going to lock her up somewhere and throw away the key. Grinding her teeth together, she stepped back and Roland nodded to her curtly, pleased, perhaps. Not that he looked it.

How could he look anything other than furious with Elodie missing?

'You three,' Roland snapped at a group of young knights Wren didn't know. 'Attend the princess. Olivier, you know what to do. Give them their orders.'

It only took moments and then they were gone, leaving Wren, with Olivier still standing behind her.

'You should go with him,' she murmured. 'He's going to need everyone he has, isn't he?'

Olivier, clearly reluctant to listen to her right now, shook his head. 'You need to be safe.'

'I'm fine. Go with him.'

He hesitated. The light shine on him, he hesitated. He wanted to go, they all did. Wanted to find Elodie and bring her home safe, wanted to follow the Grandmaster wherever he might go. They weren't going to obey her... not unless she made them.

But still Olivier protested. 'If anything happens to the queen, Wren—'

Oh Wren had had enough. 'Then go and get her back!'

She reached out, wrapping a shaft of light and a twist of shadow together. She wasn't proud of it, but it was necessary and she could do this. She could make them obey her. She only hoped they would forgive her if they ever found out.

When she spoke again, there was a touch of othertongue in her voice and it rippled with power. Threads of magic wove around them in a translucent net only she could see. It was easy, far too easy, just a little spell, a small push, with words Elodie herself had taught her in the oldest language, the words Elodie had once used on her and oh, how she had hated her for it. 'You are knights, all of you, servants of the Aurum. Go with the others and bring Elodie back to me.'

It felt like the air left her body all at once.

She shouldn't have done it. She knew that a heartbeat later, but it was far too late. Before she could act on her regret and unwind the spell, the remaining guards bowed to her and made their way after the other knights, duty- and honour-bound to her by something more than their vows. Something they couldn't begin to understand.

A wave of revulsion made her gasp. What had she done? What had she been thinking? She had used their loyalty against them.

'Great light,' she whispered out loud and the Aurum seemed to stir, as if noticing her for the first time. The light grew a little, but so too did the shadows in the corners. 'I'm sorry.'

'You should be,' Anselm replied, his voice unbearably cold.

Wren jumped, twisting around to face him like a startled cat. The knights taking him to the barracks had followed the others on her command. Everyone else seemed to have left. At the sound of Anselm's voice, however, Olivier stopped. He had been the last and now he turned back before he reached the gates, rubbing his temples vigorously.

'Anselm?' he murmured as if waking from a dream, as if some other reality still clung to his mind.

'Let him go, Wren,' said Anselm.

The thread of magic was only a fine one. She didn't have Elodie's ability with enchantments. It would have worn off in a little while anyway, by which time Olivier should have been with Roland, attacking the lower city or whatever they were planning to do. He should have gone with the others but he didn't. Somehow he had been fighting the compulsion. She severed it and Olivier took a step back from her.

'You... you *are* her daughter,' he murmured, and she couldn't shake the idea that it was an accusation. And a recognition. Like knew like, she thought, absently. Well, she didn't regret trying to get him out of the way. Now she would have to deal with both of them.

'I'm something,' she muttered. Apologies would have to

wait. She didn't have time. 'I'm angry. Now, where do you think he took her?' Wren asked Anselm. 'Where *really*?'

'I'm going to get her back,' he said. Which was not an answer. 'If I don't, my life here is over. Everything I've worked for. Besides, she is my queen.'

There wasn't time to discuss this and sooner or later someone was going to notice the three of them standing there in the courtyard.

Anselm was unarmed but he was still a knight. He was Finn's friend, and hers perhaps as well. And he knew something.

'I'm coming with you,' she said.

Olivier sighed, a long and heavy rush of air, resignation in a single sound. 'Then so am I. If I get court-martialled for this, Anselm, it'll be on your head.'

'I can help,' said a small, terrified voice from behind them. They turned sharply to find Carlotta peering around a plain door to the servants' quarters of the keep. 'You need a way out of the palace, don't you?'

CHAPTER 29
WREN

'I didn't lie to Roland,' Anselm told Wren solemnly as they made their way to the armoury. 'I swear that. My father will go to Castel Sassone in the lower city. It's a fortified stronghold, older than Pelias itself. Before the Aurum and the crown, we held that building. It is a fortress in its own right and armies have broken themselves on it. My ancestors held it in siege for years when the first queen Aelyn took Asteroth, and only relented with the promise of high office and royal marriages. Roland won't get in easily, but I can. While he's outside, distracting them, we'll rescue Elodie and get out. Easy.'

He made it sound like a childhood adventure, but his eyes were cold and hard. She didn't like it.

'Easy,' she murmured, dubiously.

'I know a secret way in. I grew up there, remember? Look, there are dungeons and there are tunnels, secret paths only the family know.'

'And you couldn't tell Roland about them?'

He grinned, that familiar reckless grin coming back now he had a plan and others on his side. 'He's hardly subtle, your father. He'd try to take an army through that mousehole. They would be on to him in seconds and cut him to pieces. It's up to us.'

A chill of concern spread up her back. This wasn't wise, was it? If it was Finn she wouldn't hesitate. But Anselm's father had taken Elodie, and now his son was proposing to enter their stronghold. And Wren was going with him. Not her cleverest move.

'I wish Finn was here,' she said, without thinking. 'He'd know what to do.' The two men looked at her, frowning. Well, if she hurt their pride so be it.

'I know,' Anselm said at last, his voice softening a fraction. 'I swear on my life, Wren, if you must come with me I will let no harm befall you and I will bring you back out safely again. He won't have you. I'd die first. Please believe me. I have to prove myself to your father again.' He raked his hand through his hair and sighed. 'But I would rather you waited here.'

Of course he would.

'That's not happening. You'll need help. Both of you.'

Olivier's smile turned gentle, indulgent, and she thought he would argue as well, though he seemed content to let Anselm take the lead. But then he didn't know what she could do, did he? Not really. He had heard rumours no doubt. But he didn't know the way Finn knew. Or Anselm. Anselm had been at Knightsford, and the Seven Sisters.

Wren changed briskly in the barracks, pulling on a pair of breeches and a tunic, while Olivier dug out a leather jerkin for her. It wasn't armour but it was something. Her hair was still short enough to pass for a boy's when tied back and some of the squires were the same size as she was. It should work.

Finn was going to kill her, she thought. Or never talk to her again. She feared it was nothing compared to what Roland would do. She could spend the rest of her days locked in her tower room, if she was caught.

And Anselm... Anselm could be headed straight for a

dungeon. Him and Olivier both. As for Carlotta... Wren didn't know what they might do to a servant. Nothing good.

But she had to do something. Finn wasn't here. Roland was bent on a full frontal assault on whatever stood in his way. She had to find Elodie. Quickly and quietly as possible.

Carlotta cleared her throat. 'The servants' stairs are clear. They'll bring you out by the postern gate to the palace walls. I can show you.'

'And then you wait for us there, all right?' Wren said firmly. It was bad enough she had to put Olivier in this danger – not that he would be anywhere else – but she wasn't risking the only other friend she had made here in Pelias.

'But I can help, my lady.'

'Wren,' Wren told her absently. 'And you can help by keeping our plans secret. And by waiting to let us back in.'

'But I...' Carlotta embraced Wren suddenly, pulling her close. She pressed a little knot of straw and dried flowers into Wren's hand. It looked like a bird. 'It's not much, but it will help. It will remind you of who you are, Wren. For luck.'

It was a charm, such as hedge witches made everywhere. Wren had seen Elodie's, learned to make them herself but it was something she had thought left far behind in Thirbridge.

The revelation made Wren stiffen in Carlotta's arms and open her eyes wide. There was an aura of something around the maid. She knew herbs and cures, and where to find certain flowers. And clearly she could make a memory charm. But she wasn't strong.

That didn't change what she was.

We are witchkind. We will live free or we die.

There were other witches in the world. Wren knew the stories about the rebel witches who didn't serve Aurum or Nox, who lived in the wild and didn't bow to anyone. She thought they would be strong and dangerous. People spoke of the witchkind of Garios as if they were monsters, inhuman, beings of enormous power. And when they mentioned the College of Winter, it was as somewhere austere and terrible, where people sought secret truths and honed their skills beyond anything else save the Chosen of the Aurum. They were masters of magic, wielding untold power. That was what witchkind was. Not a small girl with too large eyes and barely a scrap of power compared to herself, or Elodie, or the maidens. No wonder Carlotta had gone unnoticed. How was she here in the palace, living and working and hiding...?

If the knights found out...

Wren glanced at the two men to find them deep in a conversation of their own, a hushed and hurried argument from the looks of it.

An admission like that in Pelias was liable to get Carlotta locked away, or handed over to the Maidens of the Aurum for the rest of her life. If that was all she would be lucky. No wonder she had been terrified when Wren had thoughtlessly dragged her into the Sanctum behind her.

'I need you to stay here and be safe,' she said urgently to Carlotta. 'Watch for us coming back. And if we don't, you go and tell Lynette everything, all right?' And that might be as dangerous a mission as their own. Lynette would be furious. And then Lynette would tell Ylena. And who knew if anyone would survive that.

Wren turned to the others. 'Anselm? Are you ready?'

'You should stay here as well,' Olivier told her, but he didn't seem quite so adamant now.

'You know what I am, what I can do?' she said bluntly. 'You know it better than anyone, don't you? Were you born with magic?' He sucked in a breath to hear that. Well, it was almost as shocking as Carlotta's had been in its own way. Then he nodded slowly.

'I gave it up, to the Aurum. As all men must.' It was their tradition she recalled. Women joined the Maidens of the

Aurum and men surrendered what little magic they had in them back to the flames. Most became knights. Others just left. There didn't seem to be any choice in the matter but none of them seemed to care about that.

'I... I'm sorry.'

Olivier frowned, clearly baffled. 'Why? I'm not.'

She had to keep reminding herself that she was not only her powers. That she controlled them and not the other way around, just as Maryn had said. She closed her hand around the little charm and felt its shape imprint on her palm. He might have given up the magic he was born with, but she never would. She couldn't. But that didn't mean she should let them control her. Or expect anyone else to welcome such powers.

They left the palace in silence, leaving Carlotta as promised at the unmanned gate. If there were normally guards there, they were gone now, whether with Sassone or Roland. Anselm took the lead. 'He'll be keeping her in his dungeons.'

'And torturing her?' Wren had to force herself to say it.

His stalwart expression faded. Something else ghosted across his face. 'Yes. I expect so.'

'*Why*, Anselm?'

He shook his head as if to say he didn't know. 'We ruled this city once, my family, warlords and robber barons, long before the Aurum was brought here. He wants to go back to that, and as regent he had a taste of it. And more than that... I think he truly believes what he says, that Queen Aeryn deserted and betrayed us all. He knows her to be a traitor and he will not listen to reason. Her trial didn't go as he intended and the Aurum forgave her any transgressions. He's going to try to prove it wrong, by whatever means necessary.'

There wasn't really anything to say to that, Wren decided. She didn't know what had happened all those years ago, no more than she knew why Elodie had never returned, preferring to live in the wilds of Cellandre rather than wear her crown and rule, why she had preferred the life of a hedge witch to that of a queen.

'We should hurry,' she told him and that was that.

Thankfully, Anselm didn't argue anymore and Olivier followed his lead.

They trailed after him out into the city. To his father's halls. To Elodie.

CHAPTER 30

WREN

The lower city was eerily quiet in the aftermath of the knights'
charge through it earlier.

People hid indoors, Wren realised, which was not a good
sign. The same people who had thronged the streets to see their
queen come home now hid from her knights in terror.

It was not good. Not good at all.

The last time Wren had come this way, the streets had been
strewn with flowers and streamers. They passed the remains of
the market, stalls shattered to kindling, and Anselm turned
down a side street, and along a winding laneway. Up ahead,
they could hear a growing noise, the sound of a huge number of
men and horses.

'Have you seen them?' someone hissed out of a doorway
and Wren spun around to see a woman peering out through a
crack in the door. 'Is it safe?'

'Stay inside,' Anselm told her briskly, as if he had all the
authority of the knights still to back him up. 'It'll be over soon.'

'Have the knights gone mad?'

He winced. 'No. Lord Sassone has. He kidnapped the

queen.' The way he said it, so calm and factual... no one would have guessed he was talking about his own father.

'They'll kill him.'

'Probably,' he agreed. He didn't sound sorry about that either, Wren thought. No love lost there at all. She didn't blame him. They hurried on through the tangle of lanes.

At the back of a sheer wall the top of which could not be seen, Anselm dragged open a grate in the street. It was small and narrow and the smell that came out of it was eye-watering.

'A sewer?' Wren asked. He wrapped a scarf around his face and handed another to her. Olivier had his own and he scowled at the very thought of it, but didn't say a word in protest.

'Hold your breath. We'll be out of it again in a few minutes.'

The scarf did next to nothing to help, and it was as dark as night down there. The shadows pressed close, sensing her fear and worry. They stroked against her skin and threaded through her hair, teasing her, laughing at her. Water sloshed around their boots, but Anselm didn't pause, moving with a purpose, feeling his way forward.

When Wren hesitated, he reached back and threaded his fingers through hers to lead her onwards.

'Don't be scared,' he told her. 'I've got you.'

She squeezed his hand in gratitude, feeling the warmth in him, the light in him, and the shadows fell back to an almost manageable level. He was a Knight of the Aurum still. Her knight. The remnants of the Nox still followed her though, a host of shadows, scraps of a greater darkness, as if she was a lodestone for them. They wanted to help her, they sang. They would always be there when she needed them. She only had to ask.

Her hair curled against her neck, reaching far down past her shoulders now, growing and growing with the touch of the darkness all around her. It coiled around her scalp, tightening as they moved deeper into darkness. There was no shaking it off, as if her own fear and anxiety conjured it up.

'Wren?' Olivier asked softly. 'Are you all right?'

This wasn't good. But she didn't have time to worry about herself. She needed to find Elodie and fast, before Sassone could do anything more to her. Wren didn't want to waste a moment imagining what he might have done already.

'I'm fine. Keep going,' she told him as firmly as she could manage.

Anselm shifted a grate in the wall, which swung inwards, and they stepped into a dry passageway where the air wasn't so foul. There was a dim light ahead and Wren could make out the walls at last. With that, she felt the shadows dogging her footsteps draw back a little. It felt like a weight lifting off her shoulders and she let out a breath of relief.

'Not far,' Anselm whispered, but he didn't let her go either. She felt a pathetic sort of gratitude for that.

It was going to be all right, she assured herself. First she'd find Elodie, and then—

They stepped out into dank cellars and then climbed a narrow staircase. There were lanterns here, lighting the way, and up ahead Wren saw a heavy door.

'Olivier, watch the way out,' Anselm said. They fell readily into a team. Olivier took position by the top of the stairs with a view over any approaches from the corridor and their way back out covered while Anselm approached the cell. The door wasn't locked.

Anselm opened it slowly, as if a breeze moved it, just enough to see inside, and there was Elodie.

She was kneeling on the ground, chains weighing her down and a collar around her neck like some kind of brutally plain choker. Her eyes were closed tightly, tears leaking from the corners and streaking her cheeks. Every muscle was clenched in agony, but she didn't make a sound.

'Elodie?' Wren whispered in horror.

Elodie lifted her head, tears streaming down her face as she tried to focus on the darkness beyond the door, on Wren.

'No. You can't be here. You have to go away.'

Then she slumped forward, her face a mask of pain, her eyes unseeing.

CHAPTER 31

FINN

Finn was preparing to leave, to just get back to the palace as quickly as possible and as far away from Ilanthian nobility and all their machinations as he could. In all honesty he couldn't extricate himself from the embassy quickly enough. They had brought Leander back here in a stupor, Hestia healing him and cursing him at regular intervals, all the more whenever he looked like he might regain some kind of consciousness, and Finn could hardly blame her.

Leander had been willing to die to score a point. And to force Wren to reveal who and what she was. He still was. And then what? Was he so confident that Hestia would save him? Probably, Finn decided, because Hestia had charge of him and to lose him in Pelias of all places would put not only her life but that of her son on the line as well. But did Leander really think the Asterothians would let him return to Ilanthus in triumph with Wren after everything that had happened? Make her his bride or whatever he had planned for her? They'd kill her the moment her secret was revealed. Finn didn't doubt that for an instant. The sooner the Ilanthians all left Pelias the better.

As if Finn didn't already have a thousand things for which to never forgive his half-brother...

'Thanks be to the divine you were there,' said Hestia. She was still trembling, the energy which had filled Elodie having shaken her to the core. 'I had no idea, I swear to you, Finn.'

No idea. No idea what Leander planned? Or no idea what Elodie could do? He chose to believe she meant the former.

And he knew it was a conscious decision on his part. Hestia would do whatever suited Ilanthus best. He'd been a fool to forget that.

He continued packing the few belongings he had brought with him. 'It wasn't the kind of plan he'd share, was it?' And if he had that was a whole new level of problem. 'Besides, I don't think he had what you might call a plan in the first place. If you've healed him, I suggest you pack him off back to Sidon as quickly as you can. Tie him up this time. Drag him behind a horse if you have to. You might buy a cage.'

He shoved the last of the formal tunics into the bag. The fine fabric would be crumpled and lined, but he didn't care. He had no idea why he was even taking them with him. They were Ilanthian in style, gifts from his cousin, but he would never wear them except for here in the embassy or representing them, a kingdom which hated him. Something he would never do again. So why was he even packing them? Perhaps because Hestia had been so delighted to see him and had given them to him, along with that glass pendant, and for once he felt like he had family again. But *his* family? No. His father might have offered him the pendant by way of a gesture of reconciliation. It hung like a millstone around his neck now.

Of course Leander had to spoil that too.

Hestia was pacing, knotting her hands in front of her. 'You'll explain, won't you? That we didn't know. That he acted alone. The queen will listen to you, won't she? I know the Grandmaster will, surely?'

Finn gave a brief and humourless laugh, little more than a snort. 'I'll try. But to be honest, our rapid retreat from Elodie was probably an indication enough.'

Hestia glared at him. '*Elodie*,' she growled. 'Since when did you refer to the queen of Asteroth by her childhood name? She has a title, Finn.'

Finn shrugged. He didn't have the time or inclination to explain things to her.

There was something in the air, he decided, something unsettling. Ever since the scene at the trial when Elodie had channelled the Aurum like the queen she was, everything felt wrong, on edge. And it was getting worse. He could feel it under his skin, crawling like shadows with the sunset.

Was it Wren? Had seeing the Aurum fill Elodie unsettled her so much? But she herself had drawn on that power at the Seven Sisters.

Somewhere, shadow kin were stirring. They had no place in Pelias with all its wards and protections, with the Aurum awake once more and the queen back on her throne. But they were here. He knew it. Perhaps the wards in the palace weren't the only ones breaking down.

That was when Gaius arrived, slamming open the door to Finn's borrowed quarters without so much as a knock. Finn didn't mind really. He wasn't particularly attached to the embassy walls anyway. He was a prince of Ilanthus in name only as far as he was concerned. They had already squandered any goodwill he had towards any of them. Burned through it in fact like a summer fire through dry grass.

And Leander had left no goodwill at all. It was only Hestia's promise that she could control him this time that had prompted Finn to stay and act as the intermediary with the palace here in Pelias this long.

Great light he was an idiot.

'He's locked up but we have another problem,' the general growled. 'Their sham of a trial isn't over yet. That fool Sassone has taken the queen to conduct some kind of inquisition of his own. The Asterothians are going to blame us for this as well. I've secured the compound but it's only a matter of time. Castel Sassone is a stone's throw from here. Once they're done with him, they'll turn on us. We should all prepare to leave immediately.'

'What do you mean, he's taken the queen?' Hestia gasped. Her carefully engineered peace plans were crumbling in front of her and Finn almost felt sorry for her. Almost.

She had actually believed it was possible, he realised.

'He's going to make her confess and burn her. There's a full army of knights descending on him right now. I don't see how they're going to get through those walls in a hurry but they'll break them eventually. As we're right next to him, it's only a matter of time until it's our turn. Make ready to leave at once, my lady. This foolish enterprise is at an end.'

Hestia almost sagged, defeated. 'Gaius,' she protested. 'We... we can't...'

'We have to, Hestia. It's over.'

'Then we have lost everything,' she whispered.

Finn felt it again, the darkness surging beneath them, the undercurrent. The Nox was here. He could feel it, loose in the city and gloating at the chaos it had unleashed.

Leander had unleashed it. Great light, he would kill the bastard himself if Hestia didn't do it first once she recovered herself. But that was all secondary. The queen of Asteroth had been taken, the queen he had sworn on his life and soul to defend.

'The Earl of Sassone took her?' he asked Gaius. It sounded like madness, but at the same time... Sassone was a law unto himself. The general gave him a curt nod.

'Hideous little man,' Gaius said. 'Whether he kills her

quickly or not, it's his death warrant, I would think. Your father would never have let such a—'

'That doesn't make sense,' Finn said, uninterested in what his father may or may not have allowed. Alessander had spilled more blood in his court than anyone in history. 'Why would he—'

'Why do any of them do anything? Sanctimonious fools, each and every one, and their Grandmaster is the worst of them.' Gaius stalked to the window, leaning out as if it might offer him a better view. 'This embassy was a terrible idea, Lady Hestia, pointless and weak. A disaster from beginning to end. The sooner we return home the better.'

'We'll only be returning to war,' she snapped. 'And I realise that would suit you, but I am trying to give us a better future. You saw her, Gaius. You saw what she can do. With Aeryn on the throne again—'

'Maybe her own people will take care of her for us. That would solve everything. With the girl on the throne instead—'

Wren. Finn felt a surge of light flood through him at the thought of her name.

She'd be terrified, helpless. They all looked down on her, just like Gaius and the rest. They saw only a girl to be used, not a woman with a heart and mind of her own. They thought her helpless. But she was far from helpless. Yet, she … she couldn't control the power at her disposal. He knew that as well as she did. He needed to go to her now. If Elodie had been taken and was in such danger—

No, he realised, and that burgeoning darkness beneath them all grew clearer. Wren was never helpless and with Elodie in danger… she was not going to sit in the palace waiting for someone else to ride to the rescue. He remembered her when Elodie's tower burned. She would have run in there if he hadn't stopped her. She would never back down from a fight or leave it someone else. And when Wren lost herself in emotions and magic... He really did need to find her right away. Not only for her sake. For everyone's.

Grabbing his sword belt, he slung it over his body and buckled it in place, leaving the bag of unwanted belongings where he had dropped it.

Wren was in trouble, more trouble than she knew. He could feel it now, spreading out through the city, the shadows converging on a single place, like a vortex sucking them in.

Even the pendant around his neck prickled in response to that power. Like it would lead him straight to her.

CHAPTER 32

WREN

Wren ran to where Elodie lay, dropping to her knees beside her.

When she touched her face, and whispered her name, Elodie flinched back and her eyes opened, bright and bloodshot with agony.

'Wren?' Her voice grated along her throat like sandpaper.

'Yes, I'm here. We're here. We're going to get you out.'

'You can't, love. You—' She looked up to see Anselm and a look of pure loathing passed over her face. It quickly crumpled as another wave of pain lanced through her. 'You can't be here. You have to leave. Now. They'll be back soon. And the spells...'

Wren was too busy examining the chains and the collar, trying to find a catch. The metal was icy cold against her touch and as she ran her fingertips over it, she felt it hum. When she had released Elodie at the Seven Sisters, she had pulled the shadows from the steel, but this time it was too deeply ingrained and slipped through her grasp.

Elodie sobbed again, and she grabbed Wren's wrists in shaking hands. 'You have to stop, love. You're... you're making it worse. It hurts... Please... go.' Her voice rose, ragged and pained.

'But I—'

'Worse, Wren. The power in you... It's... it's feeding on it... growing... please...'

Wren withdrew, desperate now. If she couldn't free Elodie, if she was making it worse by being here...

'What do I do? You broke free of manacles like those before, Elodie. You have to be able to do it again.'

'I'm too weak and this place... too dark... with you here... no time...' Suddenly she stopped, listening intently, pain still playing out on her face but pushed back for a moment. 'They're coming back,' Elodie hissed. 'Get out, all of you. Tell Roland... tell him...'

Whatever it was she couldn't say it. Another wave of agony swamped her and she arched her back, trying to fight through it.

Footsteps outside told them their time was up. Olivier stood in the doorway. 'I can carry her,' he began but Elodie shook her head. Even though she had to bite out the words, there was no doubting the tone of command.

'...slow you down... get out.'

But Wren wasn't giving up. 'Elodie, please, we can make it. You and I—'

'Why won't you listen to me? You've never listened.' She fixed Wren with her manic eyes, wild with pain. 'I did it all for you and you never listen. You aren't even my child. You're nothing to me. We owe each other nothing. Do you understand? Now leave me. Get away from me. You... you're nothing but a monster. You always have been.'

Wren staggered back, stunned at the cruel words. Anselm pulled her into his arms, clearly as surprised as she was by Elodie's rage.

Noises from above made them all freeze, the sound of footsteps coming down the stone stairs.

Ignoring the horror on their faces, Elodie struggled to her feet. 'Get her out of here, knight,' she hissed to Anselm. 'I charge you on your vows. Both of you, protect her.'

Anselm dragged Wren back into the shadows which she instinctively pulled around them as armed men flooded the dungeon. Olivier folded in beside them and the darkness hid the three of them, for once acting in her favour. Just as it had promised, she thought, and felt like a traitor. Anselm's whole body went tense with loathing at the sight of his father, but he didn't release her. Perhaps he didn't dare to. His queen had given him a command. Even Wren couldn't counter that, no matter how much she might want to.

Sassone looked no further than a defeated queen and his own triumph.

Elodie looked up at him, pain and contempt dripping from her voice. 'I'll say what you want,' she spat out each word. 'Whatever you want. Let's get this over with.'

'Bring her,' Sassone barked at his men. He didn't question her change of mind or the reasons for it. Perhaps he thought the enchanted chains had done his work for him. Perhaps he was that arrogant. Or perhaps, Wren realised, his position was too dire for hesitation. The knights were at the gates. 'There isn't much time. We need that confession in public, now, where everyone can hear her. Her knights need to hear it. As does all of Pelias.'

Wren stifled a sob and the shadows surged around them again, angry now, upset with her. They teetered on the edge of her control and she felt it too, the wild magic in the air, exacerbating everything and sending the balance of light and dark off its axis, spinning recklessly as a drunk.

The moment Sassone and his men had dragged the still chained Elodie from the cell, Wren turned on Anselm.

And lost the last grip on her powers.

Shadows coiled around him like ropes. She flung him back against the wall, pinning him there, and felt the dark power that was her birthright erupt inside her.

'Why did you do that? Why didn't you help me free her? Do you want your father to kill her?'

She hardly recognised the man there, smothered in darkness, his eyes wide in abject terror.

'Wren please,' Anselm managed to heave out, before shadows surged into his mouth until he choked on them.

Elodie had called her a monster. Had said Wren was nothing to her. Not her child, not really. And now... now... what was she doing? What would Anselm call her right now?

Please...

Who was begging her? The man or the shadows? It almost sounded like the voice of the Nox. It was so strong down here. Now it all rebounded on Wren, drowning her in its power. And she was ready to surrender to it.

'Let him go,' Olivier snapped. His sword touched her back, Aurum-forged and icy cold. But even seeing the evidence of what she was and what she could do, he didn't panic, not entirely.

What was she doing?

The shadows recoiled, dumping Anselm unceremoniously on the cold slabs of the floor. He gasped for air, trying to pull himself up.

Olivier stepped back and she turned to see the ghost of fear on his handsome features. It didn't make him back down though. He was a knight. He took his vows seriously. 'What... what are you? We fight the Nox, with flame and sword.'

And there it was, the reaction she expected. Every time.

But to her surprise, Anselm pushed by her, and with one hand swatted Olivier's sword aside, standing between them defiant. 'She's our princess and we are sworn to protect her.'

Olivier frowned at him as if he was mad and then he exhaled slowly. 'It's magic and that is no concern of ours. Men give it up to serve the Aurum and we don't need to have anything to do with it. It is necessary, I understand that. But this...'

'Olivier,' said Anselm softly. Just his name. An admonition. And a warning. Olivier stared at him, frowned but then, slowly, he nodded.

'Very well, I trust *you*.' The word was pointed and only for Anselm, Wren knew that. 'Don't get us killed.' Then he gave Wren a curt nod. 'Princess.'

The glow of flickering lanterns reflected off his sword and armour, a brief glimmer of light. But it was *light*, here in this dark and terrible place. Wren found the breath she hadn't been able to draw into her lungs. It came with a surge of relief as she pulled herself up to her full height and fixed him with a look of gratitude and desperation.

'I'm Wren,' she told him. 'Not princess, not lady, not... not anything else and we are running out of time. I don't care what Elodie said. We have to help her.'

CHAPTER 33
ELODIE

Pain coursed through Elodie's body.

Each time she thought she had managed to gain some sort of equilibrium, had managed to reach a place where she was balanced precariously on the edge and might be able to reclaim some sense of herself, or perhaps even grab a scrap of her power, the darkness surrounding her resurged, swallowing her down again.

It was far more than the power of shadow-wrought steel. More than anything she had encountered before.

Someone had made this, created this – a spell which riddled the black manacles and collar, twisting the old magic's light and dark, blending the two and switching them back and forth in a whirlwind of pure chaos – just for her. Someone who could turn the magic she thought she knew so well inside out.

Sassone couldn't have done this. Not on his own. This was witchkind magic, but Elodie had never encountered anything so vicious. Not even the rebel witchkind or the College of Winter would willingly do this, not even the Sisterhood of the Nox. This was magic twisted and corrupted. And there was nothing Elodie could do to counter it.

Agony blinded her, smothered her voice and deadened her senses. All was pain.

The cold black power eating away at her wouldn't relent. It sucked all the light from her, chilled her to the core and there was nothing she could do. It had been made to do this, designed with her power in mind, targeting her alone. She was helpless in the face of it and the Nox's laughter echoed through her head.

Finally, it seemed to say, *finally you're mine. And the girl will be next.*

Wren... her face, pale and frightened but still determined, still so perfectly stubborn, swam up out of the shadows and pleaded with Elodie to fight, tried to help her, even when Elodie told her to run. But Elodie was nothing now. Once a queen, once a witch, she was barely clinging onto herself.

There was only one way she could still protect Wren.

Give Sassone what he wanted. A confession.

Whatever he wanted her to confess. She didn't know. She just needed it to stop.

If she could just catch her breath for even a second. Even a breath. If she could just...

They had erected a pyre in the top of the walls, a great stack of kindling and firewood. In the middle a single wooden post rose like a finger pointing at the sky. As they dragged her up the steps she could smell oil and tar.

Given to the flames... this was what it meant. Burned alive, choking, blistering, dying, consumed by the one thing that ought to give her strength. She was lost.

The light overhead was dim and night was already falling. Even if she could reach her magic, the dawn was hours away. The moon wasn't due to rise tonight.

Panic raced along her veins like acid, careening through her. The wind cut at her skin like knives and she saw the lower city spreading out beneath her. The palace was so far away, a white shining thing on the hill, out of reach. There was a noise outside the gates of Castel Sassone, the sound of war. She knew it too well to forget it. Looking down, she could see them now. The Knights of the Aurum, still faithful to her... Horses and men circling, siege weapons being readied.

She hadn't dared to hope they would come. But it was still too late.

Elodie knew this place. It had always been here, the stronghold of the Tarryns. And it was impenetrable.

A fortress as strong as the palace complex above it, and Sassone had made sure to keep it in perfect order, all his line had. They were no fools. The walls were tall and thick, not overlooked from the nearby buildings, offering no position to attack easily. All her knights could try to do was break through the gates and scale those walls, so securely defended. They would have to fight their way to her.

They would never be in time. That must be Sassone's intention. Her knights would watch her die long before they reached her.

And they wouldn't be the only ones. The whole city was watching. She could feel them, her people, some terrified, some angry, some curious and some delighted... those whose hearts were filled with hate, who blamed her for everything.

Rightly perhaps. She had taken the crown. Oh she had been young and naïve, but she had sworn vows and promised to protect them. And all she had done was plunge them into war.

They might have won it, but that was no victory of hers. She had been long gone.

No wonder they hate you, said the voice inside her which might have been the Nox, or the Aurum, or her own conscience. *You are a traitor. You always were.*

The Ilanthian embassy was in sight, all gleaming walls and gold-topped towers, pennants flying to show that royalty was in residence. Were they watching too? Was Leander even now looking on in triumph? He had everything he wanted now. She was going to die.

And Finn? Was he there? Poor Finn, so hopelessly lost between his heart and his duty and his blood...

But he'd protect Wren, surely. He had to.

The wooden pole, as thick as a tree trunk, struck her back as she was pushed against it, and her arms, still chained, were dragged up and secured above her head. The guards fell back, releasing her as if reluctant to touch her rather than eager for her death.

One of them muttered something. It sounded like a prayer, a plea to the Aurum to help them all. And well he might pray, she thought. He might not like what he was doing but that didn't stop him doing it.

Roland was coming. He would be too late for her. But not too late to exact his vengeance.

His retribution would fall on each and every one of them and it would never be satiated. Roland de Silvius, her Roland, her love... he'd break the world apart with grief to have found her and lost her again.

Below her, the city fell to an eerie silence. Faces looked up at her, so small and lost in the encroaching darkness. Waiting. They were waiting. They were as helpless as she was.

She had to protect Wren. That was all that mattered. Whatever the outcome here, she had to protect Wren.

Once more, she struggled to free herself, fighting through the agony crawling along her limbs, through every spasming muscle. Her vision blurred, the edges eaten away with night.

And then she saw him, far below her, Roland, still dressed in the ceremonial armour from the trial, gilded and etched with patterns of flames, and not even the slightest bit practical. It made him beautiful. More than beautiful. Great light, he was everything she might have hoped to see as her last vision. Her Roland. He was older than in her dreams, harder than ever, but he was still the one thing she wanted. The one thing she missed about life here. The only thing...

She still ached for him.

Tears scalded Elodie's face as she stared at him, as she studied the expression on his face, the traces of fear, the anger, the wrath...

'Aeryn of Asteroth has a confession to make,' Sassone roared through the horrified silence encircling Pelias. 'Hear her and witness her execution.'

'Tarryn,' Roland shouted back. No title anymore, no honorifics. He wouldn't sully his lips with them. 'Don't do this. Let her go and—'

'Hear her confession,' the earl shouted over him and turned to her. His face had turned florid, spit flecking at the corners of his mouth. Was he deranged? Enchanted? Or simply driven by lust for power and other delusions? 'Speak, woman.'

Elodie drew in a shaking breath but as she opened her mouth another spear of pain lanced through the whole length of her body. Laughter echoed in her ears, distant and invisible, but still there.

They'll burn you, and scatter your ashes as you burned and scattered me. You will be nothing but a hated memory.

The metal was an icy fire on her skin, as if the Nox threaded itself through it. No, she thought. She couldn't give it the satisfaction. Wren would be safe by now, surely? The boy would have got her clear, taken her back out the way she came in. Elodie hadn't meant a word she'd said. Wren was hers and would always be hers. She'd needed to make sure she left.

From somewhere she found her voice. It was thin and agonised but it was hers. That was all she had left now. Her voice.

Elodie locked eyes with Roland, down below her, staring up helplessly. He was saying something to the men around him, still issuing orders, but he never tore his gaze away from her. He held his horse in check, the beast straining beneath him. Nightbreaker, strapped to his back, sang out to her, the Aurum's light in it trying to give her strength. And perhaps it did.

'I am Aeryn,' Elodie shouted, her voice rising on the wind. 'I am the trueborn queen of Asteroth, the Chosen of the Aurum. Everything I have done, everything they accuse me of, was done in defence of my people, my kingdom and in service of the great light.'

She glanced at the Earl of Sassone, who was opening and closing his mouth in disbelief. 'Your confession—'

Elodie shook her head. 'That's all I have to say. Were you...' The pain surged back, clawing inside her, tearing her apart, but she didn't care. She smiled through it. 'Were you expecting something more?'

He snarled a curse at her, violent and final. 'Very well, perhaps your child will be more cooperative. I'll soon bend her to my will.'

Elodie bit her lip until she tasted blood and scowled at him. She made sure her voice carried again. Let them all hear. Let them know the truth at last. If she couldn't protect Wren it was all for nothing anyway. 'What... child? I have no child.'

Sassone grabbed the torch from the guard beside him. The flames turned his face scarlet and black, sweat gleaming. 'This is your last chance, witch.'

Elodie lifted her face to the sky, feeling the faint touch of the last rays of light lingering on her skin like a lover's caress. Roland was there, but he was too far away. She had no magic left to her.

A dreadful boom filled the air and the wall below her shook. A battering ram? He had a battering ram. Elodie almost laughed. Roland was going to tear this place apart, bring down the gates and the walls and anything in his path to reach her. Because he was Roland, her Roland.

And he would always try to save her.

Too late, the voice that taunted her seemed to say. *Far too late*.

Sassone thrust the flaming torch into the pyre, which caught in an instant. He knew what he was doing. Perhaps she wasn't the first woman he had burned.

The boom of the battering ram again, shouts of rage, the crackle of flames, and the pain, the endless waves of pain coming one after the other. They swirled to a crescendo and then one sound cut through them all.

A scream, high and desperate, so scared... a voice which had brought Elodie running no matter what was happening to her for twenty years now. A sound she would always put first. Wren's voice, Wren's scream, and all around the darkness howled in triumph. Wind whipped around Elodie, lashing her hair across her face, but all it did was fan the flames underneath her. Smoke rose, black and choking, and even as she reached for the light the flames ought to embody, the metal turned cold as ice and the smoke closed on her, smothering her.

Wren was down there somewhere and all the light left in Elodie's world rushed to the girl's command. And all the darkness too.

They would all know what Wren was. They would all see.

Everything Elodie had done, all she had given up, had been in vain. She screamed, her voice breaking as she threw back her head, trying to warn Wren, trying to stop her and failing.

A terrible crash told her the gates had shattered, either the ram itself or helped by Wren's power, Elodie no longer knew. There was no magic left to reach for, no light, nothing.

Hooves thundered on stone, and Elodie saw the flash of a sword, a line of pure white light arcing through the night. The heat beneath her was unbearable and she was locked in the cold embrace of shadow-wrought steel. Fire caught on her skirts, rising around her, and she tried to take its light, tried to use it to protect herself, but the enchanted metal sucked that away in a moment and turned it back on her in agony. It was voracious and unstoppable, this spell. It would devour her.

She was lost. Darkness surged up around her and Elodie felt the last glimmer of light in her heart flicker out.

And Roland... her Roland...

The sword crashed against the post above her head, severing the chains holding her there. She slumped, falling towards the flames, helpless to stop herself. Her meagre strength was gone, the fight in her all but done. But strong arms seized her and pulled her clear. Someone hauled her over the withers of a horse and they were moving again, riding through the night. Hooves struck stone and the stone walls of the fortress fell away.

A body clothed in metal held her against him like she was something precious. And his voice... she knew his voice...

'Elodie?' he panted, adrenaline and exertion making him breathless. Or maybe that was fear. But he had never been afraid. Not her Roland. Never. 'Elodie, can you hear me?'

She tried to answer, tried to find words, but there were no words and there was no more air in her lungs. Only smoke and shadows, only darkness. She had failed to protect Wren and now they all knew.

There was nothing else she could do. She had lost and the Nox had won. That was all she knew.

Elodie finally let the pain take her into unconsciousness.

CHAPTER 34

FINN

'Where are you going?' Hestia cried out, hurrying after him as far as the main entrance hall. Finn stalked onwards, ignoring her. The Sassone house wasn't far from here.

His ancestors had chosen the embassy with care, near to the outskirts of Pelias's lower city in case they had to leave in a hurry, but still in a rich and prosperous area populated by the old families. Being almost next to Castel Sassone had been the concession that got them the location.

No one from the court of Sidon would stand to be accused of slumming it. And the people of Pelias could feel safe knowing their strongest nobleman guarded the way. But if Sassone had turned on the crown now...

Finn didn't make it outside. Something unseen wrapped itself around him, something dark and determined, and oh so powerful.

'Stop, Finnian. I can't let you leave.' Hestia held out her hands, shadows tangling around her fingertips and flooding her eyes. She held him. He knew she was powerful but he had never considered how powerful. 'It's too dangerous. And you are too important to us now. We need you.'

She thought she was protecting him? Furious, he tried to tear himself free, not caring what she had to say, not now. There was no time for this.

Light burned up through him, bright and desperate, the Aurum reaching out for anyone who would serve it. All of the knights had to be feeling this, a wild and desperate urge to get to the fight, to defend Elodie. They would break themselves apart on the gates and the walls until they reached her.

And beneath it... laughter, dark and terrible laughter. With its power wrapped around him he could hear the Nox, feel its sense of impending victory. Elodie would die and Wren's defences would crumble and he... he...

It would take him as its slave. It would make him love it.

He wrenched words from his throat. 'Hestia, stop. I have to help Wren. Let me go.'

As if using her name summoned it, light filled him as it had once in the forest, when Wren had filled him with the blessings of the Aurum. Bright and terrible, blinding him from the inside, it roared along his veins. It tore through the spell holding him as if it was no more than smoke.

Had he done that? No, not possible. He couldn't do anything of the sort. That kind of magic wasn't possible for his line. Leander could wield shadows and summon shadow kin to do his bidding, but not Finn, and none of them could command light.

When he looked back at his cousin, she was on her knees, the effort of holding him draining her.

'Hestia,' he tried again. 'Wren needs me. Please...'

The light grew even brighter, like a blade in the heart of a forge, white hot and transforming to something new. The force holding him recoiled so suddenly that he stumbled forward as the spell snapped, ploughing through the open doorway.

'Come back,' Hestia called weakly, but she couldn't hold him now. 'You have to come back. You don't understand.'

There wasn't time for this. No time at all and no one from Ilanthus needed him. They had made that more than clear over the years. But the pendant felt cold and heavy around his neck, an unwanted weight he should shed, if only there was time.

The light in him subsided to a dull glow and he knew there were a thousand questions to answer. No time for that either.

Laurence, Hestia's son, was in the courtyard outside, peering out through the gates. He ran back to Finn as he emerged from the building, ignoring his shaken expression. 'You're going to help, aren't you? Prince Finnian, you have to help.'

'Tell me what you know,' he said.

It was amazing what an adolescent boy could discover in the lower city. Quickly, and with an efficiency that shouldn't have been a surprise given he was Hestia's son, the boy told him that Sassone had put out word that the queen would confess, that he had taken her to Castel Sassone and planned to execute her there. He was calling on the people to rise up, to follow him instead of the false queen. Finn closed his eyes, imagining for a moment the chaos that was going to unleash across Pelias. Sides taken, old grudges reawakened, and loyalties torn apart. Sassone must have lost his mind. Or he truly believed Elodie a traitor and that was its own kind of madness.

'He's going to kill her,' Laurence said. 'They say he's already torturing her and when he's finished... and the knights can't get inside.'

Where was Anselm? Finn wondered. He'd know a way. He'd spoken about secret passages and—

The currents in the ground beneath him twisted and bucked, trying to wrench themselves free. Shadows and light, tangling together, torn from their paths and redirected by sheer force of will. And rage. Blind rage. Such fear.

It might have been Elodie, or the Aurum itself.

What happened when someone tortured the Chosen of the Aurum so close to its heart?

Then again, it wasn't only the light he was feeling. The Nox was there too and the shadows were rising. Everything twisted and confused, as if someone had grabbed both powers and tangled them together. It all felt wrong.

Wren would be feeling this too, all the wild rage, grief and loss. It would funnel up inside her and if it came out…

Wren wouldn't let anything happen to Elodie. And she had been with Anselm.

He could feel her, her scent tangling around him, her voice calling him. And he wasn't entirely sure if it was Wren, the Aurum or the Nox, or something else entirely. It was power. And it was dangerous.

Now he knew where she was. All he had to do was follow those currents rippling through the ether.

'Stay inside,' he told the boy.

'I can help you, guard your back. They're going to kill her. There isn't much time.'

Just what he needed. A boy in tow. And yet he felt a surge of relief that at least someone in his light-forsaken family had some sort of priorities. It didn't matter to him that she was the queen of Asteroth or anything else.

He grabbed Laurence and pulled him into an embrace, kissing the top of his head. 'You go to your mother right now and protect her. She's… she's exhausted and won't be able to help herself if anything happens. Lock the gates after me and tell Gaius to double the guards. Tell him he's right and everyone should get out as quickly as they can once this is over. Understand? I charge you as…' He couldn't remember the honours and knighthoods of Sidonia. He'd never learned them. They had never mattered and he had not cared. 'As my cousin,' he finished. 'As a member of the line of Sidon. Will you obey me in this?'

The boy stepped back, face shining with gratitude and faith and something Finn didn't even want to consider. 'Yes, Prince Finnian.'

Light, Finn hated that title.

Outside, the city was in chaos. The noise was already deafening, armed men everywhere, and every knight in Pelias converging on the area.

There had to be a way in. Finn could feel the current of shadows pulling him onwards, faster and faster, the urgency of it roaring through his mind. The light Wren had planted in him burned now, brighter and brighter. He had to find her. He had to protect her.

Probably from herself.

Screams filled the air, people crying out for their queen or venting their anger, and he heard the gates breaking before he reached them. There was a blast of something powered by a scream, something made of rage and terror. He felt it shake the air and the earth and forced himself to run.

The knights charged through the breach as he reached the broken gates, pressing the advantage. It felt like an earthquake shook the city. Lost in a whirl of darkness which suddenly rose from the stones and descended with the fall of night, Finn ran, sprinting through the chaos of the attack. He caught sight of Roland leading the charge and then lost him as he raced inside the courtyard himself, sword drawn. Sassone's guards fled or fell before the Knights of the Aurum.

But the river of shadows beneath them was still there, surging like rapids, driving him on. The light in him grew even brighter, like its own beacon, reaching out for her in return.

'Finn!'

It was Wren, her voice frantic. Finn plunged towards her without a moment's hesitation, heedless of danger.

CHAPTER 35

FINN

Wren ran towards him, right across the open courtyard, flung herself into his arms. Tears silvered her face and she trembled. Finn pulled her into the lee of the west wall, as a group of armed men tore past them.

Anselm and Olivier joined them, covered in sweat and blood, their eyes too wide.

'What are you doing here?' Finn snarled at them all, knowing the answer before he asked. He couldn't help himself.

'She brought the gates down,' Olivier supplied, as if that was some kind of excuse. 'When they tried to burn the queen. She just—' He glanced at Wren with a newfound respect in his eyes. 'She wielded light... and shadow. As one. I've never seen anything like it.'

'I can't hold it all together,' she hissed. 'It's like... there's magic at work here. The magic that trapped Elodie and cut her off from the Aurum. It's all running wild. I can't... I can't...' Her eyes were too large, too dark, and Finn could feel her control slipping away even as she clung to him. She couldn't hold on much longer, he could see that. It was old magic, both light and dark and everything in between, but it was tangled and vile.

'Let's get out of here.'

'But Elodie,' Wren protested. 'We came here for Elodie. It's centred on her.'

'Roland has her,' Anselm supplied. 'They'll get her to safety first but then they'll be back. We don't have much time. Finn's right, if my father finds you here…'

Too late, Finn wanted to say. Sassone's guards were regrouping as the knights withdrew to the gates, covering Roland's retreat with Elodie. Which left them trapped inside.

And if this spell was centred on Elodie, it should be subsiding. But it wasn't. He could feel it building, like a vortex looking for a new focal point, and centring on Wren instead.

They couldn't make it out of the gates, not now. The battle was focused there.

'How did you get in?' he asked Anselm. 'Can we go back that way?'

But Anselm had frozen, staring past Finn with an expression of dread on his face. He smothered it quickly, pulling on an unreadable mask instead.

'Olivier,' he said in a strangely calm and quiet voice, 'you need to get them out of here.'

'Anselm?' Sassone roared. He bore down on them, his men fanning out around him to cut off any hope of escape. 'Did you bring her here, boy?' There was wary joy in his eyes, a kind of relief and the realisation that all might not be lost. 'Well done, my son. I knew you wouldn't fail me.'

Anselm stepped forward on his own, sword bare. 'You will not have her, Father. The princess is not a tool for you to use.'

Hope and pride twisted into something terrible instead. 'I might have guessed. You never do anything right, do you? Too much your mother's son.'

Anselm flinched, his shoulders tightening, though only Finn, standing so close to him, would have been able to spot it.

'My mother was loyal to the crown at least. Up to the day you killed her.'

'Stand down, boy. I won't tell you again!' Sassone's voice, enraged and thwarted but not yet defeated. Finn understood his thinking in an instant. If he could take the princess while Roland rescued the queen, he still had a hand to play. Desperate now, and dangerous, because without this last victory, he had lost everything. He had no idea how bad it could yet be.

Anselm Tarryn didn't move. 'It's over, Father. You've failed. Stand down and yield to us in the Aurum's name.' It was an audacious demand given the numbers surrounding them. But Anselm didn't hesitate to make it anyway.

Finn blinked, realising that he'd always dismissed Anselm's loyalty as more convenient than anything else. But not now.

Sassone scowled and gave a curt signal.

The first arrow took Anselm in the shoulder, and he was flung to one side, almost off his feet but not quite. He spun back, the shaft jutting from his body, his face white with shock. He had no armour, no more than Finn did, but that didn't stop him as he squared up again to block the way, to protect his princess.

Men rushed at them and Olivier stepped up to meet them. He drove them back, his sword a line of light, holding the line to the left. Finn took up the right flank.

Anselm still stood between his father and Wren.

Sassone nodded and the archer fired again. Another arrow punched into Anselm's side this time and he sank to his knees. Olivier gave a howl of dismay, torn between defending Wren and his beloved comrade. Finn took three of Sassone's guards, sweeping his sword around in a blur of light, but there were too many of them.

Anselm keeled over and Wren dropped to her knees beside him, her hands coming away bright with his blood as she tried to help him.

Behind Finn, from the city outside, a great shout went up.

'To arms, Knights of the Aurum! The queen is saved. To arms against the traitors.'

The knights were coming back and the ground shook with their charge. Sassone and his men broke off, faced with the full fury of the forces of Asteroth. The fortress was broken and all they could hope for now was to escape with their lives. They ran.

But a wave of darkness rose up behind them. The nearest ones fell without even a sound. The screaming of the next group would haunt him.

He'd forgotten Wren, forgotten what might happen to her in the wild maelstrom of magic that had been cast in the Castel Sassone. Dark and terrible, Wren now lost herself in it. Her arms spread wide, and her head flung back, shadows flocked to her, ready, at her command, to tear apart those who fled.

Finn had seen her do this before, when she hadn't even realised what she could do. The shadow kin she had summoned that time had turned the forest into an abattoir in moments. Perhaps she didn't realise she was doing it now. That was his one hope.

She tore through the twisted spell and pulled out everything she wanted or needed. Her hair flowed out as if she was underwater, black ink in the night, and her eyes blazed darkness. She was gathering more power, more than he had ever seen her channel before and unleashed it, sending it after Sassone, tearing through all the wards around her like paper to summon more.

So much power. So many shadow kin. Everything that hid in the dark corners of the city, born of fear and despair, nursed on injustice, it all flocked to her now. They would all die. Everyone. Not just those who threatened her, Finn realised. Not just those running away, but those charging into the castle as well. And those outside the walls. And everyone hiding in terror. The knights, the people of Pelias, everyone, friend and foe.

Those who didn't die would know what she was. And then they would kill her.

But there was light as well. Everywhere she dragged away the darkness, there was light and she somehow gathered that together as well, focusing it as if through a prism, pouring it into Anselm's still form. The more darkness she pulled into herself, the more light she could force into him. Into all of them, Finn realised. It sang in his veins, in his and Olivier's, in Roland's and the knights', the light of the Aurum filling them as they battled their way forward. All because she was trying to save Anselm, trying to heal him. That was what she was doing, without thought to the consequences.

'Wren!' he yelled. 'Stop!'

He was too late. Far too late. He knew it at a glance. His knees longed to drop to the ground before her, and his heart screamed at him to submit to her, to be hers and let her take him and do with him whatever she wanted.

And maybe Wren was already gone. She was saving his friend's life. She was sending retribution after those who had threatened Elodie and hurt her. But in doing so, she'd lose herself to the Nox.

At the sound of his voice, her head snapped forward, long black strands of hair snaking over her face. She fixed her attention entirely on him and smiled. Her eyes were dark and endless. Empty now of all that was Wren.

Olivier held Anselm in his arms, trying to staunch the flow of blood, his eyes clenched shut against the light that poured through them both.

Finnian, my beloved, the voice purred. It wasn't her voice. But it was all around him, rippling through him. The wild magic lashed against his will, and only his need to help Anselm let him withstand it.

'You have to stop,' he shouted desperately at the Nox, praying it would understand him. Those traces of the Aurum's light still lingering in him flared like wildfires and went out. 'The knights will see. They'll kill her. If they see what you're doing here, if they see what your creatures can do to Sassone, they'll burn her and then what will you do? The knights are coming and they will know. They'll see the dead, what you've done to them. Everyone will know. Please, stop. Just stop and think.'

If they hadn't already seen. If they didn't already know. And here he was trying to reason with the darkness.

Anselm's strength, such as it still was, gave out as the light surrounding him flickered out and Olivier couldn't hold him up. He lowered Anselm to the cobbles as gently as he could so both of them wouldn't fall. Then Olivier dropped down beside him, his hands shaking.

'He's dying,' he shouted. 'Finn, do something. He's dying.'

Wren watched them, her head tilted to one side like a cat's, her eyes unbearably dark, holes into an endless night. The wave of shadow kin subsided, but it didn't depart. It drew back to her, a cloak of seething, hungry night, waiting. Any moment now the Knights of the Aurum would arrive. His friends, his comrades, all full of holy light and ready for battle... Any moment...

Finn dropped to his knees. He didn't know what else to do. His friend was dying, Wren's friend. She'd never forgive herself. He had to reach her somehow. 'Help him. Please.'

She tried. She cannot. And what do you offer?

Offer? What could he possibly offer?

'Whatever you want...' He knew what it wanted, what it had always wanted. He whispered it like a dark admission and closed his eyes in acceptance. 'I'm yours. Hers. Gladly. You know that.'

Everything went quiet. Far too quiet.

Cold hands touched his face, hands that trembled. Wren. It

was Wren. She drew in a shaky breath and her voice was weak. 'I think... I think he's stable. I thought it wouldn't—' And then she saw his expression and the devastation around her. 'What – what did I do?'

The darkness around them had gone. They were only four people, cold and shivering in the night, drenched in blood and sweat. Bodies were strewn around them. He didn't want to think about that. He'd killed some. So had Olivier. But not that many.

He couldn't tell if Sassone was among them. He couldn't tell if some of them had ever been human.

Finn couldn't tell her what had happened. 'Help me, love. We've got to get Anselm out of here. We have to get you away before...'

The knights were coming. Even if no questions were asked, they would never find a healer in time, not if they waited here in the ruins of Castel Sassone. And there would be questions. So many questions. They'd have to explain why they were here, with the son of a traitor and the heir to the throne dressed like some kind of stable boy. And as for explaining what happened to Sassone's men... or the remains of them...

'But where can we go?' Wren asked. Olivier lifted Anselm's limp form as if he was no more than a bundle of rags and looked to Finn for direction.

There was only one place close enough. They didn't have time to go any further. Anselm certainly didn't.

Finn only hoped he wouldn't eternally regret this.

CHAPTER 36

ROLAND

Roland paced the corridor, from one end to the other, never stopping. He couldn't stop, couldn't allow himself to have a moment when he might rest, and think, and consider what might have been. What had almost happened...

People came and went from the bedroom, Maidens of the Aurum, various physicians and nurses, but no one who wasn't thoroughly checked first. His Paladins patrolled the corridors and there were knights posted at every doorway. Sister Maryn, still bloodied and bruised, had all but snarled at him when he challenged her but he let that go because she was almost as frantic as he was.

Elodie was like a sister to her. And Maryn had been there when Sassone had taken her. She had failed to protect her. She couldn't fail now.

The rest of the regents' council were under heavy guard, in spite of their many protests. Even Ylena. Perhaps especially Ylena. Roland didn't know if she was involved in this or not but right now he didn't care. Let her stew for a while. It served her right and her arrogance could do with taking down a peg or two. Or more.

If they had planned this together, he would gladly see them all hang. He would put the nooses around their necks himself.

There had never been a coup in the history of Asteroth and it had come so close to succeeding.

'Roland?' Maryn opened the door and beckoned to him. 'She's asking for you.'

He moved without thinking, like a raw recruit summoned to his first parade.

They had brought her to her old suite of rooms. The maidens still clustered around her, but she lay in the bed of the queen now, a raised confection of a thing draped in silk and cloth of gold, not in the narrow and stark cell where he had last seen her. And she looked so small. Almost childlike.

Her golden hair spread out on the pillow around her and the white nightgown didn't help the illusion. Her skin was too pale, but there were no signs of injury or burn marks now. They had cut the collar and shackles from her skin and laid healing hands on her. Elodie opened her eyes and gazed at him for so long he wondered if she still knew who he was, or if instead she had lost her mind completely. When they tried to stop her sitting up, she waved them away imperiously and there she was, his Elodie, the look of pure irritation almost making him laugh out loud with relief.

'Out,' she tried to say, but her voice was strained.

He had heard her screams. They had almost driven him to distraction. In all honesty he had lost any sense of reason as the gates had shattered – he had no idea how as the battering rams alone should have taken twice as long to break through but he blessed the light for it. He had ridden his warhorse up the stone steps at a gallop, trampling the guards beneath him, and plunged into the flames to reach her.

And then the Aurum had erupted through them all. As if by taking her from that vile fortress, he had let her call it. But she hadn't. She couldn't have. Elodie had barely been conscious.

She couldn't have raised a spark. He knew that. It had to have been someone else and he suspected who that might be. But how could she have done that from up here?

He remembered Finn telling him of the madness that had overcome him when Wren was in danger and Roland knew now he should have been more sympathetic. He knew the feeling just as intimately. Only then it had seemed something lost to the past and another lifetime.

Now it was fresh and ragged and raw. It still churned in the pit of his stomach.

He would have done anything to spare her. Anything.

He still would.

The servants and the healers backed away, leaving the two of them alone. He hardly noticed when the door closed behind him. All he could see was Elodie.

'You're alive,' he said.

She gave him that look again, the one that called him an idiot of the highest order. She still had that perfected. He might be Grandmaster of the Knights of the Aurum, but Elodie would always see the boy he had been. The same way as he saw the girl instead of the queen, the witch and the Chosen of the Aurum.

'Thank you,' she said, and he wondered for a moment if he had misheard her. 'If you hadn't come...'

She closed her eyes again, trying to push away the memories of what had happened to her. Her brow furrowed and, the next thing Roland knew, he was on the bed, holding her in his arms.

He shouldn't. It was a terrible idea. All their shared and separated past, all the lies and deceptions, everything they had done and every way they had hurt each other told him that.

But right now he wasn't listening to anything but her.

'I will always come for you,' he told her, his voice rough in his throat. He took her hand and pressed the cold metal of the locket into her palm.

Slowly, Elodie curled in against him, taking a deep breath. Her hands came up to his chest and rested there, so cold through the fabric of his shirt. But oh, that touch was worth anything. Anything at all.

'I thought...' Her voice shook and she couldn't go on. He could hear her fear now, feel it the way he had felt it in those terrible moments before he pulled her free. Trauma still racked her body and it would haunt her for years to come. He knew the way of it.

Carefully, he cradled her cheek in one hand and pulled back so he could look her full in the face, to fix her with his gaze and hold her full attention.

'I will always come for you,' he repeated, a new vow, one just for her. 'That was always true, El. It still is. Always, just as I promised.'

Tears spilled from her eyes, falling like jewels down her cheeks. 'I had to go, Roland, all those years ago. I can't explain everything but I-I simply had to. If I had stayed... if I hadn't taken Wren...'

He knew he ought to ask all his questions, get those answers that no one seemed willing to give him. But right now, he didn't care. Or rather he didn't care enough. Elodie was here, and she was safe. She wasn't dead and for those dreadful moments after that bastard Sassone lit the pyre he had thought that he was about to lose her forever. Again.

But Elodie, his Elodie, was here. Safe. In his arms.

'Later,' he told her. 'You can tell me later. I'll wait. I'll wait as long as you need me to. I've waited twenty years. What's a little more time?'

'But you...' She looked so delightfully confused. Elodie, who always thought she knew everything and who usually did. 'You need to know. They're going to want to put her on the throne and they can't, Roland.'

'She's your daughter – *our* daughter... Of course she's going to sit on the throne after you, but not for many years, my love.'

But instead of comforting her, his words made it worse. He could see that in her blue eyes, the shattering of hope, the desolation of despair.

'That's the problem... She is our daughter, but not... not actually...' She pulled back, cursing, and he let her go, because fighting her at a moment like this would never work. She wrapped her arms tightly around her chest and her teeth worried at her lower lip, like she used to when she was young, when she didn't want to tell him something or own up to anything wrong. 'You must have suspected. After the trial. You must have guessed.'

'What happened, Elodie? All those years ago? If you don't want to tell me yet, I will wait, but one day... one day you'll have to tell me. Please. I've waited, I've searched, I've guarded your kingdom for you. Yes, for duty too, but mainly for you. And when I saw Wren, the moment I saw her, I knew. I just *knew*. She looks like the women of my family, all of them. My mother's eyes, my aunt's build, my sister's—'

Elodie shook her head. 'I know what she looks like. But it isn't as simple as that.'

'Then explain it to me.' He sighed and raked one hand through his greying hair. 'Use the simplest words.'

At that, she laughed, a bitter and broken sound that was almost relief but was also something else, something lost and sad.

'You won't understand.'

He raised an eyebrow at her. 'I know where children come from, love. And we did enough to create a child, didn't we?'

Her lips wobbled and she dropped her gaze to the bedclothes. And that was somehow worse, because a rosy blush spread up her neck to her face.

She looked up sharply, as if a thought had occurred to her.

Her hands closed tightly on the fabric of his shirt, her grip as strong as ever. 'There was never anyone else but you,' she told him adamantly.

'I didn't think there was.' He tried not to sound bewildered. All these years, and she was a beautiful woman, one with needs and desires. And yet, he believed her. Because how could he not? 'Nor was there anyone else for me but you. You know that, surely.'

Any other woman would be pleased to hear that, he thought, but Elodie nodded glumly. 'I'm sorry, Roland. I'm sorry for everything. It's all my fault.'

She opened her arms to him again and waited until he settled himself beside her to curl in against him. He stroked her hair, freshly washed and brushed to a sheen like silk. He just wanted to hold her, now that he could.

'What grievous sins have you committed now?' he asked. 'The Aurum didn't seem to think there was any blame. It hasn't roared to life like that since—'

He stopped, remembering. It hadn't acted like that since the last time she was here, when Evander had killed himself and summoned the Nox, and Elodie had fought it and won, vanquishing their ancient enemy in the holiest place in Asteroth.

'Since I fought the Nox,' she whispered.

'You defeated it.'

Please say yes, he thought. Please, Elodie, just say yes. Tell me you broke it and scattered it, and the dark goddess was banished forever. Tell me the pretty story about our triumphant queen who sacrificed herself to save us all, the one the maidens had spread throughout Pelias before Evander's corpse was yet cold.

'It... it was almost defeated,' she whispered, staring up into his eyes. 'It took a thousand forms, each more terrible than the last. It came at me like a dragon, like a whirlwind, like a thing from beyond our world with a million teeth. It tried everything and I drove it back.' Her hand closed on his shirt, her knuckles going white around the locket. 'It made itself great and terrifying, and still I drove it back. I broke it to pieces, chipping away at it with the Aurum blazing through me. And then...'

Roland held his breath, listening because there was nothing else he could do. Part of him wanted to cover his ears or tear himself away from her. To call her a liar. But his voice was lodged in his tight throat, useless, helpless. Like him. And he couldn't let her go anyway.

'It was almost done. Only fragments of it remained. I had all but banished it to the beyond. But at the last it took one more form. A baby. A little girl. With... with eyes and hair and skin like yours... Our child. The one we would have had. Should have had. It looked into my heart and my mind and it took the form I would never be able to hurt. It locked what remained of its power inside her and... I couldn't kill her, Roland. She's part of you and part of me, and I couldn't harm her. It knew that. It has always known. She is our child, the one we might have had in another lifetime, if we were different people. But...'

'But?' He didn't know how he managed to ask. Elodie was a taut wire against his body and his pulse was thundering through his brain.

'But at the same time, she isn't. She's the Nox. The last, vital part of it. And if she succeeds me, if they place that crown on her head and she stands before the Aurum...'

The words were ancient and hollow and had never felt more real or more terrible. 'Then the lost queen stands alone,' he whispered. 'That's you. But you won't be alone, Elodie. I'll be there. I'll—'

'You'll be dead. You'll all be dead. Asteroth will be at the mercy of Ilanthus and it will exact such vengeance on us... I'll be all that's left. Because it will want me to see our utter destruction. Alessander will want that. So will Leander.'

235

Of course they would. Elodie understood the prophecy better than anyone. She had studied it all her life. It was about her, wasn't it? Her and Wren...

'Where is she?' Elodie asked after a moment of aching silence. 'I need to see her. I need to explain it to her as well.'

'She doesn't know what she is?'

He watched her swallow hard, pushing down her fears, her regrets. 'I think she suspects and she is terrified.'

'Shouldn't we be the ones who are terrified?'

'Of Wren?' Elodie shook her head with a soft surprised laugh. 'No. Not ever. You've met her, spoken to her, seen her. There is such goodness in her, Roland. She has been all that was good in my life since I left you. Oh, she has made mistakes but what child has not? No, Wren is the one thing I have done right. But I need to explain it to her as well. All of it. And reassure her.'

He dragged himself from her embrace and made for the door, summoning the squire and sending him running to fetch Wren.

But she was nowhere to be found.

ILANTHIAN PROVERB

When you step into the stronghold of your enemy,
Be prepared for everything you know to change in a
moment.

CHAPTER 37
WREN

It was full dark when they reached the Ilanthian embassy, dodging through the chaos of the lower city and avoiding the knights and guards who were still trying to seek out anyone connected with Sassone, and anyone who had seen what happened in the fortress. It wasn't a time for discussion.

Wren knew if they realised who Anselm was, who his father was, he would be lucky to make it as far as a jail. It felt like, by trying to kill their now beloved queen, Sassone had driven the people of Pelias to the brink of madness with a rage that would not be quelled except with his blood.

And failing that, surely his son's blood would do.

It was possible the Earl of Sassone was no more than a smear in the courtyard of his ancestral home now.

Olivier had found a cloak and wrapped it around Anselm as they half carried and half dragged him through the narrow lanes. It wasn't far, Finn assured her, which was just as well, because Anselm wasn't going to last much longer. When Olivier began to tire, Finn took over, carrying Anselm in his arms.

The embassy was a tall, gated enclosure, around a building

topped with a cluster of bright towers. Wren stopped, staring at its willowy structures up close now, and she thought of the tower in Cellandre with a strange sense of familiarity and longing.

Finn spoke to the guards outside, stiff and impassive Ilanthians who looked long and hard at his companions but were quick to obey him. The gates opened silently, and they slipped inside.

This was a mistake. It had to be a mistake. But what else could she do? There was no way they were going to make it all the way back to the palace with Anselm. And Finn assured her that this would be safe. He was a prince of the line of Sidon here.

The servant who greeted them at the door bowed so low, Wren couldn't doubt him.

'Fetch Lady Hestia,' he said, in a calm and quite different voice to the one she had come to love. This voice was cool and precise, used to commands. There was no please, and no if you will. It was an order. He didn't hesitate in his advance either, hurrying inside the building. The servant vanished at once. 'In here,' he told her, and gestured towards a door which led to an elaborate reception room. Fabric lined the walls, rich damask the colour of blood. They laid Anselm on a chaise longue and Wren sank into the chair beside it.

'What do we do?' she asked.

'First, we need to get the arrows out. And I hope Hestia can heal him. Then... then we'll try to send word to Roland. Tell him we're here and we need help.'

'You said we'd be safe here.'

'And we will. To a certain extent. Please, Wren, trust me. I'm doing what I can. I won't let anyone harm you.' There was a subtle emphasis on the word anyone. No doubting who Finn meant.

Leander was here somewhere.

Wren shuddered, curling in on herself, lifting her knees and wrapping her arms around them like a cocoon.

Footsteps outside brought Finn to his feet but Wren couldn't move. Perhaps if she stayed still, no one would notice her. She was still in breeches and a jerkin, dressed as a boy. She grabbed her hair, pulling it back from her face. It was too long, far too long, out of control. If she could find a knife, she could cut it here and now.

But there wasn't time.

The door opened. 'Finnian,' said the cultured voice of a woman, a voice like a song. 'You're back. You're safe, thank the—'

Her beautiful voice fell still.

'We need your help,' said Finn. 'He was hurt, defending—'

He glanced at Wren who tried to shrink back again. Shadows rose around her like smoke and her hair moved, her scalp tingling as the magic began to weave itself against her will. Fear did that, she realised, and she could not help but be afraid.

'Oh,' said the woman who had come to the ball, still beautiful and graceful. She looked harried now, exhausted and somewhat shaken. 'This is...' Without needing an answer, she sank into a deep curtsy. 'Your highness, there's nothing to fear here. I swear, we are at your service. Now and always.'

Wren really didn't like the implications of that. It wasn't her position as the supposed princess of Asteroth that made the Ilanthian woman say such things and they all knew that.

'Wren, this is Lady Hestia Rayden, my cousin, daughter of—'

'That doesn't matter, Finn,' Hestia cut him off. She had straightened. 'I am blood of Sidon, yes, but more importantly I am sworn to the sisterhood of shadows. I studied at the College of Winter and sought out all the secrets of witchkind I could find but I am forever happily bound in the service of the Nox. I gave vows at the Caves of Deep Shadows when I was only a child myself, where I knelt before the feet of the divine and promised to serve her. I never imagined...'

She broke off, as if she was struggling not to fall to her knees.

'Imagined what?' Wren asked, her voice strange and alien to her own ears. She rose to her feet slowly and advanced on Hestia. It almost felt like someone else was making her move. 'Say it.'

Hestia stared at her, as if trying to figure her out. 'That I would see you incarnate. That I would know you.'

'You know me?' She didn't like the cadence in her voice, the way it reverberated around the still air of the room.

The Ilanthian witch smiled. 'Lady of the Darkest Night, I know you like I know my own heart. I was wrong to try to stop you, Finn. I... I had no idea... She called you, didn't she? That was how you broke free.'

Wren froze, every nerve in her body quivering. This was wrong. She didn't want this to be true. And... broke free? Had Hestia been holding him here against his will?

'Hestia,' Finn began warily, a note of caution in his voice, but then, behind them, Anselm let out a groan and they all turned. 'He's going to bleed out at this rate. Help him.'

The noblewoman wasted no time, examining him as efficiently as Elodie might have.

'Call one of the servants, Finn,' she said. 'Tell them to bring me a knife, hot water, bandages and as much lark's root as we have in the store. And poppy milk. He's going to need it.'

'How can I help?' Wren asked, kneeling down again and running a hand over Anselm's brow while Finn went to the door and called out for help, passing on Hestia's commands. The other knight was already feverish. This wasn't good. Wren knew that much.

'We need to get the arrows out first. Then get his shirt off so

I can see the wounds. Finn, I may need both of you to hold him down.'

One of the shafts had already broken in their rush here and jutted from his side like an old tooth. The one in his shoulder shook with his fitful breath. None of this was good.

Anselm opened his eyes weakly, fixed them on Wren and winced. 'I... I can feel them inside me.'

What was he talking about? Were the arrows poisoned? She glanced at Finn but he looked just as mystified.

'What can you feel?' Wren asked.

The word was a long, low hiss but it made her blood turn cold.

'Shadows...'

CHAPTER 38

WREN

Finn took the other knight's hand, wrapping it with his own, holding him down while Hestia set to work. 'It's going to be all right, Anselm. I promise. We're going to help you. Wren is going to help you. Aren't you?'

He didn't have to sound like he doubted her, she thought, and it must have showed on her face. Anselm turned his gaze to her and all she could read there was terror.

What had she done? What had happened when she lost herself back there?

Hestia's servants arrived with all she had demanded. She tipped the contents of a small amber bottle into his mouth, and then she cut the arrow from his shoulder with a terrible efficiency. Anselm cried out, unable to stop himself. His back arched but a moment later, Hestia's hand on the wound stilled him completely. He took a deep breath, his eyes wide.

'Wren?'

'Yes,' she blurted out, a bit too loud. 'Yes, I'm not going to let anything happen to you. You helped me. You came with me for Elodie. Of course I'm not going to let anything happen. You're my friend. Do you hear me?'

She focused her attention and reached for the light, any she could still find inside and beyond, pulling it into her body and ready to release it. There wasn't much. It was the dead of night and she was exhausted and they were in the Ilanthian embassy and...

Hestia's hand closed on Wren's wrist like a metal band. 'Not here, my lady. You can't do that here.'

'What do you mean?'

'It will likely kill him. There are shadows threaded through him. You must have... I'm sure you were trying to help but... Tearing them out will do more damage than even you can heal.'

'But I didn't...' What had she done? She didn't know. She had acted on instinct and now look at the mess she had made.

'Without them he would probably be dead already. And even if you succeeded, all you would do would be to bind him to your service as securely as...' She glanced at Finn again. 'Well...' she finished and dropped her gaze.

'What do you mean, bound?' Wren asked.

'It doesn't matter,' Finn replied, far too quickly. 'Hestia, can you help him? Please?'

'I can and I will. We must do something to allay suspicion after that fiasco today. If Roland de Silvius believes we had anything to do with Sassone, we will be in trouble indeed. No amount of diplomacy will help me then. Go, rest, refresh yourselves. I will see to him. You have my word.'

And healing Sassone's son was going to help how? Wren thought grimly. But Anselm was one of Roland's knights. That had to count for something.

They held him as Hestia removed the broken arrow and set about healing his wounds. She called for more water and bandages and a flurry of servants came to her summons.

Helpless, unsure of what else she could do other than get in Hestia's way, Wren stood and looked for Finn. He took her hand and then, without warning, pulled her against him, holding her close.

'I could have lost you,' he whispered into her hair and Wren felt all the strength go from her body. What had she been thinking?

She should have stayed in the palace and waited, done as she was told. But then... but then Elodie would have burned. She knew that as surely as she could still breathe.

'I'm here,' she told him. 'I'm safe. With you.'

And she was. Seeing Finn had brought her back to herself. He grounded her in this reality and whatever else was trying to claw its way out through her had no power when they were together. Where they belonged.

Finn stroked her hair and strands of it tried to twine themselves around his fingers, sliding like silk over his skin.

'Your highness,' said a uniformed man, from the doorway. 'What do we do about the other one?'

Finn glared at the Ilanthian and his interruption. 'What other one?'

The man nodded out into the hall where two of the other guards were holding a struggling Olivier. Wren and Finn had barged in here, intent only on the wounded man in Finn's arms, leaving Olivier, an armed Knight of the Aurum, at the gates of the Ilanthian embassy. The moment he charged after them, as no doubt he did, they had taken him prisoner. From the shaken look of some of them, that capture had not happened quickly enough.

When Olivier saw Finn and Wren, he fell still. 'What have you done with him?'

'He's in here. With a healer,' Finn told him firmly. Then he glanced at the Ilanthian guards. 'Let him go.'

They reluctantly released Olivier at Finn's command.

He staggered forward, unarmed and clearly dishevelled. They hadn't been gentle with him, but then Wren figured that went both ways. Her knights would never go quietly, none of them. Perhaps Roland had taught them that.

She moved towards him. 'Were you hurt?'

But even as she reached out Olivier shied back from her, wary as a horse about to bolt. 'Lady...' he began nervously, and then seemed to lose sight of whatever he had been about to say to her. He glanced helplessly at Finn who was no help at all. 'I don't know what happened back there. The things I saw...'

The monster she had become, she wanted to say, the creatures she had summoned. 'I know,' she whispered. 'And I understand.' She stepped back, withdrawing from him. If he needed to leave so be it. She couldn't ask him, someone with his faith and belief, to stay with her now, to help her, someone who had willingly surrendered what the Aurum gave him in order to serve it, to accept how she used its power.

'Do you?' he sounded incredulous. 'Because I don't. But we would have died in there without you. So would the queen and any number of my brother knights. I know that much. Is Anselm... is he...?'

'He's sleeping,' said Hestia, coming to the door behind them. 'And you're all making far too much noise.' But as she noticed Olivier, she hesitated, reading something on his face. 'We can move him to a bedroom now. I'll have the servants see to it. Go with him, if you must, Paladin, but he needs to rest. Can you supervise that for me? Watch over him?'

'I'm not a Paladin,' Olivier replied, almost automatically.

'Oh but I think you are,' said Hestia firmly. 'Both of you. And now he needs your care. You have my word as to your princess's safety. And that of Prince Finnian, of course.'

To his credit, Olivier hesitated, looking towards Wren. He had sworn to protect her, had given Roland his word. But clearly Anselm was all he could really think about.

'I've got her now,' said Finn and relief spread over the other knight's features.

'Thank you,' he murmured to them, and made for the door, both of them forgotten.

'Poor boy,' Hestia murmured as he vanished inside. 'The Aurum is a cold and hard thing to follow. He would be happier without it. Then he could be what he was meant to be and love freely where he wanted.'

'He can love where he wants,' Finn replied in curt tones but she shook her head.

'Can any of you really? So many strictures. The Aurum took the magic he was born with, didn't it? It would take every-thing. What do any of you know of freedom? Come, let's get a room sorted for them. And send word to the palace that you are safe. Otherwise we'll be accused of kidnapping Wren to compound all of this.'

Finn wrapped his arms around Wren and held her close, long after his cousin was out of sight.

'You must be exhausted,' he murmured, but Wren shook her head. 'What do you need? We can supply anything. You're our honoured guest. More than that.'

We, she thought. Our. He was even sounding like an Ilanthian.

'I need you,' she told him and pressed her lips to his, like she might somehow be able to claim him back.

CHAPTER 39

WREN

It had been too long. Finn was her addiction, the one thing she craved more than anything, more than air. Wren was hardly aware of the two of them moving, but everything was suddenly a rush of motion. He took her hand in his, and they all but ran up the grand staircase in the centre of the house.

Wren had no idea where they were going but Finn moved unerringly, without hesitation. They fell through a doorway into a stately bedroom and she was in his arms again, right where she wanted to be. He kicked the door shut behind her and brought his mouth down on hers, kissing her with a degree of focus and determination that would never be rivalled. She returned that kiss with a burning need of her own.

There was no one like him. There never would be. Great light, she had missed him. It had only been a matter of days, but it felt like months.

Wren buried her hands in his hair so she could pull him to her, hold him. His own hands were busy with her clothes, pushing back her boyish garb to caress the soft skin beneath, revealing each inch like it was a precious gift. She shuddered against him, and gasped as one questing hand curved around her breast. The pad of his thumb brushed against the sensitive skin of her nipple, which tightened, aching for him. She gasped out loud and let her head fall back as the warmth of his mouth closed over it and that deep drawing heat shot through her with each stroke of his tongue.

In moments she was pressed against him, crying out her need, and Finn didn't pause, not for a moment. She could feel his erection through his clothes, trapped between them, his cock hard as steel. He was as determined as ever, dedicated to their mutual pleasure but focused in the first instance on hers alone.

He walked her back until she came to the bed and kissed her body everywhere he could as she lay back on it, hands and lips exploring, as if he would claim her by touch and taste alone.

Wren's desire pooled inside her, rich and intense, driving any other thoughts from her mind. His scent encircled her, tangled itself with hers, a rising musk of desire and need. They were together and that was all that mattered. All efforts to drive them away from each other, and to keep them apart, had failed and there was a sense of triumph in that.

His clever mouth and artful fingers brought her to ecstasy, arching off the bed, crying out his name heedless of who might hear. It didn't matter and she didn't care, not this time. She wanted the world to hear, to know.

Finn was smiling down at her, watching her with those beautiful eyes as she came back to herself.

'What is it?' she asked, a little wary.

He shook his head. 'Nothing. Just... just wanted to see your face.'

'I think you can see a lot more than that,' she teased, reaching for him. He was still clothed. 'You have me at a disadvantage. You really need to take these off.' She tugged at his shirt, pulling it from his belt so she could slip her hands beneath it, eager to touch him.

The necklace with that peculiar pendant fell out from

beneath the material, and hung between them, swinging like a pendulum. The wave of cold that came off it made her freeze. It was dark and she felt that unpleasant shiver like something shadow-wrought had pressed to her skin.

'What is it?' he asked, suddenly concerned.

'What's that?'

He frowned, his dazed eyes struggling to focus on it in irritation. 'A... a gift. Nothing.' And he took it off hurriedly, dropping it onto the clothes he had already shed, before kissing her again as if determined to rid her mind of any thought but pleasure.

He was good at that. Far too good. He could make her forget anything when he touched her like that.

Wren ran her hands down the line of his back, tracing her way across the scars she knew too well, old and new. The shadow kin had bitten him there, when he had been trying to defend her. She had poured the Aurum's light through him to save him. She had made him her own.

He shivered and caught his breath as she tormented his skin, warm and soft, stretched over the iron of the muscles beneath. His body was a marvel, honed to perfection, sleek and strong.

She didn't know how he got himself out of the rest of his clothes so quickly, but he did. He shed every remaining item and then he gathered her in his arms again, the two of them entwined together on the bed, skin to skin and body to body.

'Great light, I missed you,' he murmured as his mouth claimed hers again, his kiss stealing her breath. He moved against her, sending a ripple of warmth and pleasure throughout a body she thought already sated, but moments later that hunger was back with a vengeance. That was his magic, his effect on her. Nothing would ever be enough where he was concerned.

'Show me,' she told him. 'Show me how much.'

Light poured through her, racing along her veins, filling her with fire. It burned away the shadows that still lingered, and with it came joy, with pleasure. Her hands stroked his sides as he rose over her. She could see the glow that came from her playing over his flesh like iridescence.

'You're made of magic,' he whispered in awe, and then he entered her, slowly, deliberately, taking his time to savour everything. His cock stretched her and filled her, and made her complete. It was like exhaling after holding her breath for too long, this sense of relief, of rightness. He held himself there, as if caught in a spell, frozen by pleasure, letting it wash through him and trying to adjust to this new reality where the two of them were one. Her body was not so patient. How could she be? She squeezed herself tightly around him, feeling every inch, that deep delicious slide of skin on skin, and Finn opened his mouth in an *oh* of surprise.

Her hair curled around his hands on the sheet, binding him close as if never to let him go. Shadows were coiling up from the corners of the room, thrown into sharp relief by the light in her, and she couldn't stop them. She couldn't stop any of it. Part of her didn't want to. He was hers and she was his. They belonged together.

She couldn't stand it any longer. She couldn't wait.

'Finn!' she cried out, desperate now. 'Please!'

It was all he needed. Finn surged into her, deep and hard and hungry, as if he no longer had a will of his own or a mind to reason. His cock filled her over and over and all was need and desire. His pace was intense, driven by that endless hunger she created in him, which was reflected back in her.

She shouted his name again, and other things. She didn't know what. There were words of othertongue in there, and words of joy and need, words which owned him and which gave him all she was.

It was bliss. It was everything. She broke apart in light and darkness, in waves of dazzling pleasure, and even as he started

251

to lose his rhythm in release, she rolled over, taking him with her, seizing control of their lovemaking. Beneath her, Finn arched on the bed, desperate to please her and racing to match her pace. She pinned him down as she rode him, binding him with body and with magic, with love. Great light, she had missed him, missed this. He was hers and she was his and the light flooded through both of them, blinding and terrible, while shadows coiled against their skin, weaving untold enchantments, leaving them both enraptured. He cried out her name, helpless and overjoyed, aglow from within as her power surged through him, lost to himself as he came.

Magic and desire were a potent combination and, adrift in it, Wren didn't care where it led and what it did to her. But this was Finn, her Finn, her everything. She was safe with him. She always would be.

She tumbled over the edge with him and cried out his name over and over. He wound himself around her, as she slumped down onto his chest, little aftershocks still shivering their way through both of their bodies. He cradled her close like she was something precious, a treasure.

Wren found that she had tears on her face, and her hair, long and dark and far too wilful, fell loosely around her. It still teased his skin, like it was stroking him, and he lay beneath her, clearly trying to remember if he had ever had a name to begin with.

Magic, she recalled. There was a vital part of her that was magic. And when she made love to him, it was part of that too. It filled him as it filled her. Part of that addictive pleasure, part of that hunger, came from something far beyond either of them.

He looked dazed. Lost.

'Finn?' Concern speared her. What did she do to him in moments like this? What could she do to him? 'Finn, are you all right?'

'You...' he whispered hoarsely and words seemed to fail him.

'You are more than life itself, Wren. More than anything. I was lost until now, lost without you. But that was...' He lost himself again, gazing up into her eyes, adoration plain on his handsome face. 'I am yours, body and soul. You know that, don't you?'

She did. Of course she did. How could she doubt that, looking at him right now?

And for the first time she truly understood what that might mean. And all the dangers that might entail.

Finn was Ilanthian royalty, the blood of Sidon, no matter how he might want to deny it. And she... she was something else.

Finn dozed, drained, and Wren watched him, searching for signs that she might have harmed him in some way, that she might have stolen something from his spirit or changed him. But he just sprawled there, loose-limbed and sated, breathing softly. She had pulled the bedclothes over the two of them in the night, but as dawn sent seeking fingers of light through the tall windows, she slipped away from him, wrapping herself in one of the silken throws which had slid onto the ground while they made love again in the moonlight. The city was waking up outside the walls of the embassy and reality was going to come thundering back around them at any moment. She knew that. It was inevitable.

She slept a little. Her head was filled with Finn. When they had been in the forest – scared, desperate, running for their lives with only each other to rely on – it had been so easy to fall in love with him. And now they were together again, she knew that she was never going to want another man. Not like him.

Because there was no one like him.

But she also knew that she was not entirely human. Not really. There were shadows threaded all the way through her and a dark goddess claimed she was her child. Her creation, anyway. Elodie had never explained that. Perhaps she couldn't. Wren had command of ancient powers, threads of light and darkness that warred against each other and seemed intent on making her their battleground.

And she woke once more with thoughts full of creeping shadows.

❧

Wren stared up at the palace on the mountain as the sunlight struck its white walls, blue roofs and golden domes. It was perfection, cold and beautiful, but it would never be her home.

Strong arms slid around her, and Finn's body pressed to hers again, all the comfort she could ever need. He kissed the top of her head gently.

'Couldn't you sleep?' he asked. There was a wariness to the question, doubts underpinning it.

She nodded. 'I just woke up before you.' It sounded so simple, but as a statement it held a multitude of meanings she didn't want to go into. 'We have to go back,' she told him after a long moment of thought. 'And they'll try to pull us apart again.'

'Roland? The council?'

She gave a brief and bitter laugh, although it wasn't from humour at all. 'Everyone.'

Wren felt him shrug, a gentle roll of his shoulders. 'They'll do the same if we stay here. Or worse.'

'So what do we do?'

There were so many answers to that. Run away, face them down, do as they were told, and all the iterations in between.

'We do what you want,' he said at last. 'And I'll be there with you. But for now...' He pressed his mouth to her bare shoulder, kissing her there. His lips moved up slowly, inexorably, to the column of her neck, then to her jaw. 'Come back to bed, heart.'

The clothes Wren found waiting for her were far simpler than the elaborate affairs she had been forced into at the palace.

A long sweeping sheath of a dress, made of the finest silks, shimmered with a touch of lustrous threads. She could dress herself in clothes as simply cut as this, which suddenly seemed like the greatest luxury. And it was beautiful, the type of dress designed to make a woman feel beautiful. There was a discreet pocket in the seam into which she could tuck the little twist of straw and flowers in the shape of a bird Carlotta had given her. That seemed important somehow. She didn't want to lose it.

She plaited her long hair as tightly as she could and it fell in a braid down her back, tamed with a silk scarf at the end in midnight blue. It was all she could do with it for now. It wasn't as good as cutting it all off, but it was a start.

Finn had been gone when she finally awoke in the light of late morning, the bed cold beside her. She vaguely remembered him kissing her forehead, telling her he had things to do but she could sleep on for now. She had tried to reach for him, too sleepy to stop him, but he was already gone.

A murmuring sound outside the room called to her, and

Wren frowned. It was almost like music, like a half-remembered tune that toyed with her senses, always on the edge of her hearing.

Shadows drew close, teasing skin made sensitive from Finn's lips, from his touch. And all she could do for a moment was stand there listening as the sound swept in over her. Calling her.

She needed to follow it. That was suddenly clear. It swelled softly, a little more urgently now. *Come to me.*

But it wasn't threatening or demanding. Not this time. It was gentle, cajoling. It needed her.

Wren slipped out of the door, the silken dress whispering around her, echoing the song that drifted on the air.

The embassy was silent and still. As she wandered tentatively along the long corridor, with its bright tapestries and plush carpeting, she realised she didn't know where she was going. Was this area for guests? Or just for Finn? Or his family... which meant she might run into Leander at any second. She was about to turn back but then she realised she didn't know where to go. It had seemed like one corridor but now... now it looked strange, as if she was on another floor or in another part of the building.

At the sound of soft, approaching footsteps, Wren froze and stepped back into one of the recessed doorways, holding her breath. She could find Finn, couldn't she?

A whisper of othertongue played across the back of her mind in that disconcerting way it would when the Nox was trying to manipulate her. Or help her. She tried to breathe calmly, tried to slow her racing heart. The Nox's promises of help were always a trick. Weren't they?

What had she been thinking, wandering off on her own? She didn't know where she was going.

Wren reached into her pocket and felt the little charm in

her fingers. It stilled her racing thoughts and she took a deep breath, calming herself.

A figure passed her without noticing her hiding there, dark and drifting, dressed the same way Wren was, moving like her, but her long black hair loose and unbound.

And Wren followed.

She couldn't help herself.

She followed a shadow of herself down the stairs and along another corridor, and then down again, down and down, into the cellars below the house. Into the darkness.

It was like a dream. Or a nightmare.

But she had to follow the song and the shadow. And that vision of herself.

Herself as she might be, or as she might one day be, herself as someone else might see her.

The figure moved like a queen, like a goddess.

It stopped in an open doorway and Wren reached out to grab the shoulder, to turn this dark-haired woman around and finally know for sure who or what she was.

But the moment she did, the figure dissolved into shadows which slid away and Wren found herself staring into a dark, cave-like room, lit with tiny flickering candles.

In the middle of the chamber, another woman was kneeling in prayer or meditation. Head bowed as if waiting.

Wren tried to step back and her foot scraped on the floor.

Hestia looked over her shoulder at Wren, as if woken from a dream, her pale eyes wide in surprise.

'Your highness?' she said. 'What are you doing here?'

There was nowhere to go, nowhere to run. The woman knew it was her and Wren had clearly interrupted her. Whatever she was doing here in the almost dark. She was witchkind as well, a member of the Sisterhood of the Nox. One of their highest priestesses.

'I-I'm sorry,' Wren gasped, suddenly embarrassed. 'I didn't mean to – I'll go back.'

But Hestia smiled gently. 'No. Please, you can join me if you want. You would be more than welcome here.'

Wren glanced around again. 'What... what is this place?'

'Our household shrine, nothing sinister, I promise. It simulates the caves of the Nox in Sidonia, our holiest of places. I was praying for balance, and patience, I'm afraid. It doesn't come naturally to me.' The diplomat seemed so completely at peace with herself that Wren frowned and Hestia gave a small laugh. 'I mean it. Sometimes I want to scream at everyone and break some dishes rather than sit down and discuss things calmly.'

The comment made Wren smile in return. 'I wish I could learn that. Elodie always said—' The thought of Elodie cut her off. Was she all right? Had she been hurt?

'Word came to us this morning that she is safe and unhurt. The maidens are tending her and she wears her crown once more. There's no need to be afraid for her.' Hestia rose to her feet and held out her hands to Wren. Her touch was gentle and comforting, in the way Elodie could be comforting. Not soft or mawkish, but reliable. The type of strength on which you could depend. 'They were looking for you. We assured them of your safety and that we would bring you back to them as soon as you were ready.'

As soon as she was ready? How could Wren ever be ready to set foot back in the Sacrum? The Aurum would destroy her. It knew her now. And she had let the Nox take control in that courtyard. She'd seen the destruction, the remains... Finn might not be willing to tell her what happened but that spoke volumes about what he must have seen, what she had done. She was a threat to him. A threat to all of them. Even someone like Hestia.

Before Wren knew what she was doing the words came rushing out. 'I was so afraid. I couldn't... I couldn't get to her. I couldn't stop it. And I couldn't control the darkness in me. The shadow kin were everywhere. I couldn't keep them in, or make them obey. I couldn't help myself. I would have done anything, hurt anyone to get to her. But I... I wasn't in control. And I didn't know what to do. It was only afterwards that I... that I knew who I was again.'

To her surprise, rather than being horrified, Hestia drew her into an embrace, her hand soothing her trembling form, and it seemed like a pulse of peace rippled through her. Almost the way Finn calmed her. Nothing sexual, but it was almost like love.

Again, like Elodie. It was disconcerting.

'You are so very young, my poor dear girl. And there is so much magic in you that...' she sighed. 'No wonder it spills out when you're scared. It's all right. It's perfectly natural. And it is not your fault.'

Wren drew back, staring at the woman. 'But you... you serve the Nox.'

Hestia nodded. 'All my life.'

'But it... it's...' She couldn't say evil. Not to her face, but it was. Wasn't it? All her life she had been warned against it, had felt it trying to lure her into its traps.

'Wren,' Hestia said calmly, still holding her hands. 'You have only ever been told about one side of the old magic. To us the Aurum is just as dangerous, as we saw at that farce of a trial. If you stare into the fires of the sun you go blind, after all. Light can drive a person mad. But in darkness there is peace and calm. The darkness of the womb, or the grave, the darkness of the night...' She released Wren and lifted her hands up to indicate the small room in which they stood. 'The Nox and the Aurum went to war, we know that. But we don't know why. A madness overtook them both perhaps. I don't believe in war, religious or otherwise, not humankind and not for gods. I'm a diplomat. I believe in peace. And that is why I'm here. Will you help me?'

'Help you?'

'I need to speak to your mother. I believe between us we can help you and come to an accord. You're a daughter of two worlds now, a meeting point. You can bring balance. You are one of the few who can.'

'But I can barely manage to control my magic.'

'Because you are trying to suppress half of it. Or push it away. I'd like to help you as well if you will let me. Show you how to use it properly, the darkness as well as the light. It's easy, Wren. So easy for someone like you. Let me show you.'

Her hands spread wide, and her long elegant fingers moved in an intricate dance. The darkness behind her rose like an inhalation of breath and then subsided. Wren felt it inside her, moving in time with her own heartbeat. And then, just as suddenly, it fell back, a wistful sigh.

'What did you do?' she asked, trying to stop her voice shaking.

'It's an invitation. There's trust involved as well. But you can trust it, and me. I promise. Try.'

Wren swallowed hard. If Hestia was right she had hope of some measure of control. She hated the way the Nox spiralled out of control and tried to overwhelm her, but if there was a possibility of something else...

She closed her eyes, inhaled, and the shadows responded. For a moment, panic seized her but then Hestia took both her hands and held them gently. 'Just breathe,' she whispered. 'Let it in and then let it go. That's it.' Wren followed her voice and the power slowed its advance. It lingered in her, at the back of her mind, flowing through her like an underground river. She exhaled, and the magic receded. It was like the balls of light Maryn had had her conjuring. It was the same thing, she realised. Two sides of a single coin.

She opened her eyes to see Hestia smiling affectionately at her. 'You really are a wonder. Your control is sublime. When you don't panic.'

She had never had control before. She longed for more.

'When it cooperates, perhaps. It isn't like that normally. That was nothing like when the Nox tries to come through. It's... she's... She doesn't care what happens to me.'

'We can change that. There is always a risk with any great power and she was once the greatest. Well, the Nox and the Aurum. But such magic can consume you, burn all the way through you and leave nothing behind. It's as dangerous for them as for us. But they don't have the capacity to understand that. They see things differently. I thought Elodie would have taught you that. She would know better than anyone.'

Wren shook her head. Elodie had left out so much. She'd seen the Aurum fill Elodie at the trial and now she knew why. If Elodie had her way, they would still be back in the forest behind all her wards, protected by whatever agreements she had made with the trees and the rocks and all its living things, and Wren would never have had to face any of this.

'That's why you came? To teach me?'

'One of the reasons. Even in Ilanthus the sisterhood felt what happened between you and the Nox, felt her reawaken, mad and desperate. I knew we had to help you or it could destroy you both.'

'And the other reasons?' Wren flexed her fingers again and felt tendrils of shadows wreathe around them. Her hair drifted, alive with magic, a mass of living shades.

'I am here on behalf of my king and my country, as I said. Ilanthus wants peace and that is going to take work on both sides. The other reason is Finn. He is the other key to all of this.'

A chill spread up Wren's spine. She didn't like the sound of that. What did the Ilanthians want with Finn now? She knew the stories. He'd told her, everyone had told her. They'd tried to kill him, as a boy, to sacrifice him to the Nox. And ever since he had been promised to the dark goddess which sought to steal Wren's body.

'Finn? What do you want with Finn?'

CHAPTER 41
FINN

Wren's scent lingered around him. There was no denying the way she wound through Finn's mind and around his heart even after only one night back together, how she was a part of him. His everything. He could sense her still, as if at any moment she would walk around the corner, as if he just had to reach out with his mind to find her.

If Roland had thought separating them would make it lessen, what Finn felt for her, he had been sorely mistaken. There was no diminishing this.

She enchanted him without even trying. They were bound together somehow. Perhaps they always had been.

And he wasn't the only one. The other Ilanthians couldn't help themselves either. From the lowliest servant, right through the guards to the highest ranks, all the various diplomats, the general, Hestia and of course Leander himself, they gazed on her with a kind of wonder which ought to be deeply disturbing.

He should never have brought her here. Never. He should have known better.

But at the time it was the only option, without leaving Anselm to die and braving whatever madness had engulfed the palace. She certainly would not have been safe there. If Sassone could reach into the Sacrum itself and take Elodie.... Take the queen in her place of power...

And Wren had almost given herself away. She had no longer been herself and he feared he knew what had taken her place.

Of course he knew. Pretending otherwise was fooling himself. He knew what she was. He had known from the beginning. He had felt the magic that ran through every part of her reach out and claim him effortlessly and he had welcomed it.

In the courtyard of the embassy, he waited with the horses, the guards mustering around him. It wasn't far, he told himself. They would take Wren to the palace. They would explain the situation. And then he would do his best to get Hestia and Leander out of Pelias as quickly as possible. Because everything was going wrong; throw an Ilanthian into the mix and it would mean war.

Especially if that Ilanthian was Leander.

So when he realised his brother had not yet appeared and neither had Wren, he knew instantly that something was wrong. Again. He bent his mind to her, to the sense of her, and found only shadows.

That could not be good. He ought to go and find her, he thought, and turned back towards the building. Laurence was hurrying towards him, an expression of concern creasing his young features.

'Prince Finnian? Please, you're needed. The guards told me to tell you your knights are asking for you.'

His knights. If Anselm and Olivier heard called themselves called that, he would never hear the end of it. But they were in enemy territory as well and he had brought them here. He had sworn he would protect them.

'I'm not... I mean... they're not...' It wasn't something he could explain to Laurence, not when he stared at him with such unguarded awe. Stories had been spreading about what had happened in Castel Sassone. He didn't want to think what Laurence would do if he saw Wren.

'Help Gaius get everything ready to leave,' he told the boy. 'We will join you as soon as possible.'

'But I can help you.' He was so earnest. Finn wondered if he had been the same at that age. He'd idolised Roland. He still did, if he was feeling like being honest with himself.

What would Roland say about all of this?

He fixed Laurence with a stern glare.

'Help me by helping the others and following orders. We need to make sure everyone is ready to move.'

Laurence swallowed down his obvious disappointment. 'Yes, your highness.'

He headed off, so outwardly obedient that Finn worried about him. Was he as compliant with Hestia or was this just with him? No way to know, not without spending more time with them, and that wasn't on the cards. He turned back into the main building.

The ground floor was deserted. Anselm and Olivier had been given a room upstairs, with Ilanthian guards placed outside it.

Finn hadn't argued against it. How could he? Gaius wasn't about to take a chance of two Knights of the Aurum wandering around the embassy. He was having a hard enough time with Hestia's insistence that Finn have free rein here. And Finn was a member of the royal family.

The two guards manning the door watched him approach with a keen wariness which made his skin itch. Finn was armed. He wouldn't go anywhere without his sword and a knife at his belt, especially not in these halls. All his life had been a study in risks, the threat of danger ever present.

Among his own people that danger was greater than ever.

The guards didn't step aside from the door and Finn slowed, unease growing with every step.

'I wondered how long you'd take,' a voice drawled from behind him. Leander. Of course it was Leander. 'I thought even Hestia's idiot son would find you more quickly than that.'

Finn turned, suddenly feeling world-weary. He'd been expecting this since he first laid eyes on his brother. It was almost a relief. Leander wanted him dead. Leander had always wanted him dead. Nothing had changed there.

The crown prince wasn't only armed with a belt knife this time. He had twin swords strapped across his back, curved and lethally sharp.

Behind him Finn heard the guards unsheathe their own weapons. Three against one then, all highly trained swordsmen. Leander would have picked only the best for this. He'd been waiting to find Finn alone, lured him here with a mention of the knights who were more like brothers to him than his own blood. He'd even sent Laurence – innocent, willing, Laurence – to deliver the summons.

'And how will you explain this to Hestia and Gaius?'

Leander smirked. 'You and your knights attacked us. It was terrible. Such underhanded treachery. But what else would one expect from Asteroth? They'll understand. Well Gaius will. He's pragmatic.'

Finn lifted his hands away from his weapons. 'You don't have to do this, Leander.'

But Leander advanced, his long legs carrying him close, his white-blond hair aglow in the morning's light streaming through the stained glass and a look of murder on his face.

'Oh, I really think I do. In fact, I'm looking forward to it. A shame we had to kill you all. But there it is. A tragedy.'

Anselm and Olivier were locked in the room! Were they already dead?

Finn snatched his weapons free and whirled around, plunging towards the door. He took the first guard out with a kick to the groin and a knife to the throat, but the second was waiting for him. The clash of weapons rang out and from behind the door he heard shouts. They were in there, still alive, still safe, but not for long. Leander wanted to finish Finn off first. They would be next.

Leander and the remaining guard only needed to get lucky once.

The door banged hard as someone shouldered it, trying to batter it down. Olivier, it had to be. He had the brute strength. Finn couldn't help, couldn't hesitate, or Leander would be on him. Always the better swordsman. No matter how hard Finn trained.

His brother lunged towards him, swords coming so close to his throat that had Finn not bent back like a reed, they would have taken his head off. The movement left him exposed and he twisted again, barely avoiding the remaining guard's weapons slicing through the air towards him.

The door rocked again and this time something splintered. The knights beyond didn't have weaponry and Leander was already summoning reinforcements.

'Get back,' Finn tried to yell to them. It wouldn't do any good, he knew that. His brother knights would never give up. They'd arm themselves with whatever they could. 'Anselm, you have to get out of here another way.'

What that might be, he didn't know.

Something struck the small of his back, sending him lurching forward. Leander was waiting, a blow knocking his sword from his suddenly numb hand and bringing him to his knees.

Why did he always end up on his knees?

The two curved blades closed against his neck and he swallowed, his Adam's apple brushing the edges. He fell still, perfectly still, because he had to. It was over. Breathing hard, Finn looked up into Leander's triumphant face.

The door gave way and he heard Anselm cry out a warning while Olivier ploughed into the remaining assailant. Too late though. They were too late.

'Let him go,' Anselm snarled. Hestia had been as good as her word. But for his pallor and the shadows under his eyes, no one would have known him for the man they had dragged from death's chill embrace last night. He circled Leander, holding the sword from the fallen guard, but there was nothing he could do to help Finn and he knew it.

Leander laughed. 'Now? I don't think so. It's time I dealt with you for once and for all, Finnian. Before it's too late.'

'Too late for what?' Finn asked.

Leander had that reckless light in his eyes, malice and vengeance combined. 'She still hasn't told you, has she? Hestia and all her plans within plans. She thinks she's so clever. But *I'm* not giving everything up that easily.'

All the same Leander didn't land the killing blow. His hands shook. Finn could feel the trembling all down the blades, almost as if some other force held him in check.

'What plan?' he asked in as calm a voice as he could. If he could keep him talking, keep him gloating even, he might still have a chance. 'Is this about Wren? Did Hestia have something to do with Elodie's kidnapping?'

At that, Leander howled with laughter. 'Elodie? Oh, I have no idea what the sisterhood intend for Elodie. Even Hestia has no idea and she's meant to lead them. They've been laying plans of their own, some of them. But I'll tell you this, I'll look after Wren. You have my word on that. I'll make her mine if it's the last thing I do. I'll make her forget you ever existed.'

He leaned into the swords, as if trying to force himself on, and froze, his expression changing from crazed obsession to bewilderment. And then pain.

Blinding, furious, pain.

Leander screamed as he fell and Finn rolled aside, narrowly avoiding the swords. They clattered on the flooring beside the crown prince, who lay there, writhing in agony.

Behind him stood Wren and Hestia, and the eyes of both women were as black as a moonless night, and shadow kin, eyes aglow and teeth bared, wound around them like a pack of hunting dogs.

CHAPTER 42

FINN

Finn struggled to his feet, checking on Anselm and Olivier. They weren't hurt, but they looked as wary as he felt. The other guard crawled away silently. And Leander sobbed in rage and fury as he curled around his right arm where the bracelet seethed with dark magic.

He'd never seen Hestia display power like this before. She belonged to the Sisterhood of the Nox, he knew that, but even so...

Wren stood beside her, in a dark green Ilanthian gown, the sleeves falling from her wrists like fronds of weeping willow, her hair coiling and moving like smoke in a breeze. Power radiated from her and filled the sorceress.

'What is going on here?' Finn said, in as calm and determined a voice as he could muster. 'Hestia? What have you been doing?'

'Stand down, Finn,' Hestia snapped without so much as glancing at him. 'This is witchkind business and I will have answers. I want to know everything, Leander, all your petty plots and machinations. Someone will blame us for Sassone's ridiculous coup. If you know anything—'

'How could I know anything?' Leander spat through clenched teeth. 'I've been on your leash since I got here.'

Hestia scowled at him and words of othertongue filled the air, flowing like whispers and songs, jarring against the ear and making Finn's skin recoil against his muscles and bones. The shadow kin around her surged forward and Leander's face blanched. He snarled in agony again, his body arching back like a drawn bow, as shadow kin wound about him, holding him in place, crushing him, tighter and tighter. They didn't bite, but their teeth grazed his skin, a threat, a promise.

Wren didn't move. She watched Leander, as if his pain and fear fascinated her. Perhaps it did. Finn wasn't even sure if this was Wren anymore. She seemed to flicker in the shifting shadows, sometimes the woman he loved and other times...

He had to stop this. Now.

'Wren, please,' Finn whispered. 'Stop. You're helping her, aren't you? Making her stronger. Please stop. This isn't the way, love.'

'He almost killed you,' she said softly as if waking from a dream. 'He would have killed you. I had to stop him, Finn.'

So it was her then. Her magic. Not the Nox itself but its power. And it was pouring along her veins now, swallowing her up more and more by the second. It would burn its way through her, destroying all that there was of her, of the Wren he knew and loved. He'd seen her almost lose herself before, and he couldn't let it happen again. Not for him.

He wasn't worth that.

'He's almost killed me more times than I can remember. And he will try again. But this isn't you. We need to go, leave this place. It isn't good for you. It isn't safe.'

'Good,' she murmured. 'Safe... they're just words. Maybe I'm not good. Maybe nowhere is safe. Maybe I belong here. The Nox can help us.'

Was this Hestia's doing? He glanced at her. Had she

enchanted Wren or... or what? His cousin was furious, he could see that and understand it too. All her plans had come to naught and if Leander was to be believed her sisterhood was plotting behind her back. But would she use the incarnation of her goddess to have her answers? Would she destroy Wren to get them?

Of course she would. Hestia wanted peace and she'd have it at any cost. Even if it meant destruction.

He reached for Wren's hand, carefully, cautiously, advancing on her as if she might explode, and lifted it in his. The air between them crackled and he felt that sweeping maelstrom of need in him again, rising like the storm. How he longed to give in to it, to be hers and do whatever she commanded without thought and without hesitation. One day he would. He knew that. When Wren lost this fight, so would he.

But not yet. Not today. She wasn't gone yet. And he wouldn't let her go. Though everything in him longed to fall at her feet and worship her, there was enough of his own will left to let him do this one thing. For her. For Wren.

He pressed his lips to her skin. She felt so cold, it was like kissing ice. But he didn't care. 'Maybe you belong with me. Maybe somewhere else. But Wren, not like this. This isn't you. Let him go.'

Her eyes flickered again and she glanced at him. A look of confusion passed over her beautiful features and she frowned.

'Why would you save him?' she asked.

'I'm not saving him. I'm saving you. Let's go and find Elodie. She can help you. She'll understand. She loves you. Please?'

Wren sighed and her body gave a shiver, but she didn't pull away from him. Abruptly the power holding Leander vanished and he slumped down onto the crimson carpets of the gallery floor.

'We still need answers,' Hestia protested. 'The Asterothians will demand them. Or blame us.' The shadow kin were gone.

The power in her was diminished now and though she was still a sorceress, she couldn't sustain that sort of spell alone. Wren had been fuelling her power. That was a conversation for another time and Finn would get her explanation for it. But not now. What answers was she after? What did she suspect Leander of now?

'And I don't have answers.' Leander's voice came out between a sob and a snarl. 'I've tried to tell you, Hestia. None of this is my doing. Yes, I tried to kill Finn. I want him dead. But none of the rest of it.'

Finn narrowed his eyes, suspicion making him listen even more closely. He was missing something, something they had deliberately kept from him ever since they arrived here. 'What are you two talking about?' This wasn't about Sassone and Elodie. It wasn't even about Wren. There was more to this. 'What else has happened?'

Leander had picked himself up again, still in obvious pain but he dusted off his fine clothes and glared at them all. Anselm and Olivier had fallen back behind Finn, flanking him. Guarding him.

Hestia gave in first. She sighed and then lowered her hands. 'We weren't only here for the trial, or for Leander to apologise, and certainly not for him to pull his petty little stunt in the Sacrum. We weren't even just here to meet Wren or to attempt to broker a permanent peace. There's a problem back in Sidonia, Finnian, and the sisterhood sent me here to find out the truth. Someone has been passing our secrets to the rebel witchkind through Pelias, and sold shadow-wrought steel to Sassone here, clearly. The College of Winter may be involved and we have servants there trying to find out the truth. They are moving against both kingdoms, trying to destabilise us and disrupt the powers themselves. They seek to destroy the Aurum, the way Elodie destroyed the Nox. We came to find out who, and why.'

'And so far all she has done has been to torture me,' Leander growled at her. 'And now she's brought your beloved in on the act. Promising to teach her and help her embrace the dark, as if she can control the Nox. There's no control, when it comes to that power. It will burn through you and destroy whatever is left of you. And it will laugh as it does so. You'd have to be a naïve fool to believe that kind of power can be controlled by one woman.' He sneered at her and Wren took a step back, her face very pale. Fear or anger, Finn wasn't sure. He put himself between them all the same. 'Believe me, I am going to remember this. When I take the crown, Hestia—'

Hestia snarled at him and flexed her fingers. He flinched and this time she smiled. He wasn't as brave as he pretended. Not anymore. The Ilanthian court was intent on flaying the arrogance out of him, the sisterhood most of all, it seemed. Had he crossed them as well? How great a fool had Leander become?

'Don't let your father hear you talking like that or I will be the least of your worries, you stupid boy. He'll hand you over to the sisterhood completely to do with what they will and all this will seem like a pleasant dream. Well?' She turned to Wren. 'Can you tell?'

Wren shook her head and Finn studied her. She seemed more herself again. When she saw him watching her she curled in against him once more.

'I'm sorry,' she said. 'Hestia offered to help me control the shadows instead of fighting them. And then Leander attacked you... And I—'

Hestia offered to help. Well, Hestia could be persuasive when she wanted to be. Oh he should never have left Wren alone. She had wanted to know more about her powers, about the people who would accept the darkness in her. Finn understood that and he should have predicted it. He didn't have to like it but he at least could understand. And there was Hestia, of the Sisterhood of the Nox, offering to explain it all.

He could imagine. The betrayal burned in the pit of his stomach. He should have expected it. She was blood of Sidon too, after all.

'Let's go home,' he told Wren softly, more a plea than an order.

'But it's not my home, Finn. It never will be.'

'It's all we have,' he replied, trying not to hear the pain in her voice. She truly hated it here. Pelias was nothing but a cage to her. Coming here had cost her everything, as she had always feared it would. 'We have to see Elodie and Roland. They need to know about this as well. Your investigation, Hestia, should have been explained in detail from the start.'

'It's an Ilanthian issue,' Hestia told him curtly. Of course, they didn't want it widely known that the security of the Ilanthian court had been breached, or that someone was trading with witchkind.

But this was not an argument anymore. If they were all intent on treating him like a prince here, then he would embrace it. This so-called 'issue' affected all of them. And if the rebel witchkind were trying to disrupt the old magic itself, if they were trying to take over the sisterhood, or if they were after the Aurum, he had to raise the alarm. He was duty-bound.

'Clearly not. Sassone used Ilanthian steel on the queen. You have no choice but to tell them everything and let Elodie and Roland handle it. If they believe you had a hand in it, that's going to make your mission all the more difficult, Hestia. Impossible in fact. You'll be lucky to get out of Pelias, ambassador or not. And Leander will have the war he always wanted.'

'I don't want a war,' his half-brother muttered. 'Only a fool would want that.'

Which was, Finn reflected, the most sensible thing he had ever heard come out of Leander's mouth. It wasn't as if he had been demonstrating that the last time they met though, and he had learned long ago never to trust a word his brother said.

'Really? I thought that was what this was all about. Conquering Asteroth, securing power, the triumph of the Nox.'

'It doesn't have to be like that,' Hestia interrupted. 'Does it? None of you understand. How many times do I have to explain to get it through your thick royal skulls? We can achieve a balance instead.'

She looked plaintively at Leander who gave a growl and rolled his eyes. 'So you say. And Hestia knows these things. She certainly convinced our father anyway.' His voice took on a grandiose tone. 'She has looked into the darkest places and been shown the path of things to come. All must obey or we face utter ruin. Not everyone agrees with her though and that is the problem.'

Finn turned his attention to his cousin who had the good grace to look embarrassed.

Mystical and ominous portents from the sisterhood. He should have guessed.

'And what is that?' he asked, raising an eyebrow to let her know how dubious he found all of this. 'A vision?'

'I can't tell you. Not everything. Just that peace is possible and it is imperative. Without peace I saw a wasteland where our fair kingdoms should be.'

Hardly a surprise. That was what war did. Hestia knew that as well as anyone. He'd had enough of this nonsense.

'You need to leave,' he told her. 'Get out of Pelias and back to Sidonia. Spin your foretellings to Alessander instead if he's of a mind to listen. They'll do more good there.'

'I have. He sent us here, Finnian. For you.'

Those two words made him stop, his body frozen. Wren's hand tightened on his. Did she know about this?

'And why does Alessander want me?'

He dreaded to think. He may have visited the royal court

and been treated with casual disdain at most over the years, but his last clear memory of his childhood was his father dragging him to the sacrificial chamber, knife in hand. That was his one abiding memory, the thing that brought him awake screaming from nightmares in the darkest hours of the night. Alessander had tried to kill him and Roland had been the one to save him.

Then the king of Ilanthus had handed his youngest son over as a hostage without a single qualm. The boy was dead to him anyway.

But it had been Hestia who had sent Roland to save him. Finn had always known that. And for what? For this? He'd thought it was love, or at least affection. But had she always known? Had this, in fact, been her plan? Not to let him die then, but to save him up for the future, for when the Nox returned in a human form.

Daily, Finnian thanked the light of the Aurum for Roland's intervention. He had been a man by the time he had been able to return to Sidonia without an escort for his own safety. And in those prayers, he had thanked Hestia as well. Now they felt like ashes in his mouth.

Oh he could imagine why Alessander might want him back after so long. Blood of Sidon. The expendable son. The one doomed to die...

He stared at Hestia, desperately ignoring Leander. He could lay hands on a weapon again in moments. He trusted his hated brother knew that.

Anselm and Olivier moved closer. He'd almost forgotten they were there. They were Knights of the Aurum. They could be silent and unseen. It was part of their training.

Anselm... Anselm who would tell Roland everything. And even if he didn't, Olivier would. Oh great light, how was he going to explain all of this to Roland?

'Finn,' Wren whispered. It sent a shudder through him and he glanced to her. Her dark eyes were fixed solemnly on him, and she looked as worried as he felt. Her hand, cold and shaking, tightened on his again, as if she felt the need to hold him back.

He trusted her, more than trusted her. He would do anything for her. She was part of him and he was part of her. They had to get out of here.

'We should go,' she said, her voice trembling.

Had they already told Wren? Before him? Or had she sensed it? Her magic could do so much. Why not peer into Hestia's mind and read her intentions? Or maybe Wren had figured it out. She was clever, intuitive as well. Everyone seemed to forget that.

'Why's that, little bird?' asked Leander with a sarcastic drawl. 'Why not let him hear the future?'

She turned on him angrily and Finn felt the shadows snarl around her, rising in an instant. Her hand almost pulled away from his, but he held onto her, which made her pause.

'No one knows the future,' she replied, almost evenly. 'It is not yet written. It can only be guessed.'

The prince smirked at her, a deliberately infuriating expression. He thrived on such behaviour. 'You'll find Hestia is *remarkably* good at guessing.'

'Enough, Leander,' Hestia snapped, her tone all warning. 'You're impossible.'

Leander scowled at her, his face tight with pain, loathing in his eyes. She was using the bracelet to try to stop him but this time he was fighting his way through the pain. 'She didn't see the crown of Ilanthus on my head when Father dies, brother dearest. She saw it on yours. Happy now?'

CHAPTER 43
WREN

Finn wouldn't even consider it or discuss it. He stalked from the gallery, heading back down the stairs to the door and the outside world, and Wren hastened after him while Hestia remonstrated with Leander. The crown prince was about to lose that crown, and all hope of a future one. He'd seized his chance to kill Finn and almost succeeded again.

No wonder Hestia thought he had to be part of this plot in Pelias, let alone anything happening back in Sidonia.

But if not Leander, then who?

There were not many people who could produce shadow-wrought steel. Perhaps it was old, left over from the last war. Or perhaps Hestia was right and witchkind were somehow involved.

The courtyard outside was deserted, the other Ilanthians having already left as instructed. It seemed they had been eager to follow those orders.

'Finn, please wait.' Wren hurried after him. His legs were long and his pace was fast, especially when he was upset.

'For what?'

'For me?'

That did it. His step faltered and he did stop, looking back at her, his face apologetic. 'Wren, I... it isn't true. It can't be true. It's a trick or a lie or... or a mistake. She can make mistakes.' He didn't sound convinced.

'Everyone can,' she told him. Her hand touched his face, trying to comfort him, and he leaned into her touch, his long-lashed eyes flickering closed.

'If I'm to be king of Ilanthus... what would that mean for us?'

It was the one question she didn't want to think about, the one that had roared through her mind the moment the words were said. How could they be together? How could they have any future at all? How could Finn continue to serve the Aurum and remain himself if he was made king of a country dedicated to the Nox?

Balance, Hestia had said. There was a way through to be found if they could find balance. But giving him up entirely to the darkness wasn't balance at all. How could it be? It would make him a slave. That had always been its plan.

'I don't know,' she replied, truthfully, and stepped in close, letting his arms come up around her, needing to feel his touch. 'But you could say no.'

He half laughed, a bitter and slightly twisted sound. 'I'm not sure it works like that, my love.'

Wren kissed him, pressing her lips softly to his. 'Really? Because it's the only hope I've got left, in my case.'

Finn returned the kiss with a fire, pulling her to him and devouring her. She returned it full force, needing this, needing him, wanting him to know that she was still his and praying that he was still hers.

If she was queen of Asteroth after Elodie and he was king of Ilanthus...

This was wrong. It was all wrong. It had to be. There was

no balance to be had in any of this. It was all or nothing. It wasn't fair.

Reluctantly, Finn pulled away, gazing at her, his eyes so deep and dark they were almost black as well. She could see herself reflected there.

'Running away and hiding in the forest is starting to sound like a definite plan,' he told her.

'I would leave with you in a heartbeat.' She would if it would work. And why not? Why shouldn't they? Just go, right now, and never look back. But then the pang of remorse hit her. 'But... but I need to make sure Elodie is all right first.'

Finn had seen her embrace the darkness and be prepared to use it. She saw that knowledge flicker across his eyes. 'Is that safe? To go back to the palace? To be so close to the Aurum?'

She let out a long, shaking breath. 'I have to. And Hestia is right. We need to find out how Sassone got the steel and why he thought he would get away with it.'

'Then we go back to the palace,' Finn sighed, his expression troubled. 'And hope for the best.'

'That is all we can ever hope for.' She glanced at Anselm and Olivier, lingering behind them, on constant guard among the Ilanthians. She didn't blame them. All of them were lucky to still be alive. 'The sooner we leave the better.'

The thundering clatter of horses' hooves on the cobbles beyond the gate made them all look up to face a new threat. The Knights of the Aurum had arrived, with Roland at their head. The gates were already open so there was nothing the Ilanthians could do to stop them. And it would have ended in blood if they had tried. Gaius and the main force had already gone, leaving Leander and Hestia with a small, largely ceremonial group who wouldn't have stopped Roland.

Especially not with Roland enraged like this. Even Wren could see it.

He pulled his horse to a halt and glowered down at them all.

Without a word spoken, Finn, Anselm and Olivier dropped to their knees, offering up their swords in silence, heads bowed. Hestia and her guards still surrounded Leander as they emerged from the main building and she didn't look in the slightest bit cowed by Roland's presence. But she didn't say anything either.

Which meant it was left to Wren.

'They helped me. They rescued me and gave me sanctuary.'

Roland stared at her for a long moment, studying her. His face unreadable. Wren didn't like what she saw there, even if she didn't quite know what it was.

Nothing good.

'Very well,' he said at last, his voice surprisingly calm. 'Take them all into custody. We can sort this out back at the palace. The Aurum can decide.'

'You can't do this,' Hestia protested. 'I'm an ambassador, a diplomat. We were helping her. And you certainly can't take him prisoner. He's a prince of Ilanthus.'

She didn't specify which of the two princes she meant. What would Roland do if he learned of Hestia's offer to Finn? Wren glanced at Anselm and Olivier but they said nothing, for which she was profoundly grateful.

Roland turned his glowering attention to Hestia. The knights behind him bristled, reading his mood and ready to attack. The remaining Ilanthian guards shifted uneasily. They were vastly outnumbered. They were not hardened soldiers but clearly little more than a ceremonial military division. These men had not signed up for any of this. But they were sworn to the crown, and to defend their ambassador. If it came down to it, they would try. And they would fail.

Finn saw it too. 'Stand down,' he told them in an unwavering voice.

Roland didn't spare them so much as a glance, nor offer

Finn any comment regarding the order. All his attention was fixed on the ambassador now.

'Save your lies, Lady Hestia. The Aurum will demand the truth or burn it from you. I will know how the princess came to be here, and I will know how shadow-wrought steel was used on the person of my queen. You will find I always get answers.'

Wren felt all the blood sliding away from her head, leaving her dizzy and scared. She didn't know this man. Roland had always been terrifying but Roland enraged... Had something else happened to Elodie? He had saved her, hadn't he? He had saved her and carried her to safety like something from one of the old songs but maybe... maybe...

Elodie had to be all right.

'Wren, come here,' he snapped and held out his hand. She didn't dare disobey this time. He pulled her up onto the horse behind him, away from Finn and the others.

'What happened?' she asked urgently now she was up close and didn't have to raise her voice.

'Enough,' Roland said and his tone silenced everyone. 'The queen will decide all their fates. She is not best pleased.'

Hestia lifted her chin, defiant. 'She is the queen again, then, your lady? Your witch-queen is recognised once more by the people who would have let her burn?'

Roland narrowed his eyes. 'She was always our queen.' He gestured to his men. 'Bring them. All of them.'

ON BALANCE

BY PILAGIA OF SIDON

In the end the balance of light and dark is a simple thing. It hangs by a thread, or on the point of a needle. It can tip either way.

Everything lies in the eye of the beholder. To someone trapped in a lightless hole, a candle is the sun. To someone lost in a desert where the sun blinds them and burns them, the night is blessed relief.

This then is the balance. This is what the wise will seek.

True power lies in that balance, in maintaining it, in holding it, like an acrobat balanced high above a ravine.

In the balance. In the corruption of that balance. In the entangling of dark and light.

And in its untangling comes chaos.

CHAPTER 44
FINN

Roland arrived, and all Finn could do was fall to his knees beside the others and pray no one told his guardian that Ilanthus wanted him back. That they wanted to put a crown on his head.

Finn wanted none of it and Roland had to know that. He had to.

But Roland looked like he could happily order the immediate execution of everyone right there at the gates of the Ilanthian embassy.

Including Wren.

Something had happened. Something terrible. Finn knew that without even asking. He just had to look into the eyes of the man he had thought of as his true father to see the desolation there.

'The queen?' he asked one of the other knights as they were hustled through the city, towards the gates of the palace. The man glanced down at him from horseback.

Roland had taken Wren up on his mount, riding ahead with her. Finn had been left to walk with the others.

This was not good. Not good at all.

'What happened to the queen?' he asked again.

'She lives. He rescued her. And she's angry. Understandably. Your Ilanthian friends were helping Sassone. They provided the shadow steel with which they bound her power.'

But they didn't. Hestia and even Leander had insisted that was not the case. They were as mystified about it as anyone else, desperate to find out how it had happened and who was behind it before something happened. Something like this. Finn had seen nothing while at the embassy to believe any differently. He didn't think they were lying to him. That was almost a surprise. He had always expected lies, especially from Leander.

But not this time.

Hestia had been his only friend in the Ilanthian court. She was a powerful sorceress, true, and a devoted member of the sisterhood. His father trusted her like no one else. Hestia had never harmed him.

There was always a first time, some dark voice inside him whispered. And Hestia seemed determined to put him on the throne. The last thing he wanted.

The last thing anyone else wanted. If that wasn't harm he didn't know what was.

This was all a terrible mistake. All Ilanthus had to know that.

The gates of the palace opened silently. No rain of flowers this time, no cheering crowds, no great ball to welcome them either. The Ilanthians were ushered inside like captives rather than guests and Finn remembered long ago when he had first arrived here, the feeling of those gates closing behind him, like the doors of a tomb.

'But they saved me,' he heard Wren's voice, strident in the still courtyard between the palace and the Sanctum. 'This is madness.'

'If you had stayed where you were you wouldn't have needed saving,' Roland growled at her, more frustrated than

Finn had ever heard him. Honestly, he couldn't blame the man. He'd thought the same thing himself. Not that Wren would pay a blind bit of notice. 'And besides—'

They never heard what else he was going to say because the main doors to the keep opened and Elodie emerged. Silence settled over the whole gathering. She glided forward, head held high. She was a sword, in human form, crowned with a circlet of gold which gleamed in the sunlight. Lynette and several of the ladies-in-waiting came after her, clearly distressed that she had left whatever safety they had managed to construct around her. This was the main courtyard of her own palace. She had already been taken from the supposedly most secure place in Pelias so what did she care for security now? And Finn knew better than anyone at this stage, nothing would stop Elodie if she had set her mind to something.

Not Queen Aeryn, he thought. Elodie the hedge witch of Cellandre. She was the real power here.

'Wren,' Elodie said and her voice rang out like a bell.

Wren ran to her. She didn't even hesitate or glance back, all fear gone. Finn almost felt a pang of grief at the thought. But Elodie had always been there for her. She was her mother and her fiercest protector. She always had been.

Why did anyone doubt that?

The queen of Asteroth enfolded her daughter in her arms and held her close. She lifted her chin over Wren's bowed head and her eyes locked with Roland's. 'Did you find him?'

Roland half-shrugged his shoulders. 'What's left of him. Perhaps.'

Finn thought back to the shadow kin in the keep of Castel Sassone and tried not to glance at Anselm. No telling what he thought, or what he might have to say on the subject. They both knew what Wren had done there.

'And his conspirators?' she asked in a voice that could have come from the wintry wastes. Roland shook his head.

Elodie turned her attention on the group from the embassy. Her tone didn't change. The fearful authority that threaded through her words made it even worse.

'Bring them to the Sacrum. Let them face the fire of the Aurum and speak truth whether they like it or not.'

'Your majesty!' Hestia cried out in protest. 'We have nothing to do with this. Prince Finnian brought the princess to us for safety. That was all.'

'Did he?' Elodie's voice was so cold and Finn felt something inside him tighten in fear. She had once defeated him without so much as breaking a sweat, without drawing a weapon, with no more than a handful of dust. It had been humiliating then and he still felt the sensations of that cloying dust in his mouth and nose as his consciousness had slipped away. She had almost killed Leander in a swordfight. In the Sacrum Finn had seen her at her full power, channelling the Aurum, bright and terrifying as any nightmare spun for wayward Ilanthian children. If she thought his people were to blame for even the slightest part of this coup, they were in trouble. If she thought it was his fault...

Wren straightened, said something soft and low, and confusion flickered over Elodie's beautiful face. Her gaze strayed to Finn, bored into him as if seeking confirmation. He held himself still and strong, as if he could convince her of his faithfulness by appearance alone. Elodie's eyes narrowed.

'Very well.' Her voice had gentled. It was barely perceptible, but it was there. He could feel it. The gratitude that she believed in him should not have felt quite so much like relief. 'We will get to the bottom of this. Come, Prince Finnian, Prince Leander. And Lady Hestia.'

Finn didn't like to say what might have happened if she had tried to separate Hestia from them right now. She, too, was witchkind, and very high in the Sisterhood of the Nox. Perhaps she was even a match for Elodie, had their goddess not been broken and scattered. And she had Leander's keeping. He might be a monster, and she might be controlling his magic with the bracelet, but she was also responsible for him. And if anything happened to him, Alessander would make her suffer indeed. Worse, he would take it out on her son as well. Finn's father made Leander look like a saint. And Gaius had taken Laurence with him, not through any altruistic motive. He was a bargaining chip, an offering. Hestia had to know that too.

Elodie's use of Finn's title, and giving him precedence over Leander, didn't bode well at all. His heart felt like something had speared it, something cold and dark indeed. He could almost hear the taunting laughter of the Nox. He'd always been an Ilanthian here.

As they stepped into the cool interior of the keep, he felt Wren take his hand. He hadn't even seen her lingering in the shadows beyond the door

'Are you all right? They didn't hurt you?'

He shook his head. He didn't even know what to say to her.

'Will Hestia and Leander tell them you're to be king?' she whispered, as if she didn't dare to say it any louder.

He didn't want to say it out loud himself.

'My family lies as soon as they breathe,' he replied. 'I don't know what they're planning, none of them. This could all be another trick. Never trust them. I mean it, Wren. Don't ever trust anyone from my family. It will only end in misery.'

She wrapped her arm around his and pulled him closer, folding in against him, warm and intoxicating. Perhaps she meant it to be a comfort, but it reminded him of the way he lost himself in her, in his desire for her, and in the ingrained need to do whatever she asked of him without question.

It reminded him that he was destined to serve the Nox, no matter how much he struggled against that fate, and the pendant around his neck felt heavy.

With Wren so close, the darkness teased at the back of his mind, and he thought he heard a ripple of laughter.

Laughing at him.

Will you bring her misery, little king-in-waiting? Oh how we long to see it. In her despair she will embrace her darkness and then we will be whole again. By all means, break her heart.

He sucked in a breath of alarm and she pulled back to look at his face, confused.

Where had that come from? It had sounded like the Nox but that dark power couldn't be here. Not right in the heart of Pelias.

The doors to the chamber of the Aurum closed behind him, the sound echoing in the high-ceilinged room hewn from white stone, lit by its flickering light, and the dark whisper was cut off.

He could feel the light in his veins, pulsing inside him, calling to him, as if an invisible string drew him forward. He longed to drop to his knees before the flames and proclaim his faithfulness to it. To at last have it accept him as a Paladin, as its servant.

And yet something else held him in place. Wren. And what Hestia had told him of the future.

'Someone,' said Elodie in that voice like the north wind, 'needs to explain the meaning of all of this to me right now.'

CHAPTER 45
ELODIE

Elodie fought to control her rage. Every time she thought everything might be all right again, something else happened, another disaster, another mess to clean up. At least Wren was here, and safe. Finnian had been with her. That had to be a good thing.

Except it didn't look that way. Something had happened with the Ilanthians. They wanted him to lead them, Wren had said. They wanted to take him back. Once, Elodie would have said it was the perfect solution, but now she was not so sure.

Leander stood there, defiant still, his magic contained but that was all. Leander, who had tried to imitate his uncle the last time he was here, when they had stupidly extended even a little trust. He had used his own blood to summon the Nox in the Sacrum to face the Aurum, leaving her burning and so blind and weakened Sassone had taken her without a struggle.

And every time she closed her eyes she could still see the earl's leering face, still feel the flames burning higher around her and the icy embrace of the shadow-wrought steel on her skin stealing away her defences.

Not anymore. Never again. That steel had to have come

from somewhere and Ilanthus was the only place to produce it. The regents should never have agreed to allow the Ilanthians here to reopen their embassy, should never have invited them when they sued for peace.

They were not to be trusted. They could never be trusted. Not even Finnian. Not when it came down to it. He was still of the line of Sidon. He had slotted back in among them without a murmur and Hestia, as close to a high priestess as the Nox had, was already sinking her claws into him. And into Wren as well... Elodie really did not like that.

Making her way to the place where Prince Leander stood beside his cousin, Elodie glared at him, looking past the handsome arrogant face to the young man behind. She'd faced him in battle at the Seven Sisters, and defeated him. He wielded what little magic he had almost as well as he wielded the sword, except...

Except the magic of shades and darkness was gone from him, locked away by a bracelet similar to the metal which had bound her.

Elodie pulled back, wrinkling her nose with distaste. No one deserved that.

'Oh believe me, your majesty, the feeling is mutual,' Leander muttered, instantly taking her reaction the wrong way.

So the arrogance was still there. Chastened, perhaps, a bit battered, but still so deeply ingrained in him it would never be completely gone. He used it to hide his fear, but she saw through him. He was deeply afraid right now.

'Your own people took your magic from you?'

He lifted his chin defiantly. 'Such as it was. I wasn't lying about being here to apologise. It was the only way I might be able to convince them to take this off.' He lifted his arm to show her the bracelet. It seethed with power, all his, she suspected. The light of the Aurum bounced off it, sliding away, and leaving the shadows clearly visible with othersight.

Elodie lifted her hand to it almost idly, even though everything in her wanted to recoil.

'I wouldn't do that, your majesty,' Hestia warned.

'Oh? You know more than me, do you?'

'I know more about shadow-wrought steel and its properties. And what it does to you. To our kind.'

Elodie tilted her head to the side, looking at the witch. Not quite forty, more or less her own age and equal. Hestia's mind crackled with power. Among the Ilanthians she was formidable. If the Maidens of the Aurum had found her first, she would stand high among them by now. As high as Maryn perhaps. Or higher.

So much promise. Wasted in the darkness.

'I don't hold with people being chained like this,' Elodie told her, 'not even princes of Sidon. I've experienced it myself far too recently. Remember where you are this time, Leander. That is all I ask. No more attempts at a grand but pointless gesture.' She gestured towards the flames. 'You have seen that the Aurum does not take well to betrayal. And my knights have lost all their patience, as have I.'

Elodie touched the bracelet and it came apart, falling into her other hand. The shiver that ran through her wasn't unexpected and it wasn't pleasant either. Shadow-wrought steel... A loathsome material. She passed the heavy bracelet to Finn who held it like it might burst into flames at any second. Wren took a step back from it, wary of its presence.

Good.

Leander rubbed his wrist absently, but then bowed deeply. 'Majesty, I am in your debt.'

'Remember it. At least it taught you some manners.' She deliberately left off any form of a title. He didn't deserve one. The Ilanthians were far too free with their shadow-wrought steel as a means of control. No wonder he had been driven to desperation. She turned on Lady Hestia, the architect of this particular situation. 'I want answers and I want them now.'

Behind her Roland drew Nightbreaker. What she had said about patience was no lie. He had thought the Ilanthians had taken Wren when they found out she was missing. He would have razed their embassy to the ground had they not immediately relinquished her. Their entire country, perhaps. She knew the feeling.

The Aurum roared, the flames rising to meet her anger.

Elodie hesitated. All of them here – the heirs of Sidon, a high witch of the Sisterhood of the Nox, the Grandmaster, Wren and herself, all standing in the light of the Aurum... something felt off. As if they had been brought together by design. A group who should probably never be brought together...

'If you please, majesty...' said a voice from the far side of the chamber.

A serving girl stood there. One of the girls who attended her and Wren. How had she even gained access to the chamber at a moment like this?

'Carlotta?' Wren said, starting towards her, but the maid shied back from her.

'Please, I... I must speak with the queen.' She stumbled forward, her eyes wide, pupils so dilated they filled her sockets with pools of darkness. Her body trembled, skin shivering, gleaming with a sheen of sweat as she struggled against something unnatural. It wasn't right, Elodie realised. There was something wrong with her, something crawling within her. She moved like a marionette. Otherness surrounded her, grey and nebulous, strands of light and dark magic twisted together in unnatural knots.

And Wren was still standing directly in front of her.

The maid stopped, and then reached out a shaking hand. 'Please, princess,' she whispered. 'Please move aside. You've been kind to me and I... I don't want... please...'

Wren reached for her and a long-honed instinct made Elodie react, ready to lash out with her power before the servant could touch her daughter. As the air crackled between them, she felt others respond as well, Hestia raising a shield around both her princes, Roland and his Paladins surging forward in response to her, and Wren...

Wren reached out to Carlotta, for the only real friend she had made here.

Tears streamed down the other young woman's face. It made her look much younger, no more than a child. A lost child. Her mouth moved. 'She made me. I'm sorry, Wren. She made me.'

Her voice sounded ragged and desperate, broken, as if her own words were being forced out under great duress.

She was fighting a magical compulsion. Elodie could see the threads of magic woven around her. She was witchkind, young, vulnerable, compelled to do something against her nature and her will and fast losing that battle... and no one would be able to stop her in time.

Carlotta's fingers touched Wren's, a look of anguish on her features. She said something, something which made Wren's expression turn from confusion to horror. Wren tried to pull away, but it was too late.

Carlotta drew a knife, a long blade like a silver leaf reflecting the light of the Aurum, and pulled Wren against her, a hostage... or bait.

The princes of Sidon were here as well, along with a high priestess of the Nox.

And Wren was in mortal danger.

Finn threw himself towards her, heedless of the threat, desperate to stop the serving girl from hurting Wren. Because of course he did. What else could he do? But he wasn't alone.

Leander reached her first, nearer and faster to begin with, and Carlotta buried the knife up to its hilt in his guts. The prince staggered back in shock, so that the servant wrenched the knife free again. Blood spilled everywhere. The blood of Sidon.

Come, oh divine darkness and be made whole once again.

The shadows stirred, the Nox coalescing, and through Elodie, already on alert, the Aurum answered without hesitation.

Carlotta's eyes – huge and unnaturally dark – held her gaze and from somewhere Wren heard the laughter of the Nox. It was everywhere, all around her, inside her, thundering with her blood.

'I'm sorry, Wren,' Carlotta whispered, silver tears scoring lines down her face. 'I didn't mean to... I didn't want to... I couldn't stop her...' Her eyes glazed and another voice came from her mouth, one familiar and strange at the same time. It snarled and growled the words and all Wren could hear was its vindictive tones, echoing through her head.

We are witchkind. We will live free or we die.

Magic boiled up through Carlotta's frail body, lines of lightning crackled across her skin, dancing and dispersing into the servant's form. Carlotta wasn't doing this. She couldn't.

She turned the knife on herself, the razor-sharp edge sliding across her throat without hesitation. Blood spilled down her front and she crumpled like a pile of rags.

But Carlotta's blood, while that of a witch, while spilled against her will, didn't matter. Not now.

Leander's blood, on the other hand, blood of a prince of Ilanthus, blood of Sidon...

It pulled power out of Wren as if she was nothing but a well. This wasn't the balance Hestia had spoken off. There was no breathing her way through it. This was more than a summoning. This was an assault.

Wren flung up her hands, trying to draw her power around her to protect herself. She didn't mean to call on the shadows but they always answered first in her time of need. They were always eager to help her. Shadow kin answered her, so many.

Instantly, light blasted through her defences, sending her sprawling backwards. For a moment she couldn't breathe, couldn't draw in any more air. Everything hurt. Everywhere.

'Wren!'

Hestia grabbed her, held her close, frantically trying to control the magic running rampant through the girl, to fix it back in its division of light and dark. She grabbed Wren's arms and pulled her to her feet, dragging her to one side as blinding light erupted where she had been only moments before.

'I've got her!' Hestia shouted, pulling Wren after her as she plunged towards the doorway.

Finn stumbled ahead of them, carrying Leander. He almost fell, as he ran, but Hestia yelled something at him and he staggered up and somehow kept going. The other knights were on their knees, light coursing through them, light so bright, all focused on one figure, on a being made of flames and blinding brilliance.

All except for Roland. He stood in Finn's path like a tree in a storm, clinging to his great sword. Light pulsed down the length of the blade, the light of the Aurum. His eyes were closed, his face screwed up tightly in concentration as he fought to hold onto himself.

'Go,' he told Finn. 'Get him out of here.' Finn skidded

around him and flung himself for the door, a trail of his brother's blood splattering behind him.

'Roland!' Wren cried out. Her father opened his dark eyes and saw her, eyes so like her own. And he tried to smile.

'Run, Wren,' he said. 'As fast and as far as you can.'

Elodie and Roland had made her whether they knew it or not. Her not-quite mother and perhaps-never father. It didn't matter. They were all she had.

Now Elodie was coming after her and Roland was in the way.

Wren was the only defence he had now. And perhaps all that might possibly stop Elodie. She couldn't leave him. He wouldn't stand a chance. Roland would never raise a weapon against Elodie, Wren knew that much. And if Elodie killed him she would never forgive herself.

Except, the thing bearing down on her wasn't Elodie anymore. One look in the shining face told her that. She took her time, almost as if it was a procession. There was nowhere Wren could go anyway. That terrible power would hunt her down and destroy her. It was only a matter of time.

The Aurum filled the queen's body and burned Elodie away. She was righteous vengeance, the Aurum incarnate. Everyone always talked about the Nox, about how terrible it was when it took form, but no one mentioned the Aurum. Perhaps they had forgotten it was possible. But Wren had seen it take Elodie like this twice now and she knew her mother had no control. If she was even there anymore. What had Hestia said? Stare at the sun and you went blind. Fire burned. Right now, Elodie didn't know anything more than the Aurum allowed her to know.

And Wren was part of the Nox. She always had been. Carlotta had stabbed Leander, spilling the blood of Sidon to summon the Nox in the chamber of the Aurum, in its Sacrum.

299

Finishing the job he had tried to start at the trial. Perhaps he had given her the idea.

No, not her. This had not been Carlotta's idea. She'd been forced to do this.

A second later and it could have been Finn.

'Elodie, stop!' she cried out, even though she knew that Elodie couldn't hear her. Wouldn't hear her. And wouldn't know her if she did.

Elodie might as well be gone.

Roland stood beside her. Her father, or the man who should have been her father if she was really flesh and blood and not some kind of magical creation. The man she sincerely wished was her father. He held Nightbreaker and hid her behind the great sword. Elodie's relentless advance appeared to have stalled. Roland, or the sword, seemed to be the only thing holding the Aurum back from her now. How, she didn't know.

'Wren, you need to get away,' Roland told her. 'It isn't safe.'

'Nowhere is safe,' she replied. 'Not anymore. Look at her.'

'My darling girl,' he whispered, and awe saturated his voice. 'Look at yourself.'

She started and tried to glance at her body. Her hair whipped wildly around her like a nest of shadows. When she held out her hands she saw her skin was suffused with stars and the night's sky, alive with its own dark light. But she didn't feel the Nox taking control of her. It was held off beyond the veil still, a world and a half away on the other side of her reality.

Balance, Hestia had said. They needed to find balance.

Elodie struck, lightning arcing through the crackling air, and Wren barely managed to raise some kind of shield around the two of them in time. It was shaky and uncertain, woven somehow around the sword itself, its light and her shadows twisting together. It wouldn't hold for long, she knew that instinctively. It wasn't meant to be possible.

Elodie, or the being that had been Elodie, tilted her head to one side as if examining this oddity.

'What's wrong with her? What is she doing?'

'She doesn't know us.' Roland's voice shook as he steeled himself. 'She's looking for a weakness, I think. When I give the signal, run.'

'What about you?'

He didn't have an answer for that. He didn't know any more than she did what the Aurum might do to him now. 'I can give you time to escape. The sword can only shield you for so long. It's her power, after all. She sees the Nox in you, Wren. She knows the truth of you. She told me.'

'But I—' And what could she say? That it wasn't true? She might not know exactly what happened and how it happened or anything else. But he was right. 'Roland, I—'

His hand fell on her shoulder, strong and firm, but oh so comforting. She had never expected that. 'I know the truth of you too, Wren. And it has nothing to do with whatever made you. I'd have to be a fool to ignore what I've learned of you. You're brave, and you're strong, and loyal. Loyal to a fault. I won't let Elodie hurt you. She would never forgive herself. But she doesn't remember right now. She doesn't know who you are. So you have to run. Understand?'

She nodded as bravely as she could manage. If Roland thought she was brave, she could be brave. She had to be.

'You aren't my father, are you?' she asked, and she couldn't keep the heartbreak from her voice.

That made him pause. He glanced down at her and suddenly he wore that grim smile. It meant so much to her. More than she had realised. 'Elodie said that the Nox formed you based on her dreams, her wishes, on what the two of us once had. It reached into her heart and took what it found there. So I am your father in every way that counts. Just as she is your mother. Always remember that. Finnian?'

'Here, Grandmaster.'

And there he was, by Wren's side again. She didn't know where he'd brought Leander. Outside the chamber somewhere, hidden, she hoped.

'You need to get Wren out of Pelias. As far away from the Aurum, and the regents' council, and the queen, as you can. Understand?'

Finn stared at him as if he had lost his mind. 'Are you telling me to—?'

'You know what to do, your highness. I believe you have the means. On my mark.'

Roland raised Nightbreaker and stepped straight into the full force of Elodie's magic.

CHAPTER 17
WREN

Wren screamed as the light of the Aurum licked around her father like the white-hot flames of a forge. But Roland stood there, unmoved, holding his sword in front of him, legs braced against the onslaught.

'Elodie,' Roland called again. 'Elodie listen!'

Something flickered in the flood of power, in that blinding light, a candle flame in the inferno. Elodie seemed to hesitate, as if she recognised him. As if for a moment she might be herself again.

'Now, Wren,' Finn said, and took her hand in his, ready to run as his guardian had ordered.

But she couldn't.

They were her family, Roland said, in every way that counted. Elodie had always been there for her. Always.

Wren couldn't abandon her now. She reached out with everything she had in her, light and dark, all her emotions and everything she ever owed to the woman who had saved her and raised her and taught her to be herself.

All her love.

But even as she did so, she knew she had made a terrible mistake.

Oh Elodie stopped. And Elodie stared. Her arms fell to her sides and her mouth moved, forming Wren's name.

And then something else, something dark and terrible, something twisted and barbed, rose out of the shadows in the corners of the room, grew from the gaps between the stones and dropped from the rafters on black-feathered wings of darkness. All of it focused on Elodie. All of it tearing through the pitiful remains of her defences.

She stood against it for a moment, her expression horrified, betrayed.

And then she fell.

The light of the Aurum flickered and died. Roland and the knights shuddered, and dropped like stones to the Sacrum floor.

Wren cried out her name and tried to run to Elodie. She had to reach her, had to help her.

Finn grabbed her and pulled her back, dragging her through the doorway to a small antechamber on the other side. Leander lay in the middle of the floor, still convulsing, holding his stomach, his face a mask of agony as he bled out.

The door slammed shut and Hestia barred it.

Suddenly everything went quiet. Far too quiet.

'Let me go!' Wren yelled, and reached out for the shadows which clustered around her. They were the only weapon she had, the only way she could tear herself free.

'Wren, listen to me, please,' Finn said. 'You don't know what you're doing.'

Hadn't he seen what had happened back there? Hadn't he seen Elodie and Roland fall? There wasn't time for this. She had to go back. She had to help.

And if Finn wouldn't help her willingly...

What had Elodie said?

Use any means necessary. I don't care if you have to summon every shadow in the place to help you.

She had been talking about Wren escaping, of running away from Pelias if they tried to crown her. But if something had happened to Elodie that was exactly what would happen next.

Othertongue danced on Wren's lips, words of power and command, words which would bind Finn and make him obey her. She didn't think, didn't hesitate. She had to help Elodie. She had to put a stop to this nightmare, and he was standing in her way.

Finn shuddered and froze, a look of horror crossing his face as he realised what she was doing.

'No,' he tried to say. He could barely force the word out.

The dark laughter that hung on the edge of her hearing flooded her mind and Wren embraced it. It made her strong, and drove away her fear and panic. She let the shadows fill her. She could do this, she could make him obey her. She could do whatever she wanted. The words of othertongue were there to be used. The glimmering strands of magic easy to weave. She remembered Elodie using them on her. Remembered the humiliation, the anger...

She pushed that thought away. It didn't matter now. Only this. Only commanding Finn, and helping Elodie.

'Wren, stop!' That was Hestia. 'You don't want to do this to him.'

Her own voice pounded through her head as she replied. 'What do you know about what I want to do? What do you care? No one cares.' Wren felt a flood of relief as she finally said it. No one cared. Not even Finn, not really. He was trying to tell her what to do as much as anyone else. No one cared about her but the thing that had created her, the thing now rushing into her and making her strong. Unstoppable.

And it felt good. Overwhelming, passionate, fulfilling,

endlessly exhilarating. It raced along her veins like the crackling of lightning. She was strong and powerful. The magic was part of her and she was part of it. She heard the cry of triumph that the Nox roared, and realised that it came from her own throat. She threw back her head and let it loose. The Aurum was gone and the Nox rushed through her.

You make him help you. You command him.

That was what Elodie had told her. So she did. Wren bent her will around him.

Othertongue danced through the air between them and Finn's eyes turned jet black, the blue vanishing as his pupils grew huge, devouring all the colour of his irises. His mouth opened in shock and his body sagged but didn't fall because she held it. She held him.

He wavered on his feet and his face filled with that wild desire, endless and intoxicating. He leaned towards her and she kissed him. He returned the passion with everything he had in him. He was hers. All hers. Her Paladin, her champion, her lover and her servant. Her slave. The ferocity of the triumph coursing through her could have shaken the foundations of the world but she didn't care. He was hers and she was his. His beloved, his queen, his goddess.

He jerked back suddenly, as if on a string, his eyes still so wide and dark, endless. Abruptly, Finn dropped to his knees, his hand catching hold of hers. So simple a touch of submission and defeat. He lifted it to his lips and pressed a kiss to the inside of his wrist, his breath a whisper against her skin. The gesture was courtly and gentle, not the action of the wildness which infected him at other times when her power filled him. It was almost tender. Almost apologetic. She tried to pull away, suddenly wary, unsure. Something was wrong.

But she was too late.

The bracelet snapped closed around her arm and the magic was cut off as if a blade had severed the connection. A blade made of shadow-wrought steel. The metal closed around her wrist, as cold as ice, and at the same time burning with thwarted rage.

'I'm so sorry, Wren, my love,' he said, his voice his own, his eyes their familiar stormy blue. 'Forgive me.'

Her borrowed strength fled and he caught her as she wilted against him.

Hestia staggered back a step, her face pale. She leaned against the wall, ready to collapse, and wound back traces of her magic, of tendrils of shadows with which she had wrapped Finn. Hestia had protected him, Wren realised. She'd countered the spell and given him the time to snap that cursed bracelet around Wren's wrist, cutting her off from the power of the Nox. Wren grabbed it, trying to tug it free, but it clung to her skin, hot and cold at the same time. Beneath it the magic surged and coiled like eels beneath her flesh.

'What... what did you do?'

There were tears in Finn's eyes. She could see them glistening there, but something else as well. A hardness like diamonds.

'What I had to do. To stop you. I couldn't let the Nox have you. I won't. Ever.'

'But... but Finn...'

The confusion and betrayal stole her voice. There had to be a way out of this. She struggled free of him and fell onto the hard ground, her strength gone. Finn rose to his feet, towering over her, and he didn't look like her Finn anymore. His face was cold, hard.

The face of a Knight of the Aurum, the face of a prince of Ilanthus.

What had she done?

CHAPTER 48

FINN

How could he have been so stupid?

He could feel the shadow kin in the chamber beyond, seething and roiling, taunting him. They were voices on the edge of his hearing, speaking a language he almost remembered from his nightmares.

He couldn't lose Wren. And at the same time, Finn knew Wren would never forgive him. Not this.

But he did it anyway.

He didn't dare take his eye off Wren as she dragged herself back to her feet and tried to fling open the door. But Hestia had seen to that. No one was getting in or out of this room until she decided they could.

He turned to Hestia, who was bent over Leander and desperately trying to save him. Even now. He was still her family, still her prince. And for once, this was not his fault. Finn dropped to his knees beside her.

'Hestia, help me,' he hissed. 'Can't you talk to her, explain... I don't know. Please.'

The look his cousin gave him would have quelled the arguments of a king. 'I'm trying to save his life.' But then she seemed to shudder and looked back down to Leander. 'But I can't.'

'She can. She saved me.'

Hestia rolled her eyes at him. 'Before you bound her power. The things you boys do... Here.' She grabbed Finn's hands and pressed them against Leander's wound. 'Keep the pressure on. He's lost so much blood already. He can't afford any more.'

Leander squirmed beneath him, delirious with pain now, as Finn pressed down. His blood was hot and sticky on Finn's hands but he didn't hesitate as Hestia drew herself to her feet and turned to Wren.

Shadow magic still flowed around Wren, her hair waving gently in the air as if underwater, and her eyes were endlessly dark, as if filled with the Nox already. The bracelet was still holding it in check, thank the light, holding her in check, but Finn could see the strain in her face, the pain he had caused her. Was still causing. Just by locking her magic away with that damned piece of metal.

Leander's blood had called it forth but Finn was the one who had locked it inside her. It was still devouring her but now it had nowhere else to go.

But what else could he have done? It was that or give up his free will. And he was not about to do that.

Even for her.

But it hurt more than he could say. He knew what she had tried to do and she almost succeeded. She had tried to control him, to make him her slave, no more than a puppet to her will. Wren, of all people. He would never have believed it of her. And yet, he'd looked into her eyes and seen her intention.

Or seen the intention of the sentience that lurked behind her mind.

It was here now as well. He could feel that. Drawing closer from the beyond, ready to tear through the veil and claim her, but without her magic she couldn't help it.

The bracelet, right now, was the only thing still keeping Wren herself. And the only thing keeping him a free man.

'Finn...' Leander hissed, and Finn's attention snapped back to his half-brother, dying on the floor of the antechamber, his blood turning the exquisite carpet scarlet. 'Finn, listen to me.'

He reached up, his hand closing on the glass pendant.

'What?' Finn asked, leaning closer, but Leander winced, his teeth bared. And the words that came out weren't intelligible, a series of whispers and sighs, like the othertongue Wren and Elodie sometimes used, but not even that. It slurred together and then, finally, he slumped back down. His hand was the last thing to fall, sliding away from the pendant and leaving it smeared with his blood.

'Hestia,' Finn gasped. 'Wren... he's... help him.'

Even though it was Leander, even after everything, he couldn't just stand by and let him die.

Hestia opened her mouth to speak but Wren lifted one hand, like an empress, and to Finn's horror, his cousin's voice stilled in her throat. She dropped to her knees, her face lifting with an expression of abject adoration.

Finn felt it wash over him, right there in this small antechamber, the sheer power Wren embodied. He had always known it but now... now she wasn't even trying to hold back anymore. She always had, he realised. Out of love, out of care, out of all Elodie's teachings. But it didn't matter to her now.

Had Leander done this with his dying breath?

Wren dropped her chin a little and looked up at him through the fall of her long black hair.

'*I can save him,*' she murmured, her voice softening. And it wasn't Wren anymore. Not really. '*But I have a price.*'

She was beautiful. She had always been beautiful. And so very dangerous. Right from the start she had enchanted him, her magic coming close to enslaving him from the very first time they met. She was everything to him, and part of him – that deep, dark and secret part of him – wanted nothing more than to be hers, to obey her every command, to do anything for her. Anything at all. Even to die, if she wished it. He would suffer tortures for her sake. Gladly.

He felt that familiar sense of submission sweeping through him.

But not the beckoning call of the Nox, promising him his every desire. This was a demand.

She knelt beside him and her hands trailed over Leander's still form. The bracelet still constrained her shadowy magic but this was something else.

Something impossible.

Light flared beneath her touch. Wren could work both powers, Finn had realised that. He didn't know how, and there was no sign of pain when she did it now.

And he wasn't even sure that this was Wren, not anymore.

But it wasn't the Nox either. He wasn't sure what he was looking at.

Leander gave a low groan and his breath rattled. But he kept breathing. Barely. Wren turned her face to look at Finn, studying him with other eyes.

'Your price?' he asked. 'My obedience.'

The smile that played over her lips was a stranger to him as well. '*You are always mine, my prince.*'

Wren rose, and now he saw the light in her as well as the dark. Balance... Hestia was on her knees but Finn got to his feet. The bracelet was meant to contain the dark magic of the Nox, but now she channelled something else. Wren could access the magic of the Aurum as well. Normally it hurt her, burned her from within. Something had changed, something fundamental. As if... as if the Nox was infecting the light as well, the way it had stained the flames of the Aurum... It was cunning and ancient and it knew magic better than any of them. And now, the two powers twisted together, and filled Wren.

Wren's hands spread wide and the wind whipped around her. Long dark tendrils of her hair snaked around his arms and legs, teased at the bare skin of his face and neck. He might drown in her if he let himself.

And all it would take was a moment.

Even now.

Light save him, he wanted to.

Finn framed her face with his shaking hands and she leaned into him like a cat, a slow smile spreading over her sensuous mouth. But this wasn't Wren. He knew it wasn't her.

And at the same time it was.

She still wore the bracelet. If he released her the Nox would finally be complete. He would serve her without a will of his own, and all doubt and fear would be swept away. He would be whole, and have a purpose, and she would love him.

She did love him...

It would be so easy to let go, to do as she said.

Not Wren. This was not Wren.

The Nox... and the Aurum... both of them tangled together perhaps. He didn't know. He didn't know what she was anymore or what he was talking to. He couldn't begin to understand the magic she could embody. But he had to reach Wren, just Wren. Nothing else mattered.

'Listen to me,' he whispered and lowered his mouth towards hers. Wren had to know how he felt. That he would do anything for her. She *had* to know. He brushed his lips against hers and pulled back, searching her eyes for a sign she was still there. Anything. 'I can get away, get you to safety. We can find a way to help Elodie and the others. Someone did this, attacked us, sent Carlotta.'

'*Carlotta?*' The voice faltered. For a moment it sounded like her again, like Wren. One brief spark of hope flared up in the darkness. 'Someone used her, Finn. Enchanted her. Forced her...'

She glanced at Leander. Then at Hestia and seemed to shake herself awake. 'Elodie is trapped and the Aurum with her. But it's trying to reach out to me as well, to use me instead. It forgot the truth of what we are, and what Elodie is. She's mortal. She's dying. And if that happens it will come to me. It wants me...'

How could she know that? He dreaded asking, dreaded hearing what the answer was. Wren knew too much. And if Elodie was mortal so was Wren. Wasn't she?

'How do we release her?'

'*There is no release,*' the voice that was not Wren's voice whispered again, cold and implacable. Light filled her, flaring like fireworks in her eyes, light flowing beneath her skin, tangling with the shadows, tracing lines in her flesh. Wren's eyes widened and she struggled back to herself, the shock of it breaking the spell surging through her. A battle, he realised, and her body was the battleground. 'What's happening? Help me. What... what am I, Finn?'

Light forgive him, all he could do was love her, serve her. He pulled her against him and kissed her fully, losing himself in her, wanting her and wanting the magic that spilled out of her. She might not be able to control it, but it was still there. And she was an addiction. His downfall.

So be it.

'You are my queen,' he whispered. 'My goddess, my everything. But we need to escape this place before the Aurum overwhelms you too. Between them they'll tear you apart, love. Come with me and I will protect you.'

He had to get her out of Asteroth by any means necessary. Away from the reach of the Aurum and whatever was happening to her. The bracelet would hold the Nox at bay, but it wouldn't work on the light that was filling her. This was all he could think of.

Because that was the choice he was making now, between

his Wren and the vows he had made to serve the Aurum. That was what was being demanded of him.

And he hated himself for the decision he made.

Wren shivered in his embrace, but when her eyes met his, he saw only her trust, her love. 'Yes,' she whispered.

'Finn?' Hestia interrupted, wary now, right on the edge of realising what he was about to do. Another person who would hate him from this moment on. He was betraying her as well, wasn't he? 'Finn, what are you doing?'

What he had to do. That was the problem. And it would involve abandoning her, leaving her here with Leander, maybe even leaving her to die. 'I'm sorry, Hestia,' he said, his voice bleak as the winds of winter. 'I have to.'

All you have to do, Hestia had told him, *is break this, and it will bring you home.*

Finn broke the pendant around his neck and released the spell Hestia had woven through it. Leander's blood boiled on its surface and something sharp stabbed into his hand. Shadow kin coiled out. Stronger than any he had ever known, more powerful. He felt them burrowing through him, deep inside him.

And from that place deep inside him, from his blood and his bone, something responded. Something dark and endless, which had just been biding its time.

CHAPTER 49
WREN

Nestled in Finn's strong arms, Wren felt the rush of dark magic around her. It was like the travelling spell Elodie had cast to take her out of Knightsford. If that spell had been turned inside out. This time, instead of a place full of light and flames that danced against their skin, a sickening aura of colours spiralling around them, there was a knot of shadow kin and a whirl of blue-black light. Blood surged in her veins and the Nox laughed as they passed through its realm. Dark tendrils of consciousness wound around her, tried to drag Wren away and drown her in the shadows.

Finn's arms tightened around her and she tore her gaze from the chaos around them to look up at him. He watched her hungrily with a curious otherness in his eyes.

Something was wrong. Terribly wrong. Not just this dark version of the travelling spell, not this traverse beyond the veil and into the maw of the Nox, something was wrong with him.

'Finn?' she whispered and shook off the cloying tendrils of darkness creeping back through her brain.

'Don't be scared,' he told her. His eyes glittered in the otherlight of the shadow kin's embrace. They were blue, so blue.

Like jewels. Like flames. Like the eyes of the shadow kin all around them. 'It's going to be all right now.'

Scared? Why would she be scared with him?

She was never scared with him.

'Finn?' Something was wrong, a voice deep in the back of her mind whispered. Something was wrong with him.

Tears matted his lashes together and spilled down his cheek. He pressed his face into her hair and kissed her head, still holding her far too tightly. The bracelet on her arm burned, pressed between their bodies, hot and cold all at once.

She felt the Nox squirm with sudden concern. Something was terribly wrong. It tried to reach her again, dark tendrils which wound about her like her hair when it tried to hold him. But those shadowy strands couldn't quite find purchase, slipping from her, and the Nox's cry of rage echoed around her, shaking her to her bones. And Finn's grip just tightened further, digging into her flesh, bruising her.

Wren tore herself free of Finn just as the shadow kin unfurled around them and she fell. She couldn't stop herself, couldn't hold herself up. She was weak and wrung out, as if the spell had ripped every ounce of energy, light and dark, out of her. Her body was barely her own. Only the burning line of the bracelet on her arm gave her something to cling to, some indication that she was still real, still feeling things, still alive.

The flagstones she hit were black as night and polished to a mirror-like shine. She stared at her reflection, a strange wild girl with a fall of too-long hair the colour of raven wings around her pale and pinched face, her eyes so black they looked like holes in her head. She didn't look like herself. She barely looked human. Something fell from the pocket of the long Ilanthian dress she wore. The little bird Carlotta had given her.

It will remind you of what you are, Wren.

And it did. It reminded her of who she was, what she was...

She was Wren. Not the Nox, not the Aurum. She was more

than a vessel for magic. The Nox wanted to wipe her away and take control of her physical form. And the Aurum... now she realised that the Aurum had tried to do the same thing.

She thought of Elodie, the Aurum burning through her, of the knights overwhelmed by the powers they served, used and cast aside. And when Elodie couldn't serve it any more, it had turned on Wren, sought her out and tried to use her instead.

And Wren... she had left them behind, Elodie and Roland, Anselm and Olivier, Hestia and Lynette... all of them. She had fled with Finn and...

Great light, they needed to go back to Pelias. Elodie needed her. The Aurum blazed inside Elodie and it would burn her away, destroy her. Perhaps it already had done so.

The sound of weapons being drawn surrounded them both and she heard Finn breathe in deeply, taking a moment to ground himself. She could almost hear his heart, like an echo of her own. It pounded in her chest, a frantic staccato beat.

But he didn't panic. That was her Finn through and through. Wren glanced up at him for reassurance and froze.

Something was wrong with him. Every instinct, light and dark, everything she was, screamed it at her.

A multitude of coloured light fell around him from the high stained-glass windows which soared up the walls of the cavernous chamber in which they found themselves. Blues and purples, every shade from the palest to the depths. They illuminated him and Finn held his head erect, his features utterly impassive. His eyes had changed. They were still blue, but the blue-flame of shadow kin eyes she had seen during the spell which brought them here. They hadn't changed back but kept that unnatural brightness. He looked like a statue, a pale carving sculpted by a master's hand, not like a living breathing man, but cold and inaccessible. He still wore an Ilanthian tunic and sash from the embassy, as did the men surrounding them, though his were of a far finer quality. All men, she noticed. All dressed as he was, all stone-faced and hostile. They bristled with swords and spears, a wall of weaponry which turned on the two of them.

And then Finn spoke.

'I am Finnian, son of Alessander, of the line of Sidon. I am the lost prince of Ilanthus, hostage to the enemy Asteroth. I am the one chosen who was forsaken, the one foreseen to wear the crown. I am called home. I demand an audience with his majesty.'

There was a hushed intake of breath as everyone absorbed that statement.

Not Finnian Ward, Wren thought. Of course he wasn't Finnian Ward, not here. And certainly not Finn. Not her Finn. She had trusted him, a member of the line of Sidon. Even though he had warned her...

'Let them pass,' said a cold voice, hardly more than a murmur, but it echoed around the room as if the acoustics of the room itself had been designed to carry it. A voice used to power and obedience, she realised. A voice that did not suffer fools or disobedience in any way.

The guards snapped back to attention, weapons still bare but pointing to the far off gilded ceiling now instead of at the new arrivals. As if two people arriving in a whirlwind of shadows was nothing more than an unexpected turn of events here.

Before Wren could get to her feet, Finn seized her arm and dragged her up, propelling her across the black marble floor. No hint of gentleness now. No sign of who he had been.

There were people everywhere, staring at her, all dressed in the rich silks and satins of Ilanthus, that now familiar sweep of a sash across their bodies. The women kept their heads bowed but Wren could feel them examining her. The glow of power off some of them was muted, but unmistakable. The air reeked with their magic, though none of them wielded it openly.

It was the royal court, she realised. They had arrived right in the heart of the royal court of Sidonia at some kind of vast assembly.

And Finn walked through it, ignoring all the eyes upon him. They let him. No one tried to stop him. He walked to the steps beneath the raised throne and then stopped.

Wren couldn't help herself. He still held her wrist in a grip like iron, pressing the bracelet into her skin where it sizzled and burned.

'Well? Back again, Finnian?' the king asked and Wren forced herself to look up at him.

He had more of a resemblance to Leander than Finn, cold and hard, pale as ice and made of sharp edges. No wonder Leander was the favoured son.

But Finn met his cool gaze without wavering. 'Hestia told me of your offer, which I accept. I bring a prize with me.'

King Alessander turned his attention on Wren and she wanted to shrink back, to fall to the floor and let it swallow her up.

'A prize?'

'The living embodiment of our dark goddess, called forth by the blood of your brother Evander, Father. The Nox incarnate.' He jerked up her arm, displaying the bracelet. 'Her power bound and contained. At our mercy instead of the other way around.' To hear him say it like that, to utterly betray her secrets and lay them bare before the whole of the Ilanthian court, was too much.

She tried to pull free but he didn't release her. He didn't even react. It was like he was another person now.

He is, the Nox whispered, that now familiar laugh cutting through the words. *He is the prince of Ilanthus, heir apparent in his brother's stead. He is the new crown prince. He is your master and our slave. He is become what we made him, my little vestige, you and I.*

Its amusement echoed around her head until she wanted to scream.

But she couldn't say a word.

'Princess Wren of Asteroth,' said the king and smiled. 'What a pleasure. As our son has served as a hostage in your capital for so many years, you may now return the gesture. Well done, my boy. We are well pleased. We have waited far too long to welcome you home openly.'

He held out his hand and Finn released Wren. It didn't matter now. There was nowhere she could go. She shrank back, cradling her arm and staring as he sank to one knee at the foot of the throne, taking the offered hand so he could bow his head and kiss the royal ring in a show of fealty.

'Too many years, Father,' Finn said, no trace of emotion in his words. He rose elegantly to his feet, moving with the grace she knew to be an innate part of him but which now seemed alien and strange. 'Too long lost among our enemy and waiting for the right moment.'

'But it came at last, and you didn't fail me. Hestia did well. Go and refresh yourself. Tonight, all of Sidonia will feast in your honour.'

But Finn hesitated. He glanced briefly at Wren and she didn't know the man behind those eyes. 'And the princess, your majesty?'

The king was gazing at her, his eyes hungry and cold at the same time. Wren could feel the Nox inside her almost as if it was singing along her veins, wild and mad and dangerous.

Alessander gave a brief laugh, as if he had judged her with that glance and found her more than wanting. 'She is a treasure indeed and when she is trained, she will rain down vengeance on our enemies. But not yet, I think.' He leaned forward, peering closely at her. 'No, just a frightened girl. The sisterhood will need to break her apart and open up the way properly.' He gestured to the nearest guards. 'Take her away and secure her.'

Finn held up a hand. 'She is my prize, Father. Mine to do with as I please.' When the old man inclined his head in agreement, Finn glanced at the guards who approached her warily. 'She won't give you any trouble. She has nowhere to run to now.'

And he was right. She knew he was right.

'Finn?' Wren tried again. 'Finn, please.'

He turned back to her, one hand on her face, his other closing on her hip to pull her to him, and he kissed her. For a moment she thought that it was all a bad dream, that she'd wake up and he would be in her bed, that they would be somewhere else, somewhere safe. Then his kiss turned harsh and demanding, all control and force which left her breathless, helpless.

He released her just as ruthlessly. 'Take her to my chambers and hold her there. I'll be with her shortly.' He fixed her with a terrifying look, one which froze her to the core and stole all fight from her. She didn't know this man. She had never known him. Her gentle lover, her Finn, had all been a lie. She saw that now. 'Remember your place, little bird,' he said. 'You were warned never to trust a member of my family. You didn't listen. And now it's too late.'

'But I—' She didn't even know what she meant to say. This couldn't be happening. It couldn't be true. Her mind scrambling, she tried to call on the shadow kin but they didn't answer. Even if she hadn't been wearing shadow-wrought steel, she knew that they wouldn't.

The Nox had what it wanted now. It was back in Ilanthus, where it wanted to be. And she was helpless before it. In no time at all, with the help of its servants, it would overwhelm her defences, and make itself whole. Then Finn would take his place as its consort and Wren would be no more.

It had used her as surely as Finn had.

EPILOGUE

ROLAND

The servant, Carlotta, was dead. Roland couldn't have her questioned, but that was only the first problem. Hestia and Leander had been secured, but the prince was so close to death he might slide the rest of the way at any second.

And Elodie had not awoken.

The knights, himself included, had felt the fires of the Aurum sweep through them, had been rendered senseless and helpless, as the light they had sworn to serve had roared through them, seeking something. He didn't know what, only that it had left everything he was bare before its gaze before it had moved on. When it retreated, he felt it like loss, like heartbreak. They all did.

It had to be a mistake, surely. Elodie slept as if dead, her chest barely moving. Sometimes her eyes moved beneath her eyelids. Sometimes she winced or frowned. But she didn't wake up, no matter what they did. Sister Maryn and the other maidens hovered around her, desperately trying to heal her, but to no avail.

'I warned her,' said Maryn. 'I told her not to channel the Aurum again so soon.'

'She didn't have a choice,' Roland replied. 'The Aurum has its own will. You know that as well as I. But you can heal her, surely? In time?' It was the one hope he was clinging to. He couldn't lose her yet again.

But Maryn gave him a worried look, her face pale and strained. 'The Aurum is...' She stopped and chewed on her lower lip. 'It isn't dead, but if it was sleeping before... I don't know how to explain it. There's barely a glow. It isn't in the chamber anymore, not entirely. I think it's locked inside her, inside Elodie. It overreached itself, it went too far. And now...' She trailed off. Maryn didn't have an answer either. None of them did.

'Who might know how to heal her?' he snarled, aware his voice had the edge of an animal in pain. 'Tell me what to do, Maryn. Any quest, any deed, and I will do it. There must be a way to help her.'

'The College of Winter hold manuscripts that might guide us,' she replied, though she didn't sound convinced. 'Perhaps they may know. And the maid was witchkind. Someone had placed her under a compulsion. Though whether that was before she came here or while she served... I just don't know. Perhaps the rebel witchkind...'

But he was only half listening. Roland paced back towards the bed where Elodie lay, unmoving, but before he reached her, a disturbance outside the door caught their attention. He heard Ylena's voice and his heart sank. Looking at Maryn, the feeling was mutual.

Olivier opened the door looking harried. Anselm still barred the way but the queen's aunt and Lady Lynette bristled behind him.

'Grandmaster,' Olivier began, apologetically.

Roland waved his hand. Might as well get this out of the way because it was coming one way or the other. Ylena hated him, and always had done. She blamed him for Elodie's failed marriage, for her absence for so many years, for the recent fiasco with Sassone and now, in her eyes, he had failed to protect Elodie again.

'Let them in, Olivier,' he replied.

It only took a second. Ylena was already in full flight. 'Where's the girl, Roland? How have you lost her as well?'

Ah yes, he had known this was coming. Dreaded it. But he couldn't avoid it.

'My lady Ylena,' he said with a bow. It was not an answer, but he didn't have an answer.

Ylena narrowed her eyes. They were slivers of ice as they fixed on him. Roland held his ground.

'Mother, we do not have time for this,' Maryn said irritably. 'I need to send word to the College of Winter and Roland—'

'*Time?* Heal her or what use are you? And *you*—' She turned on Roland again. 'You brought this upon us. You sheltered that treacherous whelp and let him take the princess. You let this happen, either by negligence or design. I name you traitor, Roland de Silvius.'

He was almost surprised to realise he had expected this too. She wasn't wrong. Not in principle, just the reasons she stated.

He had chosen Elodie, and Wren, over his duty to the crown and kingdom.

'My lady,' Lynette began to protest. 'Listen to Sister Maryn. We need to send word to the College of Winter and beg their help. They will have an answer. Surely the Grandmaster should be the one to—'

'I don't want to hear from you either. Your husband will take his place as Grandmaster. That's about as high as you could hope to climb, Lynette, so hold your tongue and be grateful. You two, knights, Paladins, whatever you are.' She waved her hands to Olivier and Anselm. 'Escort de Silvius to the dungeon. Now.'

'Mother, you can't do this,' Maryn argued in vain.

But she could. Of course she could. She was Lady Ylena, a princess of the blood royal. She was now the one and only regent and her queen was laid low, incapacitated by magic. Elodie was in her power. All she needed to rule Asteroth completely was Roland out of the way.

And now she had that too.

He could denounce her, but what good would that do? All she wanted, she would argue, was to protect her niece, to defend the crown.

And to place Wren on the throne.

The one thing that could not happen.

Suddenly sending her to safety with Finnian seemed more than inspired. He had to hope they would stay far away from Pelias.

He needed to warn them. He only hoped they were safe somewhere. Hestia wasn't talking. Leander couldn't. Yet.

He was sure that Ylena would get to that soon enough.

Anselm and Olivier were joined by Yvain, who had been curtly summoned and looked as deeply uncomfortable as they did. They didn't relieve Roland of his weapons. What good would that do anyway? He could fight his way out but then what? They were his friends, his men. He couldn't draw weapons on them.

Before they led him away, he returned to Elodie's bedside, bent down and kissed her forehead. No one stopped him. Not even Ylena.

'I'll find a way to help you,' he whispered. 'Hold on, my love. I will always find a way.'

They led him away in silence, embarrassed and lost for words, down through the dungeon to a small and simple cell. Yvain opened the door, failing to meet Roland's gaze.

'This isn't your fault, Yvain,' Roland said softly, as he stepped inside. 'And... she's not wrong. I failed Elodie. I failed everyone.'

His old friend shook his head. 'This is wrong. You know it as well as I do. And without you, we're lost, Roland.'

'Yvain.' Roland rested his hand on Yvain's shoulder. 'You have to guard her now. The queen is more vulnerable than ever. All the knights need to look for a cure. Whatever the maidens say might help her. Our enemies knew they could not control her on the throne. So they took her out of their game. And now they'll look for Wren so they can play another.'

Though no one had asked for it – they had not poured that indignity on him at least – Roland unbuckled the sword belt and held out Nightbreaker. Yvain visibly paled and took a step back.

Roland thrust it towards him again. 'You need it. If you're Grandmaster.'

'We both know I'm not. No matter what they say.'

This was not good. He was a Paladin. Events may have shocked him, but he had taken vows when Roland had. He needed to be stronger than this.

Instead, Roland put the sword down between them and Yvain's gaze followed every movement. He still didn't bend to pick it up though.

'Lynette says...' he began but his voice trailed off. 'Roland, what do we do?'

What did they do? That was a question. 'You keep to your vows. Serve the queen and the Aurum. Defend the light.'

What else could they do?

The cell door closed on him and he sat down, listening as Yvain's footsteps faded away. Nightbreaker stayed on the ground in front of him, abandoned by them both.

Defend the light? How was that possible, here, in the dark?

Roland tried to still his racing mind and focused on his breath and his heartbeat. If he concentrated, maybe he could reach out to Elodie where she slept. Maybe he could dream alongside her.

He had tried this every night since he had lost her all those years ago.

The fantasy of a boy who had lost far too much. For a moment he had dreamed he had her back, that everything would be all right again, that somehow it would work out. That he had his beloved by his side again, and a child who was a wonder to him. A treasure.

And it was gone. All gone.

The ache gnawed away inside his chest, emptying him of hope.

❧

In the depths of the night, Roland heard a noise, something which, had he been honest with himself, he had been waiting for all along.

He had wondered if Ylena would send someone of her own before they got here. A knife in the dark, a garrotte or a noose and it would be over. But no. Apparently not.

The cell door opened and Anselm stood there with a shuttered lantern.

'Grandmaster? You have to admit, this is somewhat ironic.' He tried to smile, an expression Roland didn't return.

He blinked in the light, suddenly exhausted. 'This is a terrible idea. You both know that, don't you?'

'We would have come earlier,' said Olivier. Of course he was there too. The two of them were inseparable. 'But Ylena summoned every knight in the kingdom to the mustering point. She has everyone out looking for Wren and Finnian.'

Of course she did. She needed Wren to cement her control now. She had Elodie, but with Wren, there could be no doubt.

Roland frowned at Anselm who had the good grace to look marginally guilty. 'You weren't included?'

'It... it didn't seem my place. Who am I now? The son of a

traitor. Convenient, as my father, like you, was the only other balance to her power.' Anselm had always had a political acumen that few rivalled. He had been born to this world, more so than Roland. He knew the way the tides of the royal court flowed.

'I'm sorry I doubted you, son.'

Anselm tried that wavering smile again. 'Well, he *was* a traitor. He planted his own flag, made his move and lost. And I'm still his son, for what little that's worth. We should leave, before we're missed.'

We. That was a word, one word, which carried more hope than he had a right to feel.

Roland pushed himself to his feet. He picked up Nightbreaker and slipped the sword belt back over his chest.

'You don't need to come with me,' he told them. 'You have lives here, and careers. We will be hunted.'

The two young knights glanced at each other and something unspoken passed between them. As always. They counted Finn and Wren as friends, they served their queen, and their careers were already on rocky ground. Mainly, Roland thought with regret, thanks to him.

'We are with you, Grandmaster,' Anselm said. 'To the end.'

He didn't deserve their loyalty. But he would take it.

'Very well,' he said. 'Let's ride.'

'Where to?' asked Olivier.

'North. To find some answers in the College of Winter.'

PROPHECY OF VARIANA OF ILANTHUS

In the darkest realm a light will grow,
In the flames a shadow lies,
The forsaken shall be restored to us,
And the dark queen shall arise.

A LETTER FROM JESSICA

Dear reader,

I want to say a huge thank you for choosing to read *A Kiss of Flame*. If you did enjoy it, and want to keep up to date with all my latest releases, just sign up at the following link. Your email address will never be shared and you can unsubscribe at any time.

www.bookouture.com/jessica-thorne

A Kiss of Flame is the second part of Wren and Finn's story, but it also opens up their world, so we can explore it a little more. When I started this journey I always knew that the end of *A Kiss of Flame* would be a dark moment. It ended up far darker than I expected. But don't worry, *A Crown of Night* will be available soon.

If you loved *A Kiss of Flame* I would be very grateful if you could write a review. I love hearing from my readers – you can get in touch on social media or my website. I'd love to know what you think, see these characters and locations through your eyes, and of course, say hi.

Thanks,

Jessica Thorne

KEEP IN TOUCH WITH JESSICA

www.rflong.com/jessicathorne

 facebook.com/JessThorneBooks

instagram.com/Jessthornebooks

ACKNOWLEDGEMENTS

As always I want to thank my agent, Sallyanne Sweeney, my lovely editor Natalie for her insight and enthusiasm, my writing comrades of the Naughty Kitchen, and here in Ireland Sarah Rees Brennan, Catie Murphy and Susan Connolly. Writing is a solitary pursuit, so having people who understand the general chaos is always a bonus.

I would also like to thank my friends, Kari Sperring, Kate Pearce and Jeevani Charika, for their wisdom and guidance in critiquing these stories. I promise there will be a happily ever after. Somehow.

And finally thanks to my family, and especially to Pat. I couldn't do this without you.

PUBLISHING TEAM

Turning a manuscript into a book requires the efforts of many people. The publishing team at Bookouture would like to acknowledge everyone who contributed to this publication.

Audio
Alba Proko
Sinead O'Connor
Melissa Tran

Commercial
Lauren Morrissette
Hannah Richmond
Imogen Allport

Cover design
Mary Luna

Data and analysis
Mark Alder
Mohamed Bussuri

Editorial
Natalie Edwards
Sinead O'Connor

Printed in Great Britain
by Amazon